"So," he said, "you'

"Actually, I'm her b

Warmth flooded thos
You're the lady who
Josie's mentioned you.

"Then you have a distinct advantage over me,
Father, because she's never mentioned you until
now. And you're not at all what I expected. You're
so…" She paused, searched desperately for the
right word. *Dark. Intense. Intriguing. Sexy.*

He picked up his coffee cup and took a sip.
"So…?"

"Young," she said, breaking eye contact and
focusing on a single dark blue paperback sitting
on a lower shelf, just at eye level. *Catechism of the
Catholic Church.* She supposed if he ever suffered
from insomnia, the cure was readily available,
right here on his bookshelves.

Also by LAURIE BRETON

FINAL EXIT

*Watch for LAURIE BRETON's next
novel of romantic suspense*

LETHAL LIES

Available March 2005

LAURIE BRETON

MORTAL SIN

MIRA®

If you purchased this book without a cover you should be aware
that this book is stolen property. It was reported as "unsold and
destroyed" to the publisher, and neither the author nor the
publisher has received any payment for this "stripped book."

ISBN 0-7783-2025-1

MORTAL SIN

Copyright © 2004 by Laurie Breton.

All rights reserved. Except for use in any review, the reproduction or
utilization of this work in whole or in part in any form by any electronic,
mechanical or other means, now known or hereafter invented, including
xerography, photocopying and recording, or in any information storage or
retrieval system, is forbidden without the written permission of the publisher,
MIRA Books, 225 Duncan Mill Road, Don Mills, Ontario, Canada M3B 3K9.

All characters in this book have no existence outside the imagination of the
author and have no relation whatsoever to anyone bearing the same name
or names. They are not even distantly inspired by any individual known or
unknown to the author, and all incidents are pure invention.

MIRA and the Star Colophon are trademarks used under license and registered
in Australia, New Zealand, Philippines, United States Patent and Trademark
Office and in other countries.

Visit us at www.mirabooks.com

Printed in U.S.A.

This one's for Paul,
for more reasons than I can count.

ACKNOWLEDGMENTS

Thanks to my two dear friends, Judy Lineberger and Jamie Disterhaupt. If not for your support and friendship through a long and difficult winter, this book might never have happened. Bless you both!

Thanks to my wonderful editor, Valerie Gray, for her endless support, encouragement and faith in me.

And as always, thanks to my family for putting up with me when I'm on deadline.

Prologue

March 2003
Revere, Massachusetts

Living in the ugliest house on the block was so humiliating.

Kit Connelly hoisted her cumbersome backpack higher on her shoulder and trudged through a gloomy March dusk toward the hideous two-story bungalow that some demented previous owner had painted bright blue. The garage was ready to collapse, the roof had been clumsily patched with shingles that nobody had bothered to match, and the front steps lurched to one side like a drunken sailor. Aunt Sarah, of course, loved the place. She called it a fixer-upper, and kept saying it would look just fine with a fresh coat of paint and flowers blooming in the yard. Her aunt was obviously as loopy as the guy who'd painted the house blue. It would take a wrecking ball to improve this dump.

She let herself in through the kitchen door, tossed her coat over the nearest chair, and plodded up the stairs to her room. Dropping the backpack on the bed, she plunked down beside it and rummaged in a side compartment for the third-quarter report card that was about to destroy her life. It wasn't that bad, overall. Two C's, three D's, and one F. She'd passed everything except French. But Aunt Sarah would go ballistic when she saw it, and Kit couldn't very well hide the damn-fool thing, because her aunt knew grade reports were due today. She'd be expecting to see it tonight.

Kit lay back on the bed and stared miserably at the crack that ran across her bedroom ceiling. Her life was over. She'd be grounded until she was too old to care. Sarah was already on the warpath after this morning's go-round, all because she wanted to get her tongue pierced. What was the big deal? A lot of the kids had piercings. But Auntie Dearest, fossilized at the advanced age of thirty-three, was seriously behind the times. She'd refused to even consider it.

From there, the battle had progressed to the nasty R word: Responsibility. Something that, according to Sarah, she still needed to get straight. *Wipe your feet. Turn off the lights. Pick up after yourself.* No matter how hard she tried, she could never get it right, and every time she screwed up, her aunt was on her like a duck on a June bug.

Momma would never have treated her so shabbily. Momma would have let her take the T into Boston with the other kids to hang out after school. Momma would have understood how important it was to be seen at the right parties and with the right people. Momma would have realized she didn't need a keeper. She was sixteen freaking years old, not five. At sixteen, she was old enough to make her own decisions. Old enough to take care of herself. She didn't need Sarah. She didn't need anyone. She'd proved it last summer, hadn't she? She'd taken care of herself just fine, at least she had until the New Orleans cops had busted her and dragged her back home to live with Remy and Sarah.

No way was she going to survive two more years of living in this prison, with Warden Sarah governing her every move. She was going to have to get out before she went absolutely bugfuck.

She got up from the bed and walked to the mirror, lifted her long blond hair and pursed her lips in a sexy pout like the women did in those men's magazines that old man Giordano sold from the back room of his store. Turning one way and then the other, she critically studied her appearance. Most girls her age were troubled by acne, but she had nice skin, smooth and pink and flawless. And her eyes were her best feature: wide and blue, fringed by thick lashes.

But the good stuff stopped there. Her lips were too thin, her nose tilted to the left, and her thick, wavy hair was hopeless. And her body…well, there wasn't anything good she could say about her body. No matter how much she dieted, she still looked like a fat cow.

One more thing she and Sarah didn't agree on. "You're not fat, sugar," her aunt had said, "you're just built like me. Not an ounce of fat on you, just lots of womanly curves. All the Connelly women are built that way."

Kit didn't want womanly curves. She longed to be one of those wispy, delicate women like Jennifer Aniston, with a washboard tummy and tiny hands and feet. The kind of woman who disappeared when she turned around sideways. But it wasn't ever going to happen. At sixteen, she was already five-foot-eight and wore a size nine shoe. A freaking Amazon.

On the other hand, there were certain advantages to being tall and full-figured. With the right clothes, the right makeup, the right hairdo, she could easily pass for eighteen. She could move into the city, get her own apartment, find a job. Maybe in one of the theaters. Cleaning bathrooms, selling popcorn, she didn't care, as long as it was in the theater. Maybe, if she was lucky, she'd get a chance to audition for some bit part. Maybe, if she was really, *really* lucky, she'd get discovered.

Fueled by the sweet lure of freedom, Kit emptied her backpack onto the bed and took down the locked box she kept hidden in a dark corner of the closet. Inside was the cash she'd been saving. Guilt money. Daddy had dumped her like an unwanted litter of kittens, and his way of dealing with his guilty conscience was to send an elaborate card and a big check every time her birthday or a major holiday rolled around. In a year and a half, he'd called just once, but as long as the checks kept coming, he could continue to delude himself about being a good father. Kit pocketed the money, scrabbled around the bottom of the box and pulled out three joints in a plastic bag. She hid the joints in an inside zipper compartment of the backpack. From her dresser drawer, she scooped up underwear, socks, a few shirts, and shoved them into the bag. She added a couple pair of jeans and the black leather miniskirt Sarah detested, then crammed in her hair gel, her blow-dryer, and all her cosmetics.

Her gaze fell on the framed photo of Momma that sat atop her dresser. Kit crossed the room and picked it up. She'd been so young when Momma died, too young to understand why her mother was there one day and gone the next. Too young to understand Daddy's perplexing explanation that Momma had gone home to be with Jesus. It had made no sense to a four-year-old who knew without a doubt that Momma would never have gone away and left her, not even to sit by Jesus on his heavenly throne. She'd been certain Daddy was mistaken, that she'd wake up the next morning to find Momma in the kitchen, frying bacon and eggs and humming an old Hank Williams tune. *I'm so lonesome I could cry....*

But Daddy had been right. Momma had never come back. Her mother had been gone for so long now that Kit barely remembered her, except for the silky blond hair and the clear, sweet voice that sang her to sleep every night. After Momma died, nobody ever sang her to sleep again.

She tucked the picture of her mother into the bag, between soft layers of clothing so the glass wouldn't break, and plucked Freddy from his place of honor beside her pillow. Freddy had started life as a plush stuffed gorilla with thick, luxurious fur and bright black eyes. Now, his one remaining eye had lost its gleam, he had more bald patches than fur, and she was forever cramming his innards back into the split seam in his side.

But to Kit, he was still beautiful. During her years on the road with Daddy, she'd carted Freddy from Montgomery to Richmond, from Richmond to Tupelo, from Tupelo to Beaumont. Every time they'd packed up and moved yet again, he'd been the one solid, familiar thing in her life. They were best friends, forever friends. She couldn't leave him behind.

She locked the house behind her and stood on the sidewalk, gazing one last time at that ugly blue facade. *Goodbye, good riddance, sayonara, arrivederci.* She would miss this place the way a dog misses fleas.

Only a handful of people rode the T. At this time of day, most everybody was headed in the opposite direction, away from Boston's office towers and retail stores. As the train shuddered and rocked, she studied the blank, anonymous faces of her fellow passengers. Most of them looked bored and tired. Nobody showed an ounce of enthusiasm. Kit felt sorry for them, sorry because none of them was headed off to adventure and a new life the way she was.

She got off the train at State Street. When she emerged from the station into a cold winter dusk, the smell of roasted nuts hit her full in the face. Kit set down her backpack, pulled a five-dollar bill from her pocket, and bought a bag of peanuts from the vendor. Jostled and shoved by commuters rushing to catch the train, she stood on the sidewalk next to the pushcart and breathed in the ambiance of the city. This was more like it. This was where things happened. This was where she was meant to be.

Exhilarated, she spun around in a circle and bestowed her most dazzling smile on the peanut vendor. The young man returned the smile, and Kit knew, just *knew,* this was the happiest moment of her life. With the bag of peanuts clasped firmly in her hand, she shouldered her backpack, the vendor already forgotten. And without a single backward glance, she skipped away and melted into the bustling crowd.

1

March 2003
Boston, Massachusetts

The girl wore shiny black fuck-me shoes.

She hovered in a shadowy doorway on Essex Street, at the edge of Chinatown, between a dim sum palace and a fabric store displaying exotic oriental brocades behind its barred windows. Above the five-inch heels, her legs were bare, her dress an electric blue silk that stopped a half inch this side of indecent. Over it she wore a short white fake fur jacket that undoubtedly did little to keep out the cold. Her makeup had been troweled on in an unsuccessful attempt to make her appear sophisticated. Instead, she looked cold and tired and very young.

Clancy had spent the better part of an hour cruising the areas where girls habitually worked the streets: Park Square and Bay Village, Mass Ave and Kenmore Square, what was left of the Combat Zone. The night was bitter cold, and the pickings were slim. By this late hour, most of the working girls had given up the streets in favor of a bed somewhere, anywhere, as long as it was warm. Of the few that remained, most knew him by sight, knew what he was here for, and weren't interested in what he had to offer.

They weren't what he was looking for anyway, these girls with their hard faces and their strident voices and, more often than not, needle tracks running up the insides of their arms. It was the younger ones he sought, the vulnerable ones who still had a shred of innocence left, those who hadn't yet been hardened by the reality of life on the streets. Sometimes it wasn't too late for them. Sometimes he could still make a difference.

If he could get to them ahead of the predators.

Father Clancy Donovan believed things happened for a reason, and he was certain that God had put her in this particular place on this particular night expressly for him. He double-parked the car, the engine idling. When he opened the door and climbed out, the girl darted back into the shadows. He'd frightened her. It wasn't standard procedure for a john to approach a working girl. Customers seldom left the safety and anonymity of their cars. In street parlance, that meant one of two things: he was either the law, or somebody out to do her no good.

He approached the doorway with slow, deliberate steps. Rubbing his hands together, he said casually, "Cold out tonight, isn't it?"

Silence. He wondered if she spoke English. His Cantonese was rusty, but he'd picked up enough of it to get by during his years in the Far East. "I can help you," he said in a pidgin singsong that sounded alien to his American ears. "Help you to leave the streets. My car is warm. We can sit inside and talk."

He waited out the silence. Finally, the girl moved away from the wall and took a tentative step toward him and into the light. She was pretty, with a broad Asian face and wary dark eyes. Not a day over fifteen, she probably lived with four or five other girls in a roach-infested one-room apartment where the INS wouldn't bother to track her down. In heavily accented English, she said, "You a cop?"

"No," he said, switching back to English. "I'm a priest.

And if you're ready to leave the streets, I can take you to a safe place.''

She looked him up and down, took in the knit hat and the wool coat, the jeans and the L.L. Bean boots. "You don't look like no priest I ever seen."

"Maybe not, but that's what I am. Are you interested? It's pretty cold out here."

Again, she hesitated. "No hanky-panky?"

Sorrow and fury vied for top billing inside him, sorrow because this young girl believed the only thing of value she possessed lay between her legs, and fury because some man had taught her to believe it.

"No," he said. "No hanky-panky."

He saw it in the eyes of the little girl concealed behind the painted trollop: hope. Hope that there was something more in life than what she'd already found. She cast a furtive glance to the right, then the left, and took another step forward.

"Okay," she said. "Then I come with you."

Once the girl was settled into a clean, warm bed, he left Melody in charge of her. He always assigned a buddy to each new girl who entered Donovan House. It eased the transition, helped them feel less alone as they struggled to put together the pieces of their broken lives.

In the morning, he'd call Kate Miller's office and set up an appointment for her. Any girl who entered the program was required to have a complete physical, one that included testing for drugs, HIV, and a host of other STDs. Most of them were carrying something when they came in. Most of them were using. But his rules were firm and unbendable: no sex, and no drugs. The first infraction brought a severe warning. With the second infraction, the girl was out the door.

Tough love. He could have used some of that himself when he was young and running wild on the streets of South

Boston. But at his house, there'd been nobody home to enforce any rules. More nights than not, he'd been called down to Rafferty's at closing time to peel his mother off the bar, take her home, and pour her into bed. It was hard to act like a mother when you were too drunk to walk.

Outside the rectory walls, the wind howled. He poured himself a shot of Scotch, sat on the couch and clicked on the television. At this time of night, there wasn't much on, mostly infomercials and old sitcoms. He settled on a John Wayne movie. It was either that or a *Leave it to Beaver* marathon on *Nick at Nite*. Elbows braced against his knees, he rolled the glass of Scotch between his palms and stared into its sparkling amber depths.

He spent a long time studying the contents of that glass. His mother's drinking had ruined her life, had come close to ruining his. Yet here he sat, solitary in the black hours before dawn, slugging Scotch and wondering if he were following in her footsteps. Even if his mother hadn't been a lush, he still had a lengthy and glorious tradition to live down to. The Irish were fond of their drink, and this wasn't the first time in his life that the bottle had tempted him. After Meg died, he'd gone on a three-month bender.

But that had been a different lifetime, and he'd been a different man. Before he got the calling, before people started looking at him as though he were somehow set apart from the rest of humanity. A holy man. As though he didn't get up every morning and put his pants on one leg at a time, like every other man on the planet.

Nowadays, he drank in moderation. He didn't tipple every night—only the bad ones—and he always stopped after one drink. That was supposed to be the dividing line, the thing that separated the alcoholics from the regular sots. Alcoholics, they said, couldn't stop at just one. So far, he'd done a fine job of convincing himself that as long as he was able to stop after that first shot, history wasn't in danger of repeating itself.

He downed the Scotch in a single fiery gulp that scorched his throat and seeped, languid and lovely, into his veins. He hadn't planned on cruising tonight. He'd gone to bed early, and for a while, he'd actually slept. But somewhere around one o'clock he'd come fully awake, just as he had nearly every night for the past six months. At that dark hour, the day's niggling concerns were magnified to biblical proportions and, in his wide-eyed state of unease, sleep was reduced to an elusive fantasy.

Tonight, it was the Branigans who'd kept him awake. Mike and Iris. The Battling Branigans, as he'd come to call them, were hovering on the cusp of divorce. As their parish priest, he was expected to counsel the members of his flock when they came to him with their troubles. He should have been able to make a difference in Iris and Mike's faltering marriage. But somehow, he'd failed them.

Over the past few months, he'd become increasingly aware of his limitations when it came to counseling married couples. What did he, a celibate who lived with a mismatched pair of goldfish, know about the struggle, the intimacy, the delicate balance between two egos that characterized marriage? He'd never been married, and he'd grown up fatherless, raised by a mother who loved him, but not as much as she loved the bottle. Erin Donovan hadn't exactly provided him with a model for successful relationships.

Bishop Halloran would have said that Jesus Christ, and the teachings of the Church, were all the model he needed, but then he and the bishop had been known to disagree before. The Branigans needed something he couldn't give them and today, for the first time since he'd entered the priesthood, he'd referred a member of his congregation to a secular counselor.

But it was more than just his competence at marriage coun-

seling that he questioned. Lately, he'd begun to doubt his
adequacy in a number of areas. Did he really have any business guiding people's souls when his own soul was in such
turmoil?

A crisis of faith. That's what the bishop would call it. Or
maybe it was nothing more complicated than burnout. In either case, he'd shared his doubts with nobody. Confession
might be good for the soul, but the darkness inside him was
something he could confess to nobody but God. Sometimes,
in the wee hours, as he lay awake waiting for the sun's first
rays to penetrate his bedroom window, he prayed for guidance. So far, he hadn't received any.

Still, he gave of himself, doled out bits and pieces of his
soul until he felt drained, bled dry. He presided over bake
sales and bean suppers, authorized the purchase of new choir
robes, arbitrated squabbles between the sisters over at the
convent. He called the repairman when the church boiler
broke down, conducted Mass twice each Sunday, heard confession each Saturday. He joined couples in holy matrimony,
christened infants, administered last rites to the dying, and
prayed over the dead.

But for some time now, he'd been bone-weary and oper-
ating on automatic pilot. Going through the motions. Winter
had settled, bleak and barren, into the depths of his soul. The
joy had left him, and Father Clancy Donovan had no idea
how to get it back.

When the clock on the mantel chimed four-thirty, he realized he'd nodded off. Across the room, John Wayne's rug-
ged face filled the TV screen. He picked up the remote and
muted the actor's annoying drawl.

Silence was a distinct improvement. He ran his hands over
his face. Maybe he'd lie down for just a few minutes, rest
for a while before he had to begin the day. He stretched out
the full length of the couch. It was too short, and he had to
bend his knees to accommodate his feet. In the flickering blue

light of the television, he plumped the hideous plaid throw pillow Mrs. O'Toole had given him last Christmas, tucked it under his head, and closed his eyes.

He awoke to bright sunshine and the absolute certainty that he'd overslept, a certainty that was confirmed by the mantel clock. He clicked off the television, performed his morning ablutions in record time, dropped a pinch of goldfish food into Fred and Barney's fishbowl, and headed across the icy parking lot to the church.

When he stepped into the parish office, he found Melissa, his perky young secretary, standing on a wooden chair in a shaft of morning sunlight, humming as she watered the English ivy that hung over her desk. "Good morning, Father," she warbled.

"Good morning." He unwound the wool scarf and peeled off his gloves. "It's brutal out there today. What's on the agenda?"

She paused, watering can in hand, gray eyes magnified by owlish glasses. "You have a full morning. Tia McCauley and Jeff Stuart are coming in at nine-thirty, and at ten-thirty you have an appointment with a Sarah Connelly. At eleven, you're supposed to meet with the altar guild. After that, you promised you'd stop by to see Patty O'Malley's new baby."

He tucked the gloves into his pocket and sniffed the air. "Coffee," he said. "That's coffee I smell."

She beamed. "And I picked up a half-dozen doughnuts from Fezinger's. The chocolate ones you like."

In the four years he'd been pastor of this parish, he'd watched Melissa grow from a giggly, bubble-headed teenager to a lovely, refined young woman. Fiercely loyal, tenacious as a pitbull when it came to protecting him, she had a marked tendency to smother him with maternal concern. She also knew precisely where each paper clip and sheet of letterhead was located in the parish office, she remembered details about his parishioners that he couldn't keep straight, and she kept his life running smoothly as a Rolex. He tolerated her mollycoddling because her assets far outweighed her liabilities.

In his study, lined up with military precision on his desk, were a steaming mug of coffee, a chocolate doughnut wrapped in a napkin, a folded copy of the *Globe,* and a tidy stack of mail that Melissa had already opened for him.

He sat down, took a quick slug of caffeine, and waited for the buzz to hit. It didn't take long. One more of Melissa's attributes. If he hadn't been a priest, and nearly old enough to be her father, he might have considered marrying the girl just for her coffee.

He set the newspaper aside to read later, took a bite of doughnut, and tackled the mail. Most of it was routine: a gas bill, a committee meeting reminder, a postcard from his favorite octogenarian parishioner, Alton Robbins, who wintered with his son and daughter-in-law in Boca Raton.

Melissa had hidden the letter on the bottom of the pile, undoubtedly because she knew what his reaction would be. When he saw the Archdiocese of Boston letterhead, he closed his eyes and counted to ten. He took another swig of coffee to bolster him, leaned back in his chair and began to read.

It has been brought to our attention that you have been dispensing contraception advice to the engaged couples who come to you for premarital counseling. As you are well aware, Church policy regarding this issue is clear. The Catholic Church condones neither contraception nor premarital sex, nor does it appreciate your attempts to undermine the moral values instilled by the Church in these young people who trust you to provide them with appropriate guidance. Unless you cease this practice immediately, you will risk formal disciplinary action.

He crumpled the letter and hurled it at the wall. It hit and bounced, much like the words bouncing around inside his head, words not befitting a man of his station. "Cretins," he muttered. "Mummified, antiquated, blind old fools."

He pulled a sheet of letterhead from the drawer, picked up his felt-tipped pen, and with bold, black lettering scratched out a hasty response. He scrawled his name, a dark, illegible slash, across the bottom, folded the sheet of paper, and sealed it in an envelope.

Still steaming, he stalked to the outer office and dropped the envelope on Melissa's desk. "See that this goes out in today's mail."

"I thought about hiding it," she said, "but I couldn't see any sense in putting off the inevitable."

"They're cattle. Cattle who wouldn't recognize reality if it fell out of the sky and bashed them on the head. Fully half of this planet's woes can be directly attributed to overpopulation. Crime, pollution, abject poverty. And what's the Church's response? Make more babies! Deplete the oil supplies, destroy the rain forests, and move us steadily closer to extinction. These blind fools haven't turned on a television or stepped outdoors in thirty years. They're cloistered inside their own little fantasy world. If it rained for forty days and forty nights, do you think they'd build an ark? Of course not! They'd just stand there in the valley of the shadow of self-righteousness, milling around and waiting for the water to sweep them away!"

Melissa, accustomed to his rants, remained unmoved. "Are you sure you really want to mail this?"

He leaned over her desk, hands planted firmly on the edge. "Am I not right about this issue?"

"I think you're right. But that's not the point."

"Oh?" He narrowed his eyes. "Then what, precisely, is the point?"

"The point is you're never going to win the battle."

He stared at her for a moment before realizing she was right. "Damn it."

She raised her eyebrows, and he straightened and snatched back the envelope. "If cursing is the biggest sin I commit today, it'll be a miracle. I'll be in my study."

"One of these days," she said to his retreating back, "you're actually going to mail one of these letters. Then you'll really be in hot water."

He slammed the door behind him, opened a desk drawer and tossed in the envelope alongside a half-dozen others he'd never mailed. Unwrapping a hard candy from the jar on his desk, he popped it into his mouth, imprisoning it under his tongue while cinnamon and sugar melted into his bloodstream. Some days, it was the only thing that helped. On a good day, he'd eat only a half-dozen or so. On a bad day, he'd be on his knees under the desk at day's end, gathering cellophane wrappers off the floor and tossing them into the trash.

Today was showing every indication of being a bad day. He bit down hard on the candy and it disintegrated. How was he supposed to carry out his ministry when the Church kept throwing roadblocks in his path? Was he expected to offer only spiritual guidance, intended to herd his flock along the most direct route to heaven? Certainly the afterlife was a primary concern for all people of reason, Catholic or otherwise. But what about the lives his parishioners led right here, right now? If there were something he could do to improve the quality of their lives, wasn't it his responsibility to follow through? To whom did he owe his principal loyalty: God, or the Catholic Church?

It was a question he'd asked himself numerous times over the past few months, but he hadn't yet come up with an acceptable answer.

By the time Jeff and Tia showed up, he was on his third piece of candy. He hung up their coats, offered them each a candy to break the ice, then sat back in his chair and studied their young, earnest faces. Each year, the couples he married seemed younger and younger. It was probably a sign of encroaching middle age, something he wasn't ready to think about. Not just yet, not while he still remained far enough on the good side of forty that he could pretend it wasn't hovering on the not-so-distant horizon.

While the kids held hands with white-knuckled devotion, he talked to them about the sacrament of marriage, about its significance to the Church and to God. He discussed with them the nature of their relationship, explored their expectations of marriage and their readiness to make a lifetime commitment to each other.

He talked about the spiraling divorce rate, advised them of the gravity of the step they were considering, reminded them that the Church didn't recognize divorce. He pointed out for a second time that marriage was a lifetime commitment, and not just something to try on and discard if it didn't fit. Still livid over the hand-slapping he'd received this morning, he stuck to the party line, reminding them of the Church's expectation that as an engaged couple, they would conduct themselves with chastity and decorum.

After forty-five minutes, he closed the session with a prayer. The kids both looked somber, and he believed he'd instilled a sufficient level of anxiety in them for one day. He felt like an ogre, but he'd done his job, which was to make them think before they jumped blindly into something that might ruin both their lives.

Jeff helped Tia with her coat, his hand lingering at her shoulder in a show of tenderness. With all his heart, Clancy wished them a happy ending, even though he knew it would take a great deal of work, and more than a little luck, to achieve that happy ending. It was a misnomer anyway, that term, for marriage was a journey, not a destination. All of life was a journey. Heaven was the destination.

"We'll meet again in a month or so," he told them, "after you've had time to talk over what we've discussed today. You can make an appointment with Melissa on your way out."

Jeff held out a boyish hand. He didn't look old enough to shave, let alone get married. "Thank you, Father."

He shook Jeff's hand warmly. "You're welcome. Tia, how's school going?"

"Great. I made the dean's list last semester. Mom practically keeled over from the shock. Which reminds me." She reached into her coat pocket, long hair falling around her, and pulled out a small envelope. "For you, Father." She held it out to him. "From my mom. It's a pair of tickets to the spring flower show. It starts today. She works at the Bayside Expo, and she always gets free tickets to all the events. She said she thought you looked a little down last Sunday." Tia rolled her eyes in exaggerated aggravation. "You know how mothers are. Anyway, she thought after the winter we've had, the flower show might cheer you up."

He wondered what it was about him that made all these women perceive him as needy. The ladies of his parish, young and old, fluttered around him as though he were a lost lamb in need of mothering. They fed him roast beef and Irish stew and coffee cake, knitted him socks and scarves and mittens, sent him gifts. A prayer book, a bottle of wine, a pair of tickets to the flower show. In spite of the clerical collar and the rosary, a few of them had been known to offer him more than that, and it totally bewildered him.

"Thank you, Tia," he said. "Tell your mother I'm grateful."

He saw them out, then stood in the doorway to his study, tickets in hand, wondering what the devil he was going to do with them. It wasn't terribly practical to give two tickets to a priest. Who was he supposed to take with him? His mother was long dead, and he didn't have any sisters. He briefly considered inviting his secretary, but immediately vetoed the idea. Melissa was too much like an adoring pup, running along full-tilt behind him, and he wasn't about to open that particular can of worms.

He supposed he could give them away. Call his friend Conor, offer them to him and Carolyn. But he really couldn't picture the Raffertys whiling away an afternoon sniffing posies. It didn't seem their style. Old Alton Robbins, amazingly spry for a man of eighty-seven, would be delighted with the tickets, would probably call up the Widow Larson for a date. But Alton was in Florida, where flowers grew directly outside his door, while Clancy was stuck in Boston, with winter not only outside his door, but inside his heart. He desperately needed an infusion of spring, and an afternoon spent in a garden—even an indoor one—would suit him just fine. It seemed a shame not to share his serendipity with some other winter-weary soul.

Tapping the envelope impatiently against his palm, he glanced at the wall clock. His ten-thirty appointment was five minutes late. Outside the window, snow spiraled in a shimmering cloud, raised by the frigid March wind. "She's late," he said.

Melissa glanced up from her computer screen. "Who's late?"

"My ten-thirty. Sarah Connelly. Do you have any idea what she wants?"

"Not a clue. She's a friend of Josie Porter's. Josie called yesterday and made the appointment for her."

"Ah. I see."

It was typical of Josie. Ever since they were kids, playing kickball on M Street in Southie, Josie had practiced what he euphemistically referred to as urban renewal. She loved to take in strays and try to improve their lives. Sarah Connelly must be one of her victims. If the woman was smart, she'd escape from Josie's clutches while she still had the chance.

"I'll be in my study," he said. "Let me know when she gets here." He glanced out at the swirling snow and added gloomily, "*If* she gets here."

Melissa's watchful gaze sharpened. "Are you all right?"

He supposed the answer to her question depended on whether exhaustion, frustration, and restlessness fell under the heading of all right. "Cabin fever," he said. "That's all."

He closed the door between them, walked to the window, and stood gazing out over the parking lot. Backlit by the morning sun, the blowing snow nearly obliterated his view of the rectory opposite the church. While he watched, a powder-blue vintage Mustang pulled into the parking lot and came to a stop beside his Saturn sedan. The door opened and a woman climbed out. She struggled with the car door, wavy brown hair lashing wildly against her face, before she won the battle with the wind and slammed it shut.

With a sigh, Clancy turned away from the window, yanked open the drawer that held the letters, and pitched in the tickets.

2

A biting wind swirled in off Dorchester Bay as Sarah Connelly slammed shut the door of the Mustang and glanced at her watch. She was ten minutes late, thanks to some nitwit in a Jaguar who'd changed lanes without signaling, forcing her into an instantaneous choice between death and an I-93 off-ramp. She'd chosen the off-ramp, then she'd had to drive for several blocks until she found a place where she could pull an illegal U-turn and backtrack to where she'd started. If not for good instincts, she'd be driving around in circles right now, lost somewhere in the Roxbury slums.

Everything she'd ever heard about Boston drivers was true. They were the rudest, most aggressive and egocentric creatures on the planet. These people were impervious to such minor inconveniences as traffic lights, stop signs, pedestrians, and emergency vehicles. They double-parked wherever and whenever it suited them, would sooner die than yield the right-of-way, and traveled life's highways with the supreme confidence of sole proprietorship.

Drawing her coat tighter around her in a vain attempt to keep the wind from slicing straight through it, she glanced up at Saint Bartholomew's Catholic Church, towering above her in all its Gothic splendor, narrow spire reaching like a stark finger into the winter sky. As she stood studying the gray stone fortress with its stained glass windows and bright red wooden doors, another icy blast of wind slammed into her, nearly stealing her breath away. She'd never considered herself a hothouse flower, but back home in Louisiana, she couldn't have imagined this kind of brutal cold. Buffeted by swirling gusts, she lowered her head and marched determinedly toward the door leading to the parish office.

Inside the church, warmth hit her with almost physical force, accompanied by the rich, heady aroma of fresh-brewed coffee. The young woman—barely more than a girl—who sat behind the reception desk glanced up and smiled. "Cold enough for you?" she said.

"Lord almighty." Sarah struggled to catch her breath. "This is the craziest weather I've ever seen. A week ago, it was fifty degrees, and now this. If I had any brains at all, I would've settled in Phoenix." She pulled off her gloves and tucked them into her pockets. "I'm Sarah Connelly. I have an appointment with Father Donovan. I'm a little late, thanks to some yahoo who tried to run me down on the Expressway."

"We were wondering what happened to you. I'll tell Father you're here." The woman swiveled in her chair, stood and moved fluidly toward a closed door behind her workstation. Sarah unbuttoned her coat and spent a moment smoothing the hair that the wind had restyled into something bearing more than a passing resemblance to a nest of adders. Beside the desk, a twenty-gallon fish tank bubbled merrily, tropical fish darting to and fro. Abandoning her hopeless attempt at salvaging her coiffure, she leaned to study the tiny flashes of vivid color racing through a jungle of greenery.

"Sarah?"

The rich baritone voice startled her, and she wheeled around to face its source. When Josie had described the priest as an old family friend, she had somehow translated that to mean grizzled and arthritic. But she'd been off track. Way off track. He was somewhere in his mid-thirties, tall and rawboned and attractive. His hair was a rich, deep mahogany, too dark to be a true auburn, too awash with red highlights to be anything as prosaic as brown. There was something of the ascetic in his face, lean almost to the point of gauntness above the clerical collar, an austerity that was magnified by the stark black of his attire. The severity ended abruptly at his eyes, which were a peculiar shade of amber that reminded her of the bourbon Remy kept in sparkling crystal decanters behind the bar in his den.

"I'm Father Donovan," he said. "I hear you ran into a little trouble on the Expressway."

"I had a run-in with a Jaguar. Not the four-legged kind, although the sentiment's pretty much the same. Kill or be killed. I think that must be stamped on every driver's license issued by the Commonwealth of Massachusetts."

She crossed the room and shook the hand he offered. His hand was warm, his grip solid, the grip of a man who knew his place in life and was comfortable with it. "Your hands are like ice," he said. "Can I get you a cup of coffee?"

"I would dearly love a cup of coffee. Cream, please, and two sugars."

"Help yourself to a chair in my study. I'll be right in."

An antique walnut desk, flanked by a pair of matching jade plants in terra-cotta pots, dominated the room. A faded Oriental carpet covered the floor. The twin casement windows wore curtains of a soft green, a hue that was picked up in the fabric of the two plush chairs facing the desk. Built-in bookshelves, heavy with books, lined two walls.

The overall effect was one of warmth and coziness. She took off her coat, perched on a soft chair, and scrutinized book spines while she waited. Most of them were bulky religious tomes. Heavy reading, in every sense of the word. He returned with the coffee in a ceramic mug, and she accepted it gratefully, wrapping her hands around it for warmth.

"Thank you," she said. "That cold out there is nothing short of barbaric."

He shut the door behind him and said, "You're not from around here."

"Tell me, Father, was it the frozen hands or the tirade about Boston drivers that gave me away?"

He settled his lanky frame into the chair behind the desk. Leaning back, he studied her with those oddly leonine eyes. "I can hear it in your voice. Just a hint of it, but it's there. Deep South. Mississippi, maybe Alabama or northern Florida. It makes me think of moonlight and the scent of magnolias."

"Louisiana," she said. "Most recently, New Orleans. But I was raised in a bayou town so small, it doesn't show up on any maps." She took a sip of scalding coffee, used it as an excuse to study him further. His hair was a little too long, a little too shaggy, and he possessed the pale, almost ethereal coloring so common among the dark-haired Celts. He wasn't quite handsome; his features lacked the polished refinement that marked classic handsomeness. But he was striking, with a wild, dark beauty all his own. Heathcliff, wandering the windswept moors.

"So," he said, "you're a friend of Josie's."

"Actually, I'm her boss."

Warmth flooded those golden eyes. "Of course. You're the lady who just bought the bookstore. Josie's mentioned you."

"Then you have a distinct advantage over me, Father, because she's never mentioned you until now. And you're not at all what I expected. You're so—" She paused, searched desperately for the right word. *Dark. Intense. Intriguing. Sexy.*

He picked up his coffee cup and took a sip. "So...?"

"Young," she said, breaking eye contact and focusing on a single dark blue paperback sitting on a lower shelf, just at eye level. *Catechism of the Catholic Church*. She supposed if he ever suffered from insomnia, the cure was readily available, right here on his bookshelves.

"Ah," he said. "You were expecting someone like my predecessor, Father O'Rourke. Some crotchety priest from the old school who believes in bringing people to God by beating religion into them with a stick."

When she turned back to him, she noted the gleam in his eye. "Are you making fun of me, Father?"

"Maybe just a bit. You know, when I first meet people, they generally react to me in one of two ways. Some of them try very hard to convince me how devout they are. They're looking for brownie points that'll give them an in with the Big Guy upstairs." He tapped a fingernail against his coffee mug. "The rest are terrified I'll see right through them and send them directly to hell."

"I see. And where do I fit into this little scenario?"

"I'm still trying to figure you out. You're an anomaly. You don't fit in anywhere."

"Maybe that's because I'm not Catholic. I don't aspire to heaven, and I don't believe in hell. So I have no reason to fear you." She took a sip of coffee and studied him over the rim of the cup. "Or to impress you."

"An infidel," he said. "What a shame. So what can I do for you?"

Her gaze wandered to the desktop, worn by time to a gleaming patina. On one corner, beside an open jar of hard candies, perched a whimsical ceramic sculpture of a winged pig, poised for flight. Curious about its significance, Sarah tightened her grip on her coffee mug and met his eyes.

"Three days ago," she said, "my sixteen-year-old niece ran away from home."

"I see."

"I believe she's somewhere on the streets of Boston. It's not the first time she's run away. The last time it happened, Remy—my ex-husband—and I were absolutely frantic. Two weeks after she disappeared, the NOPD arrested her for soliciting a police officer on Bourbon Street. Kit swore it was a mistake, but I don't know what to believe. I know what happens to young girls out on the street, especially pretty ones like Kit. I'm terrified that if she gets desperate enough, she'll do the same thing again. Only this time, she'll pick the wrong man and end up—"

She paused, shook her head to dispel the images playing in living color inside her brain. "I don't know what to do. The police are useless. You know what they told me? That they'd enter her name into their database. If she gets arrested, they'll give me a call. Meanwhile, she's out there somewhere in this brutal cold. She's sixteen years old, Father. Sixteen! And nobody seems to give a damn." Cupping her coffee mug in both hands, she leaned forward. "I'm here because Josie said you could find her. She said you have experience with this kind of thing."

Silence filled the space between them. He cleared his throat. "This isn't precisely the kind of thing I have experience with. I pull teenage prostitutes off the street and place them in a halfway house. I've never gone looking for a missing girl before."

"But Josie said you know the streets. You know where to look, who to talk to, what questions to ask. You're it, Father. End of the line. I have nobody else."

Those amber eyes studied her at length. "What do you plan to do with her if you find her?"

She brushed a strand of windswept hair back from her forehead. "Bring her home, of course. Bring her home and keep her there."

He steepled his fingers on the desktop. "Forgive me for pointing out the obvious, but that doesn't seem to have worked very well so far. What's to prevent her from just running away again?"

She stared at him for a moment, then she set down her

coffee mug, hard, on the desktop. "I'm afraid Josie was wrong. I'm wasting my time here. I apologize for wasting yours."

"I didn't say I wouldn't help you. I'm just trying to find out how thoroughly you've thought this through."

"What's there to think about?" she said in exasperation. "Damn it, do you expect me to just leave her there?"

A clock ticked in the silence. He got up from his chair, walked to the window, and stood looking out. "The police won't help you," he said.

"No. They made that abundantly clear."

Turning, he said, "You have to understand their point of view. If they did an active search for every runaway teenager, they wouldn't have time to do anything else. There'd be anarchy. Chaos in the streets. Criminals would have a field day."

"That's not much comfort," she said, "when it's your teenager who's run away."

"No," he said, leaning against the window frame and tucking his hands into his pockets, "it's not. Do you have legal custody? Anything on paper saying the girl belongs to you?"

"No. When Bobby decided he couldn't handle her any more, he just dumped her on my doorstep. I don't even know where he is."

"Bobby's her father?"

"Yes." She grimaced. "My brother. Mister Responsibility."

"And her mother?"

She drew a breath and squared her shoulders. "Ellie died when Kit was four years old."

"That complicates things. Technically, custody belongs to her father. That means what you're contemplating could be construed as kidnapping if she doesn't go with you willingly."

"That's insane! Her father left her with me. Doesn't that imply consent? Are you telling me I don't have a right to protect her?"

"Unfortunately, that's precisely what I'm telling you. You have no legal rights whatsoever."

Outraged, she said, "What about a moral right, Father? What about my right to protect my own flesh and blood?"

She could hear the Mississippi Delta, thick as gumbo, coursing through her speech. No matter how hard she tried to prevent it from happening, intense emotion always exaggerated her accent.

"Sarah," he said gently, "I'm on your side. I just want you to know what we're up against. If we take her against her will, there's a possibility we could both end up in trouble. Have you notified your brother that she's missing?"

Somewhere beyond her anger and her fear, somewhere beyond the frustration of the situation, in some lucid corner of her mind, she recognized that he'd said *we*. Not *you*, but *we*. "I've tried," she said. "But he's pulled one of his infamous disappearing acts. Nobody seems to know where he is." She leaned forward. "Does this mean you're going to help me?"

"First," he said, moving with easy grace back to his chair, "I'd like to know a little about Kit. Why'd she run away?" He sat, rolled the chair back from the desk, and crossed his long legs, resting one ankle atop the opposite knee. "What's so terrible at home that she'd rather be peddling her body on a street corner?"

Fury spiked through her. She looked him directly in the eye and said grimly, "Every second Tuesday, I lock her in a closet and feed her Kal Kan sandwiches."

For the first time, she saw a glimmer of a smile on his face. "I'm trying to get a feel for the situation," he said. "I'm not accusing you of anything."

"Look, my brother isn't exactly a prime candidate for Father of the Year. For ten years, he let Kit run wild. I'm the first person who's ever said no to her, the only one who's ever had expectations of her. She's having a hard time dealing with it."

"I can imagine that would be difficult for her."

"If you want to get specific, we had a big blowout Wednesday morning over whether or not she was going to get her tongue pierced."

"Let me guess. You were the one who voted against it."

"Cute," she said. "Very cute."

"Have you checked with her school? Her friends?"

"That was my first thought. It was a useless endeavor. Her teachers all said the same thing. Kit kept to herself, didn't talk to much of anybody. She ate lunch by herself, didn't have any homeroom buddies. I tried talking to a few of the kids, but all I got was a big, fat zero."

She leaned back in the chair, crossed denim-clad legs, and sighed. "I know I'm too strict. Ellie probably would've let her do it. She spoiled Kit rotten, but in a good way. She just wanted to give Kit the world. She was a wonderful mother. Then she died, just like that. An aneurysm, at twenty-six." She paused, took a deep breath. "Bobby couldn't handle losing her. Everywhere he looked, he could see Ellie's face. I didn't blame him for leaving home, but I just couldn't see him carting Kit around from town to town while he played one-night stands with some third-rate country band. I begged him to leave her with me. Of course, he wouldn't listen. She was all he had left."

Softly, he said, "And?"

"And." She took a sip of coffee. "They both survived Bobby's haphazard lifestyle until Kit turned thirteen and all those adolescent hormones kicked in. The monster Bobby'd created came roaring to life, and he finally figured out that this parenting thing was a little more complicated than he'd thought. It actually involved work, and work is something to which my brother has always had a powerful aversion. That was when he remembered how his little sister had begged for the opportunity to raise his daughter. So he brought her to me."

"Lucky you."

She smiled, but there wasn't much humor in it. "Kit," she said, "is the teenager all parents pray their child won't turn into. Sullen, rude, impetuous and lazy. She's also smart and beautiful and talented. Strong, in the same way my mother was strong. Every once in a while, the clouds will part and I'll catch a glimpse of Momma in there. Then the clouds move back in, and I'm convinced Kit's some doppelgänger planted by aliens for the express purpose of driving me crazy."

His smile returned, turning those golden eyes of his to molten lava. "She sounds like a normal teenager to me."

"If by normal, you mean obnoxious and unhappy and thoroughly unlikable, then yes, she's normal." Sarah's voice softened. "I have to tell you this up front, Father. I'd lay down my life for that girl. I don't expect you to understand. I know you're concerned about the risks. So am I. Not for myself, but for you. If you got into trouble because of me, I'd feel terrible. But I'm desperate, and—"

"It wouldn't be the first time. Do you have a picture of her?"

"Right here." She fumbled in her purse, pulled it out, and slid it across the desk. "What do you mean, it wouldn't be the first time?"

He glanced at the picture. "Pretty girl. She looks just like you." He opened a drawer and took out a sheet of paper, picked up a felt-tipped pen in his left hand, and began writing. Even upside-down, his handwriting was distinctive. Like him, it was dark and bold and elegant. "I've been in trouble before," he said. "The sky didn't fall." Still writing, he added, "I need some information about Kit. Height, weight, date of birth, any identifying characteristics."

She answered his questions, watched his hand as it followed the words across the paper. His fingers were long and narrow, his wrist bony and lightly dusted with dark hair. "Are you sure you're really a priest?" she said.

He crossed a final *t,* capped the pen and glanced up at her. "You know," he said, "that's the same question I ask myself at least twice a day. Do you like flowers?"

"Excuse me?"

"Flowers. One of my parishioners gave me two tickets to the spring flower show. If I invite my secretary—" he glanced at the closed door and grimaced "—let's just say it's not a good idea for me to invite my secretary. We're walking a fine line already. If you're free for a couple of hours, I'll treat you to a taste of spring. While we're looking at flowers, we'll cook up some kind of game plan for finding your niece."

His offer was tempting. All those flowers. An abundance of color and sweetness to feed her withered soul and provide some respite from winter's monotony. And it wouldn't be terribly painful to spend the next couple of hours in his presence. The man was charming and intelligent, and he exuded an energy so fierce the air around him vibrated with it. The fact that he was a priest was an asset. She wouldn't have to worry that he'd make any moves on her.

"I'll have to call Josie," she said. "I can't just disappear in the middle of a busy Saturday. She'll think I got mowed down by a transit bus."

He picked up the phone, held the receiver in midair. "I'll give her a call. What's the number?"

She gave in to the inevitable and reeled off Bookmark's phone number. Standing, he pulled a shapeless black wool coat from the coatrack beside his desk. "Jose?" he said as he shrugged into it. "It's Clancy. I'm kidnapping your boss for a couple of hours."

The coat reached past his knees, exaggerating his lankiness. Cradling the phone between his ear and his shoulder, he leaned to open a desk drawer, pulled out an envelope and stuffed it into his pocket. "Fine, then," he said, shifting the phone back to his left hand. "Don't look for her until you see the whites of her eyes."

When he ushered Sarah into the outer office, his secretary looked up at them in surprise. "Where are you going?" she said.

"Out. There's something I need to do."

She glanced quizzically at Sarah, then at the clock, and raised her eyebrows. He dropped Kit's photo and his hand-written note on her desk. Looping his scarf around his neck, he said, "I'd like you to make up some flyers for me. Nice big print. Three hundred copies. When you're done with that, give Kate Miller's office a call. Tell them I picked up a new girl last night. See if you can get her an appointment for sometime this coming week. Then I'd appreciate it if you'd call the O'Malleys and tell them something's come up, but I'll stop by later today, after confession, to see the baby."

"What about the altar guild?"

He knotted the scarf, patted his pockets, pulled out gloves, car keys. "Tell them I have absolute conviction that they can make it through their meeting this morning without my input. If they need to discuss any burning issues, I'm free for a couple of hours tomorrow after ten o'clock Mass."

The secretary's eyes narrowed. "You're not going to mail the letter you wrote to the bishop, are you?"

"No," he said, pulling on his gloves. "The letter's in the drawer, with all the others I've written to the bishop. We're going out in search of spring."

"Spring?" she said, as though she'd never heard the word before.

"You remember spring. The season that falls between those six months of winter and those six weeks of summer?"

The girl looked at him, then at Sarah. Sarah shrugged apologetically. *You know him better than I do. You figure him out.*

"Oh," his secretary said, and smiled. "Spring."

3

Sarah.

I've got lunch on Sunday at what's-its-name over in
Sausalito. You know how much I hate to be disappoint—

Gus collected her and said archly, "Sarah.

"*Phaleanopsis.*"

Over the din that shook the Bayside Expo to the rafters, Sarah heard the priest speak, but his words were indecipherable. She stopped, turned, and found him absorbed in one of the exhibits. "Excuse me?" she shouted.

"*Phaleanopsis.* It's a rare orchid from—" The rest of his words were drowned out by the overhead loudspeaker announcing the winner in a raffle for a dozen bags of topsoil.

"I'm sorry. I can't hear you."

He shifted his coat from his left arm to his right, clearing a few inches of space beside him. Beckoning, he said something unintelligible that she loosely interpreted as, "Come and see."

She squeezed between an elderly woman with blue hair and a young couple pushing a squalling baby in a stroller. "This is like Mardi Gras—" she shouted "—only without the booze."

"What?"

"I said—oh, never mind."

The flower arrangement was breathtaking. *Phaleanopsis* was exquisite, with petals of snowy white, daubed here and there with red. It looked like some fancy dessert, a frothy white confection dripping with raspberry sauce.

"They grow these on Maui," he said near her ear.

"They're lovely."

"I've seen them in the wild. Simply breathtaking. Do you want to—"

Once again, the hubbub swallowed his words. She shrugged apologetically, and he inclined his head in the direction of the lobby. She nodded, and they began working their way through the crowd toward the exit.

After the saunalike conditions inside the Expo, the frigid March wind struck her damp skin with such stunning force that she gasped. "I'm sorry," he said, pulling on his gloves. "I should have realized opening day would be a zoo."

"I think it was the thirteen busloads of senior citizens from upstate New York that tipped the scales," she said as they strode briskly across acres of parking lot. "But the exhibits were lovely. What I could see of them."

Eventually, they reached his little blue Saturn sedan. He unlocked the door and she climbed into the passenger seat, grateful for the reprieve from the biting wind. She sat shivering while the engine warmed. Fiddling with the heater, he said, "How long have you been in Boston?"

"Since August. Kit and I moved here right before the start of the school year."

"Ah. Then this is your first New England winter."

"And it may well be my last."

"You'll adjust. Give it a year or two—"

"Or ten?"

Still engrossed in the heater controls, he glanced up. When he smiled, warmth swam in those golden eyes. "Or ten," he said, "and your blood will thicken. You'll start to feel like a native."

"Right now, I feel like a Popsicle."

He finally got the heater knobs adjusted, and glorious warmth flowed from the vents. "In another month, there'll be flowers blooming everywhere."

"And I'm supposed to believe you because…?"

"I'm a priest. We're not allowed to lie. Are you hungry?"

"I'm not sure. Ask me again after I've thawed out."

"I have ninety minutes before afternoon confession. Since it was too noisy to talk at the Expo, we might as well talk over lunch." He carefully backed out of the parking space. "If you'd like music," he said, shifting gears, "there's a little of everything in the console."

With icy fingers, she locked her seat belt and snugged it around her, then flipped open the hinged console cover to reveal his CD collection. Melissa Etheridge. U2. Bruce Springsteen. Tom Petty. "My, my," she said, "you have interesting musical tastes."

"For a priest?"

"I didn't say that."

"You were thinking it."

"You have to admit," she said, working her way through CD cases, "there probably aren't too many priests around who own the soundtrack to *Saturday Night Fever*."

"Bite your tongue. That's a true classic from the good old days when the Bee Gees wielded iron control over the Top Ten, and John Travolta was King of the World. I was twelve years old when I saw that movie, and I wanted to be him."

She studied him with avid interest. "As I recall, Father, that movie was rated R. How'd you get in at twelve?"

"I had a friend with an eighteen-year-old sister who drove a '66 Bonneville. It had the biggest trunk I ever saw. If we squeezed tight, she could fit four of us in there. She used to sneak us into the drive-in."

"So you were a wild child."

"That's a polite way of putting it. I was a rebellious, hard-headed delinquent, determined to ride the fast track to hell."

"How'd you end up on the road to heaven instead?"

"Sooner or later, we all grow up."

When he pulled up in front of a Chinese restaurant in a strip mall near the Expo, she studied its facade with apprehension. The plate glass windows hadn't been washed in months, and a wide crack marred the plastic sign that said All Day Buffet.

"I know it doesn't look like much," he said, shutting off the ignition, "but the food's marvelous."

"I didn't say a word."

"You didn't have to. You have an incredibly expressive face. Trust me, you're safe here. They haven't killed a customer yet."

Outside the entrance, he paused to flip open the door of a battered newspaper vending machine. He pulled out a folded tabloid and tucked it under his arm, then held open the restaurant door for her. The instant she stepped inside, heavenly smells accosted her from every direction: ginger, soy sauce, Chinese tea and the mouth-watering aromas of frying chicken and pork.

An elderly Asian man led them to a corner booth and poured them each a steaming cup of tea before disappearing through a swinging door into the kitchen. She took a sip of the fragrant hot liquid, warmed her hands with the miniature teacup and studied the man who sat across from her.

His eyes were keen and bold as he returned her assessment. "We can help ourselves to the buffet."

She set down her teacup. "Then lead the way before I expire from hunger."

The restaurant may have been small, but the quality and variety of foods on the buffet were surprisingly good. She took her time choosing from the assortment of exotic delicacies, returning at last to the table with a number of familiar items as well as tidbits from several new dishes she'd never tried before. She slid into the red vinyl booth and eyed his heaping plate in astonishment.

"What?" he said.

"How can you eat like that and stay so thin? There's not an ounce of fat on you."

He picked up the chopsticks the waiter had left beside his

plate and removed them from their paper wrapper. "I have an active metabolism. I could eat all day and not gain weight."

"If I ate like that," she said, "I'd weigh six hundred pounds." She watched his expertise with the chopsticks, eyed the matching pair by her plate, and opted for her fork. "You maneuver those things as if you know what you're doing."

"I spent a couple of years in Hong Kong."

"For the Church?" She nibbled a bite of broccoli.

He lifted his teacup, sipped, shook his head. "Before I entered the seminary." He set down the tea and picked up the newspaper he'd dropped on the seat beside him. "Are you familiar with the *Phoenix?*"

"No. What's the *Phoenix?*"

"Back in the early days, it used to be called an underground newspaper. Now the fever of political correctness has changed the term to alternative. It's aimed primarily at the college crowd. There's some pretty good journalism, a lengthy arts section—reviews of movies and theater and music and gallery exhibits. And then—" he opened it up, pulled out the innermost section and handed it to her "—there's this."

The black-and-white cover photo showed a man and a woman in a mildly suggestive pose. Inside, she found a soup-to-nuts menu of erotic pleasures, categorized for easy reference. Adult personals. Commercial ads for phone sex, exotic dance clubs, sex toys, XXX-rated book and video stores. Grainy photos of huge-breasted women with only the most crucial areas covered. Classified ads for everything from massage and escort services to fantasy and fetish. Spanking. Domination. *Hot young girls want it tonight.*

"Lord love a duck." She paged through it in horrified fascination. "Forgive me for sounding naive, but isn't most of this stuff illegal?"

He swallowed a mouthful of food and waved his hand in

a *comme ci, comme ça* gesture. "It's a gray area. Most of it skirts the edges of the law. Pornography—books, magazines, videos—isn't necessarily illegal. Depending, of course, on local ordinances. Any business that defines itself as an escort service or a massage parlor is in the clear unless you can prove the exchange of money for sexual gratification. And phone sex is an even more shadowy area. Because there's no actual physical contact, nobody can seem to decide whether or not it's prostitution. For the most part, the police look the other way. The consensus seems to be that it's a victimless crime." He set down his fork, took a sip of tea. "As you can see, sex is big business."

"I always thought of Boston as staid and reserved. Beacon Hill, old money, and all that."

"This city was settled by Puritans. It's been nearly four hundred years, and still we keep our vices well hidden. Don't get me wrong—we have plenty of vices. We just don't wave our dirty linens in front of the world. Welcome to Boston."

She folded up the newspaper. "I assume, Father, that you had some reason for showing me this. Other than shocking me."

"Have I shocked you?"

"Not particularly. I'm thirty-three years old. I've been married and divorced three times. I haven't lived under a rock."

He raised an eyebrow and studied her with keen interest. "Three times," he said.

"That doesn't mean I'm a floozy."

A smile played about the corner of his mouth. "The thought never crossed my mind."

"What it does mean," she said, "is that I have lousy taste in men. I have good intentions, but poor judgment. And why am I telling you this, anyway? I don't even know you, and I'm sure you don't give a rat's behind about my personal life."

"It's this clerical collar. You'd be amazed by the things people tell me. Yes, I had a reason for showing this to you, and it wasn't to shock you. I wanted you to understand a couple of things. First, the sex trade is a complex and pervasive issue with ramifications that extend far beyond the social or moral. There are political and economic cogs in this particular wheel. And street prostitution is only a very small part of the greater whole. The bottom rung of the ladder." He paused for a sip of tea. When he swallowed, his Adam's apple moved up and down.

"Second," he said, "Kit's an extremely attractive girl. Chances are good she won't be on the street for long."

Her stomach soured. "You think she'll be snatched up by some talent scout looking for new blood."

He picked up his napkin, wiped his fingers. "It's quite possible. If she ends up working for an escort service, finding her could be like finding the proverbial needle in a haystack."

She exhaled a hard breath. "Then I'd suggest, Father, that we don't waste any time getting out there."

A half-dozen customers browsed the bookstore shelves, and a trio of teenage girls clustered around the magazine rack, giggling over the latest photos of the boy band *du jour*. Sarah swept past the register, where Josie was flirting with a middle-aged customer buying the latest Ludlum blockbuster. Josie glanced up and raised her eyebrows, and Sarah tilted her head in the direction of her office.

She nearly tripped over Steve Merino. He was on his knees in aisle three, resetting shelves to make room for the newest Danielle Steel opus. The jeweled studs lining the college student's earlobes winked in the reflection of the overhead fluorescent lights.

"You were gone long enough," he said. "We were about to call out the search-and-rescue dogs."

She knelt beside him, frowned at a book that was shelved out of order, pulled it and reshelved it in its proper place. Eyeing the dreadlocks that had recently sprouted from his head, she said, "I do believe there are wild creatures nesting in there."

"Very Rastafarian, don't you think?" He shoved aside a half-dozen books and filled the empty space with glossy pink paperbacks from the box at his side.

"I hate to break it to you, son, but no matter how Jamaican you get, you'll still be a white boy from the burbs of Boston." Still on her knees, she followed along behind him, straightening the books he shelved, neatly lining up the spines.

Unfazed, he grinned. "Thanks for the reminder."

She ran a fingernail along the line of books. Satisfied with their alignment, she stood and dusted off the knees of her jeans, just in time to watch Josie stride briskly down the aisle. At thirty-three, Josie Porter, née Rafferty, was drop-dead gorgeous, with sleek black hair and deep green eyes, lush ruby lips, and a hard, lean body that looked equally delectable in jeans or in a slinky black cocktail dress. If Sarah hadn't liked Josie so much, she would have hated her.

"So?" Josie demanded. "What's the verdict?"

"He's going to help me look for her."

"Thank God." Josie closed her eyes, reopened them. "I knew Clancy'd come through for you."

"There aren't any guarantees, Jose. He made sure I understood that. But he has resources and experience I couldn't begin to replicate. It's a hell of a lot more than the police offered me."

"He'll find her. He has God on his side. And I have absolute faith in him. Clancy's the most amazing man I've ever met."

"Speaking of which, thanks for the warning."

"Warning?" Josie raised an eyebrow. "About what?"

"I left here this morning laboring under the misapprehension that I had an appointment with some well-meaning old geezer. It would've been nice if you'd prepared me for the reality of the situation."

Josie's slender, manicured fingers covered her mouth. "Oops."

"Oops is right. The man is so—so—" She stopped, unable to find a suitable adjective.

"Priestlike?" Josie offered.

"No, Jose, that's not quite the word I was trying to think of."

"So what's the problem?"

"There is no problem. It just would have been nice to be forewarned that the man is charming and erudite and way too easy on the eyes for a man of the cloth. Not to mention he has the subtlety of a steamroller and the edge of a freshly honed razor blade. I've never seen anybody ooze that much energy. Just being around him is exhausting. My head's still spinning."

"While we're on the subject of charming and attractive men," Josie said, "you missed a distinguished visitor. State Senator Thomas Adams IV stopped by to pay us a visit."

"I've never heard of him. Is he somebody important?"

From his perch on the floor, Steve said, "Don't you ever watch TV?"

"Not if I can help it."

"His face has been splashed all over it for months. Claims he can trace his family tree all the way back to *the* Adams family."

Sarah raised both eyebrows. "Morticia and Gomez?"

Steve grinned. "John and Samuel. Heroes of the American Revolution. I suppose you've never heard of them, either?"

"Are you kidding? I'm from the Southland. The only heroes they taught us about were Jefferson Davis and Robert E. Lee. Everybody else was a filthy Yankee. So what was the esteemed Mr. Adams doing in our humble establishment?''

"He's running for the U.S. Senate," Steve said. "He's out shaking hands and kissing babies and flashing his pearly whites at little old ladies. The man's terrifying. He's conservative enough to make Rush Limbaugh look like Dennis Rodman.''

"Oh, come on," Josie said. "I like him. He's polite, he's clean-cut, he's good-looking. He has a bit of a Kennedyesque aura to him.''

"He's a politician," Steve said. "They all have a Kennedyesque aura while they're on the campaign trail. It isn't until after they get elected that the forked tail and the little red horns start to grow. I've seen his type before. Good family man, pillar of the community. Wants to bring strong family values back into our lives. He'll probably get elected. Who among us is against family values? The minute he gets to Washington, he'll start lobbying for censorship, the overthrow of Roe versus Wade, and the return of women to the kitchen. It'll be 1950 all over again.''

In spite of herself, Sarah grinned. "Are you telling me you're an enlightened man who doesn't believe women belong in the kitchen?''

Steve pulled another stack of Pepto-Bismol pink books from the box at his side and stacked them on the floor. "Are you kidding? I'm all for women's rights. I can't wait to play Mister Mom while my wife goes out to slay the dragons of corporate America.''

Sarah glanced at Josie, who raised a single elegant eyebrow. Leaning to pat Steve on the shoulder, she said, "Good luck finding her, son.''

The North Shore wasn't his home territory, but Clancy had visited Revere often enough to be familiar with the working-class town that hugged the shore just north of Logan International Airport. Josie lived nearby. He'd been to her house numerous times over the years, for backyard barbecues and family get-togethers. When she was still married to Ed Porter, he'd been a regular at Ed's Saturday-night poker parties, until the stakes had climbed too high for a man living on a priest's subsistence salary, and he'd dropped out of the game for good.

He turned right at the liquor store, his stereo speakers thumping to a driving rock rhythm as he drove past a neighborhood convenience store that was closed for the night, past the darkened K of C hall, past a storefront funeral parlor that looked more like a restaurant than a place you'd take Aunt Greta or Uncle Giovanni to be dispatched to eternal rest. A block short of the garishly lit biker bar that was a local landmark, he hung another right, following Sarah Connelly's directions with unerring instinct. As a creature of the night, he was accustomed to navigating unfamiliar streets after dark. He found Chestnut Street easily and took a sharp left onto the short dead-end street lined with modest single-family dwellings.

Her house was the last one on the right. The swaybacked single-car garage snugged up close against a chain link fence that separated her property from the tracks where the blue line train ran day and night. He pulled into the driveway, headlights illuminating the Depression-era bungalow painted an alarming, eye-popping blue. He sat for a moment drinking it in, then turned off the ignition and opened his door, spilling vintage Springsteen into the crisp winter darkness.

The wind had died with the sunset, and the night was clear and cold. Stars swirled in a milky trail across the sky. He waded through drifted snow to the front door, illuminated by a single weak lightbulb. The porch steps were spongy, the framework sagging.

He rang the bell and waited. Light streamed from a window onto the plywood flooring, and he fingered a strip of curling blue paint that had peeled from the door frame. Hands in his coat pockets, he leaned back to study the house, admiring its old-fashioned lines and angles, the wide roof overhang that punctuated the upstairs windows. The place was a wreck, but it had potential, a charm and character missing from most new architecture. It wouldn't take much to restore the house to its former glory. A little paint, a little lumber—

"You think it looks bad now, you should see it in the daylight."

He fell back to earth with a thud. Sarah Connelly stood in the doorway, soft brown waves spilling over her shoulders as she leaned against the frame. There was something refreshing, something immensely appealing about this woman who was three times divorced but definitely not a floozy. He bit back a smile and cleared his throat. "Actually, I wasn't thinking that at all. I was admiring it."

"I thought you said priests weren't allowed to lie." In the dim illumination from the overhead light, her eyes were a vivid blue, and right now they sparkled with mischief.

"I'm not lying. This house has marvelous lines. Lovely bone structure. It just needs the right cosmetics to enhance those bones. Right now, it's just a little…" He trailed off, looked up at the roofline as words eluded him.

"Blue?" she suggested.

"Tired," he said. "A coat of paint would take care of most of your problems. A little lumber would fix the rest."

"That's what I keep telling Kit, every time she complains. It belonged to my Aunt Helen. The black sheep of the family. She was a political radical who taught English lit at Harvard. After her last stroke, she couldn't do the upkeep on the place, so she let it go to hell. It doesn't take long for neglect to do ugly things to a house. When she died, she left it to me."

"Well. I'm not sure whether to offer you congratulations or condolences."

When she smiled, a single deep dimple appeared in her

left cheek. "Just keep remembering those great lines. I fixed us a thermos of coffee. Let me get my coat."

He followed her through the snow to his car, held the door for her. As she climbed into the passenger seat, he caught a faint whiff of something—shampoo, perhaps, or perfume—sweet and wispy and feminine. Sometimes Carolyn Rafferty, his friend Conor's wife, smelled that way, like spun sugar, some sweet confection you'd find in a gift box wrapped with a red velvet ribbon. It had been over a decade since he'd buried his face in a woman's hair just to drink in her honeyed scent. Meg had been the last. Circumstances no longer allowed him to think of women in that way. But he hadn't forgotten.

He realigned his thoughts as he climbed into the car and popped out the Springsteen CD, replacing it with something less raucous, one of Dave Grusin's mellow jazz albums. Sarah picked up the stack of flyers he'd left on the passenger seat and studied the top sheet.

"Melissa did a good job with them," he said.

She glanced up, and her blue eyes softened. "I'm so sorry, Father," she said. "Dragging you out this late at night. It's not right for me to disrupt your life this way."

He backed out of her driveway and shifted the car into gear. "It's all right. I don't have much of a life, anyway."

As he drove down the darkened street, he was aware of her lengthy appraisal. "You look different in your civvies," she said. "Less…"

She trailed off, and he glanced down at the burgundy cable-knit sweater and jeans he'd worn instead of basic black. "Less what?"

"I don't know. Austere."

Austere. That was the last word he would have used to describe himself. Father O'Rourke had been austere. Bishop Halloran was austere. They'd been cut from the same mold, the two of them, dour of face and bleak of spirit. Clancy

Donovan was anything but dour. "It's not me," he protested. "It's the clothes."

"Yes," she said. "I know."

How could she possibly know? He'd only just met her this morning. He glanced suspiciously at her, wondering what else she could see, but he knew better than to ask. Women were odd creatures, intuitive in ways men couldn't begin to understand. Better he should simply accept her words at face value, and not question what lay beneath.

Route 1A was calm at this time of night, and they were both silent, soft jazz flowing around and between them as they passed parking lots and oil tank farms, weathered hangars and fuel trucks and jets lined up twelve deep, waiting for permission to take off. "Lovely scenery," she said dryly.

"Isn't it? Logan just keeps expanding, hacking away at East Boston a piece at a time."

He left the airport behind, stopped at the mouth of Sumner Tunnel to pay the toll, and then the tunnel swallowed them up. At this time of night, inbound traffic was light. He accelerated to cruising speed, heedless of the speed limit signs posted every quarter-mile. Like most natives, he considered them little more than a suggestion.

They emerged from the tunnel into the turmoil that was the Big Dig. "Lord in heaven," she said. "What a mess."

"I believe we're now in year eleven of a five-year project, with a budget that ran into the red several billion dollars ago. You have to admire the people of Boston. We're audacious, if nothing else. We leveled hills and filled swamps to hold up skyscrapers and boulevards and a high-speed highway. Now that we've recognized the monster we created, we're excavating to bury the ugliness and the exhaust fumes underground."

"Now I know why I stay in Revere."

He paused for a red light. Beside him, a bright red BMW raced its engine. The light turned green and the BMW shot forward. He followed at a more sedate pace, maneuvering through the maze of crooked streets and centuries-old buildings that was downtown Boston. "The city's not so bad," he said. "It has its moments."

"I daresay this isn't one of them."

He held back a smile. "Are you always this straightforward?"

"Only since my last divorce. I made a pact with myself."

She leaned over the dashboard and raised her face to gaze up at the silver monolith that was Exchange Place, the slender column of her neck turned alabaster by the moonlight. She had the most exquisitely flawless skin he'd ever seen.

"What kind of a pact?" he said, turning right onto State.

"The day I divorced Remy, I told myself that for the rest of my life, I'd be brutally honest in all my relationships. Most especially my relationship with myself."

"You were dishonest with yourself?"

"For six years, I lived with a man I didn't love. I kept telling myself it didn't matter, that I'd already been there, done that, bought the T-shirt. I came pretty close to convincing myself it was security that counted, above all else."

"What happened to change your mind?"

She leaned back in her seat, braced her head against the headrest. "Kit came to live with us. Remy'd already raised one family, and becoming instant daddy to a belligerent teenager at that particular point in his life simply wasn't on his agenda. I had to make a choice." She tilted her head, and he caught a glimpse of a wry smile. "The divorce was quite civilized."

He circled around the Common and picked up Commonwealth Avenue on the other side. It was broad and lovely, lined with ancient and majestic trees, and deserted at this late hour. "This is a big city," Sarah said. "She could be anywhere. How do you know where to look?"

"I grew up here. And it's not all that big. Girls work the

streets in relatively concentrated areas. I thought we'd try Kenmore Square first. There are dozens of bars in the blocks that surround Boston University, not to mention scores of testosterone-laden college boys with wads of disposable income."

It was past midnight and five below zero, but Kenmore Square was in full party regalia, brightly lit and heavily populated. The bars and most of the restaurants remained open until 1:00 a.m., and on Saturday nights they swarmed with college students and young singles right up until last call. He cruised the Square slowly, his gaze methodically and thoroughly scouring the sidewalks as he drove. They passed a young couple striding briskly, heads down and coat collars turned up against the frigid night, bare hand clasped in bare hand. A mixed-gender group clustered on a street corner, cigarette smoke rising in a cloud above their heads as they talked and laughed, expending the youthful energy they'd spent all week reining in.

He stopped for a red light, sat idling while a half-dozen drunken college students crossed the intersection in front of him. Pinpointed in his headlight beams, a heavyset blonde staggered and would have fallen if her giggling companions hadn't caught her and guided her to the other side of the street.

"A lot of college boys," he said, "get lucky before they leave the bars. They've learned that most girls, if you pour enough alcohol down their throats, will follow you anywhere. The boys who don't pick up a girl in a bar are stuck making do with the hookers who wait outside to snare the less fortunate souls in their traps. Over there."

He nodded in the direction of a slender black girl with bare legs and spike heels who leaned casually against a lamppost. His stomach soured as a lanky young man walked up to her. They carried on a brief, intense conversation before she shook her head and went back to leaning. The boy walked away, shoulders slumped in disappointment.

"How do you pick them out?" Sarah said. "I wouldn't have even noticed her. The way young girls dress nowadays, sometimes it's hard to tell the difference."

"I've had years of practice. It's not just the way a girl dresses, but the way she walks, the way she holds her body, the aura of ownership she flaunts while she's parading around inside her own little corner of the world. These girls are very territorial. You'll see them, night after night, walking the same beat. And in this case, I cheated." His mouth thinned. "Her name's Terry. She's one of my girls. Or at least, she used to be."

He checked his rearview mirror, yanked the steering wheel to the right. Double-parked and set his four-way flashers. Pulling a flyer from the stack Sarah held in her lap, he said grimly, "I'll be right back."

Terry didn't seem surprised to see him. One glance into her eyes told him she was flying high on some illicit substance, which explained why she wasn't shivering in the skimpy outfit she wore. She probably hadn't even noticed the cold. It was a situation that could prove lethal. Hypothermia was a stealthy and insidious enemy, just one of many enemies lurking on these streets, waiting for the next unsuspecting victim.

"Hello, Terry," he said.

She eyed him up and down. "Hope you're not here to peddle any of that 'Jesus loves you' shit, Father, because I ain't taking any."

"I don't peddle shit. I peddle second chances."

"Yeah? Well, I already blew my second chance, so go find somebody else to pester."

"Let me see your arm."

"Go to hell."

Her words were defiant, but they lacked bite. She didn't

even resist when he gently but firmly took her wrist in his hand and shoved up the sleeve of the thin jacket she wore. He studied the bruises and the needle tracks in silence, then tugged the sleeve back down and released her arm.

"It's never too late," he said. "I've told you before."

"It was always too late, Father. But thanks for dropping by. Next time, give me a call first. We'll have a tea party."

Ignoring her sarcasm, he withdrew a business card from his pocket, tucked it into her hand and folded her icy fingers around it. "My cell phone number's on the card. You can call any time, day or night. Even if you just want to talk. I'm a good listener."

"Right."

He held up the flyer. "I'm looking for this girl."

She gazed dispassionately at the photo of Kit Connelly. "Yeah? So what?"

"She's a sixteen-year-old runaway, and she's not familiar with the city. Her aunt's very worried about her."

"My heart bleeds."

"Her name's Kit. If you see her, or hear anything about her, I'd appreciate a call. In case you lose the card, my number's on the flyer. Remember, any time. I'm open twenty-four hours. Just like 7-Eleven." He folded the flyer and slipped it into the pocket of her jacket.

"Yeah, right. Look, would you mind getting lost now? You're scaring off my customers."

He returned to the car, slammed the door behind him, and sat unmoving behind the wheel. "You okay?" Sarah said.

Instead of answering—or perhaps it was an answer of sorts—he said, "Terry spent a couple of months last summer at Donovan House. I tried desperately to get through to her, but nothing I did or said made an iota of difference. One of the other girls caught her using the second-floor bathroom as a shooting gallery. Heroin. I couldn't allow her to stay. She could have undone months of progress we'd made with the others.''

He wondered who he was trying harder to convince, Sarah or himself. He folded his fingers around the steering wheel and sighed. ''You know the old saying about one bad apple spoiling the whole bunch? It's true. But it always breaks my heart when I have to put one of them back out onto the street.''

Softly, she said, ''I'm sorry.''

''Yes. So am I. Welcome to La Vida Loca.''

4

The Sir Charles wasn't much of a hotel, but for fifty bucks a night, Kit figured she was lucky to have her own bed and a toilet she didn't have to share with anybody but the resident vermin. The yellowed porcelain hadn't been scrubbed in a while, but at least the plumbing was in working order. The hotel slouched dejectedly on a side street near North Station, in a seedy, run-down neighborhood dotted with bars that catered primarily to winos and off-duty Big Dig construction workers. Traffic on the nearby Expressway was a constant dull roar, punctuated at regular intervals by the screech of the green line train that ran on overhead tracks above Causeway Street. The place wore an air of tired resignation, and the desk clerk had a mouthful of rotten teeth. But he took her cash without asking for an ID, and never questioned the fake name she used when she signed the register. She suspected that was because few patrons of the Sir Charles ever used their real names.

She locked herself in her room, unpacked her scanty belongings, then sat on the bed with the faded chintz spread to count her money. It was going far too quickly. She hadn't bought much: the bag of nuts, a burger and a Coke, and a copy of the *Globe* so she could look at the classified ads. But she'd paid in advance for a week in this lovely establishment, and the fifty-dollar-a-night room charge had eaten up a significant chunk of her meager stash. By her calculations, she could stay here for seven or eight nights—depending on how much, and how often, she ate—before she ran out of money.

There had to be other options. Cleaner, cheaper options. The YWCA, for instance. Maybe a youth hostel. She wasn't about to go near the runaway shelters. In the first place, she hadn't run away; she'd simply left home to start living her own life. Second, the homeless shelters would probably be the first place Aunt Sarah looked for her.

Assuming her aunt even bothered to look.

It was a shame she couldn't stay indefinitely here in this dump, because it was the last place on earth anybody would expect to find her. She would never have discovered the Sir Charles herself if she hadn't asked some guy who was pan-handling on a street corner where she could find the cheapest hotel in the neighborhood. She'd dropped fifty cents in his cup, and he'd given her directions.

There was no phone in her room, so she bundled up and walked over to North Station, where she miraculously found a pay phone that not only worked, but actually had a phone book attached. She bought a steaming cup of watery cocoa at McDonald's, got some change from the cute guy behind the counter, and began making phone calls.

It was a waste of time. She called every youth hostel in the phone book and got the same song and dance from each of them: staying there required a paid membership, and then you still had to pay a nightly fee on top of that. It was a big rip-off. The Y was even worse; the nightly room rates were nearly as high as some of the downtown hotels. So much for that brilliant idea.

But it wasn't the end of the world. She was young and strong and smart. For the next few nights at least, she had a roof over her head. It might not be the Waldorf, but her room was heated and the shower worked. The classified section of the *Globe* was huge. In a city the size of Boston, there were thousands of jobs. Tonight, she would read the want ads with pen in hand, circling the ones that showed the most promise. In the morning, she'd visit the theater district first. If nothing panned out there, she'd start following up on some of the ads she'd circled. Even if she had to wait tables for a living, she would get by.

"Good afternoon," Sarah said to the nineteen-year-old who'd come out of the back room when she asked to speak to the manager. "How are y'all doing?" He was tall and gangly, with a severe case of acne, and looked as though he should be playing high school basketball instead of managing the neighborhood 7-Eleven. But the kid wore a tie and a big plastic name tag that said Manager, so it looked like he was her man.

"I'm Sarah Connelly," she continued, "and my niece is missing." She held up a copy of the flyer, and the kid stared unblinking at Kit's photo, like a reptile sleeping in the sun. "Her name is Kit. She's sixteen years old, and very pretty. Have you seen her?"

"Nope."

He possessed all the animation of a corpse, and she was tempted to shake him just to make sure he was alive. Instead, she smiled sweetly and said, "I'd like your permission to post this in your front window."

"Uh..." He glanced around as though expecting the answer to drop out of the sky. "Yeah, okay. I guess it wouldn't hurt."

Trying to forget that kids like this were tomorrow's leaders, she taped the flyer in a conspicuous place near the front door. Back out on the street, the afternoon had grown cold as the sun sank deeper in the western sky. Sarah raised her coat collar and drew on her gloves. She'd been at this since breakfast, with just a ten-minute break for a lunch that had consisted of a cup of coffee and the world's greasiest hamburger.

The priest had mapped out a big chunk of downtown Boston, and the two of them had divvied up the territory. Armed with a stack of flyers and a roll of Scotch tape, she'd spent the last three days plastering Kit's face all over the sector he'd assigned her. Some of the shopkeepers she'd spoken with had been sympathetic and willing to help. Others were apathetic, even annoyed. One Chinese merchant actually shooed her away, flapping his apron and scolding her soundly with words she didn't understand.

Her feet ached, her toes were numb from the cold, and she sorely needed a bathroom. Glancing at her watch, she saw that it was nearly five. Quitting time. She paused on the sidewalk to get her bearings before heading for the Burger King where she and Clancy Donovan had agreed to meet.

She arrived ahead of him, made a quick pit stop in the ladies' room before she bought two cups of coffee and took them to a window seat, where she could watch the activity on the street outside. Traffic was a tangled snarl at this time of day, and the sidewalks were jammed with people who strode past with brisk determination, finished with the day's work and eager to get home for the evening. As she warmed her hands over her coffee cup, she wondered how the natives managed to tolerate this kind of cold, year after year. Winter seemed endless here in the Northeast. According to the calendar, spring was imminent, but somebody had forgotten to tell Mother Nature. Boston had to be the coldest place on earth, and March the coldest month.

In the purple shadows of dusk, she saw him coming half a block away. Head and shoulders above the crowd, Clancy Donovan moved with a distinctive, swinging stride, his long legs eating up the distance between them. He entered the restaurant and paused inside the doorway, his gaze scanning the room. She held aloft the cup of coffee she'd bought him. He saw it, rested a hand over his heart, and headed toward her. "God bless you," he said as he squeezed into the seat opposite her and dropped his stack of flyers on the table.

"I figured you were probably freezing, too."

"Who can find a virtuous woman? For her price is far above rubies." He peeled the plastic cover off his cup and tore open a sugar packet.

"Excuse me?"

He glanced up, smiling as he emptied the sugar packet into his coffee. "Proverbs 31:10."

"Of course. How silly of me to not recognize the verse. How'd it go for you?"

He busied himself opening plastic creamers and dumping their contents into his coffee. Stirring, he said, "About a seventy-five percent success rate."

"That's better than I did. For me, it was about fifty-fifty."

"It's the clerical collar. People are intimidated by it." He put the cover back on and peeled back the tab. "Sometimes I can use that to my advantage." Closing his eyes, he took a hit of steaming-hot coffee. Reverently, he said, "Nectar of the gods."

She watched him with bemusement. He opened his eyes, caught her watching, and flashed a rueful smile. "My one addiction," he admitted.

"And here I was, thinking you were perfect."

"Far from it, I'm afraid. But I have a bit of news that might interest you. There's a little Thai restaurant about five blocks from here." He took another sip of coffee. "The owner recognized Kit's picture. He says she was in there yesterday, looking for a job."

Her heart lurched, and she cupped a hand over her mouth. "Oh, Jesus," she whispered.

The priest leaned to the right, stretched a lanky arm toward a nearby condiment station, pulled a couple of napkins from their dispenser, and handed them to her.

She hadn't realized she was crying. "I'm sorry," she said,

dabbing at the corner of her eye. "I've just been so scared. So afraid she was dead. Is he absolutely certain it was her?"

"He says it was Kit. That's not the name she gave him, but he insists it was her."

She dropped the wadded napkins onto the table. "Do you think she'll come back? Did he offer her a job?"

The priest shook his head. "She refused to give him an address or a phone number, and that made him suspicious. He figured she must be a runaway, and he didn't want to get mixed up with that kind of trouble. So he told her the job was filled."

"A real Samaritan."

"Sarah, this is good news. It means Kit's somewhere nearby, and now that we've wallpapered downtown Boston with her picture, more people will come forward to say they've seen her." He set down his coffee cup, reached across the table as though to take her hand, then seemed to think better of it, retreating an instant before flesh would have touched flesh. "Sooner or later," he said, returning his hands to his coffee cup, "we'll catch up to her."

Discouragement, heavy and dank, flooded her. "In the meantime, what are we supposed to do?"

He picked his cup back up, his long fingers wrapped around it. "We've cast our bait," he said. "Now we do what every good fisherman does. We sit back and wait for a nibble."

Kit spent seven fruitless days looking for a job, seven days of aching feet and dashed hopes and continual rejection. She got absolutely nowhere with any of the theaters. Discouraged, she moved on to the restaurants and fast-food outlets, the dry cleaners and the copy shops. But they weren't interested, either. After several potential employers refused to even look at her application because she hadn't included a phone number or a home address, she wised up and fabricated them.

She lied about her experience, said she had waitressed for two years and that she knew how to type, and how to run a cash register. After all, how hard could it be? Any idiot could make change or find the right letters on a computer keyboard. She could probably type forty words a minute with two fingers.

But she hadn't counted on how many other people were also looking for work, most of them overqualified and as desperate as she was. She didn't stand a chance against some twenty-four-year-old with a master's in English and six years of waiting tables while he put himself through school. And there wasn't much call for unskilled labor. For even the dumbest of jobs, they wanted you to have either a college degree or experience, experience, experience.

So with sixty-two bucks left in her pocket and a trail of rejection behind her, Kit reluctantly packed her things and checked out of the Sir Charles. It might be a dump, but it had begun to feel like home. The noisy plumbing and the paper-thin walls had become familiar. Now her stomach was empty, her money was almost gone, and she had no place to sleep tonight. It didn't take an Einstein to figure out she had a big problem.

It was about to get bigger. As she passed a downtown restaurant, her eyes were drawn to a flyer tacked up in the window. Beneath the word MISSING, printed in huge, bold type, her own face smiled cheekily back at her.

Kit stopped abruptly, nearly causing a multi-pedestrian pileup, and gaped in amazement at her likeness. When she recovered her wits, she ducked into a nearby alley, away from the crowds of tourists jamming the sidewalks. Heart thudding, she shoved her hair up under her knit cap and scrabbled through her backpack for her Ray-Bans. With her hair and her eyes hidden, nobody on the planet would recognize her as the kid in the dorky ninth-grade school picture.

It didn't take long to discover that the flyers were taped to windows from Kenmore Square to the waterfront. Kit wanted to cry. She'd never get a job now, not with her face plastered all over the city like some kidnapped kid on a milk carton. She'd have to wear a Halloween mask if she didn't want to be recognized. How could that dried-up old witch do this to her? What the hell was she supposed to do now?

One thing she knew for sure. She wouldn't go back to the house in Revere, back to Aunt Sarah sticking closer to her than a flea on a bluetick hound. She'd rather starve to death here on the streets. Besides, it wasn't as though Sarah wanted her there. Nobody wanted her. Her aunt had only taken her in because they were blood relatives and she didn't have a choice. Sarah'd never had any kids of her own, and she didn't have a clue how to treat one. She ran the household like a boot camp, and Kit had experienced all of the military life she intended to take.

She was used to being alone, anyway. She'd always been alone. Right from the time she was a little girl, she'd known she was nothing but excess baggage to Daddy. She could see it in his eyes, could see it in the eyes of every new girlfriend who came sniffing around. None of them wanted some nosy little girl getting in the way of their big romance. They always pretended to be nice to her, but she could see straight through their lies. In the end, she always got shoved aside. They would put her to bed on a strange couch in a strange living room in a strange house, with nothing familiar except Freddy. Even the bedding smelled foreign. Daddy would go into the bedroom with the new girlfriend and close the door, and she'd be alone.

She'd lie there in the dark, clutching Freddy, terrified by the sound and feel of an unfamiliar house. Sometimes she'd have bad dreams, and wake up crying for Daddy. But Daddy never came. The bedroom door stayed shut. At other times, the noises she heard coming from behind that closed door frightened her, until she got old enough to understand what was going on. Then she just wrapped the pillow around her head, pulled Freddy tighter, and tuned it all out.

Sooner or later, every one of Daddy's relationships went south. Just about the time she started getting used to being there, the big silences would begin. Then came the sharp words. Eventually, even that would deteriorate into shouting and throwing and breaking things. About that time, Daddy would pack their suitcases, his and Kit's, and they'd be back on the road again, looking for a new place to crash.

She knew it was stupid, but for some crazy reason, every time they moved into a new place with a new "auntie," there was a part of her that hoped this would be the one who liked her, the one who'd become her new mother. Even with Aunt Sarah, at the beginning, she'd hoped. Until their first big go-round, when she'd realized her aunt was no different from the rest of them. Sarah just tolerated her because she didn't have any other choice.

The bouncing from place to place might have gone on forever if Daddy hadn't married Melanie. His new wife de-tested Kit on sight, and the feeling was mutual. Which meant that in Daddy's eyes, Kit had become an even bigger liability. He was madly in love with his new wife, but he couldn't very well dump his daughter on a street corner. So he did the next-best thing: he dumped her on his sister's doorstep and slunk back into the night.

Fuck Melanie. Fuck all of them. She didn't need anybody. She'd show them all. She'd become a famous actress and live in a gorgeous house filled with beautiful things, just like in the magazines, with a maid and a butler and a Jaguar in the driveway. And when Daddy and his snotty little bitch of a wife came to call, she'd tell the butler to send them away.

Kit Connelly was going places. Just as soon as she figured out where she'd be sleeping tonight.

"Woo-hoo! Father! Hold up, I want to talk to you."

Clancy paused at the door to the meeting room and waited

for Ruth Steinman to catch up to him. The sort of woman others described as handsome, Ruth could have been anywhere between the ages of fifty and seventy. Her silver hair looked as though it had been lopped off with a dull Boy Scout knife. She wore sensible flat-soled shoes and the same brown tweed suit she'd been wearing for as long as he'd known her. Ruth was opinionated, fiercely outspoken, and highly formidable. In the five years they'd served together on various boards and committees, he'd watched countless times as she reduced some junior board member to a quivering mass of jelly.

She was also a born leader, and indefatigably devoted to her pet causes. When Ruth chaired a committee, things got done. She had no patience for incompetence, no patience for endless theory or analysis. In her frequently stated opinion, talk was cheap, and action was the only valid solution to a crisis. When presented with a problem, she grabbed the bull by the proverbial horns and mapped a route directly from Point A to Point B to effect a solution.

Which was why he could imagine just how crazy tonight's board meeting must have made her. Tempers had flared hotly when the group failed to reach a consensus after Dickie Forsythe's painfully detailed presentation of the financial problems plaguing the downtown soup kitchen that Forsythe was struggling to keep from crashing and burning.

"You young people are always in a hurry," Ruth scolded as she caught up with him. "Running around like you're headed to a fire. When you get to be my age, you'll realize that every step you take is one step closer to the grave, and that's a place even you won't be in a rush to get to." She thumped him soundly on the chest. "If you don't have anywhere else you're supposed to be, I'll buy you a drink."

It was an offer he couldn't refuse. Hiding a smile, he held open the door for her and they stepped outside into a raw

March night. "Where to?" he said, adjusting his coat collar as the wind sliced through him.

"The Parker House. It's only a couple of blocks."

The sidewalks were treacherous, and he took her arm as they made their way up Tremont Street to the elegant nineteenth-century hotel. The bar was quiet on this weeknight, soft jazz serving as a backdrop to muted conversation. Ruth flung off her coat, and was peeling off her gloves when the waiter appeared. "Maker's Mark, straight up," she said before he could ask. "Father?"

"I'll take the same, thanks."

The waiter left. "Beastly cold night," Ruth said. "Tell me, Clancy, how do you perceive our role as board members?"

He solemnly considered her question. "To set policy," he said.

"And?" She furrowed her brow and studied him as though he were a fourth-grader who'd been given a particularly telling exam.

"To allocate budget. And to see that both policy and budgetary matters are carried out in a satisfactory manner."

"Precisely. Which is why you should be managing the damned soup kitchen instead of that idiot Forsythe. You have a brain, and you're capable of using it. It's his job to deal with day-to-day problems. They shouldn't be left up to us. If I thought we could find a suitable replacement for him, I'd recommend to the board that we fire him for incompetence."

"You know as well as I do how hard it is to find somebody who can manage a nonprofit without running it into the ground."

"Which is why Forsythe still has a job."

"But it's obvious the money's being mismanaged. Somebody needs to find out why. And how. It might behoove us to send in an auditor."

"Or a board member," she said thoughtfully, "who can function as one."

"Is that your way of asking me to look over the books?"

"You have enough on your plate, already. I'll delegate the job to Tom Adams. The esteemed senator's always complaining that his position on this board is too static. This will give him something to do. He's sharp as a tack when it comes to business dealings. If something's funky with the books, he'll find it."

Their drinks arrived, and he watched as Ruth upended hers. "Better," she said when the glass was empty. "Much better. Father Donovan, I have a proposition for you."

He took a slow sip of bourbon. It blazed a trail of warmth all the way to his stomach. He leaned back in his chair, crossed his legs, and waited.

"A few months ago, I applied for a federal grant to create a new after-school program for at-risk inner-city youth. So many kids get into trouble because they have no focus, no goals, no self-esteem. No caring adult to help them make sense of their lives, to help them figure out who they are and where they're going. This program would address that problem. I just got word yesterday that my grant's been approved. Now I need somebody to run the program. Interested?"

He turned his glass in idle circles on the table. "I already have a job."

"Oh, hogwash. You're wasting your potential with the Church, and you know it. You have so much to offer, but the Catholic Church isn't interested in letting you use your God-given talents. You'd be a natural for this job. You're smart, you're creative, you're dedicated, you have charisma up the ying-yang. You're great with kids and you don't take any bullshit from anybody. I need you, Clancy. The kids need you."

"Appealing to my Catholic guilt, are you?"

"If that's what it takes." She leaned over the table. "We

could build the program together. I'd give you carte blanche to take it in any direction you see fit. I have absolute faith in you. The salary wouldn't be huge, but it would be better than what you're making now." She leaned back in her chair. Smugly, she said, "Tell me you'll ever get another offer as good as this one."

She was right. An offer like hers didn't come along every day, and he found the idea of working with kids immensely appealing. But leave the priesthood? Inconceivable. The Church was his life, his family, his identity. Despite his patient and frequent reminders to that effect, Ruth persisted in looking at him as little more than a glorified social worker.

"Ruth," he said, "it's an extraordinary offer. I'm flattered to know you think so highly of me."

"But? I hear a but in there, don't I?"

"But. Although I'm frequently frustrated with the hard-headed Church bureaucracy, I don't really believe the grass would be any greener on the other side. Government funding also means government regulations. We all have to answer to somebody. I'd just end up answering to Uncle Sam instead of the Vatican. Plus—"

"*Pffft.*"

"—plus," he continued, "the priesthood isn't the kind of thing you just walk away from. We've had this discussion before. It's a lifetime commitment. A higher calling. I'm serving God. Keeping watch over his flock." He smiled to soften his words. "Or at least a small portion thereof."

"I don't understand why a man like you would choose to stay. We won't even get into the celibacy issue." She dismissed it with a wave of her hand. "I've never understood that one. But I'd think you'd be disillusioned by all the hoopla that's gone on lately. Pedophile priests coming out of the woodwork. The Church admitting it spent years shuffling them from parish to parish. Doesn't it bother you to be associated with that?"

He took a sip of bourbon. "For every two of them, there are a hundred like me. You just don't hear about us because we're too boring to make good copy for the evening news." Setting down his glass, he said with genuine affection, "How many years have you been trying to steal me away from the Church?"

"As long as I've known you. And I don't intend to stop trying until you say yes."

"I'd be happy to help you get the program up and running. I'll serve on the board, I'll volunteer as much time as I can possibly give you. I'm spread thin right now, but for a friend like you, I can spread a little thinner."

"You're a good man, Clancy Donovan. I suppose you realize you've taken the wind right out of my sails. Nobody else could do with this program what you could."

He patted the back of her bony hand. "You'll find someone."

"I don't want someone," she said petulantly. "I want you."

He walked her back to the lot where she'd left her Buick Park Avenue and made sure she was safely on her way before he turned back in the direction of Downtown Crossing, intending to catch the red line back to Southie. Instead, he changed his mind and took a leisurely detour through the theater district and down LaGrange Street into the heart of the Combat Zone.

There wasn't much left of the Zone. There'd been a time, not so many years ago, when walking here alone at night had been an open invitation for a mugging. But as the expansion of Chinatown and the opposition of neighborhood residents had forced most of lower Washington Street's sex trade out to the suburbs, the area had lost its sharp teeth.

There were a few holdouts: Liberty Books sat brazenly in the shadow of the historic Liberty Tree building, currently home to the city's Motor Vehicle Registry. The Erotic Entertainment Center was squeezed in between a Malaysian restaurant and an Oriental gift shop. The Glass Slipper and the Golden Pussycat, for years the only strip clubs left on La-Grange Street, had recently acquired a controversial new neighbor amid a clamor of disapproval. Prostitution and drugs were still a problem, although less noticeable than in years past. He'd heard talk of Chinese gangs, but the Chinese were an oddly insular people. They warred with each other, but pretty much left everybody else alone.

Nowadays, the odds of being mugged here were about the same as on any street corner in downtown Boston. He'd never been afraid of the streets anyway, no matter how late the hour. After all, he had God on his side. And he considered the disenfranchised—the homeless, the working girls, the teenage runaways—as much a part of his flock as any pious congregant who knelt in the pews at Saint Bart's on Sunday morning.

It was barely ten o'clock, a little early for the working girls to be out, but the street people were here if you knew where to look. He walked down Beach Street, with its neon-blazoned restaurants, past the Chinatown arch and through a maze of dark, narrow streets. Here and there, the homeless huddled in doorways or slept in alleys. Ragged and dirty, some sought warmth from tattered blankets, others from bottles held close against bony chests. On a night as cold as this, none of them should be on the street. But the homeless shelters could take only so many, and some of the old-timers, wary of the city's largesse, refused to seek sanctuary. Charity too often came with a price tag attached.

There was no telling where the man he sought might be. Or, for that matter, whether he would even be here. Willie Slattery might currently be a guest of the county, or of the state mental hospital. It wouldn't be his first time in either place. For all he knew, Willie could be dead by now. The man had to be in his sixties, and life on the streets wasn't conducive to longevity.

But he should have remembered what a tough old bird Willie was. He found the old man hunched in the entryway to a travel agency, wearing a ratty and aromatic raccoon coat he'd probably filched from somebody's trash.

"As I live and breathe," Willie said, his rheumy eyes reflecting the light from the overhead streetlamp. "How's it going, padre?"

"Hello, Willie. How've you been?"

"Can't complain too much. Rheumatism's acting up a tad. This cold weather don't do nothing good for my hands."

"I haven't seen you around for a while."

Sheepishly, Willie said, "I been inside. Just got out last week." He shrugged. "It ain't all that bad. At least you get clean clothes and three squares a day. Hot showers. And a bed that's indoors, out of the cold."

Clancy took the old man's gnarled hand in his. Even through his leather gloves, he could feel Willie's bone-deep cold. "Is there anything I can do for you?"

The old man shook his head. "I'm getting by, Father. Seems like the good Lord ain't ready for me yet."

"He's not done perfecting you, Willie."

Willie nodded keenly. "I guess you're right about that."

"There is something you can do for me," Clancy said. "I'm on a fishing expedition. I'm looking for a girl."

Willie's grin revealed a big gap where his front teeth should have been. "Looks like you're in the right place, then. There's plenty of girls to be found around here." He chuckled at his own joke.

"You're probably right. But I'm looking for a specific girl. She's sixteen years old, and her name's Kit. I'm trying to find her before she gets into trouble."

Willie's expression sobered. "She one of your girls, Father?"

"No. As far as I know, she's not working the streets yet, and I'd like to keep it that way. She's a runaway. Listen, Willie, I know there's not much happening out here that you don't see or hear about. Will you keep your eyes and ears open for me? I have a picture of her—" He paused, patted his pockets, finally located a flyer in the breast pocket of his suit coat. He handed it to the old man. "My cell phone number's on there. If you hear anything, anything at all, give me a call."

"Will do, Father."

He paused for an instant, then gave in to the inevitable and pulled off his leather gloves and handed them to the old man. He'd paid fifty dollars for them, a small fortune for a man on a priest's salary, and he'd probably kick himself later. Altruism wasn't always everything it was cracked up to be. But Willie Slattery was an old man, and priorities were priorities.

"Here," he said. "Take these. They're fur-lined. They'll help with your rheumatism."

Willie didn't even offer a pretense of argument. He snatched the gloves and tugged them on, then held up his hands to marvel at his good fortune. "These are great," he said, turning his hands from side to side to admire them from all angles. "You even warmed 'em up for me ahead of time."

"Next time I come by," Clancy said sternly, "you'd better be wearing them. If I find out you sold them—"

"Oh, no," Willie protested. "I'd never do that, Father."

"If I find out you sold them—" he said again, then gave up, knowing any threat he made would be empty. By tomorrow night, somebody else would probably be wearing his fifty-dollar gloves while Willie sucked on a bottle of Old Duke. It was the way of the world. But for tonight at least, Willie Slattery's arthritic hands would be protected from the cold.

5

Some days, all Kit did was walk the streets. She walked until her feet were on fire and her fingers and the tip of her nose were numb from the cold. She was almost out of money, so she only ate once a day to stretch her meager funds as far as possible. She spent a lot of time in Cambridge, hanging around the Harvard campus, trying to blend in with the students, pretending she lived here, in an ivy-covered brick dorm, studying economics or engineering or law, and meeting her friends after class for coffee and sticky buns at *Au Bon Pain* across the street.

She spent her nights sleeping in a shadowy corner of the Harvard Square T station, her head propped on her backpack and her coat wrapped around her like a blanket. The floor was hard and damp, and when the trains stopped running for the night, she could hear the scurrying of small animals on the tracks. But it was preferable to the very real possibility of freezing to death. Or it was until the morning when fate intervened in the form of a man who worked the drink stand near the escalator. Bent on taking a furtive leak before he opened for the day, he ducked into the corner where she was sleeping and nearly fell over her in the darkness.

She awoke to a pair of smelly boots parked a half-inch from her nose. The stranger grabbed her by the elbow, yanked her roughly to her feet, and dragged her out into the light.

"Well, well," he said as a lascivious smile played about his mouth. "Look what I just caught."

The guy had to be forty at a bare minimum, and the way he was looking at her gave her the heebie-jeebies. She jerked her arm away from him in disgust and said, "Leave me alone, creep. I was just sleeping."

He beetled thick, black brows. "Well, you can't sleep here, girlie. After hours, it's called trespassing."

"Yeah? Well, bite me!"

He turned to whistle for MBTA Security, and she snatched up her coat and backpack and bolted for the stairs. "Hey!" he yelled. "Get back here!"

But she didn't waste any time. She took the escalator two stairs at a time and burst out into the early morning dimness of Harvard Square. Behind her, the footsteps of the MBTA cop echoed like gunshots. Kit never paused, just kept running, block after block, until her screaming lungs finally forced her to stop for breath. She slumped against a light pole and sucked in oxygen until her heartbeat slowed. The cop had long since given up on her, but it had been a close call. From now on, she'd have to be more careful.

She'd run all the way to the Charles River. Cambridge was just beginning to come to life, and across the river, the tips of Boston's skyscrapers were afire with sunrise. Behind her, a sanitation truck lumbered along the curb, trolling for last night's refuse. A *Boston Globe* truck, green with gold lettering, passed by, tires scrunching on the icy street. Walking briskly because of the cold, she passed MIT, crossed Memorial Drive, and took the Harvard Bridge back to Boston.

A frigid wind swept in off the Charles, stirring up sand and leaving stinging particles in her eyes. She blinked away an involuntary tear, rubbed at the corner of her eye where the offending grain of dirt had lodged, then lifted the hood of her parka and tightened the drawstring until her face was nearly enclosed. It was the coldest walk of her life. When she reached the Boston side, she continued on to the Mass Ave T station, where she squandered a precious subway token so she could go inside and get warm.

As always, the temperature change was dramatic. The T was always steamy. Within a minute or two, her hair was damp, and she could feel sweat trickling down her neck. She lowered her hood, slipped off her jacket, and pulled out a hairbrush to try to tame her hair. She hadn't washed it in three days, and it felt icky and snarled. Maybe she could sneak into a public bathroom somewhere and wash it, once the day warmed up a bit. She'd stolen a grimy towel from the Sir Charles, so she could at least towel it dry. If she didn't, and went outside while her head was still wet, pretty soon she'd have icicles instead of hair.

She finished with the hairbrush and tucked it away as the inbound train pulled into the station. Kit had discovered that for the price of a single token, she could ride the train for hours, from station to station, getting on and off at will, even changing lines, from green to orange to red. She varied her routine so people—especially the MBTA police—wouldn't notice her sitting in the same place, hour after hour.

This morning she got off at Park Street, which was more like a miniature city than an underground train station, a place where you could buy a newspaper or a Coke or a dozen doughnuts, if you weren't flat broke like she was. There was always music, some of it pretty good, some of it simply awful. She was beginning to recognize some of the regulars, like Jamal, a scrawny black kid who spent hours every day playing on some kind of percussion instrument she couldn't identify. He was about her age, and he'd told her he'd been playing in the subway since he was eleven years old.

When she got off the train, Jamal was already comfortably ensconced in his favorite spot. Kit sat on a nearby bench and tried to look like she was waiting for a train. With one foot tapping in time to Jamal's rhythm, she picked up a discarded copy of the *Metro,* the free newspaper put out by the Transit Authority, and began reading it.

"Hiya, Princess. Read anything good in there?"

She looked up from the newspaper, leaned back against the grimy tile wall, and cautiously eyed the man who stood looking at her. She wasn't a complete rube. She possessed a few street smarts, enough to know that survival depended on a couple of things: using common sense, and knowing better than to trust strangers.

On the other hand, as strangers went, this one wasn't bad on the eyes. He was tall and lean, with broad shoulders. Incredibly good-looking, with artistically disheveled blond hair and a tiny gold loop in his left earlobe. His forehead was high, his blue eyes clear and lucid, his fingernails clean, and he wore his expensive leather coat with style and panache.

"I've seen you here before," he said. He sat down beside her and took a bite of the jelly doughnut he'd just bought from the doughnut stand across the tracks.

Her stomach growled. She watched with undisguised interest as he ate. He caught her watching him, and she felt her cheeks flame as she rapidly swiveled her head to look in the opposite direction.

He touched her shoulder, and a rush of adrenaline shot through her. Fangs bared and claws unsheathed, she wheeled around to defend herself. But he wasn't bent on attack, he simply held out half of the jelly doughnut. "A beautiful woman," he said, "should never have to go without."

The automatic fight-or-flight response subsided. While she considered his offer, the Riverside train rolled into the station, momentarily drowning out Jamal's music. The conductor opened the doors of the train and passengers spilled out onto the platform. Kit snatched the piece of doughnut and devoured it.

When the train left the station, the man was still sitting beside her. He leaned, wiped a few loose sugar crystals from the corner of her mouth, then licked it off his thumb. "Sweet," he said. "So what are you doing on the street, gorgeous? Things that bad at home?"

Instead of answering his question, she asked one of her own. "Who are you, and what do you want?"

He held out a hand. "My name's Rio. What's yours?"

She eyed the hand, but she didn't take it. "Rio?" she said. "I'm supposed to believe your name is *Rio?*"

He grinned widely. "You want to look at my driver's license, Princess?"

She hesitated, then turned away to feign interest in a movie poster affixed to the opposite wall. "Thank you for the doughnut," she said primly. "But I'm not a princess."

"You could have fooled me. You sure look like one, with all that yellow hair and those big blue eyes. You could be a movie star, like Meg Ryan or Julia Roberts. Or even—yeah, now I know who it is you remind me of. Not Julia Roberts. Julia Stiles. She is one hot chick. You look just like her. Something about the cheekbones. What was the name of that movie she made with Freddie Prinze, Jr.?"

"Down to You?"

"Yeah, that's it. You look just like she did in that movie. As a matter of fact, if I didn't know better, I'd think it was her, sitting here beside me on this old wooden bench."

"Yeah. Right."

"Honest to God. Could this face ever lie to you?"

He wore the sweet expression of a Boy Scout, and he continued to ply her with that guileless smile and those soulful blue eyes. Two benches over, a studious-looking black kid with wire-rimmed glasses and a backpack had his nose buried in a fat paperback copy of Shakespeare's tragedies. A couple of housewife types, in from the burbs for a day of shopping, studied the subway map on the wall, heads close together as they held a private conversation and avoided eye contact with anyone who might jeopardize their safe return to their safe suburban homes on their safe suburban streets in their safe suburban neighborhoods.

In the background, Jamal continued to play. The Arborway train hurtled into the station, and the man named Rio stood. "This is me," he said. "You take care of yourself, Julia."

He walked away, casually tossed a dollar bill into Jamal's open instrument case. Jamal nodded thanks without breaking rhythm. Rio climbed the steps onto the train and staked out a space near the door, stood there as several women squeezed past him to get a seat. The door closed and the train began to move. At the last possible instant, he looked up, met her glance through the dirty window, and raised a hand to his brow in silent salute. Then the tunnel swallowed him up.

The house was so empty without Kit. Instead of all that youthful energy, instead of the teenage angst and the constant clutter and the daily overdose of MTV, there was just…nothing. Sarah wandered from room to room like a lost soul, waiting for a phone call that didn't come. She hated having Clancy Donovan's phone number on that flyer instead of hers, hated it passionately, even if she did understand his reasoning. Because she bounced perpetually between the house and the bookstore, she risked missing an important call. As pastor of a large parish, the good Father was on call twenty-four hours a day. There was never a time when his cell phone wasn't with him. It made sense that they should use his number instead of hers, but she still didn't like it. Patience had never been her strong suit, and this business of sitting around waiting for the other shoe to drop was driving her to the brink of insanity.

She wasn't sleeping worth a damn at night. Instead, she lay awake, night after night, thinking about what she might have done differently. Somehow, she knew, this was all her fault. If only she'd listened more closely, if only she'd been a little less rigid. It had been a challenge, having instant motherhood thrust upon her in the form of a wayward and high-spirited teenage girl. But she'd risen to the challenge with enthusiasm, and with gratitude for having finally been given the opportunity she'd waited years for. That she'd failed so miserably at such an important task was a heartbreak she would carry with her for the rest of her life.

She paused at the dining room window and drew back the curtain. Outside, the snow gleamed bluish in the moonlight. A dried leaf, caught by the wind, scuttled across the lawn. Sarah dropped the curtain and went back to pacing. She couldn't abide sitting here like some helpless B-grade movie heroine, wringing her hands and waiting for the hero to rescue her. She wanted to be Erin Brockovich, out there on the street, kicking ass and getting things done. She needed to find Kit before something god-awful happened to her, something Sarah would never forgive herself for allowing to happen.

Earlier tonight, she'd called Remy in New Orleans, just because she didn't know who else to talk to. To his credit, her ex-husband hadn't said, "I told you so." Instead, he'd sounded concerned, for her as well as for Kit. "You can't blame yourself," he said. "If anybody's the villain in this piece, it's Bobby. If he'd been any kind of father at all, he would have handed her over to you the day Ellie died. You wouldn't be in this mess now."

"How can you be sure?" she argued. "Maybe I would've messed her up as bad as Bobby has. We come from the same gene pool, after all. And I haven't exactly lived the most stable existence. Maybe Connellys just aren't cut out to be parents."

"Or maybe your guilt's more about the past than the present."

She didn't have an answer to that, probably because he was right.

"Look," he said, "kids run away every day. Most of them

come home sooner or later, maybe a little the worse for wear, but not irreparably damaged. It's the parents who suffer, because teenagers have tunnel vision. They don't understand that the things they do hurt the people who love them. They're too self-absorbed. Kit's a smart girl. She'll be okay. You're the one I'm worried about. You need to get some sleep. If you don't, the worrying's apt to kill you.''

''Yes, Mother.''

''And call me again if you need anything. I mean it, Sarah. Just because we're divorced doesn't mean…well, you know. I'll do whatever I can to help.''

They'd ended their conversation after that, because there really was nothing left to say. She understood the truth in his words. She just wasn't sure she could apply it to her own life. Guilt was a powerful motivator. And so was love. Put the two together and you created an unstoppable force.

She wandered to the living room and turned on the television. The man whose face filled the screen was fair-haired, charismatic, fortyish. He smiled into the camera, surrounded by a young, attractive, athletic-looking family. ''Tom Adams,'' the voice-over said solemnly. ''Standing tall for the Commonwealth.''

So this was the esteemed Senator Adams. What was it Steve had said about him? *He's so conservative he makes Rush Limbaugh look like Dennis Rodman.* Adams hardly looked like the spawn of Satan Steve had made him out to be. His politics may have leaned a little further to the right than she preferred, but wasn't that what the majority of the voters seemed to want? Josie was right. Adams looked agreeable enough, if you could get past the fact that he was probably one more rich boy who would never have to worry about the demise of Social Security, because his trust fund was bottomless.

Sarah clicked a button and the senator's face disappeared. She knelt before the hearth, took a long-handled match from the box on the mantel and struck it. The match flared into flame. She touched it to the stack of kindling arranged neatly in the fireplace, fanned it with her breath, and watched the fire dance to life.

Determined to enjoy its cozy warmth, she poured herself a glass of white wine, popped in a Patsy Cline CD, and settled on the couch with her bare feet tucked up underneath her. While Patsy sang about walking after midnight, Sarah stared into the flames, absently twirling her wineglass by its stem. She'd been so sure she was doing it right this time, so sure she'd finally turned around that string of bad luck and worse choices that had followed her around for the past sixteen years.

She and Remy had parted on friendly terms. But when she'd announced her intention to pack up Kit and move to Boston to take up residence in the house she'd inherited from her father's sister, he'd been aghast. "Why would you want to do that, sugar?" he asked. "The place is falling down, Boston is an icebox, and the people there are the rudest I've ever had the misfortune of doing business with."

Dear Remy. He truly meant well. And the house had its faults, for sure: it was desperately in need of paint, and the front steps were about ready to fall off. Sooner or later, she was going to have to replace the roof. The interior could use fresh wallpaper and updated kitchen appliances. It was going to take time and money to bring the place into the current century. But she'd fallen in love with the old wreck the instant she turned her key in the lock. It was hers, all hers, and she loved it in a way she couldn't adequately explain to her ex-husband.

"Stay here," he'd argued. "I'll put you and Kit up in a nice little apartment. I'll take care of you financially. You won't have to worry about a thing."

"But that's the problem," she'd told him. "I need to pay my own way. I need to stand on my own two feet and be a responsible adult. I need to be a momma to that poor little girl.''

He argued until he was blue in the face, but she refused to back down. She needed to make a new start, needed to reassess her life. She started looking at business opportunities in the greater Boston area and found a charming little bookstore that had just gone on the market. She flew to Boston to check it out, then put together a business plan, liquidated her assets, and took the plunge.

Bookmark was doing well. And after years of being married to one man or another, she'd discovered she really didn't mind being alone. Between mothering Kit, running the bookstore, and trying to keep the house from falling down around their ears, her life was too full for the absence of a man to even register on her radar. She'd begun to flex her muscles, both physically and emotionally, had begun to plumb her inner depths and to discover her own strengths, strengths she'd never imagined she possessed. It was empowering to discover she didn't need a man to survive.

But this thing with Kit had knocked her for a loop. She hadn't realized the extent to which she'd built her life around the girl. Kit's disappearance had placed her life on hold indefinitely. If the worst happened and Kit didn't come back, that hold was likely to become permanent, because without Kit, she couldn't see much reason to go on.

She finished off the glass of wine, muted the CD player, and picked up the telephone. She knew Clancy Donovan's cell phone number by heart because she'd spent hour after hour, day after day, staring at that flyer with Kit's picture on it. She hated that picture, had always hated it. School photos were so stiff and unnatural, and Kit was such a lovely girl.

He answered on the second ring, his voice soft, mellow, familiar. For a brief instant, she wanted to give in to the aching desire to cry. Instead, she said, "Do you think I'm crazy?"

There was a measured pause before he said, "Sarah?"

"Never mind. I guess that gives me my answer. You must not know very many crazy women."

"I recognized your voice. Moonlight, magnolias, balmy southern nights."

"That's your story, anyway."

"And I'm sticking to it. Why would I think you're crazy?"

"My ex-husband thinks I'm obsessing too much about Kit. I just wondered if you shared that opinion."

"I think that under the circumstances, you're allowed to obsess until the cows come home."

"Josie's been at me, too. She keeps telling me it's time I started dating. The universal panacea. Like I have any interest in men right now." She wrapped the phone cord tight around her index finger, let it spring free, and watched the flow of blood return. "The longer this goes on, the more frustrated I get. I guess I had this naive idea that we'd just cruise downtown, pick her up off a street corner, and bring her home. Rather simplistic of me, wasn't it?"

"It's a normal expectation. Not particularly realistic, but normal. This kind of thing is an education in itself. Unfortunately, the degree comes from the school of hard knocks."

"In the beginning, I was fueled by anger. I was furious with Kit for running away in the first place, furious with the police for not being more helpful. Now—" She paused, sighed. "Now, I think I've run out of fuel. I'm so tired. And so discouraged. This is my fault, you know."

"How is it your fault?"

"I was lousy at being a mother."

"Do you think that's really fair to yourself? Have you ever had any previous parenting experience? Did you ever take parenting classes?"

"Most people don't take parenting classes. They still manage to raise normal kids."

"Most people start with infants, and work their way up to

teenagers. They have a little bit of experience under their belts before they get to Bedlam. You're being far too hard on yourself.''

''I could have made better choices. Kit's been dragged from pillar to post all her life. So what did I do? I uprooted her one more time and took her fifteen hundred miles away from everything that was even remotely familiar. I knew she was unhappy, but I didn't know what to do about it. That girl's just starving for love, and God knows, I tried to give it to her. But I couldn't get through. That's my failing, and I know it. Now I'm terrified she'll go looking for it in the wrong place, and it'll be all my fault.''

''Have you talked to anyone about this guilt you're feeling?''

''Well, Father, in case you haven't noticed, it appears as though I'm doing just that.''

There was a brief silence at his end of the phone. ''Yes,'' he said, sounding surprised. ''So you are.''

''I'm sorry I bothered you. I really wasn't looking for a therapy session. I'm not even Catholic. And you're off duty. But I appreciate you listening to me. I guess I just needed to blow off a little steam.''

''You're not bothering me. And I'm never off duty. You know, there's a local support group for families of runaway and missing children. I think it meets somewhere in Lynn. If you're interested, I can get you information on where and when.''

''Is that what you think I need? A support group? You don't strike me as the touchy-feely type.''

''I think any of us, when faced with a life-altering crisis, can benefit from the wisdom and support of people who've already been there.''

''A cagey response if ever I heard one. All right, Father, you might as well get me the information. I suppose it beats psychotherapy.''

"I'll see what I can do for you. Sarah—" He paused, and she waited, breathing a little too hard, still playing with the phone cord, trying to mold it back into its original neat coil. But it was too late for that; the damage was already done. "We'll find her," he said. "I promise."

"You keep telling me that," she said. "Maybe one of these days, I'll start believing it."

The next time she saw the man who called himself Rio, Kit was hovering at the top of the stairs inside the entrance to the Park Street T station, trying to stay warm. Every time the door opened to let commuters into the old stone building, the March wind sliced through her with knifelike precision. But she was loathe to descend those stairs and part with even a dollar in order to pass through the turnstile and rest her weary body on a bench. Last night, she'd slept in the foyer of a dilapidated apartment building somewhere in the South End. At least she'd been indoors, out of the wind and the cold. But when she woke up, her backpack was gone, stolen while she slept right next to it.

It was the closest she'd come to crying since she left home. Her clothes were gone, and so was the photo of Momma she'd carried since she was four years old. Her last joint had been in that bag, along with the candy bar she'd bought yesterday afternoon and vowed to save for morning, no matter how much her stomach gurgled and growled in the meantime. Now all she had left was Freddy, who'd been cradled in her arms while she slept, and a five-dollar bill tucked into the pocket of her grimy jeans.

For the first time, she considered the possibility of going home. Kit was familiar with the concept of hitting rock bottom, and she was pretty sure she was hovering in the vicinity, if she hadn't already arrived. But to go home now—assuming Aunt Sarah would even take her back—would be to admit she'd failed. Failure was a weakness, and only sissies were weak. Kit Connelly was no sissy. Life with Daddy had toughened her, and she would spit in the eye of anyone who possessed the audacity to suggest otherwise.

If only she wasn't so very hungry.

He materialized out of nowhere. One minute, she was standing alone, squeezed against the wall as harried commuters dashed by in a mad rush to catch the train that had just pulled into the station. The next instant, Rio was standing in front of her, a bagel in one hand, a steaming cup of coffee in the other. She wasn't sure which looked better to her, the man or the bagel, but if she voted on the basis of smell, the coffee won, hands down. Anything that smelled this good couldn't possibly be bad.

"Hey, Julia," he said. "How's it going?"

Eyeing the bagel, she said, "Hi."

He glanced down at the bagel in his hand, then back up at her face. "Buy you breakfast, gorgeous?"

Suddenly, it was more than she could stand. The cold, the hunger, her stolen belongings, his generosity. A single fat tear spilled from the corner of her eye and rolled down her cheek. She swiped at it viciously. Without another word, Rio took her by the arm and led her outside, across the street and into the bagel shop on the corner.

"Anything you want, babe," he said. "My treat."

She picked out a raisin bagel and two chocolate honey-dipped doughnuts, a carton of milk and a bottle of Fruitopia. They sat in a booth and he watched in silence while she ate every last morsel. She washed it all down with the milk, and then she opened the bottle of juice for dessert. For the first time in a week, her stomach felt satisfied, full almost to the point of discomfort. "Thank you," she said. "You can't know how hungry I was."

"Anything for you, sweet thing. I wondered if you'd still be around. I thought maybe you would've gone back home by now."

Over the rim of her bottle, she said, "I'm not going back."

He nodded knowingly. "That's what I figured when I saw you. You seem like the type of girl who knows what she's doing. If you left home, you must've had a good reason. It wasn't just to get attention."

"Hah. Like I ever got any."

He took a sip of coffee and said casually, "Folks ignored you, did they?"

She studied him, debating whether or not she should trust him. She didn't know him, not really. They'd conversed a couple of times in a crowded subway station. For all she knew, he could be a modern-day equivalent of Jack the Ripper.

But he was looking at her with those amazing blue eyes, waiting patiently for her to tell him the story of her life. And he'd bought her breakfast, the most wonderful breakfast she'd ever eaten. "All I have is my dad," she said, playing with her bottle cap. "My mom died when I was little."

"That's tough," he said. "I lost my mother when I was twelve. Never really hit it off with my old man. I left home at sixteen, and I never looked back."

"I've been living with my aunt. Daddy got married a couple of years ago, and his wife hates me. So he dumped me on Aunt Sarah. We don't exactly get along."

Sympathy flooded his eyes. "She didn't want you either?"

Kit shrugged. In spite of her conflicts with her aunt, it seemed disloyal to bad-mouth Sarah to someone else, even if that someone had bought her breakfast. "It's not that she's so bad. I mean, she took good care of me. But I couldn't even turn around without her breathing down my neck. And she blamed me for everything that's gone wrong since the Year One."

"Bummer." He pointed to Freddy, propped up beside her on the seat. "Who's this?"

She flushed hotly, tucked Freddy closer against her side,

and lowered her eyes. "Nobody," she mumbled into her Fruitopia bottle. "Just some dumb stuffed animal."

"Hey, I wasn't making fun. Really. Everybody needs somebody."

She hazarded a quick glance in his direction, but detected no levity on his face. He seemed sincere. "Freddy," she said. "His name's Freddy."

"Hi, Freddy. Nice to meet you."

Freddy just stared back with his lone eye. "He doesn't talk much," she said.

Rio laughed. "I imagine he doesn't. You know—" his expression grew somber "—I meant what I said the other day. You're as pretty as any of those girls out in Hollywood. Have you ever thought about being an actress?"

Only since she was old enough to walk and talk. But she'd never admitted it to anyone. Until now. There was something about Rio. He was so easy to talk to. "Sure," she said. "I've thought about it."

"I knew it. I could tell. You have this aura. So, do you have a portfolio?"

"A what?"

"Portfolio. You know, pictures, to take to casting calls and so forth. Every aspiring actress has to have a portfolio."

"I didn't know about that."

He leaned back, rested an arm on the back of his seat. "I do those things all the time. I'm a photographer. Maybe I could help you out, throw something together for you. Of course, I'd give you a discount."

It was probably just a pick-up line. As if he thought she could afford pictures, when she couldn't even afford to buy her own breakfast. But he was so cute. And he dressed as though he'd never had to worry about money a single day in his life. "Thanks," she said, "but in case you haven't noticed, I'm a little short on cash right now."

"No problem, Princess. We can work something out. You

know, I've been thinking about hiring a helper. Somebody to run errands, do paperwork, keep the dog fed. When I'm in the darkroom, sometimes I lose track of time. You know how it is.''

Was he offering her a paying job? The details seemed a little hazy. Then again, she wasn't exactly in a position to quibble over details.

"I don't want you to take this the wrong way," he said. "I'd never suggest anything even remotely improper, and if this makes you uncomfortable in any way, I want you to say so. But if you're looking for a place to crash, I'd be glad to put you up for a while. Just until you get on your feet."

She bit her lower lip. Rock bottom was one thing. But bad things happened to girls who were too trusting. "I don't know. I mean, I hardly know you."

"Hey, no problem." He held up both hands, palms up, and leaned backward in the booth. "I'm glad you trust me enough to be honest with me. It's just something you might want to think about." He reached into his pocket and pulled out his wallet, withdrew a business card. Sliding it across the table to her, he said, "Give me a call if you change your mind."

Kit picked up the card and studied it. In a classy font on a creamy matte background it read Design Solutions. Beneath that, a phone number. Rio stood, took his time draining his coffee cup, while Kit thought about rock bottom, about the cold weather, about the five dollars in her pocket.

"See you around," he said, and turned for the door.

The hand that held the card trembled. Kit wet her lips. "Wait!" she said. "I'm coming with you!"

6

Leaning back in his chair, his pen tapping idly against the edge of the desk, Father Clancy Donovan was brooding.

He'd come close to driving out to Revere last night, had nearly shown up at Sarah Connelly's door with a rental video, something light and frothy that would make her laugh. Make her forget, for just a couple of hours, how worried she was about her niece. She probably would have welcomed the company. There'd been something in her voice on the phone. She'd sounded tired and frightened. Frustrated. Above it all, there'd been an aura of loneliness that had driven straight through him.

But he had to remain ever mindful of his position. As a priest, he was forced to take propriety into consideration. Helping the woman track down her niece was one thing. Spending time alone with her, inside her house, late at night, undoubtedly fell somewhere on the wrong side of that narrow line he was expected to walk. No matter how innocent the situation, there were those who would easily misconstrue it. Especially when the woman in question was a three-time divorcée. Especially when she was as attractive as Sarah Connelly.

So he hadn't gone. Instead, he'd closed himself in his study, cranked Springsteen loud enough to rattle the stained glass windows of the old stone building, and spent two hours working on his homily for Sunday-morning Mass.

Odd, he thought, that this particular woman should raise

his yellow caution flag. It had happened before, but usually only if a woman had made advances toward him, or clearly established her availability, just in case he should be interested. He'd never understood why, but he'd been a priest long enough to know there were certain women who viewed the robes and the Roman collar as a challenge.

But Sarah wasn't like that. She'd come to him out of desperation, and he seriously doubted she'd ever really even looked at him. Not as a man, anyway. It was a blessing, because if she ever had looked at him that way, he would have been obligated to make a swift but graceful retreat. Sarah Connelly was as straightforward as they came, a genuine example of what-you-see-is-what-you-get. If she had designs on a man, any man, she would undoubtedly come right out and say so.

Which left him right back where he'd started. If the problem wasn't with her, then it had to be with him.

She was a lovely woman, no argument there. There was a lush softness to her, a womanly quality that camouflaged a backbone of steel. He'd have to be dead not to notice. But he knew any number of beautiful women, none of whom had ever set off flashing amber warning lights inside his skull. Take, for instance, Carolyn Rafferty. Caro was a knockout, quite possibly the most beautiful woman he knew. He'd spent countless hours alone with her, had even helped wallpaper her apartment last fall after she'd married Conor. Bedroom, bathroom, the whole nine yards.

Yet never once had the issue of propriety crossed his mind. Caro was simply there, a part of his life since they'd both been toddlers, riding their tricycles up and down the sidewalks of South Boston. He was as comfortable with her as he would have been with his own sister if he'd had one. It was only Sarah who left him keyed-up and jittery, only Sarah whose voice, with its honeyed Southern accent, made the soft hairs on his forearms stand rigidly at attention.

He was pondering this unexpected calamity when the phone on his desk rang. It was Ruth Steinman. "I know you're a busy man," she said, "but I thought I'd take a chance you might be free. I have an appointment in a half hour to look over a space on Huntington that sounds ideal for the new center. What I know about plumbing and drywall could fit on the head of a pin and still leave room to go square dancing. I thought maybe you could find time to come with me and offer a man's perspective."

He agreed to meet her there, shrugged into his coat, and stopped by Melissa's desk on his way out. "I'm leaving for a couple of hours," he said, looping his scarf around his neck. "If anybody calls, I should be back by noon."

He'd hoped to escape without getting the third degree, but he should have known better. Those keen gray eyes missed nothing. "Gloves," Melissa said. "Where are your gloves?"

"I can't imagine. I must have left them somewhere."

It was only a small lie, but it pained him that the words had slipped so effortlessly from his mouth. "Your hands will freeze," she protested. "Don't you want to borrow mine? They're a little small for you, but they'll stretch."

Sometimes, her mothering got to him. This was one of those times. "Thank you," he said firmly, "but no. My hands are fine. The gloves will show up sooner or later. Besides, in a couple of weeks we'll be seeing leaves popping out everywhere, and I won't need them anymore. Even in Massachusetts, winter can't last forever."

He left her to reflect on this gem of wisdom and made his escape. Outside, the air smelled like spring, but the wind funneled between buildings with the force of a freight train. He drove across town and parked illegally in front of a fire hydrant near Symphony Hall. A block away, Ruth and the real estate agent, Benjamin Harris, waited on the sidewalk in front of a three-story yellow brick building with a For Lease sign taped to the window.

"Excellent timing, Father," Ruth said when he joined them. The wind caught the tails of her scarf and sent them flapping about her face, and she batted them away. "We just got here ourselves."

The building had the square and uninspired appearance common to structures built during the mid-twentieth century. In its original incarnation, it had probably been utilized as office space, but in more recent times it had been converted to some sort of storefront business with two floors of apartments overhead. Cheap plate glass windows with aluminum trim had been installed at street level, destroying whatever character the original structure might have possessed.

Harris opened the door with his key and they stepped inside. The space yawned dark and cavernous, in spite of the bright sunlight making a valiant attempt to filter through the grimy windows. The agent tried the wall switch, but nothing happened. "Power's off," he said.

Rubble littered the floor: a stack of cardboard boxes in one corner, an empty Coke bottle, looking forlorn in the middle of all that vacant space, a pair of sunglasses with one bow missing. Hands tucked in his pockets, Clancy crossed the room, his footsteps echoing in the emptiness, and poked his head inside an open office door at the rear. The room was small but cheery, bright sunlight blasting through a high window embedded with chicken wire. A decapitated telephone cord lay coiled on the floor, last year's phone directory tossed carelessly beside it.

"Well, Clancy," Ruth said at his shoulder, "what do you think?"

"The space is certainly adequate. What year was it built?"

"Sometime in the thirties," Harris said. "Thirty-six, thirty-seven. They built things solid back then."

"If unimaginative. It's not cold in here. Single boiler system for the entire building?"

"That's right. Owner pays the heating costs. Electricity's up to the tenant."

"I don't suppose the wiring's been updated?"

Harris consulted his clipboard, flipped through a couple of pages. "The owner claims a full update was done in '74."

"How does he feel about renovations? Partitions, additional bathroom or kitchen facilities, that kind of thing?"

"You lease the space, short of burning down the building or manufacturing designer drugs to peddle to kiddies on the playground, what you do with it is up to you."

Inside his hip pocket, Clancy's phone rang. "Excuse me," he said, stepping away to answer it. There was a faint crackling on the line, then silence. "Hello?" he said. "Is anybody there?"

More crackling. Then a few garbled words. "...calling... girl...poster."

He made a mental note to write a letter of complaint to the FCC about the pathetic state of the cell phone industry. "Hold on," he said. "I can't hear you. Let me take the phone outside."

On the sidewalk, huddled against the wind, he tried again. "Go ahead. I'm still here."

There was silence at the other end, but he was pretty sure he could hear breathing. "All right," he said. "How about I wait until you're ready to talk?" His hands, holding the phone to his ear, were freezing. He hated it when Melissa was right.

"I'm calling about the girl. The one on the poster."

The voice was young, male, probably black. He hunched over, turned away from the wind. "Do you know where she is?"

"You a cop?"

If he had a nickel for every time he'd heard those words, he'd be on vacation in Tahiti right now, instead of freezing on a downtown street corner. "No," he said. "Where is she?"

"I don't know. But I seen her."

"Where?"

"Park Street T station."

"What's your name?"

"I don't want no trouble. Who are you, anyway? Her old man?"

"I'm a friend of the family. We just want to get her back. What'd you say your name is?"

"Jamal."

"Listen, Jamal, can we talk face-to-face? I'm on Huntington right now, and my car's just down the block. I'll meet you anyplace you want. You tell me where."

"I don't know, dude. I should stay out of it."

"This is important, Jamal. You know that, or you wouldn't have called."

For an instant, he thought he'd lost the kid. He stood there, shivering, as the seconds ticked away. Then he heard a slow exhalation of breath. "Yeah, okay. Meet me at the corner of Washington and Beach. What kind of car you drive?"

Relief washed through him. "A blue Saturn."

"A blue Saturn?" Jamal snickered. "My granny drive one of them things."

"Maybe we can start up a support group. Ten minutes?"

"Ten minutes, Bwana." And he was left holding a dead phone.

He navigated the narrow streets of Chinatown, squeezing between a double-parked produce truck and a silver BMW Z8. At Harrison, he ran the light, ignoring the angry blare of horns, and zipped past a string of Vietnamese restaurants. The light at Beach and Washington was red. He stopped this time, tapped his fingers impatiently on the steering wheel as he scrutinized his surroundings. On the corner to his right, a scrawny black kid holding some kind of instrument case slouched with deliberate nonchalance against a lamppost. Their eyes met, and the kid strolled in the direction of his car. Clancy popped the lock and Jamal opened the door and peered inside. "Yeah," he said, "this just like my granny's."

Behind them, a horn beeped. Jamal slid into the seat and closed the door, and Clancy stepped on the gas and cleared the intersection. "Where to?" he said.

"Don't matter. Hey, you some kind of priest or something?"

"Or something. What's that you're carrying?"

"Balaphon. From deepest, darkest Africa. Sorta like a xylophone, only made out of wood." Jamal checked out the interior of the car, found the button for the window, and lowered and raised it three or four times.

Clancy cleared his throat. "So...."

Jamal glanced up. "So?"

He turned left, driving aimlessly. "You've seen her. Kit. You're absolutely certain she was the girl in the picture."

"Kit, yeah, that her name. She liked to listen to me play." Jamal thumped oversized knuckles rhythmically against his instrument case. "We used to shoot the shit, there in the train station. But she stopped coming around a few days ago. I didn't think nothing of it at first. People come and go. Then I seen her picture on that poster, and that's when I started thinking maybe she went with that dude I see her talking to."

Clancy's fingers tightened on the steering wheel. "What dude?"

"Flashy white dude wears an earring. Don't know his name, but I seen him around before. Hitting on the girls, talking trash, making 'em tee-hee and giggle and turn five different shades of red. I see him talking to her one day. Couple days later, she gone. And I ain't seen him since."

Jamal reached down and turned on the radio, punched a button. Tom Jones filled the interior of the car, reminding them that it wasn't unusual. Jamal grinned. "Dude, you about as honky as it gets."

"Guilty as charged. Back to this guy. What else can you tell me about him?"

"Youngish. Pretty face. About five-ten, five-eleven. Blond hair, look like a surfer dude. He dress real slick. Leather coat, expensive watch. Great teeth."

"Let me guess. You have a photographic memory."

Jamal leaned back against the seat and clasped his hands behind his neck. "Nah. Just good at reading people. Like you, for instance. I say boxers. Plain white cotton."

He leveled a gaze at the kid. "How old are you? And why aren't you in school?"

Jamal grinned. "Old enough. And school's for people ain't got no place better to be."

He dropped Jamal off on lower Washington Street with a business card in his hand and an extra twenty in his pocket. As he drove back toward familiar territory, Clancy pondered what the boy's story might be. Jamal was cheeky, quick-witted, and eloquent, despite the occasional side trip into late-twentieth-century Ebonics. Not the kind of kid you'd expect to see walking the streets in the middle of a weekday carrying his balaphon from deepest, darkest Africa. What was keeping him out of school? Poverty? Boredom? Peer pressure?

He knew the depressing statistics, knew the kind of future lying before a kid like that, knew the odds of a young black male like Jamal winding up in a pool of blood on a street corner somewhere in Dorchester. Inexplicable sadness welled up in him at the thought. He shook it off, fought his way back, hardened his heart against his own too-tender emotions. He wasn't a superhero; he couldn't save all the lost kids. Nobody could save them all. He could only do what he could do, and right now, he needed to concentrate on one kid he might actually have a chance of saving.

He pulled out his cell phone. Steering one-handed, he dialed police headquarters and asked for Lieutenant Rafferty in Homicide.

"I need to pick somebody's brain," he said when he had Conor on the phone.

"Sounds appetizing. Any particular somebody?"

"Somebody from Vice who'll treat me with the same warmth and compassion I always get from you."

"Hard to find anybody with my kind of warmth. Prostitution?"

"Probably."

"Vince Paoletti. Give him my name, tell him I said to treat you with respect. Something special going down?"

"I'm on a fishing expedition, looking for a sixteen-year-old runaway. I have a description of somebody she might be with. He feels like a pimp, but he's not anybody who rings a bell with me. I was hoping somebody from your end might know something I don't."

"Give Paoletti a try. There's not much happening out there that he's not intimately acquainted with." Conor paused for a half beat. "When are you coming to dinner? Caro's been hounding me. And you know how Caro can be."

He knew how Caro could be, like a gorgeous blond pitbull. "Tell her to call Melissa and set it up on a night when I don't have a committee meeting. Melissa keeps my entire life in that little black book of hers."

"You going Hollywood on me, Donovan? Having my people call your people?"

"Absolutely. Thanks."

He cut across the Back Bay, circled the Common, and wove his way down the backside of Beacon Hill to Dock Square. There, he picked up the Expressway north, took the Route 1 exit that wound precariously around Boston Sand

and Gravel and under the new Leonard Zakim Bridge, and shot into the tunnel.

When he came out the other end and rolled up onto the Tobin Bridge, he dialed police headquarters again. To his amazement, Paoletti was in. Two for two, an almost unbeatable record.

"Father Clancy Donovan," he said into the phone. "I'm a friend of Conor Rafferty's. He said if I used his name, you'd tell me everything I want to know."

"Oh, he did, did he? I guess that depends on what you're looking to know."

"The identity of a possible pimp."

"In connection with?"

High above the Mystic River, he watched a red tugboat chug toward the harbor. "I'm looking for a sixteen-year-old girl, a runaway from Revere. Chances are good she's with him." Rattling off the description Jamal had given him, he shot past a lumbering tour bus, zigged and zagged around a ten-year-old Taurus wagon that was blowing blue smoke out the tailpipe.

At Paoletti's end, there was a long, thoughtful silence. "Christ," Paoletti said. "I thought I knew everybody out there, but this dude just isn't ringing any bells."

"Same here. I know most of the pimps working downtown. He's not one of them."

"You got a visual? Might be worth checking out a few mug shots."

"All I have is a description. On the other hand—" He passed the scenic slums of Chelsea and squeezed into a tiny opening in the far right lane while he considered the possibility. If he could find Jamal again, maybe the kid would be willing to spend a couple hours at the police station, playing show and tell. "There's a kid," he said into the phone. "He's seen the guy. Maybe I can convince him to come in."

"Bring him in. Ask for me at the front desk, I'll see what I can do for you."

He hung up, took the Revere exit, and merged with the flow of traffic. Calculating the distance to the Northgate mall, he measured it against the speed of the traffic, then picked up the phone again and dialed Melissa.

"I'm running late," he said. "I got sidetracked. How much time do I have before my next appointment?"

"You're free until two-thirty."

"It's almost noon now...all right, that should do it. I'll be back by then. Take a long lunch. Go shopping. Get your hair done."

"What if somebody calls?"

"They can talk to the machine. If it's an emergency, my cell phone number's on the recording. I'll see you around two-thirty."

He could have phoned Sarah Connelly instead of talking to her in person. But there was no sense in hiding from the woman. He wasn't some libidinous schoolboy, tripping over his words and his feet. He was a grown man who was quite capable of dealing with something as trifling as being attracted to a woman there was no possibility of getting involved with. Avoiding her wouldn't make the problem go away. He would simply have to work around it. He'd spent enough years running away from his problems. This one he would face like a man.

When he entered the bookstore, a bell rang over his head. The young woman behind the counter glanced up with a smile, studying him with open interest before she noticed the clerical collar. The wattage of her smile dimmed and a flush crept up her cheeks at her realization that she'd been ogling a Catholic priest.

"Hello," he said. "Is Sarah in?"

"She's in the office. Straight back, just behind the rack of Cliff's Notes."

He felt her eyes boring holes in his back as he strode to the rear of the store. He found Sarah in the cramped closet that passed for an office, the phone to her ear and her back to the door. One hand was buried in the tangle of soft brown curls. While he watched, she slid the hand southward and began leisurely massaging her neck, then tilted her head back and moved it from side to side in a slow and sinuous roll. With an interest that wasn't entirely academic, he studied the long, corded length of her throat.

"Oh, I understand," she said into the phone. "But I also have a business to run here, and if shipments don't come in when they're expected, I might as well just wave bye-bye to my whole little operation."

She swiveled around to face the door. When she saw him, she froze. He gave her a reassuring smile, watched her facial muscles relax. "Fine," she said into the phone. "What am I supposed to do in the meantime?"

Trying not to eavesdrop, he wandered a few feet away, picked up a book at random, and began thumbing through it. "Look," she said, "this book is scheduled to hit the streets tomorrow. It's already number fourteen at Amazon, and it hasn't even been released yet. First thing tomorrow, I'm going to have me a flood of people in here asking for it. What am I supposed to do? Tell them to try Stop & Shop?"

He held back a smile. This woman took no prisoners. "You do that," she said. "While I'm waiting, I'll just sit here and whistle 'Dixie.'" She replaced the telephone receiver in its cradle with surprising gentleness before she muttered, "Rat bastard."

A moment later, she appeared from around the end of the aisle. With her tousled hair and her huge blue eyes, she looked stunning in the blue V-neck sweater. "Good morning, Father," she said.

"Sarah. Having a bad day, are we?"

"I wasn't, until I got that bozo on the line. What can I do for you?"

"I thought you might like to have lunch with me."

Although her face remained impassive, she wasn't good at masking the thoughts that went on behind those vivid blue eyes. His words had been as much of a surprise to her as they'd been to him. They weren't at all what he'd planned to say, but it seemed his mouth had taken on a life of its own, one his head wasn't wholly in agreement with.

Instead of answering, she glanced at the book in his hand. A deep dimple appeared in her cheek, and those blue eyes twinkled as she returned her gaze to his. "Learn anything useful?"

He looked down at the title of the book he'd been mindlessly thumbing through. *Childbirth the Natural Way.* "Well," he said, "I think it's important for a priest to have a broad knowledge base."

"Slick," she said. "Very slick. I'll get my coat."

He took her to Fuddruckers, a few miles up Route 1 in Saugus, because he believed everybody should enjoy the Fuddruckers experience at least once. The place was humming, the lines lengthy, the burgers worth the wait. "Is that not the best hamburger you ever wrapped your mouth around?" he asked as she bit into a bacon cheeseburger dripping with ketchup.

It took her a minute to answer because her mouth was full. A glob of ketchup dribbled down her chin, and she set down the burger, picked up a napkin, and wiped it away. There was nothing of the oh-so-proper shrinking violet about her. Sarah Connelly was warm, earthy, and genuine. It was one of the things he liked best about her.

"It's absolute heaven," she said, still dabbing at her mouth. "But I thought you were kidding about the name until I saw it myself."

"Strange but true. It's a coast-to-coast chain. I'm surprised you've never heard of it before."

"Now that I know about the place—" she studied the burger on her plate with immense appreciation "—I'll be back again."

"I want to apologize," he said. "I didn't mean to frighten you, back at the bookstore. I could read it on your face when you first saw me. You were afraid I was bringing bad news."

Some of the light left her eyes. "You get used to that after a while. Everything strikes fear into your heart. Every time the doorbell rings." She picked up a French fry. "Or the phone." She dipped the fry into her ketchup and bit into it.

"Or when a thoughtless priest barges into your office in the middle of your workday without calling first. I'm sorry."

"Never in a million years would I call you thoughtless. Look, Father, I know my Southern charm is utterly devastating, but you didn't drive all the way to Revere just for the pleasure of my company. Since you're not bringing bad news, why are you here?"

He picked up a French fry, dipped it in the ketchup, and popped it into his mouth. Licked a drop of ketchup off the tip of his thumb. "I wanted to give you that information on the support group." He brushed off his hands, pulled a folded paper out of his pocket and slid it across the table. "Adrienne Thibodeau is in charge of the meetings. Give her a call and she'll fill you in."

"Thank you. I think." She took the paper, opened her purse, and tucked it inside. Closing it again, she propped an elbow on the table and rested her chin on her palm. "What's the real reason you're here?"

He abandoned all pretense of eating. "I talked to a kid named Jamal today. He knows Kit, thinks she might be with a man he saw her talking to in the T. Just under six feet tall, snappy dresser, blond hair, wears a gold earring. Does that sound like anyone you know? Someone she's talked about? Maybe a friend she brought home?''

"Kit never brought any friends home, although God knows I tried to encourage it. I kept telling her they'd be more than welcome. She told me flat out that she didn't have any friends." She paused, stared off into space. "This boy," she said, "this Jamal—do you think he's telling the truth?"

"I have no reason to doubt him. Of course, you have to realize there's no guarantee she's with this person he saw her talking to. But Jamal says he's seen him there before, hitting on pretty young girls."

"A pimp?" she said.

"That would be my guess."

She pursed her lips, exhaled sharply through them. "Shit."

"It may turn out to be a dead end, but at least it's a jumping-off point. It's more than we had this morning."

"Or not."

He picked up a French fry. "Or not," he conceded.

"So what do we do about it?"

He chewed thoughtfully. "I'll put feelers out. I have contacts everywhere. Contacts on the street, contacts within the religious community and the community at large. The girls at Donovan House. Maybe somebody can help us identify this guy. It might be a good idea for you to poke around the high school again. There's a possibility this could be somebody she already knew. Somebody there may recognize his description."

When he dropped her off in front of the bookstore, she paused, hand on the door handle, before getting out of the car. "You'll keep in touch," she said. "If you hear anything, I want to know."

"I'll let you know if I learn anything new. Call me if you turn up anything at the high school."

She strode briskly toward the building, the wind stirring her hair, golden strands mingling with brown in a riotous sea of curls. At the entrance, she paused to hold the door for an elderly woman with an armload of shopping bags. She said something to the woman, smiled, then glanced quickly in his direction. He lifted a hand, and she returned the greeting before closing the door and disappearing behind plate glass windows turned opaque by the glare of the midday sun.

Melissa was at her desk when he came in whistling some old Hootie and the Blowfish tune in a heretofore undiscovered key. "What's with you?" she said, following him into his study and watching as he took off his coat and hung it on the coatrack.

He neatly arranged his scarf on the hook beneath the coat before he turned to look at her. "What do you mean?"

She crossed her arms, leaned against the door frame, and gave him a long, speculative glance. "You've been so chipper lately, I barely recognize you."

He ran fingers through his hair, shoved it back into some semblance of order. "Chipper?" he said. "Me?"

"I haven't seen you throw anything at the wall in weeks."

He stared at her, realized she was right. Since he'd begun searching for Kit Connelly, his longstanding black mood had gone through a sweeping color evolution. He might not be quite Rebecca of Sunnybrook Farm, but it had been weeks since he'd gone on a rant or written a letter to the bishop. "Spring is almost here," he said in his own defense. "The sun is shining, the sky is blue—"

"The wind chill is nine degrees."

"I'll have you know, I saw a robin this morning. On the sidewalk in front of the rectory."

"Poor little thing. I hope he was wearing a winter coat."

"He was. And I think his suitcase had a baggage tag that said Aruba."

Those big gray eyes of hers, usually so solemn, warmed with humor. "I'm not complaining," she said. "Whatever it is, I hope it lasts. You're certainly easier to live with when you're like this."

7

The meeting took place in the basement of a church in Lynn, in a Sunday school room that smelled of school paste overlaid with weak coffee. Sarah stood just inside the door, her sweeping gaze taking in the wooden folding chairs arranged in a circle, the portable chalk board, the battered piano. Cardboard cutouts of Jesus adorned the walls. A long table shoved up against the wall at one side of the room held a coffeemaker and a stack of politically incorrect foam cups. Perhaps a dozen women milled about the table; a lone man sat stiffly in a hard wooden chair, staring at his feet, coffee cup clenched like a lifeline in both hands.

A fortyish blonde separated herself from the group near the refreshment table and came forward to greet her. "Sarah?" she said.

"Yes."

The woman held out her hand. "Adrienne Thibodeau. We talked on the phone."

Sarah shook the proffered hand. "I've never done anything like this before. I'm not sure what's expected of me."

"Relax. There are no expectations. Everybody here is friendly, and we're all here for the same reason, to share our stories and help each other cope. Just sit back and listen. If you feel like contributing something to the discussion, we'd be glad to hear from you. But remember, there's no obligation to participate. Nobody wants to add to anybody else's stress level. And sometimes just listening is enough." She gave Sarah's arm a friendly pat. "Help yourself to a cup of coffee. It's not very good, but it'll give you something to do with your hands. We'll talk after the meeting."

She got a cup of coffee and found a seat as Adrienne called the meeting to order. The first person to speak was a young Latina named Anna whose five-year-old daughter had been snatched from a shoe store while she tried on shoes just a few feet away. "Two days ago," she said in a halting voice, "Carlos moved out of our apartment. He went home to his mother. He blames me. His mother blames me." Anna's hands twisted and worried the hem of her cotton blouse. "I blame me."

The air grew heavy and the silence built as the group waited for Anna to continue. "The thing is," she said. "The thing is—" she paused on a sob, and the woman sitting next to her rested a hand on hers "—I only went out that day because Carlos and I had a fight. There was this pair of shoes I wanted to buy. Red, with little tiny heels. Real sexy, you know? I wanted those shoes so bad I dreamed about them at night. But Carlos said they cost too much and I couldn't buy them. I got mad and said he couldn't tell me what to do, and I took Juanita with me and went out to buy them anyway." She raised her face to the group, dark eyes brimming with tears. "I traded my daughter for a pair of shoes! It cost me everything. My child, my marriage, my whole life. If I hadn't been so stubborn, so goddamn vain—" She stopped, unable to continue, and the woman beside her drew Anna into her arms. She turned her face into the woman's shoulder and sobbed brokenly.

Guilt. It was something Sarah knew well. *If only I had done this. If only I hadn't done that.* Like a broken record, the intertwined themes of guilt and self-hatred played point and counterpoint through each speaker's recitation. There was the woman whose ex-husband had picked up their son six months ago for a weekend visit and still hadn't brought him home. The couple whose eleven-year-old daughter had gotten into a car with a strange man and never been seen again. The woman whose teenage son had flown to Los Angeles to visit a friend and, somewhere between LAX and Santa Monica, had simply disappeared off the face of the earth. Their pain and guilt mirrored Sarah's, and if it was painful to experience, it was excruciating to witness.

By the time the two hours were over, she was limp and drained. Her emotions felt as though they'd been dragged through a meat grinder. Her hands trembled as she gathered up her purse, slipped into her coat, and headed for the door.

"Sarah, wait." Adrienne Thibodeau wove around a cluster of gabbing women and caught her by the arm. "A little intense, huh?"

"I'm sorry. I don't think I can do this."

Compassion swam in the woman's lovely green eyes. "The first time's hard for everyone."

Sarah wet her lips and said, "I don't think there'll be a second time for me."

"This group stuff isn't for everybody. Listen, there's a diner just down the street. You look like you could use a cup of coffee." She glanced at the coffeemaker and grimaced. "A *good* cup of coffee. You game?"

"Why not? It's not like I have anything else to do."

"I've been doing some research on runaways." Sarah listlessly dragged a spoon through her coffee and then laid it on the table. "Everything I've read says the majority of kids run away because of intolerable conditions at home. Abuse. Neglect. Drugs and alcohol. That didn't happen at my house." She glanced at the photo of Kit lying on the table between them, next to a picture of Adrienne's Scotty. "I gave her a real home, the first one she's known since she was four years old. And I gave her love. So much love it almost ate me alive." She closed her eyes against the threat of tears. "I gave her normal, damn it! Why would any kid run away from a normal home?''

''It may be the trendy thing right now in psychological circles to blame the parents for everything that's wrong with their kids,'' Adrienne said, ''and most of the time it's probably true. But their fancy little theory doesn't explain the kids who come from disastrous homes and still turn out okay. Or the runaway teenagers who aren't abused, the ones who were given everything and chose to reject it.''

''That's how I feel. As though she took my love and threw it back in my face.''

Adrienne picked up her son's photo and studied it. ''Scotty was the sweetest little boy,'' she said. ''Full of love and laughter, a real joy to have around. We tried to do all the 'right' things with our kids, you know? We took them on family camping trips. Scotty played Little League, his sisters took dance lessons. Ron took him on father-son fishing trips with a couple of his friends and their dads. Our kids have never lacked for anything. We gave them a lot of stuff, but we didn't just give them stuff. We gave them ourselves, too.''

Adrienne placed Scotty's picture facedown on the red-flecked Formica tabletop and picked up her coffee. Took a sip. ''When he turned fifteen,'' she said, ''he started to withdraw. It was a gradual thing at first. He stopped wanting to do the things he'd always loved. His grades nose-dived, and he started spending more and more time in his room alone, with the door closed. We just thought it was some teenage phase he was going through. We were the typical smug, complacent parents who didn't believe anything bad could happen to a kid of ours. After all, we'd done everything right. We'd talked to our kids about drugs and alcohol and sex. We'd taught them to Just Say No.'' She smiled, but her smile was brittle. ''One day, he simply didn't come home from school. That was two years ago.'' She closed her eyes, but tears leaked from beneath her closed eyelids anyway. "Oh, damn. Excuse me."

She set down her coffee cup, rummaged in her purse, and pulled out a tissue. Dabbed at her eyes, her nose. Stolidly, determinedly, she said, "I'm sorry. I don't usually do that. Most of the time I'm okay. Holidays are hard, and of course, his birthday. But most of the time I'm okay." Adrienne paused, her eyes still too bright, and rubbed her temple. "Last week, my husband suggested that maybe it's time we did something with Scotty's room. Maybe it's time we made a conscious decision to move on and accept the inevitability that he's not coming back. I went ballistic. We've been dodging the fallout ever since."

A tear trickled in a slow slide down Sarah's cheek. "I'm so sorry," she said.

"No. I'm the one who's sorry. I thought you looked like you needed comfort, and here I am, spilling my guts to you. Some turnaround, huh?" Adrienne swiped at her nose a last time, then tucked the tissue into her coat pocket. She placed both hands palm down on the table and said briskly, "I still haven't answered your question about why kids run away from good homes. I have my own theory, one that blows the current psychological theories about bad parents sky-high. I believe some kids are born with tumultuous souls, and no matter what kind of family they're born into, no matter how hard their parents try to raise them right, those kids are going to encounter a shitload of chaos before they grow out of it. Some of them never do grow out of it. The lost ones."

She slid Scotty's photo across the tabletop, picked it up without looking at it, and tucked it into her purse. "I have to go," she said, fumbling with her coat. "But first—" She glanced back up, those lovely green eyes haunted. "I want to offer you some advice. The very best thing you can do for yourself is go back to living a normal life. I realize nothing feels normal right now, but do it anyway, even if you have to force yourself. Get up every day and go to work. Go out for dinner with your girlfriends. Watch Sunday-afternoon football or do the *New York Times* crossword puzzle. If there's some movie you've been dying to see, go see it. Take a friend or go by yourself, but by God, do it. Allow yourself to laugh, allow yourself to take pleasure from life. Stop blaming yourself for something you couldn't have prevented no matter what you did. Kit made the decision to leave home. Lay the responsibility for that decision at her feet, and don't use guilt as an excuse to die a slow death."

While Sarah silently digested her words, Adrienne stood and slid her arms into the sleeves of her coat. Buttoning it, she said, "After Scotty left, Ron and I didn't have sex for four months. I didn't think I had a right to pleasure. I didn't think I had a right to go on living when my baby was out on the street somewhere, alone and cold and hungry, and it was all my fault because I'd been such an incompetent twit of a parent." She picked up the check from the table without looking at it. "Don't let that happen to you, Sarah. Fight the guilt monster with every ounce of courage you have in you. If you don't, it'll consume you, and the monster will win."

Rio lived in a single-story loft apartment on the second floor of a converted warehouse. The only access was via a freight elevator that clanked and hummed and moved at the speed of a slug. It worked with a key that Rio kept on him all the time, so when he was at work, she was stuck inside. When Kit asked him why he didn't give her a key so she could go out, he told her it was for her own safety. Although his apartment was awesome, the neighborhood, he said, was a little rough. The liquor store down the block had been robbed at gunpoint just two weeks ago, and in the past six months, there'd been a couple of rapes and at least one drive-by shooting. There was no way he was allowing her to venture out onto that street without him by her side.

It was sweet of him to care so much about her welfare when nobody else ever had. Besides, staying in wasn't exactly a hardship. She had Pixel to keep her company. Pixel was a rottweiler-pitbull mix that she'd fallen in love with the first time Rio had introduced them and Pix had placed that soft, warm muzzle in her hand. She and Pix had the whole place to themselves, with nobody to tell them what to do or when to do it. If she wanted to sleep until noon, she could. If she wanted to eat leftover pizza and Froot Loops for breakfast, nobody cared. If she wanted to spend an hour in the shower each morning, there was nobody to yell at her about using up all the hot water. There was no school, no homework, no teachers and no stress.

She couldn't possibly get bored, not with all the electronic gadgets Rio owned. He had a forty-inch flat-screen television with digital cable, a VCR *and* a DVD player, and a stereo system that would bring down the roof if she turned it all the way up. His CD collection numbered in the thousands, and he owned enough videos and DVD movies to open his own rental franchise. He kept the fridge and the cupboards stocked with everything she liked to eat: pizza and Diet Pepsi, Dove ice cream bars, potato chips and nachos and peanut butter. The only thing off limits was the computer, which he used in his work, but it wasn't that big a deal, because what was she going to do with a computer, anyway?

Every day, she and Pix would snuggle on the plush leather sofa with a bag of Fritos and a two-liter bottle of Diet Pepsi, and watch TV for hours. *The Young and the Restless. Crossing Over With John Edward. Oprah* and *Dr. Phil.* Every night, Rio brought her a bouquet of flowers he bought in the lobby of the building where he worked, and then they'd eat a candlelight dinner together. He was an amazing cook, and one of the most romantic men she'd ever met. He bought her clothes and lipstick and jewelry. When she complained that she hadn't been outside in two weeks and needed some fresh air, he put her in his fancy car and drove her all the way to Providence to dine in a luxurious Italian restaurant with prices so high she nearly fainted when she saw them on the menu.

She was pretty sure he was falling in love with her, even though he never said it. Sometimes, she was pretty sure she was falling in love with him, too. Kit wondered how old he was, wondered where he came from and what he did for work when he left her each day. But when she tried to ask about any of that stuff, he only gave her vague answers and then changed the subject. She quickly learned which topics were acceptable for discussion and which weren't, and she was cool with that. Rio was obviously a very private man, and she respected his privacy. He worked at some kind of regular job during the day, and did his photography during the evenings and on weekends. A couple nights a week, and sometimes on Saturday afternoons, he would go out to work on special projects. When he came back, he invariably locked himself in his studio for hours. She knew, even though he never told her, that photography was his life, and she speculated that he was probably embarrassed about having to work a cruddy day job to pay the bills. That was probably why he wouldn't tell her where he worked.

Only one thing struck her as odd. Rio didn't own a telephone. Oh, sure, he had a cell phone. Nowadays, everybody had a cell phone, from the entire student body of her high school right down to the little Chinese grannies walking the streets with their shopping bags and their wheeled carts stacked with produce. But there was no phone in his apartment. Being there during the day, locked in, without even a telephone to connect her to the rest of the world, Kit felt a little like she'd been marooned on a desert island. What if she chopped off a finger and needed to call 911? When she asked him, he just laughed and said if she was worried, he could always lock up the knives. Then she forgot all about it when he went into his studio and came back with a stack of magazines. "I thought we could go through these," he said, "and look for poses you'd like to use for your portfolio."

"Really? You're really going to do a portfolio for me?"

"Of course I am, Princess." He ran a finger down the bridge of her nose. "Didn't you believe me?"

So they spent the evening poring over magazines, getting ideas to use for her own photos. He explained to her the dramatic differences he could get from different lighting conditions and shutter speeds, explained the kinds of poses models and actresses typically used in their portfolios. He told her what color combinations and fabrics would work best for her coloring (deep blues and passionate reds and mysterious blacks), what type of clothing worked best with her particular body type (just about anything, because her body, he said, was damn near perfect). If she thought she'd feel too stiff or nervous during the photo sessions, he said, they could smoke a couple of joints first to relax her, because stiff or nervous models made for lousy photos, and he wasn't giving her anything but the best. She listened to everything he said, impressed by the extent of his knowledge and troubled by the fact that a man so educated, so smart, so talented, should have to work a loathsome day job instead of being able to make a living from what he did best.

When she told him that, he just smiled and said, "Someday, babe. Who knows? Maybe you'll become a famous actress, and I can be your official photographer."

Josie locked the door behind the night's final customer and flipped the Closed sign. "Thank God," she said, crossing the room and falling like a rag doll into the chair beside Sarah's. "I've been on my feet for nine hours in these god-awful shoes." She kicked off the offending footwear, leaned back in the chair and swiveled it like a small child on a bar stool.

Her fingers rapidly working the keys of the adding machine, Sarah said distractedly, "You keep that up, sugar, you'll be staggering out of here."

Josie rubbed her temple. "My ex-husband spent years telling me I was dizzy. He'd be tickled pink." Head thrown back, dark hair spilling over the back of the chair, she swiveled to and fro in a slow, lazy rhythm.

Sarah glanced up and frowned. "I hope you set him straight real quick."

Josie opened her eyes and gave Sarah a slow, feline grin. "Oh, I set him straight, all right. Right before I booted him out the door for good."

Steve Merino came bopping down the center aisle, tossed a Granny Smith apple into the air and deftly caught it. "Set who straight?" he said, and bit into the apple.

"My ex." Josie stretched like a cat and studied him with narrowed eyes. "You're looking chipper tonight, Steverino. Hot date?"

He grinned and waggled his eyebrows. "Sizzling. But I'm not saying any more than that, because I'm a gentleman clear to the marrow."

"Sex," Josie said. "He's planning to have sex. God, I remember sex. Do you?"

"Vaguely," Sarah said, concentrating on the numbers she was running through the adding machine.

Steve leaned both elbows on the counter beside the cash register. "I already told you, Jose, any time you're interested, I'm your man."

Josie rolled her eyes. "Let me put it this way, Steven. When the day comes that you're five years older and I'm five years younger, then we'll talk."

"She wants me," he said to Sarah in a mock-confidential tone. "She's just intimidated by the idea of having the greatest sexual experience of her life with a younger man."

Sarah looked up, adjusted her reading glasses, and eyed

him over the frames. "Maybe," she said. "On the other hand, maybe she's just interested in a man who's old enough to grow hair on his chest."

Steve clutched at his heart and staggered backward. "*Augh!* That hurt, boss lady. That hurt so bad that I am outta here." He picked up his apple and headed for the back door, whistling cheerfully.

"Details!" Josie shouted to his back. "We want lots of details so we can live vicariously!" She leaned back in her chair and said, "You know, men are really more trouble than they're worth. I think women are a lot better off just getting a cat and a vibrator."

She'd finally snagged Sarah's full attention. "A cat and a vibrator," Sarah repeated, totally abandoning her adding machine. "And the reason for this is...?"

"Think about it. Between the two of them, they can do anything for you that a man can do. But neither one will ever come home smelling of somebody else's perfume."

Sarah tucked a pencil behind her ear and considered Josie's words. "I don't know, sugar. I've had cats come home smelling of a lot worse things than perfume."

Josie grinned. "You know what I mean." She slithered her lanky body higher in the chair. "So. You are coming to little Frankie's christening, right?"

Sarah had met Josie's brother Frank and his wife, Sheila, at a Christmas party. Over eggnog and sugar cookies, Sheila had confided to her about their little surprise, a souvenir from a twentieth-anniversary cruise last summer when she and Frank had gotten a little too intoxicated one night on moonlight and champagne.

They were both approaching forty, they already had three daughters—a nine-year-old and a set of twins in their final year of high school—and the last thing they'd expected was another child. But once they got over the initial shock, Frank and Sheila found themselves eager to be parents again.

"Maybe this time, we'll get it right," Sheila told her only half-jokingly. "After all, we have seventeen years of experience to draw on. And one baby at a time has to be easier than twins."

Three weeks ago, when Sheila had given birth to a baby boy, Josie had somehow managed to get Sarah to promise she'd attend the baby's christening. "Oh, shit," Sarah said now. "Tell me it's not tomorrow."

"You know perfectly well it's tomorrow. Don't even think of trying to back out. You promised."

"But—" She cast about for a valid excuse to skip the festivities, but couldn't seem to find one. She'd gotten on well with Sheila. And Josie was hell-bent on having her there to witness her shining moment as godmother to her first and only nephew.

"No buts," Josie said. "Remember what that Adrienne woman said to you? You have to go on living a normal life. Correct?"

Sarah sighed, knowing she was defeated. "Correct."

"Case closed, then. I'll pick you up at eleven-fifteen."

"Whoa, girl. Hold on just a minute. I'll go, but I'm driving my own car. That way I can make a clean getaway when I'm ready."

On a wet and dreary Sunday morning, she found herself pulling into the parking lot behind Saint Bartholomew's Catholic Church. The day was so dismal she'd almost stayed home, where it was warm and cozy and dry. But sitting alone in her living room watching *Behind the Music* and waiting for the phone to ring wasn't going to bring Kit home any more quickly, and Adrienne Thibodeau's words kept coming back to her. *Don't use guilt as an excuse to die a slow death.* A christening was a happy occasion, and right now, happy was something she could definitely use. So she'd bought a gift for the baby, pulled from her closet the only dress she owned that was suitable for church, and put on panty hose for the first time since she'd moved to Boston.

In the last week, temperatures had risen, rapidly eating away at the hard-packed snow, uncovering layer after layer of soot and muck and road sand. By midweek, Boston had reached a near record seventy degrees. Muddy water gushed in the gutters and spilled over onto the roadways, morphing into deadly black ice when each afternoon's sunset sent temperatures plummeting. This, combined with the ubiquitous potholes, made for interesting driving, rendered even more interesting by the tendency of the natives to view both as challenges to their creative driving skills.

Today's weather was a drizzly fifty-two degrees and damp, the kind of dampness that worked its way into your body and burrowed clean through to your bones. Sarah parked the Mustang amid a cluster of cars at one end of the church parking lot, opened her umbrella, and headed for the red double doors that were the only spot of color brightening an otherwise drab, monochromatic day.

Inside the church, the air was heavy with that hushed stillness all houses of worship seem to possess. Sarah folded her umbrella, shook the raindrops from it, and stepped into the sanctuary. Its ornate lushness was a far cry from the simple wooden church where she'd spent Sunday mornings during her formative years, terrified by the promises of fire and brimstone emanating from the pulpit. Here, the vaulted ceiling rose to the heavens above immense stained glass windows. A thick, blood-red carpet offset the massive wooden pews. The scent of candle wax, a remnant of the Sunday-morning service that had just ended, sweetened the air. Sarah stared in horrified fascination at the tormented and bloody Jesus who hung in eternal sorrow on the wall behind the altar. Maybe fear and intimidation weren't the sole province of the Bible Belt, after all.

In the front pews, about fifty people clustered on one side

near the baptismal font. Sarah silently crossed the crimson carpet and slipped into a vacant seat. Two rows ahead of her, Josie's six-year-old son Jake, wearing a suit and bow tie for the occasion, turned around and stared at her. Sarah waggled her fingers at him. He flashed a killer grin and wriggled back down into his seat just as the priest, followed by the parents and the godparents, proceeded down the center aisle to the front of the church. As godmother, Josie proudly carried the guest of honor, swaddled in a snow-white christening gown.

The group gathered in a semicircle around the baptismal font. From somewhere, a flashbulb popped. Father Clancy Donovan glanced up, cleared his throat, and offered a faint smile to the cluster of individuals assembled in the pews. She'd seen him in street clothes, seen him dressed all in black. But today he wore white, a flowing white robe that was both a symbol of purity and a stunning contrast to his dark good looks. Some type of deep purple scarf looped over his shoulders and fell nearly to his knees. The effect was dazzling.

The symbolism and ritual of the Catholic baptismal ceremony was as foreign to Sarah, a born and bred Southern Baptist, as it was beautiful. Candles and prayer, the renouncing of sin, the anointing of the child with some kind of oil, the holy water ladled over the head of the squalling infant, who demonstrated his displeasure at the indignity with an amazing lung capacity.

Although tiny Francis Rafferty II was the focus of interest, Sarah's attention kept wandering back to the priest. She couldn't have said exactly why, except that in the white robe, he displayed an innocent purity at odds with the sophisticated, street-smart man she knew him to be. It was a little unsettling, seeing him in his natural habitat. His movements were graceful, his hands gentle but steady as he performed the age-old ritual that would eternally bind the child's soul to God. She'd heard somewhere that a priest's hands were consecrated, blessed, incapable of sin. Watching those long, slender fingers drawing the sign of the cross on the infant's forehead, she could have almost sworn they gave off a divine glow. For some inexplicable reason, that unsettled her even further.

After the ceremony, people stood talking in clusters among the pews. Sarah lost track of the priest as she squeezed through the high-spirited crowd to pay her respects to Sheila and Frank Rafferty, who stood beaming with pride. Then she had to spend a few minutes admiring the baby. Little Frankie definitely had strong Rafferty genes; he stared boldly at her with wide, curious eyes fringed with dark lashes that would be driving girls crazy in thirteen or fourteen years.

Then Josie shanghaied her. "You have to meet my Aunt Freda," she said, and proceeded to introduce Sarah to half the people in the building. Josie had a mind-boggling array of extended family, and by the time she was done, Sarah was certain she hadn't missed a single great-uncle or second cousin. Not that she'd remember any of them by tomorrow. She was terrible with names and faces.

She finally escaped when Josie's mother dragged her daughter away to confer about the buffet luncheon waiting at Frank and Sheila's house. Grateful for the reprieve, Sarah scooted for the front door, intending to make a rapid getaway. But it wasn't fated to be; in the vestibule, near the open door, she found Clancy Donovan shaking hands with the departing guests. She tried to sneak past the portly woman in flowered silk who was pumping his hand with immense enthusiasm, but over the top of the woman's head, the priest's gaze met hers, warmed and lingered.

"Wonderful baptism, Father," the woman said. "There wasn't a dry eye in the house."

"Thank you, Mrs. Elsinore. It's a blessed occasion." His words were directed at the woman, but his eyes were still on Sarah, clearly willing her to stay.

Hell's bells. She hesitated for an instant before abandoning her getaway plan. He spoke a few more words to the woman before the petite Mrs. Elsinore fluttered away into the drab gray afternoon like a brightly colored finch.

Sarah took a step forward and held out her hand. "Father," she said. "Nice. Very nice."

"Sarah." He took her hand in both of his. His skin was warm and dry, and he smelled like altar candles and bay rum. "I'm glad you could come. Was this your first Catholic baptism?"

"Yes."

"Different?"

"Very different. Where I come from, when we baptize people, we just dunk them in the river. And they're generally a tad older than little Frankie. I'm not at all familiar with Catholic ritual, but it was a lovely ceremony."

"Thanks. Now you've uncovered my secret. I like to dress in robes and pour water over the heads of unsuspecting children."

He was teasing her. Humor danced in his eyes, and she returned his smile, wondering how anybody so closely aligned with God could be so devilishly attractive. They stood looking at each other as the wind blowing through the open door fluttered the hem of his robe. "Are you coming to the house?" he said.

She hadn't intended to. Her plan was to give Josie the gift she'd bought, ask her to deliver it to the proud parents along with her regrets, then get the hell out of Dodge. But the longer he stood waiting for an answer, the less appealing she found the idea of a long, solitary afternoon in Revere. "Will you be there?" she said.

"Absolutely. I never turn down a free meal."

The man standing in line behind her cleared his throat. She and Clancy Donovan realized simultaneously that they were still holding hands. He dropped her hand as if it had jungle rot and took a step backward.

She busied herself locating the release button to her umbrella. It popped open, and she glanced back up at the priest. He stood with feet braced apart, his hands clasped, regarding her with an odd intensity. "Maybe I'll see you there," she said.

"I'll be looking forward to it." And he turned to greet the gentleman who'd been waiting with barely concealed impatience.

She dodged puddles all the way to her car, unlocked the door and slid in behind the wheel. Shaking water off her umbrella, she closed it and tossed it onto the floor. Breathing a little too hard, she gripped the steering wheel and leaned back in her seat.

What the hell had that been all about? What devil had prompted her to stand in the damp and windy church entryway, flirting with a priest, of all people, while needles of awareness danced in her belly?

It was a momentary aberration. Nothing more. To prove it, she popped in a CD, cranked the ignition, and turned the car in the direction of Sheila's house, exorcising her demons the way she always did, by belting out a jazzy little number along with Reba.

Tell me why haven't I heard from you?

"I wouldn't let 'em put me out. Hell, I'm a grown man, you're gonna put me to sleep for something as simple as having a few teeth out? I took a local. Never felt a thing. But when he started yanking and twisting, I could hear the roots crunching. The most bizarre sensation I've ever experienced. And the blood...Jesus, it was just spurting out everywhere—"

Glassy-eyed, Sarah nodded, took a gulp of warm cream soda, and looked around desperately for a familiar face. But she'd been deserted, left to fend for herself in her hour of need. Jack Lawson was recently divorced, lonely, and movie-star handsome. He was also an interminable bore who stuck like Velcro. He had already treated her to the lengthy and convoluted story of his defunct marriage. Now he'd moved on to the recent extraction of his wisdom teeth. Perhaps Jack preferred a local, but she would have been thrilled with a few whiffs of ether, just so she could escape from this living hell.

"It's the goddamn insurance companies," he was saying. "They won't pay unless you have all four out. Can you believe that? I only had trouble with one, but unless I wanted to pay the frigging bill myself, it was four or nothing. It's some kind of collusion between the medical profession and the insurance industry. Believe me, the truth'll come out one of these days. When it does, just remember it was Jack Lawson who said it first."

Forgetting would be difficult. While the man continued to ramble insufferably, Josie's son Jake raced into the room with his cousin Brandy in hot pursuit, both of them carrying toy pistols, both of them screaming like banshees. They circled a Louis XIV armchair that was undoubtedly worth a fortune and scrambled on all fours behind the overstuffed couch. "I got you!" Brandy yelled. "I got you, you worthless scumbag!"

"That's what you think," Jake yelled back. "You're dead meat, dog breath, because I got spies watching you everywhere."

"Oh, yeah? Well, I'm the good guy, Jake Porter, and you are toast."

"You can't be the good guy. You're a girl."

"I'm three years older than you. I get to be anybody I want to be!"

In the midst of the chaos, Clancy Donovan appeared in the room's arched entry, looking relaxed and comfortable in the sweater and jeans he'd changed into before driving out here. "Jake," he said firmly. "Brandy."

The yelling ceased abruptly, and two heads popped out from behind the couch. "Take all that energy elsewhere," he said. "Right now, before you destroy the living room. Go upstairs and play."

Both kids scrambled out from behind the couch and stood before him, shuffling and contrite. Jake mumbled, "Sorry, Father."

"Go on," the priest said. "Both of you, before your mothers throttle you. And walk, please. No more running in the house."

He stood watching them until the sound of their footsteps disappeared up the staircase. Then, with a satisfied gleam in his eye, he turned to Sarah. For an instant, her breath caught in her throat as he studied her from across the room, his eyes a sea of gold, pupils wide and black in the dimness.

"—besides," Jack said, "they don't know who they're dealing with here. I don't take any of that crap from any—"

Momentarily lost in Clancy Donovan's eyes, she had forgotten Jack Lawson even existed. She exhaled and sent the priest a beseeching look across the Aubusson carpet.

Save me. Please.

He took in the situation and wasn't quite successful at hiding the smile that flitted across his face as he began moving across the carpet toward her.

"—so I told the guy he could just—"

"Excuse me. Sarah? I believe we volunteered to help with cleanup in the kitchen."

Jack Lawson stopped midsentence, his mouth hanging open. She gave the priest a look of unending gratitude. "You're right, Father," she said. "I completely forgot. Jack, it was so nice to meet you."

Jack closed his mouth. "Yeah," he said. "Sure." As if in

afterthought, he shouted to her receding back, "Hey, don't they have somebody to do that?"

The kitchen was a disaster, paper plates piled everywhere, silver and glasses and serving dishes stacked on every available surface. "You fill the sink with water," the priest said, "and I'll start tossing rubbish." He crouched in front of the sink and opened a cupboard door. "They must have trash bags in here somewhere…yes, here they are."

She raised her eyebrows and took a second look at the catastrophe. "We're really cleaning this? You and me?"

He glanced up at her, an oversized trash bag in his hand. "You wouldn't want to make a liar of me, would you? And you have to consider the alternative."

She pictured Jack Lawson and grimaced. "There is that to consider." She waited while he closed the cupboard door, then she put the stopper in the sink, squirted in dish detergent, and turned on the hot water tap. "Thank you, Father. I felt like a caged animal in there."

"It's Clancy."

"'scuse me?"

"My name. It's Clancy." He had moved to the table and was busy filling the trash bag with paper plates, empty paper cups, and disposable plastic utensils. "That's what my friends call me."

Warmth spread low in her belly. "I see," she said to the back of his head. "And are we friends?"

"I wonder if Sheila wants to save the rest of this salad." He turned, serving bowl in hand, and smiled at her. "It feels that way to me," he said, and lofted the bowl. "What do you think about the salad?"

"Toss it. Nobody wants to eat wilted lettuce."

"Good point. How are you holding up?"

He scraped leftover salad into the trash while she stacked dirty dishes beside the sink. He handed her the salad bowl and she dunked it into hot, soapy water. "I went to a support group meeting," she said, turning the ridged bowl and poking into all the crevices with her dishcloth. "I really want to thank you for that little suggestion."

"Is that a kernel of sarcasm I'm detecting at the heart of your gratitude?"

"It was awful. Heart wrenching." She lifted the bowl from the water and rinsed it. "Adrienne and I had coffee afterward. She advised me that the best thing I can do for myself is to go on living a normal life." Sarah loaded silverware into the sink and began working her way through it briskly. "So here I am. Living."

He opened a cupboard door, moved down the line of doors until he found a roll of plastic wrap. "Did you get anywhere with the high school?"

"No. I talked to the principal, and Kit's teachers, and a couple of the kids who sat near her in class. Nobody seems to have a clue about anything."

He opened the fridge and made room for a couple of bowls. "I've been pushing it," he said, returning to the table. "As hard as I can. I've been out on the street night and day, talking to people. Nobody's seen Kit, and nobody seems to know who this guy is."

He touched her shoulder and she turned. In his hand, he held a partitioned serving plate with two olives on it. "Payback for all our hard work," he said. "We get to raid the leftovers."

"My hands are all soapy."

He plucked an olive from the plate and held it out. She ate it from his fingers, then watched as he popped the last one into his mouth. "It's so hard," she said. "The waiting. I can't stand feeling helpless. I keep thinking there must be something else I should be doing. I call the Revere police at least once a week, just to make sure they don't forget I'm alive."

He slipped the plate into the sink and shoved up the

sleeves of his sweater. "I suspect they'd find you difficult to forget."

"Since I'm not sure precisely how you meant that, I'm going to operate under the assumption you meant it as a compliment."

"I absolutely meant it as a compliment. Dishcloth?"

She wrung out the cloth and handed it to him, and he wiped down the table, the counter, the stove top. When he was done, he pulled two towels from a drawer, and together they dried the dishes, quickly and efficiently. "At least spring finally got here," he said, holding up a cake pan to allow excess water to drain off. "I seem to remember telling you, just a few weeks ago, that it would."

"I didn't believe you. I still don't believe you." She glanced out the window at a dull, gray world. "This is your idea of spring?"

With a disarming smile, he said, "Welcome to Massachusetts." He dried the pan and picked up a fistful of silverware. Opened the silverware drawer and rapidly wiped and stacked knives, spoons and forks in their proper places. "The crocuses outside the back door of the church are poking their heads up through the snow. And in a week or two, magnolias will be blooming all over the Back Bay."

"Magnolias," she said with a sigh, charmed by the picture his words painted in her mind of wispy pink and white blossoms flanking narrow streets lined with brick townhouses. "I absolutely adore magnolias. I had no idea they grew this far north."

"It would be worth your while, then, to take a drive down Commonwealth Avenue to see them. They're breathtaking."

They hung up the dish towels and stood back to admire their handiwork. Clean dishes were stacked tidily on the table. Every surface was wiped clean, and the bag of rubbish was tied neatly and left beside the back door. "Now," he said, "like good little elves, it's time to steal away and leave Sheila to wonder who cleaned her kitchen for her."

It was also Sarah's cue to pack up and depart. "I have to be going," she said, sneaking a glance at the kitchen clock. "It's almost three. Thanks again for rescuing me."

"No thanks necessary."

She located the Raffertys, made her goodbyes, and unearthed her coat from the pile on the guest room bed, wondering as she did so whether the priest would still be here when she got outside. Not that it mattered. He undoubtedly had places to go, things to do, people to see. And so did she. There was that frozen turkey dinner she had to microwave for her evening meal. Several pairs of panties that needed washing. The living room to vacuum.

Lint to contemplate in her navel.

With a sigh, she acknowledged that the good Father was gorgeous. Not to mention clever and witty and smart. He oozed an innate charm he probably wasn't even aware of, and he had a deliciously off-the-wall sense of humor. She couldn't imagine being female and not finding him attractive. But as far as men were concerned, there were degrees of availability, and Father Clancy Donovan was as unavailable as it was possible to get.

Besides, her kitchen floor could use a good coat of wax, and the toilet in the downstairs bathroom needed scrubbing. That should be sufficient distraction to curb her deviant thoughts and fill the rest of her afternoon. With a renewed determination to hone her domestic skills, Sarah let herself out the kitchen door, her umbrella tucked under her elbow, and stepped around the corner of the house.

The object of those deviant thoughts was standing in the driveway, beneath the basketball hoop, giving Jake pointers on how to line up a jump shot. The breeze lifted a strand of the priest's dark hair, then let it fall. Jake nodded his understanding, bounced the basketball against the pavement two or three times, and shot for the moon.

He missed by a mile. Clancy ruffled his hair, cast her a parting smile over the boy's head, and squatted back down to explain something that apparently hadn't gotten through the first time. Heels clicking on the pavement, she moved briskly down the driveway to her car, parked on the street in front of the house for a quick getaway. She unlocked the Mustang and slid into the driver's seat. Of its own volition, her gaze returned to the dynamic duo in the driveway just in time to see the priest make a flawless shot that went through the hoop like a knife through butter. Determined to ignore her disconcerting reaction to him, she stuck her key into the ignition and turned it.

Nothing happened.

In disbelief, she pulled out the key, inhaled a sharp breath, and slid it back in. She'd been driving the Mustang for two years, and it had never even seen the inside of a repair shop. If there truly were a God, she didn't appreciate His sense of humor. Or His timing.

Please. Pretty please.

She turned the key again. Zilch. The poor old girl didn't even let out a feeble whinny. The Mustang was as dead as Elvis.

"Shit on a stick," she said.

8

The photos were amazing.

Rio had used a variety of backgrounds, working with both color and black-and-white film, and the proofs absolutely blew her away. He spread them out on the glass-topped coffee table and Kit gazed at them in awe, wondering who was this blond bombshell who stared back at her with such bold, brassy haughtiness. The poses, the lighting effects, the costume changes—for that's how she thought of the numerous outfits she wore—made her look like a different person, somebody cool and mysterious, provocative and seductive.

"The camera doesn't lie," Rio told her, reaching out to straighten one of the proofs so it lined up neatly with the others. "A good photographer can reach inside and pull out the real person hidden behind the mask they show the world. It's not the pictures that're sexy, it's you."

"Me?" It flattered her beyond belief that he thought so, even if she couldn't really see it herself.

"Look at those eyes, kitten. What do you see there?"

She studied her facial expressions, her body language, the silent message her eyes telegraphed to the camera lens. *Here I am, baby. Try me. If you dare.*

"Solid gold," he said. "The camera loves you. I have to tell you, it doesn't happen very often. But some people are born to be in front of a camera, and you're one of them. You're going places, Princess. Bigger and better places than you could ever imagine. With that face and that body, and the power that radiates from inside you—there's no way you can miss."

"But—" Excitement sizzled through her, made her heart do flip-flops. "How?"

"We start by taking more pictures. A little edgier, a little wilder. We color outside the lines a little. That's the way to get noticed. You have to take risks. You have to have something nobody else has. And you do, babe. You have the makings of a goddess."

"A goddess," she echoed skeptically. "Yeah, right."

"I'm serious. Pretty women are a dime a dozen. But the goddesses stand out. They're the women that men look at and go, 'whoa!' Marilyn Monroe. Sophia Loren. Audrey Hepburn."

The names were vaguely familiar, but she couldn't have picked any of them out of a lineup, "Or," he said smoothly, reading the uncertainty on her face, "how about Madonna? Britney? J-Lo? You recognize those names, don't you?" He reached out to toy with a strand of her hair. "I can take you to the same place they're at. You and me, babe. You let me guide your career, and I'll take you all the way to the stars."

While she stared at him in disbelief, he turned his attention back to the proofs. "Of course," he said, "you have to start small."

"Whatever it takes," she said. "I'll do anything."

He put a hand behind her head, cupped the nape of her neck beneath her hair. Leaning toward her, he said softly, "You know I'm crazy about you, kitten."

Her hands, busy straightening the stack of photos, stilled. Without looking at him, she whispered, "I know."

Beneath her hair, he stroked her scalp with the pad of his thumb, sending a thrill shooting through her. "Then you know I'd do anything for you. Anything at all."

"Would you?"

"Anything, baby. That's how much you mean to me. I've

never felt this way about anybody before. All I can think about is you. Looking after you. Taking care of you. Making you happy.''

She turned to speak, found his face only inches from hers. Those seductive blue eyes studied her face while his thumb moved in lazy circles behind her ear. She studied his eyes, his full lips, the way the light glinted off his gold earring.

"That's why," he said, lowering his eyes, "it pains me so much to have to tell you this."

Her heart began a slow pounding. "What?"

"I heard something yesterday." His thumb continued its steady seduction, slipped around to her collarbone. "I'm sorry, baby, but I thought you should know." He raised his eyes back up to hers. "It's your aunt. She's stopped looking for you."

For an instant, time stopped. She took a deep breath and tried to absorb the significance of his words. So it was true. She'd been right all along. Aunt Sarah hadn't wanted her.

It was stupid, because she hadn't been all that fond of Sarah anyway, and she'd been miserable living in that decrepit little house in Revere. Yet she felt as though she'd been kicked in the stomach. It shouldn't have hurt, but it did.

He must have recognized the stunned look on her face, for he drew her into his arms and cradled her against his chest. "I'm so sorry, baby," he said. "I'm so sorry she didn't care enough about you to keep looking for you. But you have me now, and I'll take care of you." As she fought the tears that fell in spite of the hard shell she'd built around her heart, he rocked her like an infant. "It's okay," he said. "Go ahead and cry. You'll feel better afterward."

"I don't care," she said, viciously swiping at a tear. "I don't give a damn about her."

"I know you don't, babe. Fuck her. Fuck all of 'em. Your aunt, your father, your stepmother. You don't need them anyway. You have me. From now on, it'll be just you and me. Together forever.''

She clung to him as he kissed her forehead, her cheek, the pulse beating so rapidly in her throat. When his mouth covered hers in a kiss that was warm and sweet and reassuring, she returned it with desperate fervor.

"I love you, Kit," he whispered against her lips. "Nobody could ever love you the way I do."

"I love you, too," she said. "Don't ever leave me. Please."

"Never," he promised. "I will never, ever leave you."

When he lowered her to the couch, when he tugged her shirt from her jeans and began to unbutton it, one tiny, translucent button at a time, she let him. When he sank down on top of her and settled between her thighs, she let him, because he loved her, when nobody else ever had. He loved her, and that was all that mattered. He loved her, and from now on, it was going to be just the two of them.

Together.

Forever.

"The damnable thing is, I know Adrienne's right. I can't spend all my time sitting home, waiting for Kit to walk through that door. There aren't any guarantees. I could spend the rest of my life waiting."

A gust of wind caught at a strand of Sarah's hair and whipped it around her face. She reached up and tucked it behind her ear. The sea, tinted a steely gray by the overcast sky, rose and fell with a muffled roar, washing in crisp white foam that teased and taunted before it rolled away and folded back into itself. She wasn't quite sure whose crazy idea this had been; it had simply sprung up between them somewhere between Medford and Revere. After her car had been towed to a repair shop, she'd made a brief pit stop at home to change clothes. Now, here they were, two lunatics walking the beach on a blustery spring afternoon that had lost its warmth hours ago, simply because neither of them had anywhere else to be.

Beside her, the priest bent and pried a shell from the hard-packed sand. "Life," he said, straightening, "has to go on. Sometimes terrible things happen in our lives, but we still have to keep going. Otherwise, you might as well just fold up your tent and wait to die." He drew back his arm and skimmed the shell over the water. It disappeared into the glittering waves.

"I'm not giving up on her."

"I wouldn't expect you to. You're not the kind of woman who gives up."

"I keep forgetting you have a life, too. You've done so much for me already, I don't expect—"

"I made a commitment," he said. "I'm in this for the duration. No matter how long it takes."

"And you always honor your commitments."

"I always try to. It isn't necessarily the same thing."

What she'd said was true; she did keep forgetting he had a life that didn't revolve around finding Kit. At first, he'd been no more to her than a means to an end. But somewhere along the way, he'd turned into a full-blooded, fully fleshed man, a man she found far more attractive than she should have, considering the circumstances. A man whose life, aside from the hours he spent with her, was a complete mystery.

"What do you do?" she said. "When you're not pouring water over the heads of unsuspecting children?"

"You mean besides sitting around in my robes, uttering pithy and sagacious pronouncements, like the Dalai Lama?"

"You're making fun of me. I'm serious. Give me an example of a typical day in the life of Father Clancy Donovan."

He tucked his hands into his pockets. "There is no typical day. I do a lot of pastoral counseling. People come to me for help if their marriage is in trouble, or their children, or their bank account. We talk, we pray, I try to give them advice that'll do them good without violating Church canon. I meet with couples for prewedding counseling. I spend a significant amount of time putting out fires. Whatever issues fall into my lap, I deal with. I supervise Melissa, my secretary, and Dave Murphy, the church sexton. I attend meetings at the Archdiocese office and I sit on endless committees. Church committees, community committees, the local neighborhood association. I head the church youth organization, and I coach basketball for inner-city boys with too much time on their hands. I visit shut-ins and hospitalized parishioners. I volunteer a few hours a week at a soup kitchen downtown. Oh, and of course I'm chief administrator for Donovan House."

"Stop! My head's spinning. What do you do with your overabundance of spare time?"

When he smiled, his entire face radiated warmth. "I play racquetball twice a week with Conor Rafferty. Watch a lot of boring cable TV. And I mooch as many meals as possible from my parishioners. I'm a dreadful cook."

"How do you survive? If I had a schedule like that, I'd collapse from exhaustion. How do you get through the day?"

"Prayer and cinnamon candy. In roughly equal amounts."

"Prayer," she said thoughtfully. "So you really believe in this God stuff."

"Of course. Don't you?"

They reached a huge clump of seaweed, tossed ashore and abandoned by the fickle sea. By unspoken agreement, they turned and began retracing their steps. "To tell you the truth," she said, "I'm not sure what I believe anymore. You probably think I'm headed straight to hell, don't you?"

"It's not my place to judge."

"You're not going to try to convert me?"

"I don't believe people can be converted by coercion. I believe we all come to God in our own time, in our own way. When we're ready."

"Rather heretical of you, isn't it, Father?"

"According to Bishop Halloran, I harbor a number of heretical beliefs. It doesn't bother me in the least. The Church is my home, my family, my life. But I answer to just one master, and I listen when He talks to me."

She raised her eyebrows. "God talks to you," she said.

"All the time."

"Tell me He doesn't tap you on the shoulder and sing *Yankee Doodle* in your ear."

It was the first time she'd ever heard him laugh. "He's a little more subtle than that."

"That's a relief. I really like you. I'd hate to see you carted off to a rubber room somewhere. So how does God talk to you?"

He halted his footsteps and turned toward the water. "Look out there."

She followed his gaze, out over the Atlantic, silver melding into gunmetal gray, deep and dark and endless. "It's stunning," he said, "the absolute enormity of it. It makes you realize how tiny and finite and powerless you are. When I look at the ocean, or the stars, whenever I see a glorious sunrise or a rainbow, I know it's God's voice, talking to me. I don't hear it with my ears. I feel it, in here." He lay a hand across his heart. "Faith," he said. "Pure, undiluted faith. It's the greatest power I'll ever possess."

"Is that why you became a priest?"

He tucked his hands into his pockets and they resumed walking. "I've actually given it a great deal of thought," he said, "why we turn to God. Life is so difficult. There's a great deal of beauty, but also a great deal of pain. From birth to death, our lives are rife with questions, unanswered and unanswerable. I believe that when the unanswerable becomes unbearable, we turn to God. For most of us, it's the only way we can survive inexplicable tragedy. We don't understand why terrible things happen, but when our faith tells us that only God is supposed to have the answers, not knowing becomes acceptable. We can allow God to carry the burden for us.''

''Interesting theory. Which leads to an obvious question. Did God create man, or did man create God?''

His smile was wry. ''Trying to trip me up, are you? I'm a theologian. I'll always tell you God created man, not the other way around. But—'' He paused, grew reflective. ''If you asked me if man created religion, I might give you a different answer. They're not the same, you know. God is constant, unimpeachable, unquestionable. Religion is man's way of trying to bridge the chasm between heaven and earth. We haven't yet been fully successful, but our endeavors are admirable.''

''You're right,'' she said.

''About what?''

''You do harbor a number of heretical beliefs.'' She studied his profile, the sharp line of his jaw, the chiseled lips, the slight upturn at the end of an otherwise flawlessly straight nose. ''But you still didn't answer my question about why you became a priest.''

''Yes, I did. You just weren't listening closely enough. Tell me about your husbands.''

His abrupt change of subject jarred her for an instant. ''My husbands?'' She raised an eyebrow and chuckled. ''Lord, sugar, you got all night?''

''We've talked about me. Now it's your turn. I want to hear the story of your life.''

''Well, let's see. I met my first husband, Earl Twilley, when I was eighteen. Young and foolish. Momma had just died, I was trying to figure out what I wanted to do with my life, and Earl offered me the security I was missing. He was ten years older than me, and devilishly handsome. He was a wildcatter, worked for one of the big oil companies, and he dragged me off to West Texas and left me for months at a

time in a drafty little single-wide trailer with nobody to talk
to but an old bluetick hound.''

"Sounds pretty lonely for a young girl.''

"I just about went nuts. There wasn't a soul I knew in
Texas besides my husband. My whole family was still back
in Bayou Rouillard, and they didn't even have a phone. I
wrote Daddy a letter every so often, but he wasn't the letter-
writing type. I finally got a job waitressing at a truck stop
over in the next town. It was the kind of place where redneck
truckers left big tips for the privilege of looking down the
front of my blouse and grabbing my ass every chance they
could get. I hated it, but I stayed because I was about to go
crazy all by myself in that little trailer. At least at the truck
stop I got to see other human beings. Whenever Earl came
home, we had a grand old time together. But he'd always
leave again, and I couldn't take the solitude. One fine day, I
was pouring coffee for a trucker who said he was headed to
New Orleans. The Big Easy. I set down that coffee pot and
took off my apron. Twenty minutes later, when his rig pulled
out onto the highway, I was riding shotgun.''

"You just got into his truck and left with him? A total
stranger?''

"What can I say? I was young and foolish. I must have
had a guardian angel watching over me, because he was a
decent family man. When we got to New Orleans, he and
his wife took me in while I tried to figure out what to do
next. What I ended up doing was meeting husband number
two. Jackson Forrester. We only knew each other a few
weeks before we went down to the courthouse and made it
legal. Lord, did I love that man.''

She paused, watched a pair of gulls fighting over a scrap
of refuse that had washed up on shore. "I was a little older,
a little smarter. Or so I thought. I really believed this was
the one that would last. I was cashiering nights at Winn-
Dixie. Mindless work, and while my fingers were punching

the cash register, my mind was wandering. I used to weave
these elaborate fantasies about a little house with a white
picket fence, a couple of kids, a dog. Hell, I even threw in
the minivan. Sarah Connelly Forrester, the domestic goddess.
But Jackie had a drinking problem, and when he lost his job,
the drinking got worse. It took me a while, but I finally realized that no matter how much I loved him, no matter what
I did or said, he wasn't going to quit. So I had myself a big
old cry, then I packed his things, changed the locks, and filed
for divorce."

"I'm sorry."

"Yes. Me, too." Overhead, a jet heading for the runway
at Logan passed so low she could read the writing on its
underbelly. She drew her coat tighter around her. "You sure
you want to hear the rest of this? It's not a pretty story."

"I want to hear it all."

"All right. But don't say I didn't warn you. After Jackie
left, I still had to keep up the rent on our apartment. I was
barely making ends meet. Nobody ever got rich working at
Winn-Dixie, and I had to eat. One of the other cashiers told
me about a dance club on Bourbon Street where a girl with
the right stuff could make a couple hundred bucks on a good
night. I sat myself down, took stock of my assets, and decided I had the right stuff. So I bleached my hair platinum
blonde, strapped on a push-up bra under a low-cut blouse,
poured myself into jeans that were two sizes too small, and
took the bus downtown."

She glanced at him from the corner of her eye, gauging
his response, wondering if her blatant honesty would send
him into cardiac arrest. But he was still just walking along
beside her, hands in his pockets, a tranquil expression on his
face as she painted her ruby-red picture of sin and shame.
"You still with me, sugar?"

"I'm still with you."

"Well, let's just say it wasn't the high point of my life,

being ogled by a bunch of horny old drunks while I danced on stage wearing a pair of pasties and a G-string. But the money was good. I moved into a nice apartment in the French Quarter, one that didn't have any roaches, and I bought myself a car. I wasn't exactly wallowing in dough, but I had enough money to pay the bills, tuck some away into savings, and still have enough left over to eat beignets for breakfast any time I wanted.'' She paused, took a breath. ''That's where I met Remy. He came into the club one night with a bunch of people. He was a big tipper, and he had the kindest eyes I'd ever seen. A few days later, we ran into each other at the corner grocery and discovered we lived just a few blocks apart. He asked me out for coffee. I turned him down. Remy was very persistent. Somehow, he managed to get my unlisted phone number, and over the next few weeks, he called incessantly. I finally gave in because it was easier than continuing to say no. Besides, I really liked him.''

She smiled at the memory. ''So we went for coffee, and the next thing I knew it was dinner at Antoine's, long walks through the Quarter, late nights at jazz clubs down on Bourbon Street. We became best friends. In hindsight, I can see we should've stayed friends. But Remy was determined to save me from myself. And I, with my customary flawless judgment, confused gratitude with love. One morning I woke up in his bed, with rice in my hair and a gold ring on my finger, and my dancing days were over. It was a little like hitting the lottery, because Remy wasn't just nice, he was loaded. People whispered behind my back, said I'd married him for the money. But his money was never that important to me. I married him because I liked him so very much.''

Quietly, he said, ''So what happened?''

''We were together for six years. I owe so much to Remy. He gave me the leverage I needed to pull myself by the bootstraps up and out of the gutter. He paid my way through college, took me on long vacations. Paris, Egypt, the Mediterranean. We were like two kids together, spending his money, with the entire world as our playground. But after a while, it wasn't enough. Not for me, and not for Remy either, not if he was being honest about it. We loved each other, we just weren't in love with each other. There's a big difference, you know?''

"Yes. I know."

"Still, we probably would've stuck it out if Kit hadn't come to live with us. Kit was mouthy, sneaky, prone to lying to get her way. Remy saw right through her and didn't like what he saw. She refused to show respect for the way he put a roof over her head, food in her mouth, clothes on her back. After a while, the conflict between the two of them rubbed off on us, and we started fighting. In six years of marriage, we'd never done that. When the quarrels turned nasty, I knew I had to move out. Remy was my dearest friend, and if I didn't end our marriage, I knew I'd lose his friendship. That would have broken my heart.''

"I suppose you realize that's an amazing story," he said. "Not many women, when faced with a choice between her niece and her husband, would choose the niece."

Her stomach muscles knotted. "Kit and I have a special bond," she said. "We always have."

"I'm not criticizing. I just think it's remarkable."

"It's not remarkable." Her clenched muscles relaxed as a fat drop of rain plopped against her cheek. "Just a matter of doing what you have to do." She glanced skyward as a second drop landed atop her head. "I do believe, Father Donovan, that it's raining."

He wiped a drop of wetness from the tip of her nose. "Yes. I noticed."

Without warning, the sky opened, pelting them with a frigid downpour. "This was your idea, wasn't it?" she shouted over the rain and the wind and the roar of the surf.

"My idea?" he shouted back. "I thought it was your idea."

"How far away is the car?" The rain was running in her eyes, blinding her, and her hair, hanging now in sodden strings, was already a dead loss.

"About a quarter of a mile. So tell me, Sarah Connelly, do you run like a girl?"

She raised her eyebrows while he stood there, sopping wet, his hair plastered to his head and an impish grin plastered on his face. "Like a girl?" she said. "Like a *girl?* Oh, sugar, to steal a line from your little friend Brandy, you are toast."

And she took off running.

With those long legs of his, he easily overtook her, then left her behind as she hobbled through dense sand, leaped over an errant snow bank, and scrambled up the concrete stairs to the sidewalk. Splashing through puddles, she focused on his back, a dark blur in the distance ahead of her as she ran. When she reached his car, breathless and exhilarated and soaked to the bone, he was already in the driver's seat with the heater cranked and Van Morrison on the stereo, the slow jazzy rhythm of horns and percussion keeping time with the rain tapping on the roof. *My momma told me there'll be days like this.*

He glanced up when she climbed in, then peeked casually at his watch. "What took you so long?"

Still high on adrenaline and exhilaration, she laughed in delight. "Better get that heater pumping, boy," she said, slamming the door behind her, "because I have goose bumps on top of goose bumps."

"It'll warm up in a minute." He leaned to open the glove compartment and took out a napkin. "Your mascara's running. Hold still." He cupped her chin to steady her and scrubbed gently at the smudges below her eyes.

Still exerted from running, her heart pumped a rapid beat. The pad of his thumb pressed lightly against her cheek, and his breath feathered the hair at her temple. Intent on his task, golden eyes narrowed in concentration, he seemed unaware of her rapt perusal. His eyebrows were thick and dark, the left one marred by a tiny white scar she'd never noticed before. Faint laugh lines fanned out from the corners of his eyes, and he had absolutely no business looking this good with rain dripping off him and his hair all wet and gnarly. Absolutely no business turning her inside out like this when he was inescapably, utterly unavailable.

Don't even go there, Connelly. Not even with a twenty-foot barge pole.

Her high took a sudden nosedive, and she realized she was chilled to the bone. "That's the best I can do," he said, releasing her. She fell back against the seat cushion with immense relief and released a pent-up breath. "Still cold?" he asked.

"Freezing. I don't think I'll ever adjust to your barbaric climate. I need to go home and get into dry clothes. It'd be a good idea if you did the same. Otherwise, we're both apt to end up with pneumonia."

"I think you got the worst of it," he said. "Especially since it took you so much longer to get to the car."

She closed her eyes and smiled. "You are a very, very bad man."

"So the bishop keeps telling me."

"He's right. You're rotten to the core. And your taste in music is questionable."

"My taste in music? What's wrong with my taste in music? You don't like Van Morrison?"

The heat blowing fiercely in her face from the dashboard vents had begun to thaw her out. "I love Van Morrison," she said, shoving her ruined hair back, away from her face. "It's not so much what you listen to as what you're *not* listening to. Your CD collection has some serious gaps. Where's Reba McEntire? Brooks and Dunn? Toby Keith?"

"Toby who?"

She opened her eyes and looked directly into his. The gleam she saw there told her he was toying with her again. She shook her head in mock sorrow.

"Sugar," she said, "you have truly led a life of deprivation."

9

He met Senator Tom Adams for breakfast at a little place called the Elephant and Castle, tucked away on a side street at the edge of the Financial District. They served a sumptuous buffet that was arguably the best breakfast in town. At the next table, a cluster of college students watched a soccer game on the overhead television. Every time the American team scored, they screamed and shouted and pounded the table.

"Soccer," Tom said over the uproar as he sat down across from Clancy. "Never did get it."

"Nor I. I don't even understand the game. Basketball's more my speed. So how are Bess and the girls?"

"They're great. Callie's taking dance lessons, and her first recital's coming up in a few weeks. She'd be thrilled if you could come. Geneva's madly in love with some boy at school, and Bess is going nuts as usual, trying to keep track of both their schedules." Tom leaned back as the waitress poured him a cup of coffee.

"And the Congressional campaign? How's that going?"

"It's early, but the numbers look promising. Let's say we're encouraged. What's new with you?"

"I'm looking for a runaway teenage girl. I'm trying to get the word out to everyone I can think of." He handed a flyer across the table. Tom took it and studied it, his brow furrowed.

"She's sixteen years old," Clancy said. "She took the T

from Revere into Boston a few weeks ago and simply vanished.''

"Have you checked the bus station, the airport, the train station?"

"All of the above, without a single hit. I'm pretty sure she's still here. Somewhere.'' He picked up his coffee and took a sip. ''You know as well as I do what happens to young girls out there on the street.''

Tom shook his head and sighed. "As a parent, it terrifies me,'' he admitted. ''Gen's only a couple years younger than this girl. As a concerned citizen, it makes me angry. And as a legislator, it makes me want to take strong action.''

"You can legislate until the cows come home, but in my experience, it's ineffective. You put one pimp in jail, the next day there's another one there to take his place.'' Clancy turned his coffee mug idly on the tabletop. ''It's discouraging.''

Tom set down the flyer and leaned back in his chair. Fingers threaded loosely in front of him, he studied Clancy with quiet speculation. "So what's your solution?"

This wasn't the first time they'd debated this particular issue. "I've told you this before and I'll say it again,'' Clancy said. "I don't believe you can legislate morality. And in answer to your question, I haven't yet seen any effective preventive medicine. Mostly just Band-Aid treatments applied after the fact.''

"What about better parenting skills? Stronger ties to home and church?"

"Even baby steps maintain forward momentum. But we've both been around long enough to know there's theory, and then there's reality.'' Thinking of Sarah, he added, ''And you can't always blame it on the parents. Some of these girls I work with are simply bent on self-destruction. It's heartbreaking to witness.''

Tom picked up the flyer again. "Is it okay if I make copies of this?"

"Of course. The more the better. I'm practicing saturation bombing. That's why I thought of you. Whatever agencies I'm not involved with, you are."

"I'll pass it around. I've been doing a lot with the soup kitchens and the drug treatment centers. I'm also on the boards of a couple of homeless shelters. If she's out there...well, you know the drill as well as I do."

"Thanks. I appreciate it. So tell me more about Callie's recital. I'd love to be there if I can fit it in. Callie's a great kid."

Paternal pride shone in Tom's eyes. "Yeah, she is. She's taking modern dance. I've been to a couple of her rehearsals, and it's a hoot to watch. I don't have my calendar with me, but if you give Bess a call, she can fill you in on the details. She'd love to hear from you. Just last week, she mentioned that it's been months since we had you over for dinner."

After breakfast, he drove to Braintree, where he spent the rest of the morning at Donovan House, finalizing paperwork on a girl who'd completed the program and was ready to transition back out into the community. Sheri Gordon had been clean for six months now. She was working as a receptionist for a local oil company, and she'd found a roommate to help her share expenses in the little two-bedroom apartment she'd rented above a drugstore in downtown Quincy. Her future looked promising, as long as she continued to follow the path she'd started on.

He was halfway back from Braintree when his cell phone rang. "Yo, Bwana," said a familiar voice at the other end. "What's happening, man?"

He hadn't really expected to hear from the kid again. "Jamal," he said. "To what do I owe this unexpected pleasure?"

"I happen to be in possession of a piece of information

that could prove beneficial to your cause,'' the kid said. "For the right price, I might even be willing to share it with you.''

"Of course,'' he said dryly. "And what might that price be?''

"You go tracking this dude down, I get to ride shotgun.''

"Deal. What's the information?''

"This morning, I be hanging out and shit. You know? And I see him, the surfer dude, coming out of one of them porn shops down in the Zone. Seeing as how I didn't have nothing better to do, I followed him. Discreetly, of course. Dude went into the parking garage on Beach Street and come out driving this slick red Beemer. And yours truly, being of sound mind and body, just happened to memorize the license plate number.''

"Well.'' He was duly impressed. "Good work.''

"So? We going after him?''

Something tightened inside his gut, and the fleeting thought crossed his mind that perhaps he enjoyed this cloak-and-dagger stuff a little more than he should. Wondering what that said about him, he checked the time. It would be a couple of hours before Melissa sent out the search dogs. Time enough to nose around and see what he could find out. Assuming he could get an ID on the plate.

Northbound traffic on the Expressway was backed up as usual. While he breathed in diesel fumes from the eighteen-wheeler idling in front of him, he fumbled for a pen and paper to write down the number Jamal gave him. "Look for me when you see me,'' he told Jamal. "I'm stuck in traffic.''

He tried Conor first, but Isabel, Conor's saucy young secretary, informed him in a fluid Spanish accent that the lieutenant wasn't in. Nor was Detective Lorna Abrams. That pretty much exhausted his list of contacts at the Boston P.D., at least the contacts he knew well enough to ask for an illegal plate search. He thanked Isabel and ended the call, spent a moment considering his options, and dialed Vince Paoletti.

"Father," the Vice cop said. "You're getting to be a real pain in the ass. You find your girl yet?"

"I'm still working on it. I need a favor."

"How did I know that was coming? What is it you need this time?"

"I have a license plate number. I need a name and address to go with it."

"I talked to Rafferty the other day," Paoletti said. "I asked him about you."

"Did you now? And what did he have to say about me?"

"Enough. Give me five minutes and I'll call you back."

He wondered just how much Paoletti's "enough" had to do with a thirty-year-old friendship and how much it had to do with an eleven-year-old homicide. Water under the bridge, he reminded himself as he drummed his fingers impatiently against the steering wheel and eased the Saturn ahead a car length or two. It had been a long time since his last nocturnal visitation from Meg's restless ghost. With the truth about her death revealed at last, Meg Monahan was finally at peace. And so was he. He could still look back with regret for what might have been, regret for the young girl who would never grow old. He still felt pain over her death. But the longing and the anguish were gone.

He'd just drawn abreast of the Bayside Expo when Paoletti called back. "Roger Seward," the cop said. "2301 Jameson Street, Jamaica Plain. I ran his license, too, while I was at it. Five-eleven, one-seventy, blond, blue. Squeaky clean, not so much as a parking ticket."

"Bless you," he said. "I owe you one."

"I didn't do it for you, I did it for Rafferty. You and I never had this conversation."

"What conversation?"

"Exactly. One more thing, Father. Don't go playing hero, you hear me? I doubt that your friend Rafferty has either the time or the inclination to be scraping your carcass off the sidewalk. Keep your nose clean, and leave the superhero stuff to us. *Capisce?*"

"I hear you, Detective. Thanks."

It was another twenty minutes before he reached the corner where Jamal waited patiently. "About time you got here," the boy said cheerfully as he climbed into the car and slammed the door. "I thought you was in a car wreck or something."

"Why do I get the impression that the idea of my ill-timed and bloody demise brought you immense glee?"

"Chill, dude. You get an address for Surfer Boy?"

"I did. You familiar with Jamaica Plain?"

"Not really."

"I guess we'll have to wing it, then."

He circled the block, picked up the Southeast Expressway, then exited and began working his way through block after block of unfamiliar territory. As he drove, he tried to engage the kid in conversation. "How does your mother feel about you quitting school?"

Jamal glanced idly out the passenger-side window. "Ain't got no mother." He rubbed the tip of his nose with a knuckle. "Ain't got no old man, neither."

What had happened to the boy's parents? Curiosity gnawed at him, but he felt it was more prudent to wait until Jamal volunteered the information. He cleared his throat and said, "Who do you live with?"

"My granny." Jamal turned on the radio, spun the tuner until he found a station to his liking. Rhythm and energy, in the form of hip-hop music, filled the small space that surrounded them.

Raising his voice to be heard over the music, Clancy said, "And she doesn't care that you're not in school?"

"That school," Jamal said, "seem to be of the opinion that yours truly is incorrigible. My granny say she washing her hands of the likes of me."

"Well." He wasn't quite sure what to think. "Incorrigible or not," he said, "you've just been elected navigator. Start looking for Jameson Street. It should be around here some-where."

They took a few wrong turns, assisted by Snoop Dogg and Jay-Z. "Stop!" Jamal said, holding out a hand. "This be it right here."

Clancy hung a quick right onto Jameson. They'd landed somewhere in the 2200 block. He got his bearings, then be-gan working his way westward to the 2300's. As they passed house after house, Jamal read the numbers aloud. "2291, 2293…can't read this next one…um…2297, 2299." Clancy slowed and squinted at the house numbers. They rolled past an empty lot, and the boy took up counting again. "2303, 2305—hey! What the hell happened to 2301?"

Clancy stopped the car and they exchanged a puzzled look. He turned and took a quick survey of the house numbers across the street.

They were all even.

He put the car into reverse and slowly backed down the street, past 2303, to the weed-choked lot he'd ignored the first time through. Its sole inhabitant was a rusted 1969 Chevy Impala that sat up on blocks, its tires long since be-come victims of the neighborhood. He backed a little farther down the street, to the next house, and re-read the house number. 2299. In disbelief, he turned his attention back to the empty lot where 2301 should have been.

"Son of a bitch," Jamal said.

On the drive out to Revere, he called Paoletti back, left a message on his voice mail suggesting that since Roger Sew-ard's last known address had been a '69 Impala surrounded by weeds, it might just be possible his name wasn't the real deal, either. It was a warm spring day, breezy and muddy, and he drove with the window open because spring fever had him hard in its grip. He pulled into Sarah's driveway, hip-hop music thudding at an alarming level, and turned off the car. "Holy shit," Jamal said. "That house about as blue as blue can get."

Sarah was on her knees in the front yard, dressed in a down vest and work gloves, yanking at a stubborn clump of dead milkweed. He and Jamal crossed the lawn, the ground squishing beneath their feet. "Need a little help?" he said.

She released the clump of milkweed and stood up. Brushing windblown hair away from her face, she said darkly, "You probably don't want to know the kind of language that's been coming from my mouth."

"I suspect I've heard it all before." He grabbed the milkweed in both hands, braced his legs, and yanked with brute force. The offending plant broke free, and he shook loose a few clumps of soil from its roots before he handed it to her.

"Maybe I could hire you," she said dryly, tossing the dead soldier onto a pile near a corner post of the front porch. "Think we could set a reasonable hourly wage?"

"That depends," he said. "If I didn't have to be on call 24/7, it just might be an offer I can't refuse." He crossed his arms and leaned back to survey her work. "So you're doing a bit of landscaping."

She pulled off her gloves and tucked them into the pocket of her vest. "More like excavating. But it has to be done. I'm pulling up everything that's not identifiable, raking up the muck, and then I'm planting grass seed. Once that's done, I'll start scraping the house. It's just about warm enough to start painting. So what's up?"

He introduced her to Jamal and told her about his fool's errand to Jamaica Plain. "My instincts tell me we're on to something with this guy. If he was an upstanding citizen, why would his driver's license and auto registration have a fake address?"

"If I ever catch the son of a bitch," she said, "I'll string him up by the—'' She glanced at Jamal and sighed. ''I imagine you've heard it all before, too. What's our next move?''

''I think a visit to a certain porn shop in the Combat Zone might be in order. Since Jamal's underage, I thought you might like to come along.''

''You're damn tootin' I want to come along.'' She shoved her hair away from her face and turned her back on the yard work. ''Just give me a couple of minutes to wash off some of this mud.''

After she left, he wandered over to the porch, tested the railings and found them surprisingly solid. But the steps had reached a dangerous state of deterioration. He toed them gingerly, felt the springiness that signaled rotted wood. If she didn't replace them, one of these days she'd fall right through and break a leg.

''Have you ever built a set of steps?'' he asked Jamal.

''No. And I ain't about to start now, so don't go getting no ideas.''

''It can't be that hard.''

Jamal kicked at the bottom step and a chunk of rotted wood fell off. They both stared at it. ''She your old lady?'' Jamal said.

''No, she is not my old lady.''

''She thinking 'bout it, then. I seen the way she was looking at you, like you a piece of prime, grade-A beef.''

Clancy knelt to take a closer look at the steps. ''I'm a priest,'' he said, running a finger along the edge of the top tread. ''I've taken a vow of celibacy. I'm not allowed to have a…ah…old lady.''

''Uh-huh. So how long you think it gonna take for her to get ready? It's already been ten minutes.''

''She's a woman, Jamal. I don't know this from personal experience, mind you, but rumor has it that women can take a long time getting ready.''

"My sister generally take an hour in the bathroom every morning, making herself look hot for the guys at school."

He glanced up at the kid. "You don't say. An hour?"

"Funny thing is, she don't look no different when she come out than she looked when she went in."

Clancy held back a smile. "I trust you're intelligent enough to have kept that observation to yourself."

"After the first time she whacked me with a hairbrush, I figured it out. Damn, that thing hurt! So how we gonna kill time while we wait?"

Clancy stood and dusted off his hands. "I guess when all else fails, we pull weeds."

Jamal groaned. "How did I know you was gonna say that?"

Stepping through the door of Puritan Book and Video was like landing in Oz.

There was a line of customers at the checkout, so she and Clancy wandered the aisles, perusing row after row of videotapes and DVDs that catered to every possible taste and perversion. The store carried everything from old classics— *Behind the Green Door, Deep Throat, and Caligula*—to new classics—the infamous Pam and Tommy Lee tape. From specialized fetish films (who knew feet could be such a turn-on?) to cheap and cheesy amateur productions with laughably tacky titles. Beside a closed door that led to the viewing booths she'd seen advertised outside, a row of skin mags lined the wall. Straight, gay, lesbian, swinger. Something for everyone. Overhead, artfully arranged just below the ceiling, a shelf of preposterously large male appendages circled the room, some of them as thick as her forearm. "Whoever designed those things, sugar," she said, "was either dropping acid or suffering from delusions of grandeur."

Behind her, thankfully, Clancy remained silent.

Novelty items lined the shelves. Vibrators in every shape

and size and color, from cool silver to tangerine. Penis rings—whatever the hell those were. Fake breasts and rubber vaginas. Blow-up sex dolls of both genders. Flavored condoms and anal toys whose usage she didn't even want to think about. And for the truly adventurous, leather and chains, whips and restraints.

Sarah had certainly never considered herself a prude. She'd been sexually active at sixteen, had been married three times, and she'd taken the occasional lover during the arid stretches between husbands. Hell, for a while she'd even danced on stage wearing pasties and a G-string. But apparently she possessed an innocence of which she'd been totally unaware. Or perhaps it was more ignorance than innocence. And if this place was an accurate representation of all she'd been missing, ignorance truly was bliss.

She was acutely aware of Clancy following a step behind her, acutely aware of his nearness. Acutely aware of the clerical collar he wore, and of the scent—bay rum and altar candles—that seemed to follow him everywhere. He touched her arm, and she jumped a mile. Looking cool and unruffled, he tilted his head in the direction of the checkout counter. Praying that her face didn't look as heated as it felt, she nodded agreement.

The guy behind the counter was somewhere in his twenties. He wore his hair short, shaved on the sides and blue on the top, but his biggest claim to fame had to be the silver chain that connected the ring in his nostril with the one in his eyebrow. He eyed Clancy's clerical attire and gave her a quick once-over. "Looking for something special, folks?"

"Actually," Clancy said, "we're looking for information."

Wariness entered those youthful brown eyes. "What kind of information?"

"You had a customer in here this morning. About six feet

tall, blue eyes, blond hair. Youngish, nice-looking. He may be calling himself Roger Seward. Sound familiar?''

The young man opened his mouth, then closed it abruptly as an older man with a shaved head and the build of a sumo wrestler approached from somewhere behind the counter. "Do we look like fucking Directory Assistance?" he snarled.

"He could be a big spender," Clancy continued. "Drives a flashy red BMW."

"Scott," the sumo wrestler said. "There's a guy down back needs some help."

The kid didn't waste time making himself scarce. The sumo wrestler leaned over the counter. "We don't know nothing," he said. "That clear enough for you?"

"I know he was in here this morning," Clancy said. "I have a witness who saw him leave."

"Jesus Christ, you're like a fucking pitbull. Do you have any idea how many people I get through here each day? I don't have time to keep track of customers, and even if I did, I wouldn't tell you. So take a hike, bud. I got customers waiting."

Sarah pulled a poster from her pocket and unfolded it. "This is my niece," she said. "Her name is Kit. Take a good look." And she shoved the poster in his face.

He swiped it aside, crumpled it in his hand. "I've already seen it. Be hard to miss, the way you people have it plastered all over the city."

She shoved her hair behind her ear and took a deep breath. It was either that, or reach out and grab him by the throat. "We have good reason to believe this man knows where Kit is," she said. "We have to talk to him."

"Lady, I'm sorry about your niece. But I don't know nothing. If you don't get out of here, I'm calling the cops."

"Do you have any kids?" she said. "Or don't they let mutants like you reproduce?"

"Sarah." Clancy's fingers closed over her forearm and he

tugged her gently toward the door. "It's obvious we're getting nowhere. Let's just go."

She glared at him, glared at the blue-haired kid, who had returned to witness the debacle, but she allowed Clancy to haul her out the door. Outside, on the sidewalk, she took a deep breath before deflating like one of those blow-up dolls she'd seen inside the store.

"Damn," she said. "Damn it all to hell."

"You okay?"

"I will be. I was so sure, damn it. So sure we were on to something."

"Don't give up on it just yet. Give it a little time. We've planted a seed, now let's see if it grows. How about a cup of coffee?"

She sighed. "I suppose it couldn't hurt."

She waited outside the Chinatown McDonald's while he bought two cups of coffee. "Thanks," she said, taking the steaming cup he offered her. "Maybe this'll help to restore my good humor."

They began walking toward the Common, where he'd left his car in the underground parking garage. "It's a difficult situation," he said. "You have a right to get angry once in a while."

The caffeine was already working its magic, easing its calming effects into her bloodstream. "I made a scene, didn't I?"

"Let's just say they won't soon forget you."

"My true colors finally showing through. I'm sorry."

"Don't be. I found it highly entertaining."

"You would. You're a unique man, Father Donovan."

He glanced at her from the corner of his eye. "I'm not sure whether to thank you or apologize."

"It was meant as a compliment."

"In that case, thank you."

They walked for a time in silence before hanging a left

onto Boylston at the China Trade Center. "Mind if I ask you a stupid question?" she said.

"Shoot."

She gripped her coffee cup, took a sip. Swallowed and said, "What the hell is a penis ring?"

He nearly choked to death on his coffee. He coughed and sputtered, finally got his breathing back under control. Wiped his mouth on the back of his hand. "It, ah…" He cleared his throat several times. "It's designed to increase a man's staying power. The blood flows in, the ring traps it so it can't flow back out at its normal rate, which helps him to maintain—"

Heat rushed her face. "Never mind, sugar. I get the picture." She took another sip of coffee and eyed him over the rim of her cup. "You're a priest. How is it you know this stuff?"

He tipped his head back and drained his coffee cup. She watched with great interest as his Adam's apple moved up and down when he swallowed. Avoiding her eyes, he said, "You hear things."

And he tossed the empty cup into a nearby trash can.

10

It started raining shortly after he dropped Sarah off in Revere. Despite the blessings of Daylight Saving Time, dusk still came early on these rainy spring afternoons. Water hissed beneath his tires, and the taillights of the cars ahead of him reflected in blurred and bloody pools on the pavement. Clancy stopped for a red light, pulled out his cell phone and called Father Michael Santangelo.

"Twenty minutes of your time," he told his friend. "That's all I need."

"I always have time for you," Michael said. "Stay for dinner. I'll grill us a steak."

He and Michael Santangelo had attended seminary together, had both wound up working for the Archdiocese of Boston. While Clancy had been assigned to his home parish in Southie, Michael had landed a plum assignment at a parish in the affluent suburb of Chestnut Hill. They got together once or twice a month for dinner and conversation, took in the occasional movie or ball game together. And since the day of their ordination, each had performed for the other the vital function of confessor.

Saint Vincent's was an ultramodern structure, built during the late seventies by an architect whose vision had included a hexagonal roof, white pine paneling, and stained glass windows in bizarre geometric shapes. Clancy had never been quite sure what to make of the place. He knew God was supposed to live in the heart, not in the building, but he still had a hard time looking at Saint Vincent's as a house of worship.

On the other hand, he was green with envy over the ease with which Michael was able to acquire the necessities of life. Never had a priest from Saint Vincent's had to sweat and scrape to buy choir robes or altar candles. When the controversial hexagonal roof had sprung a leak last winter, Michael had simply called a local roofing contractor and had it fixed. If the same thing had happened at Saint Bart's, repairs would probably have included a five-gallon bucket, a drop cloth, and fifty-two consecutive weekly meetings of the fund-raising committee to try and figure out where the repair money was coming from.

He parked in the empty lot and entered through the double front doors, crafted of teak, each one carved with a giant cross. He wiped his feet in the entry and continued on into the sanctuary, where he dipped his fingers into the holy water font and crossed himself before walking silently to the front of the church. At the altar, he paused to genuflect, then moved forward to light a single candle and bow his head in prayer.

When he turned back around, Michael stood waiting for him at the rear of the sanctuary. Feet braced slightly apart, hands crossed in front of his steadily expanding midsection, Father Michael Santangelo wore a benevolent expression. Without speaking, he flourished a plump hand in the direction of the confessional, and Clancy crossed the sanctuary and stepped through the door.

This, too, was as different from the traditional stuffy box as the architecture of St. Vincent's differed from that of his own stone Gothic cathedral. When Clancy heard confession, he sat in a dark cubicle, separated from the penitent by a sliding screen. Here, priest and penitent faced each other while perched on hard plastic chairs in a bland, whitewashed room about eight feet square. It hadn't been designed for comfort. Then again, neither had the sacrament of reconciliation. If the act of confessing his sins didn't make a man squirm just a bit, he obviously wasn't doing it right.

He rested both hands flat against his thighs and cleared his throat. "Bless me, Father, for I have sinned. It's been three months since my last confession."

"Go ahead."

"I've committed the sin of disobedience on a number of occasions. I counseled young couples about contraception, in direct violation of Church canon and in defiance of the orders of my bishop."

Michael tapped the fingers of one hand against his knee. "I seem to recall you were going to work on that."

It was impossible to read the expression on Michael's face. "I've tried," he said. "It doesn't seem to be working."

"Have you prayed about it?"

"I've tried prayer. But my heart just isn't in it. I'm having a great deal of difficulty accepting the Church's stand on this issue. When I think of the AIDS epidemic, I just—" He shook his head, knowing there was no sense in continuing. Michael was well aware of his feelings. He'd professed them often enough.

"All right. What else?"

"I lied to my secretary. It was just a small lie, but the Commandments don't differentiate between white lies and whoppers. It's just that sometimes, it's maddening, the way she hovers over me. I'm a grown man. I don't need a twenty-year-old girl telling me how to live my life. I already have the Catholic Church to perform that function."

He thought he saw a hint of a smile on Michael's face, but he couldn't be sure. His friend cleared his throat. "Go on."

His fingertips dug into the flesh of his thighs. "Of late," he said, "I've found myself entertaining certain…inappropriate thoughts…about a woman."

Michael shifted position, sat up a little straighter. "Impure thoughts?"

"Not so much impure thoughts as a simple awareness, whenever we're together, that she's a woman. And that I'm a man."

"Is there really a difference between the two?"

He glanced up, met Michael's eyes, carefully considered his question. "I'm not sure."

"Impure thoughts, sexual awareness. They don't seem so far apart to me. Is there a possibility of removing yourself from the situation?"

"I can't do that. She came to me for help. Her niece ran away, and the police won't help her. She has nobody else. No family, no friends who can do anything for her. Only me. I can't just leave her twisting in the wind." He paused, met Michael's eyes, read his own truth in their depths. Sighing, he rubbed his temple and said, "I suppose I don't want to remove myself from the situation."

Michael leaned forward, hands bracing his knees. "You do understand how dangerous this is? If you continue to have contact with this woman, if you continue to have impure thoughts about her, you're placing your soul in mortal sin."

"It's not that big a deal, Michael. It's not as though we're out having wild sex. I barely know the woman."

"If it wasn't that big a deal, you wouldn't be here."

One by one, his muscles began to tighten. "You don't understand."

"Then make me understand, Clancy. I'm your friend and confessor. I want to help. Make me understand."

"I was dying! Decaying, one wretched molecule at a time. I couldn't breathe anymore." He leaned forward, impatient to make his friend understand. "I'm alive again, Michael. Alive for the first time in more than ten years. I don't think I can back away. I don't think I'm willing to give that up."

"Even knowing that you're risking your soul?"

"As a priest," he said, "I walk a narrow line every day of my life. Since the day I entered the seminary, I've never crossed that line. Sarah and I are friends. Nothing more. We're both aware that anything more than friendship is an impossibility. The fact that I feel something more for her doesn't change the nature or the truth of the situation. I haven't shared those feelings with her, and I don't plan to. But there's a connection between us, a positive energy, that's truly remarkable. The woman makes me feel good, Michael. For the first time since Meg died, I wake up in the morning eager to face the day. How can it be wrong for me to want that feeling to continue?"

"Friendship is one thing. Sexual feelings are something altogether different."

He raked fingers through his hair. "But I'm not acting on those feelings! I have no intention of acting on them."

"But they're still there, festering in your heart. Blackening your soul." Michael leaned forward. "Stop seeing her. For the sake of your own salvation, stop seeing her now."

"Is that your advice as my confessor?"

"It's my advice as your friend."

"With all due respect, Father, I'm going to have to reject that advice."

"You have to reflect on God's plan for you, Clancy."

"I can't. I'm too conflicted right now to be certain any longer what His plan is for me."

Michael shook his head in sorrow and bewilderment. "I have to confess I'm not sure quite what to do. I've never been faced with a situation like this before."

"Nor have I. You know, Michael, I think we were short-changed in seminary. They taught us philosophy and theology, taught us how to deliver a homily and how to conduct all the rituals of the Church. They emphasized to us, over and over again, that lifelong celibacy is a gift from God. But they neglected one tiny detail. They forgot to tell us how we were supposed to achieve it.''

He stayed for dinner, but after the fiasco that had occurred in the confessional, awkwardness weighted the air between them, buoyed by a distance that had never been there before. Normally, they spent hours talking about everything from the sacramental mysteries to the price of fuel oil. But tonight, conversation was stilted as they both attempted to avoid treading on ground that possessed all the stability of quicksand. He made his goodbyes early and returned to Saint Bart's, where he hunched over his desk with a single lamp burning and attempted to navigate the maze of Federal paperwork Ruth had somehow coerced him into taking over.

Red tape. Everything in his life seemed to be a matter of one step forward, two steps back. He spent an inordinate amount of time jumping through hoops. Now, here he was again, only this time the hoops had been placed in front of him by Uncle Sam instead of the Vatican.

Not that he minded the paperwork. Federal forms were needlessly complex and a pain in the behind, but he'd been through this before, which made him an old pro in Ruth's eyes. Truth be told, it came easily to him. Aside from being tedious, filling out forms didn't overtax his patience or his faculties. He might prefer people to paper, but he didn't consider working with it a hardship.

Tonight, though, he had difficulty concentrating. It had been a mistake to take Sarah with him today. As he followed her down aisle after aisle of screaming sexual come-ons, it had been far too easy to imagine certain scenarios that had no business crossing his mind. The tension between them, pain intertwined with pleasure, had been torturous.

Michael was right. He should stop seeing the woman. For his own peace of mind, if not for the salvation of his soul. But how was he supposed to explain it to her?

I can't see you any longer.

I can't see you any longer because I have a crush on you, and I'm not allowed to.

It sounded ridiculous. As though he were a seventh-grader who'd been grounded for staying out too late on a school night. The embarrassment factor was more than any mortal man should be expected to bear.

I can't see you any longer because I want to bury my face in that cloud of silky brown hair and breathe in the sweet, perfumed scent of woman that emanates from you in waves whenever you move.

I can't see you any longer because I want to run the tips of my fingers over that smooth, taut flesh and find out if it really feels as soft as it looks.

It did. He knew because he'd touched her one rainy Sunday afternoon, had cupped her chin in his hand while he scrubbed mascara circles from beneath her eyes. Touching her had been impetuous and foolhardy, but he'd been compelled to do it. It was all he'd been able to think about as he stood with her in the entryway of the church and made inane conversation just to keep her in his sight for a few more seconds. All he'd been able to think about while they washed dishes and traded banter in Sheila Rafferty's kitchen. All he'd been able to think about as she clicked past him in Sheila's driveway wearing three-inch heels and a demure, calf-length skirt that showed a teasing hint of what promised to be magnificent legs.

As a priest, he wasn't supposed to look at a woman's legs.

He supposed the infatuation would wear itself out in time, since nothing inappropriate could ever happen between them. He'd been blessed with a conscience, as well as the capacity to think. Human behavior was always a matter of choice. It was what separated man from the lower mammals, what helped Clancy to maintain his faith in humanity despite the overwhelming sin and sorrow he saw in the world around him. Man had the ability to choose between good and evil, right and wrong, righteousness and immorality. As long as the potential to choose the higher ground remained intact, the earth would continue spinning in its orbit, and goodness would continue to give evil a run for its money.

He forced thoughts of Sarah Connelly and his own state of disgrace to a far corner of his mind and firmly closed the door on them. Brooding was counterproductive at the best of times, and Ruth's paperwork wouldn't finish itself. He plucked a cinnamon candy from his jar, unwrapped it, and popped it into his mouth. The candy sent a swift sugar kick through his bloodstream. With a brief glance at the clock, he settled back down to immerse himself in page after page of mind-numbing governmental gibberish.

Time passed. The clock ticked in the silence. He waded deeper into the tangle of Federal double-talk, so deep he didn't realize he was no longer alone until a voice from out of nowhere wrenched him from his stupor.

"Burning the midnight oil, eh, Father?"

Bleary-eyed, he glanced up, freezing at sight of the two men standing just inside the door to his study. Both in their mid-twenties, both of Hispanic descent, they'd moved so silently he hadn't heard their approach. The tall, scrawny one with the scraggly hair and the flinty eyes closed the door and stood rigidly in front of it, arms crossed, jacket open just enough so the butt of his gun was visible. The one who crossed the room to stand before the desk was shorter, more compactly built, a little older, a lot better looking. His dark hair was slicked back, and around his neck he wore enough gold jewelry to drag him straight to the bottom if by chance, some dark night, he ever accidentally tripped over his own feet and fell into Fort Point Channel.

Cheech and Chong, all dressed up for Halloween.

Muscle. He might have spent the last eleven years wrapped safely in the bosom of the Catholic Church, but he'd grown up on the streets of Southie, where crime was a way of life. He'd been raised by a mother whose connections were a little shady, had spent his adolescence walking a narrow line that might have taken him in a totally different direction if certain people hadn't refused to let him fall on the wrong side of the law. He'd lived in the real world long enough to recognize muscle when he saw it. But whose muscle? And why were they here?

With slow deliberation, he dropped his pen, leaned back in his chair. Propping an elbow on his armrest, he threaded fingers together over his abdomen. "Gentlemen," he said. "To what do I owe this honor?"

Apparently Cheech was the spokesman. He picked up the ceramic pig from the corner of the desk, turned it this way and that, studying it from all angles. Boldly meeting Clancy's gaze, he said, "We're here to convey a message from a friend."

"I see. My friend, or yours?"

"Could be both, *amigo*. Depending, of course, on whether or not you pay attention to the advice we're about to give you."

"By all means, go ahead. Enlighten me."

"The message is simple, padre. Back off." Cheech ran a finger along the smooth ceramic surface of the pig, traced its spread wings, its rounded belly. "Our friend would like to suggest that you stop asking questions, stop poking into what's none of your business. Drop the issue, go back to saying Mass and lighting candles, and forget any of this ever happened."

A muscle twitched in his jaw. Coolly, he said, "Or?"

"We'd hate to see anything happen to you, padre." Cheech met his eyes, raised the pig to shoulder level. "Being such devout Catholics and all, it would pain us greatly to see some kind of tragic accident befall a priest." Still holding

Clancy's gaze, he deliberately loosened his fingers. The pig fell to the floor and shattered.

"Perhaps you'd like to convey my response back to your friend." Clancy leaned forward, rolled his chair up to the desk, and rested both elbows on the desktop. "Tell him I don't scare that easily."

Shrugging, Cheech said amiably, "It's your funeral, padre. *Buenas noches.*"

It wasn't until after they'd gone that he realized his muscles were knotted into steely bands. He took a deep breath, let it out, forced himself to relax. When the adrenaline rush had settled, he got up and locked the outside door, then made a quick check of the rest of the church. Melissa was always hounding him about leaving the door to the parish office unlocked after she left at night. Too much riffraff in the neighborhood, she said. He was leaving himself too open, too vulnerable. He could be robbed, mugged, even killed. But her pleas fell on deaf ears. It was his policy to be available to his parishioners, no matter how late the hour. Whenever he was in his study, the door was unlocked.

Maybe it was time to rethink that policy.

When he was certain the building was locked up tight, he got a broom and dustpan from the janitor's closet and swept up the pieces of the shattered pig. Then he unlocked the bottom drawer of his desk and took out the Smith & Wesson .38 Special. He'd bought it after Meg died, when he'd reached rock bottom and was running on equal measures of booze and rage. Nearly a dozen years had passed since then, and still he wasn't quite sure if he'd intended to use it on himself or on the monster who'd been responsible for her death.

Its weight felt odd in his hands after all these years. As he ran his fingers along the smooth, cool barrel, dark memories swirled through his brain, memories of countless hours when he'd sat alone, bleak with despair, gun in hand and obliteration on his mind. A different man, a different lifetime. He'd kept the gun as a symbol, a reminder of how far a man could fall before God lifted him back up and gave him renewed hope.

Now, touching it, he was reminded of its sole purpose. Not hope, but death. The pistol he held in his hands was a sleek, shiny killing machine. And he was a man dedicated to peace.

He set the pistol gently on the desktop and poured himself a cup of coffee. It had been sitting for hours, and was the consistency of used motor oil. But he drank it, anyway, while he gazed at the gun sitting incongruously next to his jar of cinnamon candy and contemplated the possibility that the situation was more serious than he'd originally thought. If the man who held Kit was pimping her, why would he be so determined to hold on to her that he'd send thugs to ensure she wasn't found? In the sex trade, girls were expendable. One whore was the same as another. What made Kit so special?

Perhaps this wasn't about prostitution. Maybe there was something bigger at stake. Drugs, extortion, even murder. And who did Cheech and Chong belong to? Pimps didn't generally employ muscle. Had he borrowed them from somewhere, or simply pressed them into double-duty emergency service?

He played various scenarios through his head, but nothing clicked. There was no *aha!* moment when everything fell into place. He checked his watch. It was past eleven, late to be calling Sarah. But she probably wasn't sleeping, anyway. He suspected she didn't sleep much these days.

She answered on the second ring, confirming his suspicion. In the background, he could hear voices, the canned hysteria of a television commercial.

"It's me," he said. "I'm sorry to call so late. We need to talk."

At the other end, there was a sharp intake of breath. "Is something wrong?"

"Remember that seed we talked about planting? It didn't take long to sprout. I just had a visit from a couple of thugs who could have come direct from central casting. They were here to strongly suggest that I cease and desist."

"Cease and desist?" she said. "All you've been doing is asking questions."

"I must be asking the right ones. I've apparently stepped a little too close for somebody's comfort level. I'm just not sure if this is good news or bad."

"Oh, hell." She let out a hard breath. "Are you all right? They didn't hurt you, did they?"

"They threatened me with dire admonitions of what evil might befall me if I failed to listen to them. Then they broke my ceramic pig to illustrate just how tough they were. But I'm okay. Looks like they're trying to scare us into backing off."

There were several seconds of silence at her end before she said, "Somebody doesn't want us to find Kit. Do you think this means she's in danger?"

"I don't think so. Not at this point. It looks as though she's of significant value to somebody, enough value so they don't want us getting into the middle of things and screwing it up. I have no idea why. Or who. Listen, Sarah, I don't want to frighten you, but—" He studied the gun sitting on his desktop. Its cool, blue steel appeared innocent enough. But that innocence was an illusion. In reality, those two pounds of steel possessed the power to end a life in a single instant. "I want you to be careful," he said. "Keep your doors locked. Don't go out alone at night if you can help it."

"Be serious. I'm a businesswoman. I can't very well hide in the house."

"Until we find out what Kit's mixed up in, I can't guarantee they won't come after you. And I don't intend to let anything happen to you.'' He struggled against the sudden clenching in his belly. He hadn't been able to protect Meg. This time around, he wouldn't let that happen.

He refused to look too closely at what he meant by *this time around*.

"Nothing's going to happen to me, sugar. I'm invincible. But if Kit's usefulness to these people should come to an end—"

"Sarah," he said softly, "don't do this to yourself. Please."

"She's all I have, Clancy. I'm not sure you understand."

"Of course I understand. And we'll get her back in one piece." He suddenly realized how tired he was. Rubbing the back of his neck, he said, "Would you feel better if I came over?"

"To do what, Father Donovan? Hold my hand? Sleep on my couch? Pour coffee down my throat so I'll stay awake for what's left of the night?"

He felt a little foolish. She was right, of course. There was no comfort he could offer in person that couldn't be given over the telephone. It was eleven-thirty at night, she was a beautiful woman, and he was a priest who had no business thinking about the quick clutch of his heart every time he heard that soft, melodious voice. It would be better for both of them if he found a way to keep his distance.

"I'm a big girl," she said. "And you're a lovely man for offering. Let's just leave it at that."

It wasn't enough, but it was all he had a right to expect. "Fine," he said.

The open telephone line between them hummed. "You be careful, too," she said. "Because, you know, Father Donovan, I've grown quite fond of you. G'night."

11

She spent the day running interference between a nervous author and a book distributor who'd failed to deliver the books for an upcoming signing. With five days left until the book signing, Felicity Knowles was getting antsy. She called twice while Sarah was out running errands, and Josie tried valiantly to soothe the author's ruffled feathers. But the recalcitrant Ms. Knowles insisted on speaking with the store owner personally. Sarah did her best to reassure the seventy-two-year-old dowager that her books weren't lost somewhere. Then she called the distributor.

He hemmed and hawed about delayed shipments and computer glitches, finally admitting there'd been a screwup and the books hadn't been ordered. It took all her Southern charm, as well as a promise of two tickets to opening day at Fenway, to convince him to do a special rush order.

She called Felicity Knowles back and assured her that the distributor had promised delivery by Saturday morning, even if he had to deliver the books in person. Then she swept a pile of paperwork into her tote bag, picked up her coat and purse, and strode to the front of the store.

"I'm leaving," she told Steve. "I've had the day from hell, I feel a headache coming on, and I'm suffering from major PMS. I'm going home to suffer in solitude. If the sky falls, tomorrow's soon enough to tell me about it."

She felt a little guilty for being so blunt. Her crankiness had nothing to do with her job. The bookstore was doing

well, and she had a small but copacetic group of employees
who, right down to the last part-timer, were always willing
to go the extra mile to ensure customer satisfaction. The
problem was all with her. She wasn't getting enough sleep,
and it was starting to show.

This morning, she'd spent ten minutes ragging Josie for
stripping a box of books she'd intended to mark down to half
price to display in the entry. Once she got her temper under
control, she apologized, then she tried to make it up to Josie
by buying her lunch at the Taco Bell across the way. Josie
was a solid worker, loyal to the end, and Sarah had spent
most of the afternoon feeling guilty. She shouldn't be bringing her problems to work. It wasn't fair to Josie and Steve
and the rest of the crew. They all had their own lives, their
own problems, yet they always managed to maintain profes-
sionalism when they were on duty. She could learn something from their behavior.

It was probably foolhardy, but she'd taken to driving into
the city late at night and cruising the streets, hoping by some
quirk of fate to see Kit. Clancy had been a godsend, but he
was already doing enough. Besides, Kit was her responsibility, not his. And she wasn't the kind of woman who could
just sit back and wait for some man to rescue her. She'd
promised Clancy she would be careful, and although driving
alone in the city at night probably didn't fit into his definition
of careful, she always kept her doors locked, made sure she
had a full tank of gas, and checked to make sure nobody was
following her. After the breakdown at Sheila's house, she'd
had the Mustang checked out thoroughly by a local repair
shop. They'd replaced the ailing part that had caused the
trouble and given the car a clean bill of health. She wasn't
worried about her own safety. It was Kit's safety that concerned her.

Every time she thought about the men who'd threatened
Clancy and the implications that went along with that threat,

her throat closed up and she had difficulty breathing. Her baby was out there somewhere, and if they harmed a single hair on Kit's head, she would personally castrate the lot of them and stuff their privates down their collective throats.

But tonight, she needed to unwind, have a quiet evening, get to bed early. She'd been running for weeks on too little sleep and too much caffeine, and if she didn't get back on an even keel, she was bound to crash. On impulse, she stopped at the butcher shop and bought a single pork chop for dinner before venturing into the crush of North Shore rush hour traffic. She would sauté the chop with butter and a smidgen of garlic, and boil a couple of the fancy little red-skinned potatoes she'd bought last week at the supermarket. Maybe she'd accompany that with a sprig or two of the asparagus buried somewhere in the back of her freezer.

But first, a hot bubble bath, scented candles, a glass or two of white wine, and Tim McGraw's latest CD. It was the perfect antidote to a perfectly awful day.

The air wore the rich, muddy scent that heralded the arrival of spring. Sarah drove with the window down, passed house after house bedecked with blooming forsythia and bright, cheerful tulips. She pulled into her driveway and turned off the ignition, her mind still on dinner as she gathered up her purse, the tote bag stacked with invoices she planned to go over this evening, and the pork chop neatly wrapped in butcher's paper. She rolled up the window and locked the car, then strode across the lawn toward her front porch.

She was halfway to the house when she realized something was amiss. Sawdust littered the tender spring grass. At the end of the path, where her old, saggy stairs had squatted just this morning, a brand-new set of wooden steps, so new she could smell the pungent aroma of fresh-sawn pine, sat snugged up tight against the porch.

She stopped dead in her tracks and glanced around, half expecting a *Candid Camera* crew to step out from behind

Lizzie Figoli's honeysuckle bush and yell, "Surprise!" But she saw no camera crew, no eyewitnesses, no clue as to who had left her this unexpected gift. The street was deserted, with the exception of Lizzie's ancient one-eyed cat, Casper. And she doubted he'd be a reliable witness.

Baffled, she glanced back at the house.

And saw the magnolias.

White with a subtle flush of pink, they'd been inexpertly hacked off, crammed into an oversized applesauce jar full of water, and left directly in front of her door, where she couldn't possibly miss them.

Tiny butterflies of pleasure fluttered inside her stomach, accompanied by something else, something wispy and ephemeral that she dared not examine too closely. She wondered who the good Father had sweet-talked into allowing him to cut their precious blossoms, for she had no doubt whatsoever that was how he'd acquired them. It was a good thing he was on the side of God; had he been a con artist, he could have talked a little old lady out of her life savings and left her smiling as he walked away with her last cent jingling in his pocket.

She set down the purse, the tote bag, the pork chop, and climbed the new steps to the porch. Bending, she picked up the jar and buried her face in the sweet, fragrant blossoms. Heaven. Absolute heaven. For an instant, she felt a tug of homesickness so intense she could have wept. She unlocked the door and carried the bouquet inside, then returned for the items she'd so unceremoniously discarded on the lawn.

She briefly considered Aunt Helen's antique cut-glass vase, but decided she preferred the priest's simple applesauce jar. With a sharp knife, she carefully snipped the jagged stems so they could drink properly. Then, with the bouquet hanging heavy in the center of her kitchen table, she pulled the telephone book from the drawer and looked up the number to Saint Bartholomew's rectory.

"Clancy Donovan," she said when he answered the phone. "What have you gone and done?"

"You told me you loved magnolias. I thought they'd remind you of home."

"And steps! You built me new front steps. I can't believe it. Were you a carpenter in a previous lifetime? Maybe between your trip to Hong Kong and your stay at the seminary?"

"Contrary to what you might believe, Ms. Connelly, my Master of Divinity degree didn't render me totally incompetent. I know how to wield a hammer and saw."

"And such a lovely job you did. I have to pay you back."

"That's not necessary. It was nothing. A few pieces of lumber, a fistful of nails. I had a few hours free, and it seemed a constructive way to spend them."

"I insist. I'm from the South, where we always repay a favor. If you turn me down, I'll be obligated to consider it an insult. It might even come down to a duel, just for the sake of honor."

"Well, then. We wouldn't want that, would we?"

"I've been looking at these beautiful flowers and trying to figure out how I could possibly repay you. Then I remembered what you said about being a lousy cook. I don't know much about this Catholic thing, so you'll have to help me out here. Would there be any impropriety in me asking you over for dinner some night?"

There was silence at his end of the phone. "Just the two of us?" he said.

"Just the two of us, yes."

"Well…ah…" He cleared his throat. "Possibly."

She took a breath, decided to go for broke. "Let me rephrase the question. Would you like to come over for dinner some night?"

"Yes. I would love to come over for dinner some night."

Ignoring the fluttering in her chest, she said, "How about tomorrow at seven o'clock?"

"Seven o'clock tomorrow's fine."

"Well." She paused, uncertain how to proceed now that he'd accepted her invitation. "What should I make? I don't have any idea what you like to eat. Except Chinese, but don't ask me to make Chinese, because I wouldn't have a clue where to start. And of course, cheeseburgers, but that's not really what I'd call a meal."

She realized she was babbling, and clamped her mouth firmly shut.

"Whatever you make is fine. I'll eat just about anything."

"Spoken like a typical man. Could you at least tell me what you don't like?"

"As long as you don't feed me turnip or lima beans, I don't see how you can go wrong."

"Well, hell. There goes my whole menu down the tubes. I was planning on making lima bean casserole and cream of turnip soup."

"You have a fresh mouth, Sarah Connelly. Has anybody ever told you that?"

"I have no idea what you're talking about, Father Donovan. I'll see you tomorrow night."

When she hung up the phone, she was grinning like a fool.

"You have the most beautiful skin," Rio said. "Smooth and creamy and unblemished. Have I ever told you that?"

Kit ran a fingertip down the center of his chest. "Once or twice before," she said.

"Sweet Kit," he said, rolling her onto her back in the tangled sheets. "Sweet as honey, prettier than the sunrise over Boston Harbor. How'd I get so lucky?"

As far as she was concerned, she was the one who'd gotten lucky. All her life she'd waited for that special person, the one who would love her enough to put her ahead of everyone and everything else. And she'd found him, right when her life was a shambles and she needed him the most. She sighed in utter contentment and said, "I love you."

"I love you, too, baby." He placed a tender kiss on her forehead and then, to her surprise, rolled away from her.

She turned, propped herself with an elbow. "Where are you going?"

He sat on the edge of the bed and pulled on his jeans. "Don't make a move. I'll be right back."

Kit watched him go, mildly curious, but mostly just lazy and satisfied. She stretched like a cat. Then, with a quick glance at the door, she turned and patted the edge of the mattress. "Here, Pix," she whispered.

In a corner of the room, Pixel was curled up in his own bed, a complex wicker affair with a red plaid cushion. The dog lifted his head and studied her with soft brown eyes. Rio didn't like him on the bed, and Pix knew it. He also knew Kit allowed him privileges every time Rio's back was turned. "Come on," she whispered. "Up."

At her urging, the dog stood and stretched, then jumped up onto the bed with her. Kit sat up and folded her arms around him. Seeking a steady foothold in the jumbled bedding, Pix wriggled and shifted, turned around a couple of times, then darted upward and slathered wet kisses all over her face.

She was giggling in delight when Rio came back into the room, carrying his camera. Over Pixel's head, Kit met his glance, saw a flicker of irritation in his eyes before he said, "Just this one time. Pix can be in the pictures with you."

Smiling inwardly at her victory, Kit tugged at the sheet, drew it up and tucked it demurely beneath her armpits. She tossed her long blond hair back over her shoulder, drew Pixel back into her arms, and smiled into the camera lens.

He shot an entire roll of her with the dog before he shooed

Pix out of the room and shut the door behind him. Pouting, Kit said, "You're mean."

Busy changing film, Rio said, "I'm not mean. I don't like sleeping in dog hair."

"You could change the sheets."

He raised his head, met her eyes, and for a long instant, they challenged each other silently. Without speaking, he returned his attention to the camera, flipping shut the door and advancing the film. "Sit cross-legged," he said. "Sheet over one shoulder, falling off the other one."

She'd grown accustomed to his curt instructions when he was behind the camera lens, had even gotten pretty good at following them. "Like this?" she said.

"Like that, but more softly draped. I want to get the light and shadow in the folds."

She did as he said, followed his orders while he filled another roll. "Hold that pose," he said, and walked to the dresser to load a third roll of film. Her back was starting to stiffen. Posing for a man as demanding as Rio was hard work. He was the ultimate perfectionist, sometimes scolding her over some minuscule movement she wasn't even aware of having made. Sometimes he'd leave her sitting in the same position for so long she was lame afterward. But the end result was worth it. His photos were always brilliant.

From behind the camera lens, he said, "Drop the sheet."

Her mind had been wandering, and it took a minute to process his words. When she did, she thought she'd heard him wrong. "What?" she said.

"Drop the sheet. Let it pool in your lap, and hold the pose."

Aghast, she said, "You want to take pictures of me with my clothes off?"

He lowered the camera, flashed her a boyish smile. "It's not like I haven't seen you naked before, kitten."

"But—" Face flaming, she held securely to the sheet. She

would sooner eat worms than expose her body in front of the camera. What if somebody actually *saw* the pictures? She would die of embarrassment.

"It's not that big a thing," he said. "People do it all the time."

In a tremulous voice, she said, "Not me."

His eyes narrowed, and she saw something in them, something cold and distant that she'd never seen before. "You think this is how I want to spend my time?" he said. "Putting together a portfolio for some greenhorn sixteen-year-old kid nobody's ever heard of? I'm doing this for you, Kit. Not for me, but for you. I could be doing something better with my time, like making some fucking money. I could have made eight hundred bucks tonight, but I chose to give my time to you instead. Free. *Gratis.* You know why I'm doing it without asking for compensation? Because I think you have promise, and I really get off on helping girls jump-start their careers."

"But I don't need naked pictures," she said, her face burning with shame. "I couldn't put them in my portfolio anyway."

"Jesus," he said in disgust, "you're stupider than I thought. How the hell do you think all those actresses you worship got their start? Ninety percent of 'em started out doing nude modeling. It's called paying your dues, and everybody has to do it."

She was crying now, fat tears sliding silently down her cheeks while she stared in disbelief at this stranger, wondering what had happened to the sweet, solicitous man she loved. "If you want to be a big-name actress," he said, "you'd better start getting used to taking your clothes off. It's just one more part of the job. Everybody does it. If you refuse, word will get around that you're unprofessional, and your career will end up in the toilet. Is that what you want?"

She buried her face in her hands, unable to answer. "Grow

up, Kit," he said. "Or else be a crybaby and go running back to your Aunt Sarah, back to where it's safe and boring and nothing exciting will ever happen to you again."

Kit raised her face to him, swiped furiously at a tear. "I'm not a crybaby!"

"You can't have it both ways. You're either committed, or you're not. Personally, I don't give a fuck which way you go. It's your career. But if you're not going all the way, then don't waste my time, because I have better things to do."

And he picked up his camera and slammed out the bedroom door.

He'd barely taken his first sip of morning coffee when his cell phone rang. Clancy set down the *Globe* and its exposé of the latest City Hall political scandal and answered the ringing phone. At the other end, an unfamiliar male voice said, "Are you that priest?"

"I'm Father Donovan. And you are?"

"My name's Scott. You're the one who was in Puritan Book and Video the other day, asking about the blond guy. Right?"

Scott. Blue hair, multiple piercings, soft, brown puppy-dog eyes. "You're the salesclerk," he said.

"Right. Listen, I've had a couple of pretty lousy nights thinking about this and wondering what to do. I can't afford too many bad nights. I'm in pre-med at Tufts, and I have to stay on my toes if I don't want to lose my scholarship. I've been agonizing over whether to call you or keep my mouth shut. If Pete finds out I talked to you, I'll be out of a job. Hell, for all I know, I could be out of more than that. These guys are mean. They don't fool around."

"Then you do know the man I was asking about?"

"Yeah, but I'd rather not talk about it over the phone. I have three roommates and no privacy. Can you meet me somewhere?"

He had a nine-thirty meeting with the chair of the parish budget committee. Kendra Wakefield had a tendency toward long-windedness, so he knew he could count on her litany of complaints running at least an hour. "I'm tied up until ten-thirty," he said, "but I could meet you around eleven."

"I have a class at twelve, so that works for me. How about the pastry shop in Harvard Square? That's one place I know Pete will never see us."

Parking in Harvard Square was no better than it was anywhere else in the greater Boston area, so he took the T. To save time, he had Melissa drop him off at Broadway station. From there, it was a straight shot across the Charles to what the locals referred to—some with disdain, others with pride— as the People's Republic of Cambridge. Home to such prestigious institutions as Harvard and MIT, Cambridge was liberally populated with left-wing intellectual types who basked in their superiority and preferred to do things their own way. Unlike staid Boston, which had run for several hundred years on dual tracks of tradition and political graft, Cambridge embraced the odd, the statistically deviant, and the alternative.

At *Au Bon Pain,* he bought a cup of coffee and a jelly doughnut and joined Scott at one of the tiny outdoor patio tables. With his blue hair and his nose ring, Scott fit in perfectly with the locals. Tossing a chunk of doughnut to the sparrows who squabbled viciously over it, Clancy crossed one leg over the other and said, "I'm here. Talk."

"Like I said, if Pete finds out I talked to you, I'm dead meat. You can't tell anybody."

He dunked his doughnut in his coffee. "I'm a priest," he said. "I'm used to keeping secrets."

Scott sighed. "All right. But I'm still nervous about this." He cradled his bottle of orange juice between both hands. "This guy you're looking for. His name is Rio."

Clancy uncrossed his legs, rested both feet flat on the

ground, and leaned forward. "Rio," he said. "Is that a first name or a last name?"

"Not a clue, man. I've never heard anybody refer to him as anything but Rio. He comes in every so often to see Pete."

"He's a regular customer?"

"Yes and no."

"Explain, please."

"He doesn't buy from us. He comes in for referrals."

"Referrals?"

"High rollers. Big spenders. Guys who carry big wads of cash or American Express Platinum cards. Repeat customers who regularly drop a few hundred bucks every time they come in."

Clancy absently tore off another chunk of jelly doughnut and tossed it to the birds. "You get a lot of high rollers?"

"Man, you wouldn't believe the people who come into that place. Doctors, lawyers, judges. Cops. Politicians and clergymen. Let's just say you're not the first priest I've seen in there."

He raised an eyebrow. "Why is Rio getting these referrals?"

"Well, you see." Scott set down the bottle of orange juice, rested both forearms on the table, and lowered his voice. "Rio provides a special service for rich guys with a jones for porn and wads of cash to spend. He has a special arrangement with Pete. Petey-Boy provides the referrals, and if a referral ends in a sale, he gets a percentage. Sort of a finder's fee."

"So Rio's a pimp."

"Of a sort, but he takes it one step further. He's a cinematographer."

"You mean he makes blue movies?"

"With a twist. Imagine this, Father. Imagine your darkest, wildest sexual fantasy. Imagine having the connections and the resources to make that fantasy come true. And then imagine having it on film so you can relive it, over and over and over. That's what Rio provides. For a hefty fee, of course.''

Of late, his own wild and dark sexual fantasies had revolved exclusively around Sarah Connelly. The images were vivid and disturbing, and he shoved them forcefully to the back of his mind, where they belonged. "So he provides women for these men to have sex with, and he films it for their private collections?''

"Women, men, girls, boys, monkeys. Whatever. You provide the fantasy and Rio makes it happen. It's like that old show…what was it? The one with the midget?''

"Fantasy Island?"

"Right.'' Scott leaned back in his chair. "It's *Fantasy Island* for rich, horny men. Film at eleven.''

Traffic in Harvard Square stood, as usual, at a standstill. Clancy sipped his coffee and digested what Scott had told him. At the next table, a young Asian girl was deeply engrossed in a thick economics text. A group of passing college students laughed and called out to friends on the other side of the Square. On the corner, a black man in his fifties was selling copies of a local newspaper that raised money for the homeless.

"How often does he come in?'' he asked Scott.

"Whenever Pete has a name for him. He might come in twice in one week, then not show up again for three months.''

"Do you ever get a look at these names?''

"Never. They're always sealed in an envelope that he comes in and picks up. Look,'' the kid said, "I don't know if the girl you're looking for is with him or not, but if she is, you need to get her out ASAP. This guy is bad news, and a pretty young girl like that…let's just say she could make him a lot of money.''

Still considering the ramifications, he said, "I had a visit a few nights ago from a couple of thugs who insisted I stop snooping around and go back to lighting candles and praying. You wouldn't happen to know anything about that, would you?"

"Not for sure. But I do know the minute you walked out the door on Saturday, Pete was on the phone."

"So they might not have come from Rio," he said, thinking aloud. "It could have been Pete who sent them."

"Anything's possible, Father. If you put Rio out of business, Pete and his cronies stand to lose a big chunk of change."

Never in her life had Kit been shut out so completely. Rio refused to speak to her, looked right through her as though she wasn't even there. She wandered around the apartment like a ghost, from room to room, without even the benefit of Pixel's company, because he had locked Pix in the spare room. She knew he'd done it to punish her, and she told him so. She pointed out that it wasn't fair to make Pix suffer for her sins, but Rio refused to listen to her pleading, refused to even acknowledge that she was speaking to him.

His coldness was brutal, and she wasn't sure how long she could bear it. Eventually, she closed herself in the bedroom and sat on the bed, clutching Freddy to her breast and trying to make sense of his anger. She wasn't a crybaby, damn it! She wasn't a prude, either. Rio had taught her everything there was to know about making love, and she'd been a willing participant. But getting naked one-on-one, with somebody you loved, was a far cry from baring it all for the camera lens.

You're either committed, or you're not.

She was committed, one hundred percent. Or she'd thought she was. Nobody had explained to her that taking off her clothes was part of the package. Could it be possible he was right? That most of her TV and film idols had started their careers by posing nude? She wasn't completely naive. Anybody who owned a television and watched *ET* knew that every so often, a new crop of nude photos would surface, shedding scandal on the career of some up-and-coming young actress. The actress in question or, more likely, her publicity agent would generally explain it away by saying the pictures had been taken during a time in her life when she'd been starving and couldn't get a legitimate job.

Kit had heard it all before. But was the practice really industry-wide? She wished she knew what to believe.

I'm doing this for you, Kit. Not for me, but for you.

I think you have promise.

Word will get around that you're unprofessional, and your career will end up in the toilet.

When bedtime rolled around, Rio bunked on the couch, leaving Kit to sleep alone in his king-size bed. Not that she got much sleep. Instead, she spent hours lying awake, with a hollow, empty feeling in her belly. Was her own judgment really that whacked-out? Was she a fool to hold her ground on an issue that was apparently no big deal to the rest of the world? Would Rio come out of his snit once he'd had time to cool off?

She got her answer in the morning, when he headed off to work without even saying goodbye. At that point, she realized he was fully capable of shunning her indefinitely unless she gave him what he wanted. She sat on the couch in front of *Guiding Light,* eating Froot Loops and wondering how to fix this mess. At this point, it wasn't even about the photos anymore. She loved him, and she couldn't bear the way he was treating her. It wasn't worth the battle. Not if something as simple as giving in would return her to his good graces.

So she would extend the olive branch. She would make a special dinner, and they would kiss and make up. Rio loved Italian food, and Aunt Sarah had taught her how to make the best spaghetti and meatballs this side of heaven.

For an instant, remembering those Saturday afternoons she

and Sarah had spent in the kitchen together, she missed her aunt fiercely. Every Saturday, Sarah had come home from work early and they'd spent the afternoon in the kitchen. Just the two of them, laughing and horsing around while Sarah taught her how to cook everything from pie crust to corn bread to jambalaya. Female bonding, something she'd never had the chance to experience before. On those Saturdays, they'd declared an unspoken truce, a moratorium on arguing. It had been the only time in Kit's memory when she'd felt stability, a sense of belonging.

Until now. She reminded herself that Sarah had long since stopped looking for her, and she hardened her heart. Now, she belonged here with Rio. Her man was upset with her, and it was all her fault. She'd been acting like a spoiled child, and it was up to her to show him she was a grown woman, worthy of his love.

At dinnertime, she set the table with linen and crystal, and lit candles for atmosphere. She dressed in the red silk lounging pajamas Rio had bought her, then waited nervously, the scent of tomatoes and oregano and garlic wafting through the apartment.

When she heard the elevator humming, she squeezed her hands together to keep them from trembling. She was doing the right thing. But still she was terrified that he wouldn't forgive her, terrified of what would happen now she'd made her decision. Terrified of her own uncertainty in spite of that decision. She would stick with it. But that didn't mean she had to like it.

She heard his key in the lock, and the door swung open. Wordlessly, Rio scrutinized her appearance from head to foot, glanced past her to the table with its flickering candles. He sniffed the air appreciatively, and she took a single step forward. Trying to keep the tremor from her voice, she said, "Okay. I'll do it."

For an instant, he simply stared at her, while inside she

died a thousand deaths. And then he smiled, and it was like the sun breaking through after a storm. "That's my girl," he said.

Clancy spent twenty minutes in the shower, another half hour making sure he was clean-shaven and his hair was combed properly. Studying his reflection in the mirror, he smoothed an unruly eyebrow and decided this was as good as it was going to get. He brushed his teeth and checked his breath for freshness, then lingered at the door of his closet, debating whether to wear street clothes or clerical attire. *It's only dinner,* he reminded himself. *Not a date.* He was accustomed to eating dinner at least once a week at the home of one or another of his parishioners, and he'd been mooching meals off Fiona Rafferty since he and Conor were kids. Never, on any of those occasions, had he worried about what he wore or how he looked. He had simply combed his hair, washed his face, and focused on the meal. In theory, dinner with Sarah Connelly should be no different.

In practice, that theory was pure hogwash.

He decided on jeans and a black Henley shirt worn over his clerical collar. Comfortable, casual, but still proper. The collar was a clear statement, although he wasn't willing to examine too closely why he felt the need to make a statement.

The bottle of wine had been a spur-of-the-moment thing, something he'd picked up in Harvard Square after his meeting with Scott. It didn't mean anything. He often brought wine to dinner. As a matter of fact, he'd brought wine the last time he'd eaten dinner with Carolyn and Conor. That bottle might not have been as pricey as this one, but he was fond of this particular vintage and suspected Sarah would enjoy it as well. Maybe a glass or two would erase some of the shadows from those beautiful blue eyes.

Dusk was settling in, lovely and fragrant with the scent of

spring, when he left the rectory. He popped in a CD, hummed along with the husky crooning of Norah Jones. *Come away with me in the night.* He backed out of his parking space and shifted the car into Drive, his hand sweaty on the gearshift. His stomach felt hard, tucked up tight under his rib cage. This was probably a monumental mistake. But like the proverbial moth, he was drawn ever nearer the flame, and he was too stupid to heed the warning his instincts screamed at him.

He was halfway across the Tobin Bridge when his cell phone rang. Driving one-handed, he lowered the volume on the CD player and answered it. "Father Donovan."

"Yeah, Father," said a weary voice on the other end. "This is Sergeant McDougal of the Boston P.D."

He began easing his way into the right-hand lane in preparation for the cutoff to Revere. "Yes?"

"We have a kid here that we just arrested for lifting a couple of CDs from a record store at Downtown Crossing. He refuses to give us any information, but we found your card in his pocket. We didn't know who else to call."

Half the kids walking the streets of downtown Boston had his card. It could be anybody. Or, he realized with a sinking feeling, it could be somebody very specific. "Do you have a description of the kid?"

"Black kid, about fifteen or sixteen. Looks like he could use a good meal. Got a bit of an attitude, but underneath it, he's scared shitless. Sound like anybody you know?"

His stomach soured and his good mood tanked. Resentment, unexpected and vehement, rose up in its place as he thought about his empty stomach, about Sarah waiting for him in Revere, about the forty-dollar bottle of wine lying unopened on the passenger seat of his car.

He checked his watch. If he hurried, he'd only be a few minutes late. With a sigh, he clicked on his blinker and slowed for the upcoming exit. He would have to turn the car around and head back into the city.

"I know who he is," he said darkly. "His name is Jamal."

She made a point of wearing her oldest clothes, faded jeans and a baggy, moth-eaten sweater she'd inherited from her second ex-husband. She didn't bother to freshen her makeup, left her hair hanging in loose waves. There could be no hint of impropriety, no suggestion that this dinner even marginally resembled a date. It was merely a gesture of goodwill, payback for a kindness extended to her. She made sure the house was well lit, the blinds wide open, so if anybody looked in, they'd see nothing more than two friends eating a meal together.

The jambalaya was thick and hot and fragrant, made from a recipe that had been passed down through three generations of her family. She concocted a salad from various greens, topped with ripe red cherry tomatoes, and she'd bought a fresh-baked loaf of crusty bread at the bakery two doors down from Bookmark. The pecan pie was her own creation, sweet and elegant, the recipe one she'd learned as a girl at her momma's knee.

Seven o'clock came and went with no sign of her dinner guest. Sarah left the jambalaya on the back burner with the heat on low, wiped her nervous hands on a dish towel, and sat down with a magazine to wait for Clancy's arrival. By seven-thirty, she'd abandoned her magazine in favor of standing at the window with the curtains drawn back, anxiously watching the street. He didn't seem the kind of man to just blow her off. What if something had happened to him? He could have been in an accident, could be lying bloody and battered by the side of the road.

Or worse.

At eight o'clock, she called the rectory and left a message on his answering machine, then called his cell phone and did the same. Disappointment welled up in her, disappointment that was totally disproportionate to the situation. This wasn't a date, she reminded herself, only a friend coming to dinner. There was no sense in reading more into it. The chemistry between them was unmistakable, but it didn't matter. Nor did it matter that, had the circumstances been different, something more might have come of their friendship. The circumstances were what they were, and there was nothing left to say.

But, damn it, he could at least call. If something had come up, all he had to do was pick up that damnable cell phone that was permanently attached to his hip and dial her number. She wasn't an unreasonable woman. She understood as well as anybody that shit did, indeed, happen. But she wasn't a woman to be trifled with. She expected reason in return for reason.

At nine-thirty, she turned off the stove and dumped the jambalaya in the trash, flipped off all the lights, and sat in the dark with Patsy Cline and a bottle of Jack Daniel's. She didn't often brood, but occasionally, when she had a mad on, she liked to throw her own personal pity party, and Jack and Patsy were invariably her companions of choice. Tonight, she had one hell of a mad on, and as Patsy's voice sobbed and soared and sliced its way into her insides, Sarah took a long hit of Jack direct from the bottle. God help Clancy Donovan. He'd turned out, to her considerable surprise, to be a normal man with faults and foibles instead of the saint she'd imagined him to be. If he knew what was good for him, he'd already be dead, because if he'd stood her up for any reason less pressing than death, she was going to wrap her hands tight around his throat and kill him herself.

It took some fancy footwork to keep the kid out of juvie.

He went into a huddle with the arresting officer, O'Brien, and the manager of the record store, a fresh-faced young guy named Jerry Laughlin. After considerable negotiation, he convinced Laughlin to drop the charges as long as Jamal agreed not to darken his door again.

That was the first hurdle. The second was a little harder.

When he finally squeezed the grandmother's name and telephone number out of Jamal, the woman's response was pretty much what he'd expected. She wasn't getting any younger, and the boy was incorrigible. She already had her hands full with his younger brothers and sisters, and she simply could not take care of him any longer.

That left few options. He couldn't very well take the boy home with him, and allowing Jamal to disappear into the Massachusetts foster care system wasn't an option. The kid had potential, but a few years of being shuffled from foster home to foster home would snuff out any light shining beneath that pseudo-tough exterior.

So he did the only thing he could think of. He called Fiona.

The woman who'd been more of a mother to him than his own flesh and blood didn't even hesitate. "Bring him over," she said. "I could use somebody to fuss over. My grandkids are too busy to visit me, and I've just about given up on Conor ever giving me any new babies to spoil. I'll straighten the boy out."

He didn't doubt for an instant that she would.

The cops gave him the expected hassle. "This woman is not a licensed foster parent," McDougal said. "There's rules—"

"Bend the rules," he said. "We're talking about the boy's future."

"Look, Father, I could get my ass chewed from here to Providence if I released him to you."

"Then you'll have to put us both up for the night in your little five-star hotel, because I'm not leaving without him."

"My hands are tied. I don't have the authority to release

him to you, and if you think I'm calling my lieutenant at home over something like this—''

"Wait," he said. "I have an idea. Do you know Conor Rafferty?"

"Homicide lieutenant?"

"That's right. Fiona Rafferty is his mother. He lives right upstairs over her. What if he agreed to take responsibility for the boy while he's staying with Fiona and Hugh?"

They both glanced at Jamal, who had sat silently through-out the exchange, looking young and frightened and nowhere near as tough as he pretended. McDougal sighed. "You get Rafferty on the phone," he said, "and we'll talk."

Whatever Conor said to them, it worked. Five minutes af-ter his best friend told him, via the precinct telephone, "Any-thing happens, Donovan, your life won't be worth living," he and Jamal walked out the door of the police station and into a breezy spring night. Above their heads, a thousand stars spilled across the sky. Tight-lipped, Clancy unlocked the car and reached across the seat to open the passenger door. Jamal slid in beside him, unnaturally silent, and Clancy shoved the key into the ignition.

"I won't even ask what you were thinking," he said, his voice deadly quiet. "I don't have to ask, because I know. I've been there. I know every sneaky, slimy thought in your head, because I was just like you once."

"No way, dude."

"Shut up. You think you're bad? Hah! You're not a tenth as bad as I was at your age. You don't even have the imag-ination to think up some of the things I was doing at sixteen. But you know what? I learned. I learned that there are civi-lized ways to conduct your life, ways that won't land you in prison, or dead in the gutter with a knife in your gut."

"But—"

"I told you to shut up. I'm not done yet. I know you think

I'm just some rube, some gullible guy who'll bail you out of hot water every time you land in it. But you severely underestimate me, my friend, because this is the first and last time. I got you out of trouble, and now you owe me. And payback will be a bitch, because I now own your larcenous hide until such time as I believe you've sufficiently paid me back. And you *will* pay me back. Is that clear?''

"Come on, dude, it was only a coupla—"

"I asked if that was clear!"

There was a moment of silence before Jamal said, quietly, "Yeah. It clear."

"If it's the last thing I accomplish in this life, I'm going to teach you that you have to work for what you want. You don't have a right to take what's not yours. Are you familiar with the Ten Commandments? Particularly the one that applies to this situation?"

Glumly, the boy said, "Thou shalt not steal."

"Congratulations. You got it in one. Where do you live?"

"Huh?"

"I asked where you live. We have to pick up your things."

Harriet Washington's tiny first-floor apartment on the edge of Roxbury was spotless, mute testimony to how hard she worked, considering that she had four grandchildren ranging in age from six to sixteen to mess it up for her. While Jamal gathered his possessions, Clancy told the boy's grandmother where he would be staying and with whom. "They're good people," he said. "They'll do everything in their power to help him. The rest is up to him."

"It's not that I don't love the boy," Mrs. Washington said, a glassy sheen of tears in her eyes. "God knows, I've tried to pound some sense into that stubborn head of his. But he just doesn't listen anymore. I don't know what to do with him. And he's setting a bad example for the little ones."

On the other side of the wall, Jamal slammed things around

the bedroom as he packed. "Where are his parents?" Clancy asked quietly.

The woman shook her head in sorrow. "Killed in a head-on collision with a drunk driver three years ago. I took the kids in and did the best I could do for them, but it hasn't been easy, especially for Jamal." Sadness rolled off her in waves. "He still misses them."

"And so do you," he said, taking her hand. "I'm so sorry."

"Frederick was my only child, you know, and losing him almost killed me. I think prayer was the only thing that got me through. That, and the kids."

He squeezed her hand, released it when Jamal returned toting a boom box and a mountain of CDs, a green trash bag filled with clothes, and his balaphon in its case. "Is that everything?" Clancy said.

"This be it."

"I can take some of the load for you." He took the boom box in one hand and swung the trash bag over his shoulder. "I'll put these in the car while you say goodbye to your grandmother."

Afterward, they drove across town in silence. His stomach rumbled, and he realized he was ravenous. "Hungry?" he said.

Jamal shrugged.

"Well, I am. If you don't want to eat, you can watch me eat, instead." He saw the familiar golden arches looming ahead, and he pulled in, took the boy inside, and watched him inhale three double cheeseburgers and a milkshake. Finishing up his own fish sandwich and watered-down decaf, he wiped crumbs from his hands and said, "I'm glad you weren't hungry."

The boy smirked. "So who this Fiona person you talking 'bout? She some mean old lady?"

"As long as you behave, she won't be. But try to pull

anything on her, and she'll turn into the queen of mean. She has a finely tuned bullshit meter, and it's always ticking.''

Jamal eyed him hard and long. "How come you talk that way, dude? You supposed to be a priest.''

"I talk like a priest when it's appropriate to talk like one. Right now, I'm not in priest mode.''

Jamal raised his eyebrows. "What mode you in, then?''

"As a matter of fact, I'm in—''

He stopped abruptly as it hit him hard in the midsection. *Parent mode.* He was in full-blown, royally-pissed-off parent mode. It was an amazing revelation, especially since he wasn't the boy's father. He would never be anybody's father, and that particular truth was brutal in its finality. He would go through life being Father to many, but Dad to none.

For the first time ever, that knowledge brought him deep sorrow.

"Yo, dude. You still in there somewhere?''

He left his own jumbled thoughts behind and focused on the boy. "Never mind,'' he said, setting his empty coffee cup beside a pile of crumpled sandwich wrappers on the plastic tray between them. "Let's go.''

By the time he got Jamal settled with Fiona and Hugh, it was nearly midnight, and he was exhausted. He drove the few blocks to the rectory in blessed silence and parked beneath the giant elm tree that would provide shade and relief during the sweltering summer weather to come. When he pulled his keys from the ignition and opened the door, the overhead light illuminated his cell phone, still plugged into the charger. He'd been so revved up when he got to the police station, he'd forgotten to take it with him. That was a first. He never went anywhere without it. He unplugged it and checked the readout.

He had three missed calls.

He groaned. *Not tonight, God. Please, not tonight.* All he wanted tonight was a hot shower and twelve hours of deep, restful sleep. He wasn't crazy enough to think he'd get it, but a man could dream. For just one night, he didn't want to do any emergency marriage counseling, didn't want to hear that some elderly parishioner had died in his sleep, didn't want to deal with anybody else's crisis. For just one night, he wanted to forget he was a priest.

But thoughts like that were selfish, and he was expected to be a model of selfless behavior. Duty had been drilled into him, and God's work always came first. It had been that way since the beginning, and it would be that way until the end. With a sigh, he pulled up the call list to find out how and with whom he'd spend the rest of the night.

All three calls had come from the same number, a number with a Revere exchange. The instant he saw it, the memory slammed into him. Dinner. A favor repaid. A forty-dollar bottle of wine.

A beautiful woman he should have the sense to stay away from.

Sarah. God in heaven, he'd forgotten all about Sarah.

12

As hangovers went, this one ranked on the lower end of the scale, but opening her eyes to that first ray of morning light was still hell on wheels. Sarah groaned and pulled the pillow over her head. She'd downed too much Tennessee whiskey last night. Way too much. Now she was paying. Her head felt like a five-pound bag of sugar, rock-hard and grainy, and her stomach was singing the chorus to *Please Release Me*. There was only one solution to her problem: a hot shower, a cup of java, and five or six aspirin.

Then she was going to track down that man and kill him.

She drank the coffee at the kitchen table, her bleary eyes scanning the newspaper for any news of his untimely demise. But there was nothing. If he'd become roadkill, the *Globe* hadn't yet heard about it. Sarah supposed that was good news, since she was eager to perform the ugly deed herself. She skimmed the comics, the editorial page. Garfield was still overeating, and the locals were still arguing about the up-coming year's proposed school budget. There was a sale going on at Filene's. Maybe it was time to add a little pizzazz to her wardrobe. She didn't have to be at work today until noon. That gave her ample time to commit a homicide and then go shopping as a celebratory gesture.

A few minutes past eight, a vehicle pulled into her yard, its rumbling loud enough to pass for the trumpets of glory. Setting down the newspaper, Sarah got up and went to the window to find out what was making such a god-awful noise.

It was a blue pickup truck, circa 1975, with one red fender and a dented grill. A battered wooden toolbox was situated just behind the cab, and an aluminum ladder hung out the back. The vehicle looked like something her white-trash daddy would have been too embarrassed to drive.

The engine shuddered to a stop, the driver's door opened, and the future homicide victim himself stepped out of the cab. Sarah clamped both hands hard on the edge of the countertop as relief flooded her. Why her knees were shaking, she couldn't imagine. It wasn't as though she'd really believed the man was dead by the side of the road. And it didn't seem quite kosher to be this happy to see a man she'd planned to murder.

Hell's bells. Homicide was a messy business, anyway, not to mention illegal here in the Commonwealth of Massachusetts. It looked like the good Father would live to breathe another day. But that didn't mean she had to make it easy on him.

She flung open the front door and he stopped dead in his tracks on the other side, looking about as contrite as a man could look. Grimly, she said, "So you're alive, after all."

The morning was ripe with birdsong. A passing breeze lifted a strand of his hair and then dropped it. "Sarah," he said. "I'm sorry."

"What you are," she said, "is late. By about twelve hours, at last count."

He tucked his thumbs into the pockets of his jeans and rocked back on his heels. "Something came up. I couldn't help it."

"Ever hear of a little invention called the telephone?"

His chest rose and fell with his breathing. A little too deep, a little too hard. Underneath his open jacket, he wore a navy blue T-shirt that left his throat bare. Without the Roman collar, his neck looked young and vulnerable. That amber gaze locked on hers, and he swallowed. Hard. "I thought I'd be just a few minutes late. And then I got caught up in things and...I forgot. By the time I remembered, it was past midnight."

She raised a brow. "That hole you're digging yourself, Father, gets deeper with every word that comes out of your mouth."

It was gratifying to see him squirm like a worm on a hook. "I had an emergency."

"You're just like every other man on the planet, aren't you? Full of lame excuses. What kind of emergency?"

Color rose in his face. "It's not an excuse. It's the truth." He swung around toward the truck and beckoned. The passenger door opened, and Jamal clambered out. "This," Clancy said as the boy climbed the steps to the porch, "is my emergency. Apologize to the lady, Jamal."

The boy shuffled his feet and stared at the floor. "Sorry," he muttered.

"He got himself arrested," Clancy said. "I rescued him. Now it's payback time."

"That seems fair." She made a sweeping examination of the old rattletrap parked in her driveway. "Nice truck," she said. "Did you trade in the Saturn for it?"

She thought she saw a twitch at the corner of his mouth, but she couldn't be sure. "It belongs to the church."

"Looks like you'd better take up a collection to buy a new one, sugar. That thing is ready for the crusher. What's that you have in your hand?"

He lifted a fistful of oblong cardboard strips. "Paint samples. It's part of payback. Jamal and I are going to scrape your house, and then he's going to paint it."

"Hot-diggity-dog. Is this all part of a scheme to solicit my forgiveness for last night?"

He tilted his head to one side and gave her a lopsided smile. "That depends. Will it help?"

She hadn't intended to let him get to her. But that smile

drove itself like a fist into her heart. "I was planning to strangle you," she said darkly, "if you weren't already dead. I can't remember the last time I was stood up like that."

"Jamal," he said, without taking his eyes from hers, "go get the ladder and the tools out of the truck. The gray toolbox."

"Yes, Massuh." The boy, who'd been following their conversation as though it were a tennis match, heaved a gigantic sigh and shuffled off, dragging his size thirteens all the way.

"I can see he's really into payback," she said.

His eyes warmed, softened. "Deeply and sincerely. Sarah, let me make last night up to you."

She raised an eyebrow, took a step backward, and crossed her arms. "Wait just a minute, sugar. Let me be sure I have this straight. You want to make up for your absence at last night's dinner table by giving me a second chance to cook a meal you probably won't show up for?"

"No. I'd like to make it up to you by taking you out to dinner."

Her heart, the traitorous son of a dog, began to beat faster. This wasn't going the way she'd planned. Not at all. "Don't you care what people will think?"

"People will always think what they want, no matter what the situation. If I want to have dinner in public with a friend who happens to be a woman, that's precisely what I'm going to do. I have nothing to hide." Behind him, Jamal hefted the aluminum extension ladder out of the pickup bed. The boy struggled with it, lost his balance, and dropped the ladder with one hell of a clatter. Clancy winced. "This is a character-building exercise," he said. Then added, "I have information for you."

"Information," she said sharply. "What information?"

From the driveway, Jamal glanced over at them, yanked

his cap lower on his head, and hefted the ladder back up over his shoulder. "Make me a cup of coffee," Clancy said, "and I'll tell you."

"I've come up with a plan."

He set his coffee mug on her kitchen table and tore off a piece of cinnamon roll. "If the mountain won't come to Mohammed," he said, "then Mohammed will just have to go to the mountain. I'm tossing down the gauntlet."

Sarah scraped her fingers through her hair. She was dog-tired, and the news he'd brought her about Rio's little enterprise wasn't good. She'd seen a porno movie or two in her time, had witnessed the degradation those women underwent for the sake of titillating a large audience of overgrown boys. But the women she'd seen were fully grown, and capable of walking away from the industry when they tired of it. Kit was a sixteen-year-old girl, and it made her blood boil to think that some man might subject her to that kind of treatment.

Outside, Jamal had set up the ladder against the side of the house and was busy scraping paint. Every so often, she could see the top of his head bobbing outside the window over the sink. "What's your plan?" she said wearily.

"I don't seem to be having much luck tracking down Rio. So I've decided to turn it upside down and make him come to me." Clancy lifted his coffee mug and took a long, slow hit. "I had Melissa make up more flyers yesterday afternoon." He pulled a folded sheet of paper from his pocket, unfolded it, and handed it to her. It was identical to the last flyer, except that in bold print across the bottom, the new version read: *Last Seen With A Man Named Rio, aka Roger Seward. If You Have Any Information About Kit Or Rio, Please Call The Above Number Immediately.*

"Tomorrow morning, I'll start calling all my contacts, put out the word that I'm looking for him. Then I'm going to distribute these flyers on the street. To prostitutes, junkies, street people. Somebody out there knows him, and somebody will make sure he gets one of these. I'll put the word out, then we'll wait to see what happens."

Her mind raced in unending circles as she studied the flyer. It was a damned-if-you-do, damned-if-you-don't situation. "I'm not sure this is a good idea," she said.

"You have reservations?"

She set down the flyer. "You have no idea, sugar, how much I want to get my hands on this son of a bitch. The very idea that he might put Kit into some sleazy porn movie makes me want to rip off his testicles and watch him bleed."

He took another sip of coffee. Dryly, he said, "Remind me to stay on your good side."

"But I'm afraid we'll make the wrong move. You already got this guy pissed off at you once—"

"We don't know that for sure. According to what I learned yesterday, it could very well have been the guy from Puritan who sent the muscle."

"But it could also have been Rio."

"Yes," he conceded. "It could also have been Rio."

"You could be stirring up trouble. I want his ass fried, but I don't want Kit paying for our sins."

"No. Neither do I."

Outside the house, Jamal moved the ladder with a heavy thud. "I know this is a silly question," she said, "but has it occurred to you to go to the police with what you have? What this guy's doing is illegal."

"I've already tried. I've been in touch with a Vice detective named Paoletti. He says it's not enough to go on and, he reminded me, not for the first time, that I should back off and leave the detecting to him."

"So we're really on our own with this."

"We're really on our own." He set down his coffee mug and tapped his fingertips against the table. "I think we have to take the risk. We don't have any alternatives at this point."

She thought about it, realized he was right. With a sigh, she said, "Shit."

"I think it'll flush him out of hiding, if only for the ego boost he'll get from thumbing his nose at us. And on the slim chance that Kit isn't with him, it will give him an opportunity to clear himself." He scraped his chair back from the table, shot a quick glance at the window, and picked up his coffee mug. Carrying it to the sink, he said, "Try to remember one thing."

"What's that, sugar?"

He set the mug in the sink, filled it with cold water, and turned to look at her. "I have God on my side."

Over dinner, Rio promised that if she found the nude photos objectionable, he'd incinerate them, and that would be the end of it. "I forgot to mention," he said casually as he speared a meatball and cut it in two, "I have a special project shoot coming up in a couple of days." He studied her over the table. "Want to come along and be my assistant? It would be a great experience for you, a chance to start getting familiar with the filmmaking industry."

If he was trying to mollify her, it was working. "You're making a movie?" she said. "What kind of movie?"

"Nothing too fancy, Princess. Low budget all the way. It's no *Schindler's List*, but technique is technique, whether you're shooting high drama or a car commercial."

She'd never heard of *Schindler's List,* but from the title, it sounded dull as dirt. And she didn't care if he *was* filming a car commercial. Just being there on the set as his assistant sounded way cool. It was a fantasy job she would have paid him to let her do, and she agreed before he had time to change his mind.

The shoot took place at a seedy motel in Peabody that made Aunt Sarah's house look like the Ritz. The single-story concrete block building reminded Kit of some of the places she and Daddy had stayed while they were on the road. Rio pulled around to the back side and parked between a row of shrubbery and an anonymous-looking blue panel truck. He turned to her, cupped her chin in his hand, and kissed her hard on the lips. "Remember, kitten," he said, "you're here to watch and learn. That means you stay out of the way, do what I ask, and keep your mouth shut. You got that?"

He didn't wait for an answer. Inside the motel room, a dark-skinned guy with a ponytail and a pitted face was setting up a trio of spotlights directed at a chair set in the middle of the room. The bedding had been removed from the bed, all but the bottom sheet, and draped over the room's single window. A video camera sat on a tripod next to the chair. Rio walked over to it, knelt and looked through the viewfinder. He made a minor adjustment to the camera, then stood back up. Glancing at his watch, he said, "Where's Terry?"

"Beats me," ponytail said. "I got here a half hour ago, and I ain't seen nobody."

"Damn it. She'd better show up pretty soon. Our client's due in twenty minutes."

"She'll show," the other guy said. "She always does."

A moment later, there was a knock at the door. Rio opened it, and a lanky black girl sauntered in, a small overnight bag swinging from her shoulder. Rio eyed her long and hard, then said, "Cutting it kind of short, aren't you, Terry?"

"You said seven-fifteen, it's seven-fifteen. And here I am."

"Get ready," he said, then swung around to Kit. "Go in the bathroom with her," he ordered. "Help her get dressed."

Kit had experienced his disfavor once, and once was enough. She scurried to obey. Terry shut and locked the bathroom door behind them. The tiny room held a faint odor of urine. "Pee-yew," Terry said, waving her hand. "This place is the pits." She dropped the overnight bag on the floor, walked to the window behind the toilet, and opened it. Then she lowered her lanky body onto the toilet seat. Crossing one long leg over the other, she pulled a pack of cigarettes from the overnight bag and lit one.

"So you're the flavor of the month," she said, eyeing Kit critically as she exhaled a cloud of blue smoke. "I heard Rio had a new cookie. What's your name?"

"Kit. What do you mean, flavor of the month?"

Terry took another long draw on the cigarette. "There's been a long line of girls before you, sweet thing, and there'll be a long line behind you after you're gone." She leaned forward, elbows braced against her knees. "You look familiar. We ever met before?"

Coolly, Kit said, "I'm sure I'd remember if we had."

"A little big for your britches, aren't you? What you doing with that no-good son of a bitch outside? The one with the movie camera?"

She felt a flush climb her face. "I happen to be in love with Rio. And he loves me."

"Jesus, are you for real? Why do you think he brought you here today?"

"I'm an actress," she said, raising her chin. "I'm here to learn about filmmaking."

"Right," Terry said. "And I'm the queen of Sheba. He got you brainwashed, girl. There ain't no way to go from here except down. And if anybody can take you there, Rio can."

"If you think he's such a creep," she said hotly, "what are you doing here?"

Terry blew out a cloud of smoke. "I don't have to like the man to work for him. The work's easy, the pay's good. The customers don't smell like stale sweat. I put in a few hours here, that's eight hours I don't spend standing on a street corner. I got no complaints. But you look like some sweet young high school girl ought to be going to the prom with her sweet young high school boyfriend. Didn't your mama ever tell you if you lie down with dogs, you wind up with fleas?''

Flatly, Kit said, "My mother's dead."

"Yeah, well, life's a bitch." Terry eyed her hard enough to make her squirm. "You want my advice? Get the hell away from that man. His girlfriends have a nasty habit of disappearing when he's done with 'em." Terry crushed out her cigarette on the lip of the lavatory and peeled her T-shirt off over her head, revealing a body Kit would have given her eyeteeth for. "Help me get this damn-fool outfit on," she said. "Don't want to keep Mister Spielberg out there waiting too long."

"So how's the character-building going?"

"Slowly." Clancy leaned back on his tailbone, one hand on the stem of his wineglass, and rotated it slowly on the tabletop. "Jamal's hardheaded, just like I was at that age. He has some difficult lessons to learn."

The restaurant exuded an old-world elegance and charm. Soft music, soft lighting, hushed atmosphere, lots of dark wood. The flickering shadows from the candle at the center of the table threw his face into sharp relief. There was nothing soft about Clancy Donovan. He was all lines and angles, all strength and decisiveness. He'd worn his clerical collar tonight, and Sarah wondered whether it was his way of thumbing his nose at the world, or if it was intended to remind her—and him—of just who and what he was.

She took a sip of white wine. "Yes," she said. "I seem to recall you saying something about being on the fast track to hell. Somehow, I can't picture it."

The waiter arrived with their dinners, prime rib for him, poached salmon for her. When he'd gone again, Clancy picked up his napkin and arranged it on his lap. "Excuse me," he said, closing his eyes, and Sarah realized with a start that he was blessing the food. She was instantly swept back to her childhood, to Sunday dinners at Gramma Connelly's house. Gram had been a devout Southern Baptist, and every Sunday after church, the entire family had gathered at her house for dinner. Aunts, uncles, cousins, the occasional neighbor. Anybody who exercised the poor judgment of lifting fork to lips in Loretta Connelly's house before the blessing had been said suffered a punishment severe enough that the offense was never repeated.

Clancy opened his eyes. Picking up his fork, he said, "I was a monster in the making. Smoking, drinking, stealing. Getting high and ditching school. The list is endless. I thought I was tough and cool and sophisticated. My mother was ready to tear her hair out. She couldn't do a thing with me."

It was hard to imagine, and she wondered what other secrets he hid behind that bold amber gaze. "What turned you around?"

He sliced his prime rib, took a bite. "Fiona Rafferty got her hands on me."

"Josie's mom?"

"Yes. She basically put her size-eight foot up my scrawny arse and kept it there until I got the message." His smile was wry, and utterly charming. "It took a while."

It explained a lot. Why he'd taken such an active interest in Jamal. Why he'd brought the boy to Fiona. She took a bite of salmon. "So you grew up here?"

"Born here, grew up here. Except for my time in Asia and then in seminary, I've lived in South Boston all my life. I made my first communion in the same church where now I say Mass every Sunday."

"How long were you in seminary?"

"Seven years." He wiped his hands with his napkin. "In a little town a few miles west of Springfield. Along the way, I earned a bachelor's degree in counseling psychology, and then of course my Master of Divinity. It was a long, arduous road.''

''But worth the journey?''

He picked up his glass of wine, took a sip, leveled a glance at her. ''I'm still on the journey. Priesthood is just one stop along the road.''

''My, my, Father. We're thinking deep thoughts tonight.''

''It's not me, it's the wine.'' Humor flickered in his eyes as they examined her face. ''So, Sarah Connelly, tell me. Are you collecting information to write my biography?''

She set down her fork. ''I'm just curious, sugar. I don't mean to pry.''

''Pry away. I'm teasing you. Ask whatever you want, and I'll try to satisfy your curiosity.''

''What was your family like? Any brothers or sisters?''

''No brothers or sisters. My mother died six years ago, while I was still in seminary. She didn't live long enough to see my ordination. I've always regretted that. She would have been proud. As for my father—'' He picked up a dinner roll, pulled it apart, busied himself buttering it ''—I haven't seen him in thirty years. He left when I was…oh, two or three, I guess. I have vague memories of him, but that's all. So it was just my mother and me.''

''That must have been hard.''

''At times, it was brutal.'' He glanced up from the dinner roll. ''But you do what you have to do, and the sun continues to come up every morning. How's the salmon?''

She glanced down at her plate, at the food she'd barely touched. ''Delicious.''

''I bought a ridiculously expensive bottle of wine to bring to dinner the other night. I was trying to impress you. I should have remembered what the Bible says about pride going before a fall. I got my comeuppance. The bottle's still sitting in the back seat of my car.''

In the pit of her stomach, something warm and tremulous

fluttered to life. "If I wasn't already impressed with you, sugar," she said, "I wouldn't be sitting here."

The atmosphere between them was suddenly supercharged, and her words floated in it, invisible but palpable. She'd said too much. Gone too far. Stepped over the line and turned a harmless flirtation into something dark and dangerous. Overhead, from some distant time and place, Frank Sinatra was singing about flying to the moon. Clancy's keen gaze pinned her in place while she cast about desperately for a way out, a way to rewind the tape and take the words back.

To her immense relief, the waiter interrupted with an offer to freshen their drinks. *Loose lips sink ships,* she thought, and shoved her wineglass aside. "No more wine," she said, "but I'd dearly love a cup of tea."

Clancy ordered the same, and the waiter left silently and discreetly. "I'm sorry," she said. "I didn't mean that the way it sounded."

"No offense taken."

But the intimacy she'd felt between them was gone, flattened by her own carelessness. He'd withdrawn smoothly and, she supposed, wisely. It was what she deserved for momentarily forgetting herself and the uncrossable boundary between them. The clerical collar should have been a patent reminder. But she'd always been a slow learner.

Flirtation wasn't the reason they were together, anyway. There was only one reason she and Clancy Donovan were sitting at this table together, and once Kit was found, that reason would no longer be valid. Sarah wanted Kit back so bad she ached inside with it. She needed to make up for all those lost years. For Kit's sake, for her own. She desperately needed to fill up the emptiness she'd carried inside her for so long. She hadn't expected that her need to find Kit would come into direct conflict with her need to keep Clancy Donovan in her life. The thought of never seeing him again filled her with a sadness so profound it bordered on despair.

She picked listlessly at her salmon. Set down her fork. "Any nibbles on the flyer?" she said briskly.

"Not yet. I spent a few hours Sunday night liberally distributing them. I imagine that sooner or later, one will fall into Rio's hands. But the wait is frustrating."

"I just don't understand what would make Kit stay with someone like that. She's a smart girl, no more naive than any other girl her age. Probably a little less than some. She's done a lot of living in her sixteen years. Was life with me that bad?"

"Of course not. It has nothing to do with you." He reached across the table and took her hand in his, a gesture meant to comfort. As a priest, he probably did it so often the action had become automatic. His skin was warm, and needles of awareness skittered up her arm, raced past her heart, and settled somewhere in the vicinity of her stomach. The nape of her neck was suddenly damp. He gave her hand a squeeze and withdrew, and Sarah struggled to settle the Ping-Pong tournament he'd set off inside her.

"A man like Rio," he said, leaning back in his chair, "is a master of manipulation. An amateur psychologist, experienced at reading people, able to zero in on a girl's weaknesses and play on them. He'll seduce a young girl with his charm, make impossible promises, build her trust by showering her with gifts, even as he's subtly but effectively breaking all her emotional bonds and redirecting them toward him. If he's good enough at it, and if the girl is malleable enough, eventually he'll become her whole world. Then he can make her do anything he wants."

The waiter returned with their tea. Sarah waited while he set both cups on the table and cleared away their plates. Sorrow weighing heavily on her shoulders, she said, "It kills me to think about it. Wondering what kind of pain she's suffering at the hands of this bastard. What kind of permanent damage he'll inflict."

Clancy poured milk into his tea and stirred it. "From everything you've told me about Kit, she sounds resilient. We have to concentrate on getting her back. Then—" he lifted his cup, took a sip of tea "—then, whatever transpires, we'll deal with it. One day at a time."

Rio had lied to her.

Not so much by commission as by omission. *Nothing too fancy. Low budget all the way.* At least he'd told the truth about that. The total cost of this movie was a hundred dollars to Terry, $39.95 for the room, and a few bucks for a roll of film.

She must be a moron, because it hadn't once occurred to her that they were making a porno movie, not even after she stepped into the motel room and saw the camera and the lights aimed at that hard wooden chair. After all, as far as she knew, even in a porno flick, people generally did the nasty in bed, not in a chair.

It wasn't until she saw Terry's outfit that Kit figured it out. The girl looked like a reject from *The Rocky Horror Picture Show*. She wore a black leather bustier that laced up the front, with dangling garters attached to black fishnet stockings. With it, she wore a matching black thong, five-inch heels, and black lace gloves that reached to her elbows. That in itself was enough to qualify her as a look-alike for Elvira, Mistress of the Dark. But Terry took it one step further when she pulled out a whip, a paddle, and a black eye mask. The end result was a cross between the Lone Ranger and Catwoman.

Kit could have laughed it off if Rio hadn't taken it so seriously. But when they emerged from the bathroom, he was pacing and glancing at his watch. He eyed Terry critically, made a couple of minor adjustments to her costume—that was the only way Kit could think of it—and nodded his approval. "You know the routine," he said.

"Been there, done that," Terry said. "I could do it in my sleep."

The client arrived shortly thereafter. A tall, distinguished-looking gentleman starting to go gray at the temples, he took off his overcoat and tossed it on the bed, then handed Rio a thick envelope. His eyes were on Terry from the instant he stepped through the door. Rio opened the envelope, smiled, and stashed it in his briefcase. Picking up the camera, he nodded. *Let the games begin.*

With seductive grace, Terry crossed the room to the client, touched a fingertip to his chin. "I hear you've been a bad boy," she purred.

In a breathy voice that betrayed either great excitement or great fear—maybe both—the man said, "Very bad."

"Sit!" Terry commanded as though she were training a dog. And like a dog, eager to please its master, the man walked to the chair and sat. As Kit watched in mounting horror, Terry proceeded to do bizarre, abusive, and humiliating things to him. All for the benefit of the camera lens.

She took as much of it as she could handle before running to the bathroom, locking herself in, and losing her dinner. She retched and retched, her head hanging over the rusted john while tears welled up in her eyes and poured down her cheeks. When there was nothing left in her stomach, she flushed the toilet and ran cold water in the sink, splashed it over her face, rinsed out her mouth. For the first time in a long time, she actually felt sixteen years old.

Kit met her eyes in the mirror over the sink and shuddered. Did people really do that kind of thing to each other? What kind of sicko would pay a woman dressed in leather and lace to abuse him? If this was what adulthood was really about, she didn't want any part of it. She'd rather be sixteen forever.

She stayed in the bathroom for the rest of the shoot. When Terry rapped at the door, Kit escaped to the relative safety of Rio's BMW. When he came outside a few minutes later, whistling nonchalantly, she was sitting in the passenger seat, feet tucked up beneath her, curled into a huddled ball of misery.

"Poor little Kit," he teased as he started the engine, wheeled the car around, and shot back out onto Route 1. "Did she bite off more than she could chew?"

Still curled in a ball, she clung to the door because it was the farthest she could get from him without climbing into the back seat.

"Oh, for Christ's sake," he snapped, "stop being a baby. Don't tell me you didn't know exactly what we were doing."

"I didn't! And you didn't warn me! All you said was that you were making a low-budget movie! How was I supposed to know?" She swiped furiously at a tear. "I hate you!"

For an instant, she flashed back to her last battle with Aunt Sarah. She remembered how angry she'd been over something that now seemed petty and trivial. They might have had their differences, but at least Sarah'd been concerned with her welfare. If her aunt knew where Rio had taken her tonight, she would probably whip his ass single-handedly.

"Don't blame me," he said. "I'm just the guy who runs the camera. I'm a businessman, Kit, and the first thing you learn in the business world is that the customer is always right. Whatever the client wants, that's what I film. I go where the money is, and sometimes that means dirty movies. You know how much money I made tonight? Three grand. That's three thousand dollars, Kit. I can buy you a lot of pretty baubles with that kind of money. So quit your sniveling and grow up. This is the way the world works."

She sat beside him in miserable silence, and Rio turned on the radio and proceeded to ignore her the rest of the way home. When he pulled up in front of the old industrial building that housed his loft apartment, a black Camaro waited at the curb. When she saw the man leaning against the driver's door, Kit's stomach muscles clenched. She'd met Rio's friend Gonzales before, and he reminded her of a greasy, slicked-up gigolo. All that ridiculous gold jewelry. And the way he looked at her, with those hard, cold eyes, gave her the creeps.

''What's he doing here?'' she said.

Rio turned off the ignition and released his seat belt. ''I don't know,'' he said, ''but I'm about to find out.''

They both got out of the car, and Kit waited on the sidewalk while Rio conferred with Gonzales. Then both men approached her. ''We have business to discuss,'' Rio said. ''Gonzales is coming upstairs for a while. You'll have to make yourself scarce.''

While they rode up in the elevator, Kit avoided making eye contact with Gonzales. She didn't like this, but what choice did she have? It was Rio's apartment, not hers, and he called the shots. All of them. She was getting a little tired of Rio calling all the shots.

He unlocked the apartment door, then patted her on the bottom. ''Run along like a good little girl. Go to bed or something. I'll be along in a few minutes.''

She hated being sent to her room like a child, but it beat the hell out of pretending to be a gracious hostess to that gorilla Gonzales. Kit shut herself in the bedroom and changed into her pajamas. She'd just turned down the bed when she heard Rio's explosion from the living room. Whatever Gonzales had told him, it hadn't gone over well.

Curious, she tiptoed to the door, opened it a crack, and stood there listening. ''How the fuck does he know who I am?'' Rio fumed. ''There's no way he could know she's with me. I've been so damn careful. No way!''

''Looks to me like somebody blabbed.''

''Nobody knows she's here! Why the hell do you think I've kept her locked up and out of sight? Fuck, fuck, fuck!''

Mildly, Gonzales said, ''You want me to take care of it?''

''You were supposed to have already taken care of it.''

"You told me to give him a warning. You wanted him roughed up, you should've said so."

"I thought a warning would be enough. He's a freaking priest. They're not supposed to be pushy. He should have backed off. Any other priest would have."

"Doesn't look to me like this one's planning to back off, *amigo*. Not until he finds the girl."

Kit's heart began to beat double-time. This priest they were talking about was looking for her? She didn't know any priest. That could mean just one thing. Aunt Sarah hadn't given up on finding her. Rio had lied about that, too.

"Take care of him," Rio said in a tight, controlled voice.

A shiver ran down Kit's spine. "Permanently?" Gonzales said.

There was a long pause before Rio said, "Christ only knows how many of these flyers he's put out on the street with my name on them. If we kill him now, the cops are apt to put two and two together and start sniffing around, looking for me."

"Maybe it's time to get rid of the girl. Women are seldom worth it, *amigo*. In the end, they all become liabilities."

"Not yet," Rio snapped. "I'll get rid of her if and when I decide it's time."

"Hey, you're the boss," Gonzales said. "So what do you want me to do?"

"Work him over," Rio said. "Work him over real good. Make the sorry motherfucker wish he'd never been born."

13

Silence blanketed the church. At this time of night, there was no clattering of computer keys from the parish office in the north wing of the building, no distant whine of the ancient Electrolux that Dave ran twice weekly over all the carpets. Just a profound silence broken only by his own thoughts.

Clancy moved soundlessly toward the altar, lit a candle and spent a few moments in prayer. Hands braced against the smooth surface of the altar table, he opened his eyes and looked out over a vastness of crimson carpet and oak pews. He'd grown up here, had sat in one of those hard wooden pews every Sunday morning of his childhood, awed by the mystical powers held by the priest, the earthly incarnation of a God too gigantic and too powerful for a young boy to comprehend. Now, as a grown man and a priest, he still didn't understand the immensity of God's love. Now he was the one who carried that mystical power, and he never failed to be both humbled and honored by the privilege.

He loved it all. Loved the God-given power he held in his hands to guide men's souls. He loved the stirring beauty and drama of the Mass, loved the pomp and circumstance and the familiar, comforting rituals. Loved the candles and the music, the sense of purity, even the vestments that changed according to season and function. Here, within the cavernous sanctuary that was Saint Bart's, with the voices of two hundred souls rising to a ceiling as vast as the universe, he always found peace. He never felt closer to God than he did here, on a Sunday morning, as he led his flock in prayer. His faith was rock-solid, unshakable.

But the flesh was weak. He was living with one foot in the Church, the other in the secular world, and it was tearing him in two. Sarah and Kit were taking up all his time, all his thoughts. His part-time search for a missing girl had turned into a full-time obsession that was cheating his parishioners of his time and energy. And the situation with Sarah was getting out of hand. His duty as a priest was to lead his flock in the paths of righteousness, a duty that simply could not coexist with wining and dining a beautiful woman.

If I wasn't impressed with you already, sugar, I wouldn't be sitting here.

It was time to break things off with her. He'd allowed the attraction to go too far, allowed himself to believe in its innocence because that was what he wanted to believe. He'd thought himself capable of a friendship with a woman, but he'd grown far too comfortable with her, far too intimate. He'd begun dreaming about her, dreams that were disturbingly sexual in their nature. Before it went any further, before one or both of them got hurt, it was time to disengage.

He wouldn't stop looking for Kit. That was a given. The girl was in trouble, and if he gave up on her, he'd never be able to live with himself. He'd keep searching until he found her. But the relationship with Sarah would have to end.

He had a five-day retreat coming up next week, and Bishop Halloran had made it clear that his attendance was mandatory. The retreat would afford him the opportunity he needed to clear his head and realign his priorities. While he was there, he would pray for the strength and the wisdom to find the right words to say to her. Somehow, he would make her understand he was withdrawing from their friendship not because of her, but because of his priesthood. Somehow, he would make her understand the inherent difficulty in a Catholic priest attempting to maintain a platonic relationship with a woman whose nearness made him ache deep inside.

He'd just stepped away from the altar when he heard a noise coming from the north wing of the church. He felt a prickling at the nape of his neck. Had he locked the door behind him when he came in? Or had he forgotten because he was in his usual state, his mind a million miles away from where it should have been?

It was probably nothing. A tree branch scraping against the side of the building. The closing of a car door out on the street. He moved stealthily along the dark, carpeted corridor that ran between the sanctuary and the wing housing the parish office. Light from the parking lot spilled through a window onto Melissa's desk. Except for the computer and a black mesh cup that held writing utensils, the desktop was empty, smooth and shiny in the bluish light. A hushed bubbling sound came from the fish tank in the corner. The fish hovered, motionless, their fins swaying gently in the wake from the bubbler.

The door to his study was closed. That was odd. He was sure he'd left it open earlier. Clancy grasped the doorknob, cautiously opened the door, and stepped across the threshold.

He never saw it coming. Some hard object slammed into the back of his head with such force, his vision went red. Before he had time to react, he was hit again, this time across the shoulders, and he went down like a fallen oak.

Need to get up. Need to fight back.

But he was incapable of moving, incapable of thinking. His attacker crouched near his head, gagging him with the scent of cheap aftershave and affording him a first-rate view of a pair of shiny black boots with pointed toes. "We tried to warn you, *amigo*," the shadow said, "but you didn't listen. This time, you listen."

He knew that voice, understood now why they were here.

He tried to open his mouth to retort, but his mouth, like the rest of him, no longer seemed connected to his brain.

The first kick landed square in the middle of his diaphragm. White-hot pain shot through him, and all the air left his lungs. He gasped for breath, struggled to crawl away, but his limbs were incapable of following the instructions issued by his brain. Helpless, he lay on the hard, cold floor while they kicked him in the abdomen, the kidneys, the face. One well-placed kick to his nose brought a screaming pain that reverberated and magnified inside his head and sent a rush of tears to his eyes. He wet his lips, tasted his own blood. Cold fury enveloped him, fury at their audacity, fury at his own helplessness as he lay here and waited for them to kill him.

Bless me, Father, for I have sinned.

But they didn't kill him. Instead, when they tired of the game, Cheech knelt by his side again. "Just in case you were wondering, padre," he said casually, "this is your last warning. We have to come visit you again, we kill you. And if you go to the cops, we kill the girl. Just think about how pretty she'll look with her throat slit."

Cheech turned and spoke a couple of words in Spanish to the other man, and they left silently, wraithlike, the scent of cheap aftershave lingering in the air behind them.

He wasn't sure how long he lay there. It seemed to take forever to regain his breath. When he finally did, he hauled himself to his knees, struggled to his feet, and landed heavily on a chair. His ears were ringing, and his ribs felt like they'd been trampled by an antelope. He rubbed his temple and his hand came away bloody. Stupidly, like a movie running in slow motion, he looked down and saw that the front of his shirt was saturated with blood. It still flowed from his nose at an amazing rate, fat crimson drops that left a dark, wet spatter on the carpet.

He rose on shaky legs, swayed a bit before he got his

bearings. It seemed to take an inordinate amount of time to cross the room, one laborious step after another. He snatched a fistful of tissue from the box he kept on the corner of the desk and pressed it against his face. Wincing at the contact between soft tissue paper and a nose that felt as though it had slammed into a concrete wall at eighty miles an hour, he wondered if there were some limit to the number of orifices through which a man could hemorrhage before he bled out and died.

He stumbled to the door. Outside, it was raining, a soft spring rain that seeped through his shirt and left dark blotches on the tissue box clutched in his hand. Like some aged sot, he walked with an unsteady gait to his car, parked in the shadows of the rectory. For an instant, he leaned against the door, folded his arms on the roof and rested his aching head on them. He tried to remember whether he'd locked the church, but he wasn't sure. He didn't remember walking out the door. He'd been inside, then he'd been out here, in the rain, with no memory of how the transition had taken place.

He opened the car door, managed somehow to fold his battered body into the driver's seat. When the dizziness passed, he took stock. Ignition, brake pedal, accelerator, steering wheel. Taking comfort from the knowledge that everything was here, and in its rightful place, he cranked the ignition and backed the car around. He drove by instinct, grateful the Saturn was an automatic. No clutching, no shifting. All he had to do was steer. Steering was a relatively simple feat, even for a man holding a wad of tissue paper to his nostrils to keep what was left of his brains from leaking out.

The trip was a blur. Traffic was light, but still it seemed to take forever to get to Revere, probably because he was driving somewhere in the proximity of the speed limit. He pulled into her driveway and sat there with his window open, watching the dark, slumbering house. Through his open window, the rain carried the rich scent of lilacs, overlaid with the metallic tang of his own blood. He opened the door and hauled himself, inch by painful inch, out of the car, took his time crossing the lawn, took longer to work up the strength to climb those three steps to the porch.

He leaned heavily on the bell, his forehead propped against the door frame. Above him, the porch light came on. He heard footsteps on the stairs, and a moment later, she flung open the door. "Lord in heaven," she grumbled, "you could at least give me time to—" she saw his face and gasped, her hand fluttering to her mouth as her eyes went wide with horror "—sweet Jesus. What—oh, sweet Jesus."

Her skin wore a soft, slumberous glow that said she'd been asleep. Her hair fell in a loose tangle of burnished golden curls around her shoulders, and she was wearing a Tweety Bird nightshirt. Her legs were spectacular. It wasn't the first time he'd noticed. She was still looking at him as though he were something conjured up from a Vincent Price movie, and he wondered if he really looked that bad. He opened his mouth to speak, realized his lip was split. He found it with his tongue, dampened it. Thickly, he said, "It's not as bad as it looks."

"Dear God. Tell me you didn't drive here in this condition."

"Yes," he said. "Yes, I did." And he might add, if he were so inclined, that he'd done a rather fine job of it. He hadn't hit so much as a guardrail along the way. As far as he could remember.

"You idiot. It's a wonder you didn't pass out behind the wheel and kill yourself. Or somebody else. Get in here."

He stepped inside and she closed the door. "Bathroom," she ordered, and like an obedient child, he followed her instructions. She pointed to the commode. "Sit."

Because she wasn't the kind of woman a man argued with, he sat.

She stood before him in the tiny bathroom with her hands pressed to her mouth, fingers clasped together so tight the knuckles were white. "All right, Sarah," she said with a distinct tremor in her voice. "Think. Calm down and think. Take a deep breath—" She inhaled, held it for several seconds, then exhaled. Did it again. "You can handle this. You've handled worse, you can handle this. You just have to figure out where to start."

Maybe it was a trick of the light, but he could have sworn he saw the glimmer of a tear in her eye. "Ice," she said. "We need ice. I'll be right back. You move an inch and I'll skin you alive. What's left of you to skin."

She returned with ice cubes wrapped in a dish towel. "Your nose is bleeding like somebody opened the gates to hell. Put your head between your knees. It'll help."

He did what she said, accepted the cool, damp cloth she offered, allowed her to rest the makeshift ice pack against the nape of his neck. She knelt before him, touched soft fingers to his face. "Look at you," she said, her voice rising into a register he'd never heard her use before, one that bordered on hysteria. "You're a wreck. Some of these cuts should have stitches. Why'd you come here instead of going to the hospital?"

He raised his head, wet terry cloth still pressed against his face, and said, "I don't know." He had his suspicions, but he wasn't about to admit them to her. Not when he hadn't even admitted them to himself.

Still holding the ice pack against the curve of his neck, she said brokenly, "Put your head back between your knees, sugar. Who did this to you?"

"Cheech and Chong," he said to the floor.

"'scuse me?"

"Cheech and Chong. They had boots. The kind with the pointed toes."

"Lord in heaven, you're delusional. How many fingers am I holding up?"

"I don't have a concussion." Which may or may not have been the truth, since the drive out from Southie wasn't exactly permanently fixed in his memory. He thought he remembered some of it. "Cheech and Chong are—"

"How many fingers?"

"Two. Sarah, listen to me—"

"I think you should see a doctor. I can call an ambu—"

"Sarah." With his free hand, he caught her wrist in a tight grip. "It was the same two clowns who dropped by before. This time, they didn't bother with small talk."

She sat back on her heels, and he released her wrist. "Oh, hell," she said.

He'd been right about the tears. "I can't believe they did this to you," she said. "Lord in heaven, your face. Your poor, beautiful face."

"It'll heal." He sat back up, waited until the room stopped spinning, and removed the washcloth from his nose. Was she really that fond of his face? He thought there might be some significance to that, but he couldn't quite wrap his mind far enough around the concept to figure out what it might mean. He looked at the washcloth. The bleeding had stopped, but the cloth was ruined. "I'll pay you for this," he said.

"That makes twice in one night you've been an idiot. Better you should keep your mouth shut, before you say something really stupid and I pitch you out on your ass." She got up, tossed the bloody cloth into the bathtub, opened the medicine cabinet and rummaged around. She came back with bandages and iodine and a tube of ointment, set it all down on the toilet tank, then filled the lavatory with warm water. She dunked a fresh washcloth into it, wrung it out. Kneeling between his outspread legs, she applied it to the gash at his temple.

He flinched. "I'm sorry, sugar," she said tenderly. "I have to do it."

"I'm tougher than I look."

"Oh, really? So that's what you call it. I'd be more likely to call it crazy, but what do I know?"

Her words might have been sharp, but her hands were gentle, more gentle than anything he'd ever felt as she began to wash away the blood that seemed to be everywhere. "My second ex-husband, Jackson," she said conversationally, warm wet cloth gliding along his bruised and battered skin, "he used to go out drinking and brawling all the time. There wasn't much of anything Jackie liked better than a good fight." She dipped the cloth into the sink, wrung it out again. "He'd get drunk as a skunk, and some yahoo'd look at him the wrong way, and they'd smear each other all over the barroom floor. Turn your head." He turned. "No, the other way. That's better."

She applied iodine to the gash along his cheek, and he nearly went through the roof. "Hold still," she said as she taped a butterfly bandage to his face to keep it from falling off. "We'll get through this a whole lot quicker if you do." He gritted his teeth when she parted his hair to examine the crater they'd carved in his skull. "This one's pretty bad. I'll clean it, but there's not much else I can do." Wielding the washcloth with a featherlight touch, she continued, "Seems like I was always getting called downtown to drag him home and patch him up. Believe it or not, sometimes he actually looked worse than you do right now."

"Is my nose broken?"

"Whoa. Is that a trace of vanity I see rearing its ugly head? Does it feel broken?"

"It feels like an elephant stepped on it."

"I don't think it's broken, but if it is, it'll just give your face a little more character. Take your shirt off. I want to get a look at those ribs. You need any help with it?"

It had been a long time since any woman had offered to help him undress, but he decided that under the circumstances, it would be wiser not to share that information. He unbuttoned the shirt, wincing as he tried to lift his arm to shrug it off. Without being asked, she helped him, easing it down off his shoulders and tossing it onto the floor. "How bad is it?" he said.

Her sharp intake of breath gave him his answer. "Those bastards," she said, her voice rising again. "Those low-life, rotten sons-of-bitches." He held his breath as with the gentlest of touches, she explored his rib cage, fingers testing for tender spots, up and down and side to side. The tips of her hair tickled his bare skin. To distract himself, he said, "With me, it was my mother."

"Hurts right here, does it, sugar? What about your mother?"

"She used to get shitfaced on a regular basis down at Rafferty's bar. Around midnight, I'd get a call to come down and fetch her. I'd drag her into a taxi, take her home, and pour her into bed."

"Shitfaced," she said, still prodding. "That's pretty colorful language for a priest."

"I haven't always been a priest." She prodded hard enough to send a white-hot poker of pain shooting through his chest and into his shoulder. "Christ almighty, Sarah!"

"I'm sorry. I don't think anything's broken, just bruised all to hell. Jesus, they got you all around the back, too, didn't they? Those little bastards kicked the shit out of you."

The odor of sleep still clung to her, a musky Sarah-scent that reached into his chest and plucked at his heart. Her hair smelled of some subtle floral fragrance, and her left breast, soft and unfettered beneath the Tweety Bird nightshirt, pressed agonizingly against his arm as she examined the welts on his back. Goose bumps popped out all over him, from stem to stern, and sweat gathered in his armpits. He swallowed hard and fought the desire to reach out and take.

"Right here," she said, tracing a tender spot with her fingertip. "It must hurt something awful."

"Everything hurts something awful." And some things, he realized, were worse than physical pain.

"The way they went at it, you could have kidney damage. Listen, sugar, the next time you go pee, you check to make sure there's no blood. If there is, I want you to promise to go right to the hospital."

She rocked back on her heels and looked up at him, soft curls tumbling about her shoulders, enormous eyes the color of the sky on a perfect day in June. For a single, tenuous instant, the earth stopped revolving. Inside him, something shifted, some monumental rearranging of his universe took place as he tumbled headfirst off the edge of the precipice where he'd been teetering for so long.

It was an odd time to fall in love with a woman, in the middle of a discussion about his bladder functions. But then, he'd never done anything the way other people did. And everything about tonight had been bizarre, so why should this be any different? He had no business falling in love with her, anyway. He had no business falling in love with anyone, and he didn't know whether he should take her in his arms and kiss her senseless or run for his life in the opposite direction.

"Clancy?" she said. "Are you listening to me?"

He reached out and lifted a single strand of her hair. "Yes," he said. "I'm listening."

"I think you should report this to the police."

Her hair was thick and glossy, soft between his thumb and forefinger. Not quite brown, not quite blond, but a stunning amalgamation of both. An hour ago, he'd planned to walk away from her. An hour ago, he'd planned to push Rio as far and as hard as he could. It was remarkable how a single hour could turn a man's life upside down.

He dropped the strand of hair. "I can't go to the police," he said.

"Why?" she demanded. "This isn't some silly game. This is real. These people hurt you."

He sighed, ran a hand through his own hair, and winced. Everything hurt. His head, his body, his heart. And the pain was about to get worse. "I can't go to the police," he said. "Cheech said that if I did, they'd kill Kit."

14

Clancy considered skipping Callie's recital. Although he didn't look quite like a refugee from *Night of the Living Dead*, his cuts and bruises were still noticeable enough to raise eyebrows and elicit questions. But Callie'd been so excited when he'd talked to her on the phone that he didn't have the heart to disappoint her. She was expecting him to make an appearance. Besides, a couple hours of normalcy would provide him with a much-needed distraction. So he dressed in street clothes so he wouldn't stand out from the crowd, put on a pair of fake Oakleys to cover the worst of the bruising around his eyes, and brazened it out.

He'd expected Swan Lake, so he was surprised—and delighted—to see instead a troupe of energetic, preteen flappers gleefully dancing the Charleston. Callie Adams, with her fair-haired good looks, was a standout in this group of awkward twelve-year-old girls. She'd inherited her coloring from Tom, her graceful, leggy elegance from Bess. But her smile, that heart-grabbing, ear-to-ear grin, was all her own.

"You did come!" she said the minute she saw him. "I knew you would!"

Backstage was utter chaos: a dozen young girls in sequins and beads in a multitude of colors, all of them excited, talking and giggling and bouncing around, flanked by proud parents and bored siblings, and for the most part oblivious to the shouted instructions of one extremely frazzled-looking dance instructor. "Of course I came," he said. "You didn't think I'd miss this, did you?"

He and Callie were special friends. The first time Tom had brought him home for dinner, Callie had been a freckle-faced, eight-year-old beanpole with a wide gap where her front teeth should have been. She'd talked Clancy's ear off all the way through dinner, while her more reserved older sister had satisfied her curiosity by sneaking wide-eyed glances at this strange man dressed all in black and wearing a clerical collar. After dinner, Callie had entertained him with her impressive collection of baseball cards. When he'd told her about his own, more modest collection—including a Babe Ruth that had been his most treasured possession when he was nine years old—their friendship had been cemented.

"I know I look like a geek in this outfit," she said. "I can't believe people ever really dressed like this." She did a quick pirouette, the fringed hem of the short red dress swaying merrily. With her face lit by a rosy flush and her hair curled in tiny wisps around her cheeks, he could see, somewhere beneath the tomboy he regarded with such great affection, a glimpse of the woman she would turn out to be. Tom and Bess were obviously doing something right.

"You look lovely," he said. "Like a young lady."

"Yes," Tom seconded, "you do. Although I could live without the bright red lipstick and all that gunk around your eyes."

"Oh, Daddy." Callie rolled her eyes. "You know the makeup's part of the costume."

"I know. But you're only twelve years old, baby. I'm not ready yet for you to look like a temptress."

"Twelve isn't so young. Half the girls in my class are dating already."

"Ye gods," Clancy said, clutching his heart dramatically.

"Don't worry," she said cheerfully. "There's nobody I want to go out with, anyway. I'm not like Gen, sitting on the sofa playing kissy-face with Matt. They make me want to hurl.''

Geneva, standing quietly beside her mother, promptly turned the color of a ripe tomato. With the lofty disdain that only a fourteen-year-old girl could pull off, she said coolly, "At least I don't run around in cleats and a baseball uniform, with mud all over my face.''

"I'd rather be playing baseball than draping myself all over some boy. Gross!''

"Your time will come," Clancy predicted. "No need to rush it.''

"When she's thirty," Tom said firmly. "She can date when she's thirty. Sound good to you, Father?''

"I think you're severely deluded, my friend. And that's all I'll say on the matter.''

Callie giggled, then narrowed her eyes. "Geez," she said, "what happened to your face, Father? You look like you ran headfirst into a Mack truck.''

Both Tom and Bess had looked at him oddly when they first saw him, but thanks to a lifetime of ingrained etiquette, neither had been willing to broach the topic. Count on Callie to get right to the heart of the matter. "It's nothing," he said. "Just a little work-related accident.''

"Maybe you need a new line of work," she suggested.

"It's not that serious. Just a little foolishness. Callie, sweetheart, I can't stay, but I want you to know that you did a spectacular job. I'm proud of you.''

"Thanks for coming." She gave him a quick, hard hug, a half-dozen plastic beaded rope necklaces rattling between them. "I gotta go talk to Heather now. Bye!'' And she was gone, a whirlwind of red sequins, fringe, and colored beads.

Tom and Bess exchanged glances, and Tom's mouth thinned. "What?" Clancy said.

"I'll walk you to your car," Tom said.

"That's not necessary. Bess, it was nice seeing you.''

He tried to make a graceful escape, winding his way through a noisy crowd of kids as colorful as a fruit salad, but Tom dogged his footsteps, and he reluctantly gave in to the inevitable. Outside the recital hall, the evening was balmy, with just the hint of a breeze. "Nice night," Tom said, falling into step beside him.

"Beautiful," he agreed.

Car doors slammed and engines revved as the parking lot rapidly emptied. "Do you intend to tell me," Tom said, "or am I going to have to drag it out of you?"

Clancy tucked his hands into his pockets. "What?"

"Stop being obtuse. What's this baloney about a work-related accident?"

"It's nothing." They paused to let a late-model gas-guzzler pull out from its parking space in front of them. "Like I told Callie, it was just—"

"Foolishness. Yes, I heard. Forgive me for being blunt, Clancy, but it's pretty obvious that you didn't walk into a wall. More likely somebody's fist." The gas-guzzler accelerated and pulled away, and they resumed walking. "Which leads to an obvious question—who would beat up a priest? And why?"

They reached his Saturn, and Clancy leaned casually against the driver's door with his arms folded in front of him. "I stuck my nose someplace where it wasn't wanted, and got a little too close for somebody's comfort."

"And they did this to you?" Tom said incredulously. "Good God! And if I know you at all, I imagine you conveniently forgot to call the police."

"I don't need any police. I can handle this on my own."

"I can see that. The evidence on your face makes it painfully obvious. Who did this to you?"

He studied his thumbnail. "I'd rather not say. These people are mean. And serious. All I'm willing to tell you is that it's connected with the missing girl I'm looking for."

"Kit," Tom said. "The girl on the flyer."

Clancy nodded. "If you hear anything," he said, "anything at all, bring it to me. Stay as far away from it as you can get. I don't want to drag you, or your family—" he shot a quick glance at the recital hall "—into it."

Tom ran a hand through his hair. "I don't like this. I don't like it at all. Is there anything I can do?"

"Just keep on doing what you do best. Win the election." He patted Tom's shoulder and turned to unlock his car door. "We need more people like you in Washington." He paused with the door open. "Tougher anticrime legislation may not be the solution," he said, "but it certainly can't hurt. G'night."

He leaned back in his chair, stretched out his legs, and thumbed listlessly through a month-old copy of *The Pilot*, the official publication of the Boston Archdiocese. He'd been waiting nearly an hour, and there were a half-dozen things he should be doing elsewhere. But when the Archbishop of Boston requested an audience with one of his priests, there was only one possible response. So here he sat, killing time reading outdated magazines and trying not to think about the hundred and one priorities waiting for him back in the real world.

"Father Donovan?"

He glanced in the direction of Bishop Halloran's bulldog of a secretary, who had initially gaped at his appearance, then spent the last hour avoiding his eyes. "You can go in now," she said stiffly.

"Thank you, Dora." He dropped the newspaper, crossed the room and knocked on the door to the inner sanctum.

"Come in," said a gravelly voice from the other side.

Clancy opened the door and stepped inside the bishop's private office. "Your Excellency," he said.

"Father. Close the door behind you."

In his younger days, Bishop Gerald Halloran had been solid and muscular. But the intervening years, combined with a three-éclair-a-day addiction, had turned that brawny build to pudgy. His close-cropped steel-gray hair perfectly matched the eyes that studied Clancy now like an insect under a microscope. "Let's take a look at you," he said.

Clancy clasped his hands in front of him and silently, grudgingly, allowed his bishop to examine the healing cuts, the bruises, the still swollen nose. "From what I've heard," the bishop said finally, "I'd thought it would be even worse than it is. What happened?"

"I'd rather not say."

"You do realize this kind of thing should be reported to the proper authorities?"

Clancy cleared his throat. With his eyes focused on a point beyond the bishop's head, he said, "What kind of thing?"

Bishop Halloran sighed. "Sit," he said. "I don't approve, and we'll discuss this at some point, but I didn't call you in here today to ask who used you for a punching bag. I have something else on my mind."

Surprised, Clancy sat, crossed his ankles, and waited.

The bishop clasped his hands on the desk in front of him. "I had a call yesterday from an old friend, Bishop Livingston of the Detroit Archdiocese. One of his parishes is about to lose its priest. Father Brezinski is seventy-two years old and he's just been diagnosed with prostate cancer. He's been there for forty-two years, and his retirement has been a shock to the diocese. They're hoping to find a permanent replacement as quickly as possible. It's a very needy inner-city parish, with all the accompanying joys and headaches. But a challenging opportunity for the right individual." He paused, those gray eyes studying Clancy keenly. "Bishop Livingston is looking for somebody young and vital, somebody a little brash, somebody who's tough enough and experienced enough to stand up to the teenage gangs who run the neigh-

238   *Laurie Breton*

borhood. He asked if I knew anybody who fit that description.''

"And you thought immediately of me."

"I thought immediately of you. Although, looking at you now—" the bishop leaned back in his chair, a pained expression on his face "—I suspect you may be guilty of turning the other cheek a bit too far. Is Detroit anything you might be interested in?"

Grimly, he said, "Do I have a choice? Or is this your way of telling me I'm your biggest headache and you'd just as soon pass me on to somebody else?"

A small smile played about the bishop's mouth. "Yes and yes," he said. "Certainly, I think you're a headache. The truth is, you've been a thorn in my side since the day you were ordained. But you're still here at Saint Bart's because you have a gift, a gift valuable enough that I've managed thus far to overlook your failings."

Clancy discreetly adjusted the leg of his trousers. "A gift," he said cautiously.

"You have a way with people, Clancy. You may be a little too outspoken, a little too radical, a little too bullish. Blind obedience isn't one of your strong points. But there's an innate goodness to you, and people respond to that. Your parishioners, young and old, love you. Church attendance has doubled in the four years you've been here." The bishop tapped his fingers idly against the desk. "And despite your full-speed-ahead-and-damn-the-torpedoes manner—or perhaps because of it—you manage to get things done quickly and effectively. I may not always agree with you." The bishop actually allowed himself a genuine smile, the first one Clancy had ever seen from the man. "But I admire you. I think you'd be perfect for Detroit, but it's your choice. And as much as it pains me to say this, if you should choose to leave, the Archdiocese of Boston would sorely regret the loss."

Stunned, he sat back in his chair and said, "Thank you, Your Excellency."

The bishop waved his hand, as though embarrassed by his admission. "So what do you think? Are you at all interested?"

He thought about the ennui he'd experienced over the last year, the boredom that had been relieved only by his search for Kit Connelly. Once Kit was found, he'd be left hanging once again. Maybe it was time to move on. It excited him, the thought of pulling together an ailing parish, of stretching out a hand to those inner-city gang members who so badly needed God in their lives. He would thrive on the challenge. And after being in the hands of an aging, old-school priest for so many years, the Detroit parish undoubtedly needed new blood, needed somebody with his expertise and his talents.

But what about his own parish? What about the people who'd come to depend on him? He had responsibilities he didn't take lightly, responsibilities not only to the members of his congregation, but to the community at large. Not to mention lifelong friendships that would be difficult to leave behind.

And then, of course, there was Sarah.

"I'll need time to think it over," he said. "It's a difficult decision."

"I understand." The bishop paused. "Correct me if I'm wrong, Father, but I've sensed, over the last year or so, that you've been a bit lost. Afloat."

"That would be an accurate assessment."

"You can come to me with your problems, you know. I'm really not the curmudgeon you think I am. I may be old, but not so old I don't remember the difficulties that come with those first few years of priesthood."

"Thank you, Your Excellency. I'll get back to you about Detroit after the retreat."

His mind churned as he drove back to South Boston. So much to process, so many people to consider. This wasn't just about him. He impacted so many lives, had so many commitments. So many friends he would have to leave behind. Not to mention a woman who had become his greatest source of both joy and pain, a woman who shouldn't even figure into the equation. On a whim, he pulled onto M Street and found a parking spot. He had an hour free before the neighborhood boys would descend on him for basketball practice. He'd already lost most of his afternoon. He might as well blow the rest of it.

He knocked on Fiona's screen door, opened it and stuck his head in. "Anybody home?"

Fiona Rafferty bustled into the kitchen, wearing a flowing caftan of teal and purple that clashed screamingly with her bottle-orange hair. "If you're looking for Jamal," she said, "he's not here. He's down at the pub with Hugh."

"That's all right. It's you I came to see."

"That's some pretty face you have there," she said. "Run into a door, did you?"

Grimly, he said, "Something like that."

She eyed him long and hard. "How about a cuppa joe?"

He stepped inside and silently closed the door behind him. On the stove, in a dented aluminum kettle that was a dead ringer for the one she'd been cooking out of when he was a kid, something smelled heavenly. He edged nearer as she pulled a mug from the cupboard and filled it with coffee. He accepted it with a brief nod of thanks, sipped, then said casually, "I haven't seen you at Mass lately."

Fiona snorted. "And you're not likely to see me until the Church reverses some of its Medieval thinking and realizes this is the twenty-first century." She returned the coffeepot to its spot on the sideboard and studied him with shrewd eyes. "You're too damn thin. Sit down. I'll fix you a bowl of stew."

He knew better than to argue. Men had fought wars over lesser things than Fiona Rafferty's stew. He pulled out a chair and sat at the worn wooden table as Fiona bustled about the kitchen. She plunked a plate of stew in front of him, steamy and fragrant and thick enough to eat with a fork. He picked up his fork and dug in, suddenly ravenous. From somewhere, she produced a crock of butter, a jar of jam, and a huge slab of homemade bread, followed it up with a tall glass of cold milk—the real thing, none of this 2% crap for Fiona Rafferty. He wondered, fleetingly, if his cholesterol level would manage to survive her, and then he forgot to wonder because the food was so good.

She poured herself a cup of coffee and sat down across from him. Blood-red nails ticking rhythmically against the table, she watched him devour the plate of food. When he was done, she got up and wordlessly refilled his plate from the kettle on the stove, then set it back down in front of him.

"If it weren't for you," he said, "I never would have survived childhood. I would have starved to death."

"You turned out to be a good man, Clancy Donovan. No thanks to that drunken fool who called herself your mother."

He cut off a slice of bread and slathered it with butter. Mildly, he said, "It's not nice to speak ill of the dead when they're not here to defend themselves."

"I'm no hypocrite. I'd say it to her face if she was standing here."

"Besides—" he spooned strawberry jam onto the slice of bread and folded it in two "—I've made peace with my mother. She may have been a pathetic excuse for a parent, but she loved me."

"Yes. She did. That's the only thing that kept me from telling her what I thought of her while she was still alive."

"Water under the bridge, Fiona."

"It's a credit to you that you turned out okay in spite of her. So what are you doing here, Father Donovan, besides mooching a meal and prodding me about missing a few Sunday mornings at Saint Bart's?''

He took a huge bite of bread and chewed thoughtfully. Swallowed and said, ''You and Hugh. You've been married for how long now?''

Fiona raised an eyebrow. ''Thirty-nine years.''

''Thirty-nine years. That's amazing. Can I ask you something? Something really personal?''

''Shoot.''

He lofted a forkful of stew, paused with it in midair. ''When you met him all those years ago…how did you know he was the one?''

''Easy,'' she said as he chewed. ''He was the best-looking boy in school.''

''But that was initial attraction, right? Chemistry. There has to be more to it than sex.''

''Of course there's more to it than sex. There's friendship, and respect, and trust. There's feeling right together, feeling as though the two of you as a couple are somehow more than just the sum of one plus one. But the sex is always there. It's always part of the equation. You can't separate it from the rest.''

''But—'' he swallowed and gestured with his fork ''—that kind of thing doesn't last. What happens when it's gone? What holds two people together for thirty-nine years once the sexual attraction wears off?''

Her booming laughter surprised him. ''Oh, sweetie,'' she said, ''I don't mean to laugh at you, but you are so young. When do you think it disappears? At forty? Fifty-five? Sixty-seven?''

''I suppose I never really thought about it. I just assumed—''

''You assumed wrong. Oh, sure, you get older, the kids come along and drive you crazy, life intrudes. You get aches and pains where you never had them before, gain a few pounds, lose a little hair. Sometimes you're so tired that sleep is more important than sex. But the feelings don't go away. Ask any couple who're still together, still in love, after twenty, thirty-five, even fifty years. They'll tell you they're as attracted to each other as they were at the beginning. Time doesn't change that. I look at Hugh and still see the strapping young boy I married almost forty years ago.''

It was an amazing revelation. He'd never thought of older people as sexual beings. Was it a naiveté he hadn't realized he possessed, or simply the result of too many years spent in the Church? Whatever the reason, he'd somehow automatically presumed the sexual arena to be the sole property of the young.

''All right,'' she said. ''I've answered your questions. Now it's my turn. Why do you want to know these things?''

He set down his fork, the meal forgotten, and wiped his mouth on the napkin she'd provided. ''You're the closest thing I have to a mother,'' he said. ''Fiona…I'm in trouble.''

''Trouble?'' She leaned on both elbows over the table. ''What kind of trouble?''

''The worst kind a priest can get into, I'm afraid. I've met a woman. Somehow, I've managed to fall in love with her.''

She picked up a slice of bread, buttered it, and took a bite. ''That doesn't sound so terrible to me.''

''It's bad enough. You have to understand, it's not just about sex. If it was, I'm sure there are any number of ladies in my flock who'd be more than willing to help me out with my little dilemma.''

Her mouth thinned. ''And I bet I could name most of them without even having to think about it.''

''But it's more than that. When she walks into a room, the rest of the world disappears, and it's just the two of us. We could be standing in the middle of Copley Square at high noon, and there'd be just Sarah.''

''That's her name? Sarah?''

He picked up his coffee cup, took a sip. "Sarah Connelly," he said, setting it back down. "You met her at the christening."

"Josie's Sarah? The one with the missing niece?"

"Yes. I've been helping her, and—" he paused, sighed, ran his fingers through his hair "—it's senseless to lie and say it took me by surprise. I saw it coming miles away, like a loaded freight train. I had plenty of opportunity to step aside and avoid the collision. Instead, I just stood there on the tracks and waited for it to mow me over."

"You have good taste, I'll give you that. I liked her. She's not a wimp. I can't stand wimpy women. I assume this is a mutual thing?"

He thought about the tenderness she'd displayed the night he came to her, bruised and beaten, the night he'd looked into those blue eyes and fallen head over heels in love. "I'm quite sure it is," he said. "And I have no idea what to do."

"Don't ask me for advice unless you're looking for brutal honesty."

In spite of his misery, he smiled. "If I hadn't wanted brutal honesty, I wouldn't have come to you."

She got up from her chair, fetched the coffeepot. "Fine," she said, refilling first his cup, then hers. "Here's what I think." She returned the coffeepot to its spot and sat back down at the table. "When Meg died, you packed your heart in a box, locked it up, and put it on a shelf way in the back of the closet, in the dark, where you could pretend it didn't exist." She stirred sugar into her coffee, set down her spoon. "But it couldn't stay there forever. You're a warm and caring man. That's what makes you so successful as a priest. It was inevitable that sooner or later, that warm and caring man would find somebody special to care for."

"But I'm not allowed to have somebody special to care for."

"Sweetheart, do you really think you're the first priest to

have a woman on the side? Men weren't designed for celibacy. It's the most ridiculous notion I've ever heard."

"But what—"

"Shut up. I'm not done yet. I think it's a disgrace for the Catholic Church to take a beautiful young man like you, strong and healthy, in the prime of his life, with all that testosterone racing through his veins, and turn him into a eunuch. They're asking you to deny who and what you are. It's unnatural."

"I can't change the Church, Fiona. It's been that way since the twelfth century."

"Why should you have to choose between serving God and being with the woman you love? Why can't you have both? It doesn't make sense."

"Because I made a promise to the Church. I don't take it lightly."

"Of course you don't. You're a man of integrity. But integrity won't take you far on a cold winter night." She leaned back in her chair and studied his face. "You're thirty-five years old, Clancy. You're looking at the possibility of another forty or fifty years on this planet. Maybe even longer. That's a long time to be alone."

"That doesn't make it right."

"Just because the Church says so doesn't make it wrong, either. If I were you, I'd think hard before I let this chance slip away."

"Moral ambiguity," he said, more to himself than to her. "You honestly don't believe what I'm feeling for her is wrong?"

"There's too damn little love in this world. That's what I think is wrong. And we all deserve happiness. But this is a decision you have to make for yourself. You and Sarah together, since it impacts both of your lives. As much as I love you, this isn't something I can help you with."

He considered her words. "It gets worse," he said. "An hour ago, the bishop offered me a transfer. To Detroit."

"Oh, Lord. You're not going to take it, are you?"

He picked up his coffee cup, took a sip. And sighed. "I'm afraid I may not have a choice."

"I heard a rumor."

Sarah looked up from the invoices she'd been working on, lifted her reading glasses, and leveled a glance at Josie. "What kind of rumor?"

Josie carefully unwrapped a delicate blown-glass angel and placed it on the display shelf behind the counter. "I heard you were seen a few nights ago in a very exclusive restaurant, having a romantic dinner with a sinfully handsome man—" Josie glanced up from her work, pinned Sarah with her gaze "—who just happened to be wearing a clerical collar."

Sarah's mouth thinned, and she returned to her invoices. "It was nothing."

"My source tells me it didn't look like nothing."

"People talk too much," she said, without looking up. "They should find something useful to do."

"Is there something going on that I should know about?"

"No."

"Because, you know, I feel at least somewhat responsible. I'm the one who introduced you in the first place. I'm the one who dragged you to the christening. From which you left, I might add, with Clancy."

"My car died. I couldn't exactly walk home."

"I've seen the two of you together, and it seems to me there's some pretty heavy chemistry going on there. If I inadvertently started something, I'd really like to know, because—"

"Damn it, Josie!" She slammed her pen down on the stack of invoices. "The man is a priest. A priest! Black suit, white collar, no sex. Maybe with all that heavy chemistry, we can spend every Saturday night for the next forty years playing canasta together!''

Josie calmly unwrapped a second figurine. "So," she said with deliberate nonchalance, "you admit there's something going on between you."

"No! Goddamn it." She gave up on the invoices, ran a hand through her tangled hair. "Oh, hell. To tell you the truth, Jose, I really don't know what's going on."

"Aw, honey." Josie set aside the box of figurines and sat down beside her. "Want to talk about it?"

"It's such a mixed-up mess. This thing with Kit is tearing me apart. I'm so afraid of losing her." She rubbed absently at her temple, where a headache was beginning to take root. "Lately," she said, "I have more mood swings than Joan Crawford. This thing with Clancy...at first, it was just that he was the only person I could turn to. I could call him at any time of the day or night, and he'd always listen, even when I was being a damn fool. But, then—'' She paused, gazed absently at a customer who was browsing the self-help section. "But then, it started being about more than that. For me, anyway. Maybe it's just pheromones. Or the thrill of falling for a man who's the ultimate in forbidden fruit. I know it'll never go any further than fantasy. He's married to the Catholic Church. End of story." She sighed, decided she might as well pour out the rest of the god-awful truth. "The other night, at dinner, I pretty much laid it out in front of him."

The sympathy in Josie's eyes gave her courage to continue. "He said something about wanting to impress me, and I told him if I wasn't already impressed, I wouldn't be sitting there." She shook her head, still unable to believe those words had come from her own mouth. "When I realized what I'd said, and how it sounded, I nearly died of mortification."

Josie blew out a hard breath between her lips. "I can see where that could be potentially embarrassing."

"Embarrassing? Sugar, I wanted the floor to open and swallow me up, right then and there."

"Can I ask a stupid question? If I'm prying, feel free to slug me."

"Go ahead. Ask."

"Are you on any kind of birth control?"

"Jesus, Josie, I can't believe you said that! The man is a priest. There must be some kind of sacrilege in even thinking it."

"He's also a man, my friend, and you're a woman, and there's a strong attraction between you. You need to protect yourself, just in case."

"There won't be any 'in case' because nothing's going to happen between us."

"Don't be an idiot. You do remember high school? Back when girls used to say—" she scrunched up her face in an expression of mock horror, and put on a squeaky falsetto voice "But if I use birth control, then it'll be like I'm *planning* to have sex." In her own voice, she added, "I never did quite understand that approach. Shame versus protection, with shame winning by a mile."

"Josie…"

"Let me put it another way. Would you rather be the paramour of our favorite parish priest, or the mother of his child?"

Sarah's headache took an unexpected turn for the worse. "I hope you're happy, Jose. After that remark, God will strike us both dead for sure."

Josie patted her arm. "You're in the clear, hon. You're not Catholic." She got up, rummaged around the shelf below the cash register, found a pen and a piece of paper. "Here's the name and phone number of my ob/gyn. He's a peach. Give him a call, tell the receptionist I sent you. She'll squeeze you in." Josie held out the slip of paper.

Sarah hesitated, her stomach turned upside down by the

image of what Josie was suggesting. She already came close to detonating if the good Father so much as touched her arm. What would happen if he ever touched her more intimately?

Suddenly, she was damp everywhere. Under her arms. Beneath her breasts. Between her legs. Panic took over as she stared at temptation in the form of a tiny scrap of paper that amounted to a license to sin. "I can't," she said. "Really, Jose. If I took that, it would be—no. I'm not ready to think about that yet." She quickly corrected herself. "Ever."

"You, my friend, are in deep, deep denial."

"And that's exactly where I'm planning to stay. But I appreciate the offer. Really."

"If you change your mind, it'll be right here." Josie punched a button on the cash register and the drawer opened. She lifted the change tray and tucked the paper beneath.

Sarah blew out a hard breath. "Can I ask you something? Something I've been wondering about?"

"Sure. Anything you want to know. My bra size? I.Q.? The names of the last three men I slept with?"

"Very funny. I'm serious, Josie. Who's Meg?"

Josie's expressive face went suddenly, carefully blank. "Meg?" she said. "Where'd you hear that name?"

"He has a tattoo. On his arm." At Josie's raised eyebrow, she felt a flush climb her face. "Will you stop it? Lord almighty, you have such a gutter mind! I happened to see it under purely innocent circumstances. I just thought it was a little odd, for a priest to have a tattoo of a woman's name on his arm."

"I didn't know he had a tattoo."

"It's on his left bicep. A heart with her name inside."

"I see. And he hasn't mentioned Meg to you?"

"No. Is there some reason he should? Is she some deep, dark secret?"

"It's no secret. If you ask around long enough, sooner or

later somebody will tell you the whole sordid story. But it won't be me.''

''What the hell do you mean, it won't be you?''

Josie returned her attention to the box of figurines she was setting on display. ''It's not up to me to tell you.'' She reached into the box and met Sarah's glance, and the sadness in her eyes made Sarah clamp her mouth abruptly shut. ''When he's ready to tell you about Meg, he will.''

''So that's it?''

''That's it.'' Josie unwrapped a blue dolphin figurine and set it on the shelf. ''You know, when I said you needed to get out and meet men—'' she glanced up, the sadness in her eyes replaced by pure deviltry ''—this wasn't quite what I had in mind.''

The phone rang, and Sarah reached to answer it. ''Book-mark.''

At the other end, there was no response, just the crackling of an open line. ''Hello?'' she said. ''Is anybody there?''

And a small, hesitant voice said, ''Aunt Sarah?''

15

The boys were rowdy today, loaded with after-school energy they needed to burn off one way or another. Clancy assigned them ten laps around the perimeter of the church parking lot and thanked the good Lord he did this only once a week. At thirty-five, he hadn't started slowing down yet, but keeping up with a dozen rambunctious thirteen- and fourteen-year-old boys placed demands on his body that it hadn't seen in a long time. That, combined with the aftereffects of his encounter with Rio's henchmen, convinced him he'd seen better days.

He blew his whistle to gather the kids back together and set them to work practicing jump shots and defensive maneuvers. Most of the boys were still pretty shaky, but he wasn't trying to make NBA stars out of them. He did this for other reasons: to build their self-esteem, to help them develop camaraderie, to keep them off the streets and away from the temptations presented by drugs and gang membership. Most of their families belonged to his parish, but any kid who needed a little guidance was welcome. He never turned away anybody in need.

After they'd warmed up, he separated them into two teams and put them through a rigorous practice session. The boys were loud and boisterous and they didn't always follow the rules, but their enthusiasm was infectious. By the time they'd finished a full game, he was as much into it as the kids were. He played for one team and then the other—taking caution with his still painful ribs—gave them pointers, demonstrated proper court behavior, and kindly but firmly corrected their mistakes.

After a quick break, he stood Jimmy Muñoz in front of the basket and lined him up to demonstrate a proper free throw while the rest of the crew stood by snickering and poking at each other. The tallest of this motley little group, Jimmy also happened to be the best player, and the boy had the makings of a leader, if he didn't fall on the wrong side of the law and screw up his life before it even got started.

"All right," Clancy told them. "I want you to watch Jimmy and see what—" He glanced up, over Jimmy's head, and everything went still inside him. While the boys continued to laugh and shove and trade insults, he stood frozen, the basketball still in his hands. For an instant, he thought he'd imagined her, leaning against the door of the Mustang and watching him while the flirtatious sun teased golden highlights from her hair. Then a passing breeze lifted a strand of that hair, and with a fluid motion, she tossed it away from her face.

Sarah.

His knees buckled, and his hands, still holding the basketball, trembled like a junkie's. She looked fresh and cool and together, while he was clad in the ratty gray Harvard sweatshirt he only wore for basketball practice. His hair was damp and mussed, he was sticky from two hours of running and jumping and dribbling, and he could feel grit clinging to him, under his arms and in the folds of his skin between neck and shoulder. He probably smelled like the hind end of a horse.

He willed his hands to stop trembling. This was absurd. He was a grown man, shaking like a kid who'd never seen a woman before. And she was—

Exquisite. Magnificent. Perfect in every way.

"Hey, Father, you grow roots or what?"

He returned to reality, to eleven scruffy boys who studied him with varying levels of curiosity. He glanced at his watch, surprised to see it was nearly five-thirty. He tossed the basketball to Jimmy. "Practice is over for today. Make sure the ball goes back in the storage closet when you're done with it." On shaky legs, he began walking across cracked and pitted asphalt to where Sarah waited.

She stepped away from the car and stood in the late-afternoon sunshine watching him approach. There was something in her face he couldn't decipher. "Everything okay?" he said.

"I tried to get you on your cell phone, but you didn't answer. She called me, Clancy."

Temporarily lost in the play of light and shadow in her hair, it took him a moment to catch up. "Who called you?"

"Kit. She called me. About a half hour ago." Tears welled up in those blue eyes. "Damn it," she said.

He reached out and caught her by the arm, guided her back against the fender of the car. "Take a deep breath," he said.

She took a breath, held it, took another. "I'm sorry," she said.

"There's nothing to be sorry for. What did she say?"

She took another hard, shuddering breath. "That she wanted to come home. That he won't let her." There was a mixture of fury and sorrow in her eyes. "She's a prisoner, Clancy. He keeps her locked in. This is the first time she's had an opportunity to make contact with anyone. He left his cell phone out while he was in the shower, and she used it. I don't know what to do."

"First of all, you need to calm down."

She nodded agreement, and he awkwardly rested a hand on her shoulder and waited for her to gain control. From the corner of his eye, he saw several of the boys still on the basketball court watching them with interest. He glanced over at the rectory. He thought about privacy, about propriety, about smelling like something that had crawled up out of the sewer.

About the wrath of God raining down on his head.

"Come inside," he said. "I'll make us a cup of tea."

Inside the rectory, it was cool and dark. They paused just inside the door, and Sarah glanced around the foyer, paneled in a rich mahogany and decorated in an ornate Victorian style in keeping with the design of the church. "This is where you live?" she said.

"Actually, this is the public area of the rectory. My private quarters are upstairs." He considered and immediately vetoed the possibility of entertaining a female guest in his monastic little second-floor suite. There were times and situations when it was acceptable to push the boundaries. This wasn't one of them. "I'm sorry," he said. "I can't take you up there."

Instead, he led her into the front parlor, which was furnished with antiques upholstered in rich brocades and polished to a righteous gleam. Abby Sullivan, the rectory housekeeper, took to heart the truism that cleanliness was next to godliness. Religious artifacts were scattered about the room: a simple candelabra on the mantel, a crucifix above it. A photograph of the Pope. On a long inner wall, a reproduction of da Vinci's *The Last Supper*. "Sit," he said, and she perched on the edge of a hard Victorian sofa. "Are you all right?"

"I'll be okay. It was just such a shock, hearing her voice after all this time. I sort of went to pieces."

And came running to you.

She didn't say the words, but he heard them just the same. He sat down beside her on the sofa, leaving a safe margin of space between them. "How did she sound?"

"Young. Scared. Regretful. I tried to reassure her. I told her to hold on, that we were coming for her, that we wouldn't give up until we found her. I'm not sure how much of an impression I made. We didn't have long to talk.''

''She's young and smart and resilient.'' He took Sarah's hand in his and squeezed it gently. ''I'm sure she was comforted by what you had to say.''

''Lord.'' She took a deep, shuddery breath. ''I thought for sure I was tougher than this.''

''You're rattled. It's understandable.'' He squeezed her hand again, then dropped it. ''What else did she tell you? Anything at all that will help us?''

Sarah ran her hands over her face. ''Not really. She's in a warehouse somewhere that's been converted into apartments. Or at least an apartment. He has a friend named Gonzales who wears too much gold jewelry. She heard Rio tell him to take care of you. Sound familiar?''

''Gonzales,'' he said thoughtfully, remembering a pair of shiny black boots with pointed toes. ''If we can find him, maybe he'll lead us to that pot of gold at the end of the rainbow. I wouldn't mind seeing him go down right along with Rio.''

''Kit says she's been to his house. It's in a crummy neighborhood out near the airport.''

''East Boston. That should be easy enough. There can't be more than a couple hundred Gonzales families in East Boston.''

''Not much to go on, is it?''

''It's more than we had an hour ago.'' He thought longingly of a hot shower to wash off the *eau de basketball* that clung to him, but came to the reluctant conclusion that at this particular moment, comfort was a higher priority than cleanliness. ''Why don't we go find that tea now?'' he said.

She followed him to the rectory kitchen, a place where he spent very little time. His private quarters had a kitchenette that was more than sufficient for his needs, and it took him a few minutes of searching before he located the tea bags and a pair of cups. He set them on the marble countertop beside the gargantuan old commercial gas range, filled the teakettle and put it on a front burner, and turned the knob.

Nothing happened. Behind him, Sarah said, "I think you need to light the pilot."

He swiveled around, puzzled. "The pilot?"

"You really don't know much about cooking, do you, Father?"

He shrugged, unembarrassed. "You can't say I didn't warn you. Besides, I have other, much more significant qualities."

"Uh-huh. Find me a match." She knelt and opened the massive double oven doors. He stepped back, more than willing to let her take over. "My momma used to cook on one of these things," she said from inside the oven, "until Daddy finally decided it was time to enter the twentieth century." He handed her a wooden match from the box on the sideboard. She struck it, and he heard a poof. Retreating from the oven's cavernous interior, she brushed her hands together and stood back up. "There," she said. "Now you can run the stovetop."

"Slick maneuver," he said. "You'll have to show it to me sometime."

"I don't know, sugar. You're really good at that helpless little boy thing. I bet it goes over big with the ladies in your congregation." She paused, took a deep breath, then said briskly, "So what do we do now?"

He lit the burner, adjusted the placement of the teakettle, killed a little time waiting for it to start heating. "Now," he said, "I call Paoletti. Run Gonzales by him and see if he rings any bells."

She moved away from him, crossed the room to the window, stood looking out while she absently ran a hand back and forth along the smooth marble countertop that Abby kept spic and span clean. "Gonzales told you not to go to the police," she said.

Beside him, the kettle whistled. He busied himself pouring hot water over tea bags, then carried one of the cups across the room and handed it to her. "Careful," he warned. "It's hot."

She took it from him without speaking, and went back to gazing out the window. He returned to the stove, where he swished his own tea bag around in the hot water. To the back of her head, he said, "I'm just going to do a little discreet checking. Gonzales won't ever know."

She turned away from the window. "I'm afraid," she said. "Don't you understand? Bone-deep afraid. For Kit, and for you." Her voice broke. "They've come after you once. What's to stop them from doing it again?"

The hand that held the teacup trembled, and it was that, more than anything, that got to him. She was a strong woman, and there was nothing so heartbreaking as watching a strong woman disintegrate. He crossed the room, took the teacup out of her hand, and set it on the counter.

And took her in his arms.

It was an idiotic thing to do, but then, he'd been acting like an idiot since the day they met. Heedless of his disheveled state, he held her hard against him, tuning out the instantaneous protest from his bruised ribs. Warm. She felt so warm. Warm and soft and pliable. He buried his face in her hair, inhaled the faintly floral scent of her shampoo, and felt the rapid, steady rhythm of her heart.

With a sigh, she settled into him. Was it a sigh of contentment, or one of resignation? He couldn't tell. Breathing hard, he reminded himself that this was comfort. Nothing more, despite the rapacious urgings of his body. He lowered his head and brushed his cheek against hers. Her skin was like silk. He slid a hand up her smooth, slender neck, cupped it beneath the heavy fall of hair. With the pad of his thumb, he traced the line of her jaw, the distinct bow of her upper lip.

She raised her head. Those blue eyes met his, and all the breath left his body. He knew it was a cliché, but he could have sworn that for an instant, the earth stopped revolving. His stomach turned inside out, and his heart hammered erratically against his ribs. His gaze still locked with hers, he took a sharp, shallow breath and leaned imperceptibly closer—

And remembered, belatedly, who and where and what he was.

He froze, stricken by what he'd done, by what he'd nearly done, by what he wanted, more than anything, to do. Her eyes went suddenly soft and bruised, the eyes of a wounded doe. A pink tinge crept up her cheeks, and she pulled away.

He released her instantly, but the damage was already done. "I have to leave," she said, avoiding his eyes. "Kit might call again, and I have so much to do tonight, I'll never get it all done. I'll be up until midnight if I don't get started. Thank you for the tea."

"Sarah," he said, "don't."

She turned on him, the pain he'd caused imbuing her words with a harshness she probably wasn't even aware of. "Leave me alone, Clancy! This situation is embarrassing enough without you making it worse. I'd like to leave with some of my dignity still intact."

Her words were like a slap to the face. He didn't try to stop her. Instead, he stood clutching the cool, hard edge of the marble countertop, trying to ease the ache in his gut, trying to figure out how he'd managed to get himself into this mess. Wondering how he was supposed to cope now that he'd stepped over the invisible boundary they'd drawn in the sand between them. She was hurt. And furious. He'd seen the fury smoldering in her eyes, just beneath that outer layer of pain. He couldn't blame her for being angry. He had no business holding her, no business leading her on. No business feeling as though he would expire without her touch. It would serve him right if she simply walked out of his life the same way she'd walked into it, a whirlwind of blue eyes and golden hair, soft Southern vowels and that sweet essence that was simply Sarah.

He wouldn't blame her if she did. He just wasn't sure he had the strength to bear it.

The rectory door thudded behind her, and he waited for the sound of her car engine, waited for her to drive away, out of his life, forever. But all he heard was the soft ticking of the kitchen clock. After what seemed an eternity, there was a brisk knock on the door. He took a deep breath, ran a shaky hand through his hair, and went to answer it.

She was standing on the steps, her spine ramrod straight, her chin high in the air. "May I use your phone?" she said, as though they were strangers, as though he hadn't just held her in his arms and nearly handed his soul to the devil for her.

"Why?" he said. He glanced past her, at the Mustang, still sitting where she'd left it earlier. "Is there a problem?"

"It's my car," she said wearily. "The son of a dog won't start."

It took nearly two hours for the tow truck to arrive, two hours of pacing and stewing and avoiding him as much as was humanly possible. He tried to make amends, tried to be a gracious host. He offered her coffee, tea, hot cocoa. Scotch. A peanut butter and jelly sandwich. Take-out pizza. She refused them all, too angry and hurt and humiliated to accept anything from him, ever again. Eventually he gave up and left her to brood alone while he took a shower and dressed in clothes that didn't smell like a stale locker room.

By the time the tow truck got there, it was seven-thirty, and it had started to rain. For the second time in a matter of weeks, she stood by the window and watched the Mustang being towed away. Tomorrow, she would call the repair shop and make them wish they'd never heard her name. In the meantime, she had a more immediate dilemma.

"May I use your phone again?" she said stiffly. "I need to call a taxi."

"A taxi?" He raised those thick, dark eyebrows in disbelief. "Do you have any idea how much it would cost you to take a taxi from South Boston to Revere? Don't be ridiculous. I'll drive you home."

"That won't be necessary. I'll just take the T. If you'd be so kind as to point me in the right direction?"

"Stop being an ass. I said I'd drive you home."

Her mouth fell open. She tried to formulate a snotty retort, but the words wouldn't come, probably because he was right. She was being an ass. "Fine," she said. "Thank you."

At some point during that endless, silent ride, her anger dissipated, leaving in its place an emptiness that was somehow worse than the anger. Sarah couldn't look at him, couldn't speak to him, for fear she'd dissolve into tears. She couldn't understand why, for she wasn't the kind of woman who wept and wailed and grieved for things that might have been. She was the straightforward, solid kind of woman, the kind who made her decisions and burned her bridges and lived with the consequences of her actions. She'd made a mistake getting involved with Clancy Donovan. Goodlooking, charismatic men had always been her downfall. It was time to admit the truth, once again drag herself up by the bootstraps, and move on with her life. So why couldn't she do it?

The tension between them was so thick she could have sliced it with a knife. He pulled the car into her driveway and turned off the headlights. Rain pattered gently against the roof, and the windshield wipers slapped back and forth with a hypnotic rhythm while they sat, two statues frozen in time and place.

"The way I see it," he said into the darkness, "we have

two options. We can go on pretending this isn't happening, or we can bring it out into the open and try to figure out what the hell we're supposed to do about it.''

On the radio, Bob Seger's raspy voice sang quietly of love and loss. ''There isn't anything we can do about it,'' she said. ''What we're feeling for each other...what we're thinking...it's an absolute impossibility.''

Metal tinkled against metal as he toyed with the keys that dangled from the ignition. ''There are things I'd like to say to you. But I'm not supposed to even think such things, let alone speak them out loud to a woman.''

She focused her attention on the sweep of the wipers for fear that she'd implode if she looked at him. ''What things?'' she said.

''If the situation were different...I'd tell you that I dream about you at night. Vivid, erotic dreams. That I wake up in a sweat with my fists clenched and the smell of you still in my head. I'd tell you I want to lie naked with you, flesh to flesh, and draw in the very essence of you through my pores. I'd tell you that the instant you walk into a room, I forget how to breathe. My chest tightens, my lungs contract, and I can't for the life of me remember how to draw breath. If the situation were different, I'd tell you all these things. But the situation is what it is, so I can't.''

Inside her heart, elation warred with despair. ''How am I supposed to respond to that? What do you expect me to say?''

''That I should stay away from you? Never darken your door again?'' His misery was palpable, a living, breathing entity. ''I don't know, Sarah. You tell me.''

She hovered at the edge of a dangerous precipice. One step in the wrong direction would produce devastating results. But which direction was the right one? It seemed that no matter which path she chose, heartache lay at its end.

She wet her lips and said, "Do you want to come in the house?"

He lifted his gaze to hers. Amber eyes locked with blue and held, while her heart hammered so loudly she could hear it inside her head. *Boom-boom. Boom-boom.* Without speaking, he turned off the car, reached for his seat belt, and released it.

It took her trembling hands three tries to get her key into the lock. The door opened, and she stumbled across the threshold in the darkness. Behind her, he quietly closed the door. She reached for the light switch, and his hand closed over her wrist to stop her.

"Sarah," he whispered. Just her name, but that single word, the touch of his fingers, incited a riot inside her. For an endless instant, they stood frozen, his fingers locked around her wrist, her chest rising and falling with her heavy breathing. Then somebody took the first step—maybe him, maybe her, maybe both of them—and she moved into his arms in a motion as fluid and seamless and inevitable, as right and natural, as the sun coming up tomorrow morning.

So close they breathed in tandem, they gazed into each other's eyes, her body thrumming with terror and anticipation and delight, all rolled into a single jagged entity that danced in her belly like a porcupine on speed. The thick night air spilling through the open living room window carried the moist, fresh scent of the rain. In the distance, sharp and quick as a knife, a siren tore the velvet fabric of the night. She lay the palm of her hand against his cheek, ran exploring fingertips up the bridge of his nose, traced his eyebrows, a little too thick, a little too shaggy, one after the other.

He caught her wrist in his hand, brought it to his mouth, kissed the spot where her pulse beat so rapidly. Her breasts were crushed against his chest, and his ribs—his poor, bruised ribs—rose and fell with his breathing. His heart thudded erratically. He plowed his fingers into her hair, took her face in his hands, and dragged her mouth up to his.

Dear God.

She'd waited so long for this.

How many men had she kissed over the years? He instantly erased them all, this exquisite, forbidden man who tasted of heaven and hell and everything in between. She forgot all the reasons why they weren't supposed to be together like this, forgot everything but the magic of his mouth on hers in the velvety blackness of a warm May night ripe with the scent of honeysuckle and punctuated by the chirping of a cricket in the tall grass behind the garage. She locked her arms around his neck in desperation, in mortal danger of tumbling headlong into a place from which she'd never find her way back again.

He broke the kiss, pressed his face into her hair as she struggled for breath. "I saw this coming weeks ago," he said. "I could have done something to prevent it. I could have backed away. I should have. But the simple truth is that I didn't want to. What does that make me?"

"Human," she said, curling her fingers in the hair at the back of his neck, where it grew dark and thick and silky. "It makes you human."

He pressed a kiss to her temple. Her cheek. The corner of her mouth. She closed her eyes and let her head fall back, drifting with the exquisite sensations his mouth evoked. Weakly, without conviction, she said, "You should leave. Before we do something incredibly stupid."

He dipped his head lower. "It's too late," he said. "We've already done something incredibly stupid."

"Clancy, we can't do this."

Against her skin, he murmured, "I've waited so long to touch you. To taste you."

A shudder raced through her. "You have to leave now,"

she said breathlessly, desperately. "If you won't, then I will. One of us has to be the voice of reason."

"Fine then." His mouth continued doing incredible things to her flesh. "Go ahead. Leave."

"Fine, then. That's just what I'll do."

He pressed his cheek to hers. His skin was warm, rough in places with a hint of whisker stubble, and he smelled so wonderful, clean and fresh and male. She swallowed hard, ran a hand down his shoulder to his biceps, explored smooth, muscled flesh.

"You're still here," he said.

"Oh, shut up. Shut up and kiss me again."

His tongue tangled with hers. Lust, raw and yearning, sliced through her like a knife, raced through her veins, pooling thick in the aching hollow between her thighs. She let out a soft whimper and tightened her hold on him. Her thighs opened instinctively, without asking her permission, and wrapped themselves around him. Even through all their layers of clothing, she could feel that he was rock-hard and fully erect. They rocked together, driven by blinding need, frustrated by the inability to touch flesh against flesh. *Too late,* she thought. Too late to try to save herself, for she'd already fallen, and there was no longer any possibility of finding her way back.

Terror shot through her, and she tore her mouth from his. "Stop!" she said harshly. "Enough!"

"God, Sarah—"

"No! Not like this. If you don't leave right this minute, I'm going to drag you upstairs and tear off your clothes and give you what we're both screaming for. As much as I want to, I can't do that. Because the God's honest truth is that I don't believe you have any idea what you really want."

She knew the instant he regained control, felt his emotional withdrawal even before the physical one. With immense relief she escaped, amazed by how closely relief resembled disappointment. She fumbled with the light switch, snapped on the overhead light. He was still standing by the door, chest heaving, fingers buried in his hair.

In a tremulous voice, she said, "I do believe, Father Donovan, that you need to go home and do some serious thinking. If you ever figure out which side of the fence you want to land on, you give me a call and we'll talk."

His struggle clearly written on his face, he said, "And what will you be doing while I'm thinking?"

"I suspect I'll be taking a lot of cold showers."

"God in heaven, Sarah, I'm so sorry. I never meant for this to happen."

"I know, sugar. But it's happened anyway. And now you have to leave."

He closed his eyes, nodded, let out a pent-up breath. "Walk me to the car."

They walked side by side, close but not touching. The rain had stopped, and the air felt moist, reborn. He opened the car door and stood facing her, the door a safety barrier between them. "This isn't about sex," he said.

The hot roiling inside her said otherwise. "Isn't it, Father?"

"No. I'll tell you what this is about. When I see you walking across a room toward me, sweet and bright and gleaming like a new-minted penny, everything and everybody else disappears, and there's only you." He reached across the top of the door and ran his thumb along the curve of her bottom lip. "That's what this is about. Good night, Sarah."

He got in his car, started it up, and backed out of the driveway without looking at her again. Standing in the damp grass, her arms crossed, she watched him go. Long after his taillights had disappeared from sight, she still stood there, staring after him down the deserted street.

Eleven years.

He stared into the glass of Scotch clutched between hands that trembled so hard the liquid sloshed over the side, leaving a spattering of dark spots on the carpet. It had been eleven years since Meg died and the planet had come to a screeching, shuddering halt. Eleven years since he'd entered the seminary, naively believing he could simply shut off his sexuality like a hot-water spigot and never turn it back on again. He'd spent those years in an emotional deep-freeze, his heart and his body encased in a solid block of ice. He'd never been tempted. Not even once. Not until Sarah Connelly came along, with warmth and heart and determination, and thawed him out.

He still wasn't sure how it had happened, knew only that he wanted her, wanted to bury himself inside her, wanted to feel the slow, silken slide of her skin against his. Wanted to tangle his fists in her hair, breathe in her spent oxygen, and swallow her cries when she came.

Sweet Christ.

He tossed back the Scotch, closed his eyes and waited for its warmth to seep into his veins. Three men had let her go. Fools, all of them. He could have laughed at the irony. Of them all, he was the only one who understood her worth. The only one who couldn't conceive of setting her free. The only one who couldn't possibly have her.

The booze wasn't doing its job. He was still shaky, still tightly wound, still rock-hard and aching. He set the glass on the coffee table and peeled off his T-shirt, dropped it on the couch, and kicked off his shoes. Barefoot, he headed for the shower and finished undressing while he waited for the water to heat.

He stood under the spray, let it pummel his back, his shoulders. Turning, he raised his face to its surging warmth, warmth that reminded him too much of the woman he'd left behind. Water rolled off his shoulders, slithered through the dark delta of hair on his chest. Warm fingers of wetness caressed his groin, torturing and tormenting him in his flagrant state of arousal.

There was only one possible solution to his problem, one he hadn't utilized in a very long time. With his forehead braced against slick wet tiles and hot water punishing his back and shoulders, he took matters into his own hands and dealt with the issue the same way he'd dealt with it as a frustrated fifteen-year-old.

It didn't take long. A half-dozen grim, uncompromising strokes with a wet, soapy hand, and he exploded in a burst of guilty pleasure and collapsed face-first against the tiled wall, his heart thundering, his open mouth exhaling sharp, jagged breaths.

The guilt quickly smothered the pleasure. His action might have taken care of the immediate physical ache, but it had no more effect on the ache in his heart than a Band-Aid would have on a gaping wound. It was a pathetic substitute for the real thing, and in the eyes of the Church, just as wrong. Worse, he suspected he'd already broken his promise of celibacy by lusting after her in his heart, for it had been Sarah's face in his mind, Sarah's name on his lips, in that final instant of blinding release.

When his heart rate slowed to normal, he finished showering, dried off with a thick towel, and threw on clean clothes. Then he walked out into the sticky night and crossed the parking lot to the church.

The foyer was enveloped in velvety darkness. Clancy swung the door shut behind him, tugged it to make sure it had latched, and snapped the lock before making his way, surefooted in the darkness, to the sanctuary. He flipped on a single light and stood considering the crucifix hanging on the wall behind the altar.

Only here, in this familiar, comforting place, could he restore his equilibrium. Only here could he recover after his inauspicious tumble from grace. Walking silently on plush crimson carpet, he moved to the front of the sanctuary, pausing before the altar to genuflect. Tears burning behind his eyelids, he went down on his knees to pray for wisdom, for grace, and for guidance.

Bless me, Father, for I have sinned.

16

She was at Bookmark the next morning when Clancy called from the road. "I'm on my way to the Cape," he said, "but I'll be back Friday night. If you need me for anything, call my cell phone and leave a message. I'll be checking it regularly. The timing couldn't be worse, but I don't have a choice. If I don't attend this thing, the bishop will have my hide."

"You have a job to do," she told him. "I've already monopolized way too much of your time."

"You haven't monopolized any time I wasn't happy to give you. I called Paoletti this morning. Gonzales and his silent sidekick didn't ring a bell. He's checking around to see if anybody who covers East Boston can give us a handle on either of them. If he comes up with anything and can't reach me, he'll call you." He paused, and for a moment there was only the hum of the open line between them. "Sarah," he said, "about last night..."

A hard knot formed in the pit of her stomach. "It's all right," she said.

"No, it's not. We have to settle this. We can't just leave it hanging."

"And precisely how do you propose we settle it, Father?"

"I don't know, but I'll figure something out. I just didn't want you to think..."

"What?"

"That I'm some kind of opportunist."

"One who took advantage of my purity and my innocence?"

At the other end of the line, he uttered a soft, breathy laugh. "When you put it that way," he said, "it does sound ridiculous."

"There's no blame on your part, sugar. I was a willing participant in last night's activities." She paused, took a breath. "I probably shouldn't say this. I imagine it's not appropriate, but I'm saying it, anyway. I'll be thinking about you. Have a safe trip."

Before he had time to reply, she disconnected. She marched directly to the cash register, opened the drawer, lifted the change tray and removed the folded piece of paper on which Josie had written the name and number of her gynecologist.

Behind her, Josie said sweetly, "Change your mind, did you?"

Sarah crushed the piece of paper in her fist and slammed shut the cash drawer. "Oh, shut up."

Dr. Sheldon's receptionist, a sweet-voiced older lady named Mildred, efficiently squeezed her into a one-thirty time slot. "Now be sure to come a few minutes early," she warned. "There'll be paperwork to fill out since we haven't seen you before."

The minute Sarah hung up the phone, it rang. "Luis Gonzales," Detective Paoletti told her. "Pretty well known to the boys over in District 7. He's been hauled in a few times over small stuff, no felony charges. Hangs with a guy name of Tico Santana. Also had a number of petty charges, but nothing big. They both sound like small-time punks if you ask me."

"I don't suppose you'd happen to have a home address for Gonzales?"

"Look, I'm only helping out Donovan because Rafferty asked me to, and I owe him a couple of favors. But if you have any intention of going out looking for these two, I'm not about to contribute to your stupidity. The District 7 guys have better things to do than hose your blood off the sidewalk."

"Trust me, sugar, I'm not that crazy. This is strictly for informational purposes."

"You get in trouble, don't come running to me. Gonzales lives with his mother at 5 Bay Street, first-floor apartment. Listen, you tell your buddy Donovan that I don't care how long and intimate his association is with Rafferty, I'm done feeding him information. My lieutenant catches me at this, I'll be back in uniform, walking the streets of Chinatown."

At noon, she left the store in Josie's capable hands, with a promise to return eventually, and took a taxi to the repair shop to pick up her car. The mechanic assured her that with the alternator replaced, she should have no further troubles. She paid him and drove to McDonald's, where she picked up a salad and ate it in her car. Then she drove to the health clinic, where she filled out three pages of new patient information and submitted to the indignity of a pelvic exam before the doctor would renew her Depo-Provera shot.

Then she went in search of Jamal.

She found him around the back of her house, working among the arborvitaes, slapping butter-yellow paint onto the clapboards with a huge brush. His painting technique had grown exponentially since he'd started, but he still had a tendency to get more paint on his clothes than he got on the house. "Are you tired of painting yet?" she said.

Those chocolate eyes studied her with suspicion. "Why?" he said. "You got something else for me to do?"

"I'm headed to East Boston to stake out a house. I thought you might like to come along to keep me company."

His mouth fell open. Heedless of the paintbrush that dribbled yellow droplets all over her shrubbery, he gaped at her.

"You shitting me," he said. "You mean we going spying? Like that James Bond dude?"

"Not spying, sugar. Surveillance."

His grin was sudden, wide, and gleeful. "And Father Donovan just happen to be conveniently out of town. He ain't gonna like it one bit, you being his woman and all."

"I'm not his woman," she said. "Will you come with me? I'd feel safer with a man along." Even if said man was only sixteen years old.

"You kidding?" He set down the paint can and covered it, pulled a rag from his pocket and wiped the spillage from the rim of the can. "You think yours truly gonna miss something this good?" He carried his paintbrush to the outside water faucet and turned it on. While the water ran in a pale yellow puddle around his feet, he said, "Just promise me one thing. I get to be there to watch the fireworks when he find out about it."

He'd forgotten what it felt like to live in the company of men.

As a parish priest, he worked daily with a variety of people. Old and young, male and female. The faithful and the sinful, the good and the bad. But in this priestly convocation, he was plunged solely into the company of others who shared with him the distinction of possessing a Y chromosome. He'd grown accustomed to it during his days in seminary. As a patriarchal institution, the Catholic Church reserved its hierarchy for the male of the species. For years, he'd taken it for granted. But over the last two days, in this hotel and conference center in a small town on Cape Cod, he'd found himself longing for the companionship, the tenderness, that only a woman could provide. Camaraderie was all well and good, but it seemed so monochromatic. Everything and everybody here was either black or white. Nothing and nobody possessed any of the vivid and brilliant colors that fell between the two extremes.

And he seemed to be the only one who noticed.

After an exhausting four-hour afternoon session, he escaped early and drove to the beach, where he spent an hour walking in solitude. He'd thought this retreat might recharge his batteries, renew his energy and enthusiasm for his chosen vocation. Instead, it had just the opposite effect. He felt distant, separate. A hummingbird in the midst of a flock of crows. He'd thought coming here would ease his doubts, but it had magnified them instead.

The ocean lay calm, shimmering and serene at this time of day. As always, its vastness overwhelmed and humbled him. It reminded him of his bond with God, the slender golden thread that kept him connected to his Creator. Reminded him of the boundless possibilities God had bestowed upon humankind. Each man's life an open slate, vast as the ocean before him, waiting to be written upon. In genuine perplexity, he considered the strictures of the priesthood which man had bestowed upon himself in the name of God, and wondered how the two could be so far apart.

He pondered the nature of his feelings for Sarah, the inherent rightness and wrongness of them. Did his love for her reflect a purity of soul? Or was it a dark carnality that drove him? He'd told her their relationship wasn't about sex, but he'd lied. To himself, to her. For the two—the purity and the carnality—were so closely interwoven as to be inseparable. It was impossible to have the one without the other. It had been that way between man and woman since Eden, and would remain that way until the end of time. Heart, soul, and body, all distinct parts of the same whole.

After a soul-wrenching hour of prayer, reflection, and brooding, he drove back to the hotel, showered and changed into street clothes, and met Michael Santangelo for dinner. There in the hotel restaurant, bolstered by a double Glenfiddich on the rocks, he dumped the whole bloody mess in Michael's lap.

His friend listened in silence while he poured it all out. When he was done, Michael leaned forward in his chair, propped his chin on his hand, and said, "Need I remind you that I told you so?"

"Not the answer I was seeking, my friend. It's the one I expected, but not the one I was looking for." He picked up a dinner roll from the basket in the center of the table and tore it in two. "I don't suppose you'd care to remind me again about the significance of priestly celibacy?"

"Aside from the fact that it's supposed to be good for the soul?"

"Hah!" He buttered the roll and ate half of it in a single bite.

"Correct me if I'm wrong," Michael said, "but I believe the original concept had something to do with purity. That at certain times of the month, a woman was deemed unclean, and therefore a man who had relations with her, by virtue of that contact, also became unclean. Since it wouldn't do for an impure priest to be conducting Mass and serving the Eucharist, the concept of priestly celibacy was established."

"For God's sake, Michael, don't tell me you believe all that misogynistic claptrap. Tell me, have you never had a relationship with a woman?"

"I'm committed to my promise of celibacy."

"Before you were a priest," he said impatiently. "Have you never been in love? Have you never had a physical relationship with a woman?"

Michael eyed him balefully, then picked up a roll and began buttering it. "Of course. But that was before I was ordained. Before I entered the seminary. Before I got the calling."

Clancy leaned over the table. "Do you honestly believe that relationship tainted your purity? Do you believe it impaired your ability to celebrate the Liturgy? Or rendered you unfit to serve the Eucharist?"

"That's a ridiculous question."

"It's an honest question, and I'm looking for an honest answer."

Michael pointed the butter knife at him. "That was then, my friend, and this is now. I've been absolved of my sin. It's a nonissue."

"Then I suppose you also don't believe love can make you a better man? You don't believe that the love of a good woman can take half a man and make him whole?"

Michael snorted. "Do you want to know what I believe, Father? I believe in God. I believe in the Sacraments. I believe there are things in this universe that we aren't meant to know. And I believe that you're a fool if you allow a woman to sway you from the course God intended you to follow."

"But what if it's not the course God intended me to follow? What then, Michael?"

"Damn it, Clancy, what you're doing is wrong!"

"I haven't done anything except fall in love. Are you telling me there's something wrong with that?"

Michael picked up his fork and studied him thoughtfully. "Has it occurred to you that God might be testing you?"

"It's occurred to me. It's also occurred to me that He might be giving me a second chance at something I thought I'd left behind years ago."

"You'll do what you're determined to do," Michael said. "I know better than to try to stop you. Just let me go on record as saying that if you give in to temptation with this woman, you'll be making a terrible mistake."

"But it's my mistake to make. Not yours, not Bishop Halloran's, not the Church's. Mine. I'm the one who'll have to live with the consequences."

Michael studied his face, then sighed. "You're right," he said. "Just be sure you're prepared to face those consequences, because nobody gets a free ride. *Nobody*.'' He picked up his knife and fork and cut into his steak. ''Right or wrong,'' he said, ''no matter what you decide, there'll be consequences.''

''Stakeouts never this boring on TV,'' Jamal complained. They'd spent most of the last five days parked near a hydrant in Maverick Square, where they had a bird's-eye view of the front door of 5 Bay. So far, the highlight of their outing had been watching an old woman hanging laundry to dry in an alley outside her second-story window. They'd listened to enough noisy car mufflers to last a lifetime, they'd watched a stray dog do his duty on the fire hydrant, and they'd seen two pretty young girls, both with babies in strollers, court further trouble by flirting with a couple of neighborhood punks. What they hadn't seen was any activity at 5 Bay Street. Nobody had come in, nobody had gone out. All in all, it had been a pretty unproductive stakeout.

Sarah tapped her fingernails against the steering wheel. ''Read the newspaper if you're bored.''

''I already read it twice through. This be Boring with a capital B.''

''Stop whining and remind me once again why you're not in school.''

''That be part of payback. It being so late in the school year, our mutual friend Father Donovan say it best if I work for him until fall and start fresh in September. Besides—'' he stretched his endless legs as far as they could be stretched within the confines of a 1965 Mustang ''—if I be in school, then who be here protecting you from the bad guys?''

While she pondered a suitable reply, the front door of number 5 Bay Street opened and a man stepped out. He was of average height, compactly built, with dark hair and a swarthy complexion. Around his neck, he wore a phalanx of gold chains. ''Bingo,'' she said.

Jamal straightened and peered intently. "That him?"

"Who else could it possibly be? Don't let him see you looking."

Jamal ducked back against the seat, and they both watched Luis Gonzales walk briskly down the sidewalk to a black Camaro parked at the curb. He unlocked the car, got in, and started it up. "We following him?" Jamal said.

"Of course we are. Fasten your seat belt."

"Yes, ma'am."

She turned the key and started the Mustang. Gonzales stopped at the end of the street before pulling out into traffic. Sarah eased away from the curb and pulled into the line of traffic behind him. "I got one question," Jamal said.

"What?"

"We following this dude. I got that part down. But what we gonna do if we catch him?"

"I'm not trying to catch him. I just want to find out where he's going."

"Then I got a even better question. What we gonna do if he catch us?"

"Oh, be quiet," she said. "Bodyguards aren't supposed to express their opinions. You're here for the purpose of protecting me from the bad guys. Remember?"

"I remember. But I be sixteen years old. I ain't ready to die just yet."

Gonzales led her on a circuitous route around East Boston that ended at the mouth of the Ted Williams Tunnel. Sarah scrambled to find a few loose bills in her purse. She paid the toll and dropped into place a couple of cars behind the Camaro. They exited the tunnel in South Boston, where she immediately got stuck behind a lumbering cement truck and nearly lost Gonzales in the confusing crisscross of streets.

Ahead of her, Gonzales turned right. Trying to look inconspicuous, Sarah did the same. They were in a commercial section of town, following some sort of truck route that twisted through an inhospitable piece of real estate near the docks. Gonzales maneuvered the tangle of streets without hesitation. He obviously knew where he was going. Sarah looked around, thankful it was daylight. In a place like this, after dark, the rats came out. Both the two-legged and the four-legged varieties.

Four cars ahead of her, the light turned red. A white SUV gunned it and ran the light. Behind the SUV, Gonzales did the same. "Shit!" she said.

When the light turned green, she shot through. But Gonzales and his Camaro had vanished into the maze of empty lots, chain link fence, and deserted warehouses. Kit had said Rio lived in a renovated warehouse. Could that be where Gonzales was headed? She drove around for twenty minutes, hoping she might get lucky and run across either the Camaro or Rio's BMW. But all she got for her efforts was a leering grin from some off-duty dockworker standing on a corner with his lunchbox, waiting for the walk signal.

"Don't look so sad," Jamal said when she dropped him off at the Rafferty house. "We know where he live, we know what kind of car he drive, we know he hang out in bad neighborhoods."

"All of which leads to a big, fat zero."

"Sometimes shit happen when you least expect it. Wait and see. After all, tomorrow be another day."

In spite of her disappointment, she grinned. "The Scarlett O'Hara of Boston," she said. "See you tomorrow."

"You bet. I be the one carrying the paintbrush."

She found Josie in the sci-fi/fantasy section, stocking shelves with new books from a rolling cart that she pulled along behind her. "How's business been?" Sarah asked.

"Steady. Nothing Steve and I couldn't handle." Josie glanced up from her perch on the floor. "Hand me that stack of Asaros."

Sarah picked up the pile of paperback novels and handed them to her assistant. "I'm sorry to keep deserting you like this."

"Not a problem." Josie cleared a space on the second shelf and tucked the books neatly into it. "You have things you need to do. Stevie and I can handle the store. Oh, I almost forgot—Clancy called."

Heat flooded her body. It was absurd that she should have this kind of physical response to the mere sound of his name. She was a grown woman, thirty-three years old, with three ex-husbands and few remaining romantic illusions. It was insane that she should be this happy about a phone call from a man who was off-limits not just to her, but to every female on the planet. Ridiculous that she should feel like a giggly teenage girl with a major crush, like those girls she'd seen in East Boston, still wearing that fresh-faced look of hope in spite of the babies they pushed in strollers.

Trying to affect a cool casualness she didn't feel, she said, "Really? I thought he wasn't due back until tonight."

"He isn't. He called from the road." Josie picked up another stack of paperbacks and tucked them into an empty space. "He wants you to call him."

She strode nonchalantly to the front of the store, squeezed past Steve, who was talking books with a customer, and used the phone behind the counter. Clancy answered on the second ring. "Hey there, sugar," she said. "Where are you?"

"Right now, I'm sitting in bumper-to-bumper traffic on Route 3, headed back from the Cape. Are you free to talk?"

She stepped aside to allow Steve access to the cash register. "In a manner of speaking."

"Then I'll talk. You can listen. I've spent the last five days thinking about this little problem we've been having."

Her breath strangled in her throat. "And?"

"And I've decided we're going to resolve it tonight."

Her mouth went as dry as a double vermouth martini. Suddenly, in spite of the air-conditioning, she was damp all over. Carefully, she said, "Would you care to clarify that statement?"

"You know what I'm talking about."

She must have made some kind of odd noise, for Steve glanced up, eyebrows raised. Sarah blew out a breath and turned away from him. Into the phone, she said quietly, desperately, "You have lost your mind."

"Maybe I have. Or maybe I've found it. Sarah, I've looked into my heart, my soul, about as deep as a man can look into himself, and I haven't found anything wrong, anything sinful, in the way I feel about you. I'm not a saint, I'm just a man, a man who's been alone for too long. And I want you with every fiber of my being."

Her heartbeat thundered in her ears. At the other end of the phone, she heard the purr of his engine as he moved forward in the line of traffic and then stopped again.

"Any time you'd like to chime in with a response," he said, "the floor's open."

"What are you expecting me to say?"

"Damn it, Sarah, don't make this any harder on me than it has to be. I'm sitting here in the middle of the traffic jam from hell, breathing in diesel exhaust, with a box of Trojans in a bag on the passenger seat and my heart in my hand. Give me something. Anything."

His words struck her like a hard blow to her stomach. In a strangled voice, she said to nobody in particular, "I have to take this call in my office."

Cradling the cordless phone to her chest, she walked on unsteady legs to the back of the store and into her cluttered office. Heart thudding, she dropped into the swivel chair behind the desk. In disbelief, she said into the phone, "You bought condoms?"

"In a little drugstore in Provincetown. Hiding behind dark glasses, my hands shaking like a junkie in need of a fix. I'd have worn a paper bag over my head if I'd had one. It was the most terrifying experience of my life. I kept expecting the heavens to open up and a bolt of lightning to plummet to earth and strike me dead. I've finally figured out why so many teenage girls wind up pregnant. It's because teenage boys can't face the terror of buying condoms.''

She didn't know whether to laugh or cry, and she didn't have the heart to tell him just yet that his purchase was totally unnecessary. Instead, she said in a tremulous voice, "You're serious about this."

"God in heaven, Sarah, would I joke about something like this?"

"You're obviously not thinking clearly. You haven't considered the ramifications."

"I'm thinking more clearly than I have in months."

"What about the Church?"

"Let me worry about the Church. It's not your concern."

"Of course it is. If we do this…if we take our relationship to the next level…if we become—" She clamped her mouth abruptly shut, unable to continue.

"Lovers. It's all right to say the word out loud. God won't strike you dead for saying it."

"If we do this," she said doggedly, "then everything that affects you affects me. All your concerns become mine."

"It's too late," he said. "Everything that affects you already affects me."

"Damn it, Clancy, I don't want to hurt you! Don't you understand? You have so much more to lose than I do!"

"And so very much to gain by loving you."

She closed her eyes, bit her lip, blinked back the tears welling beneath her eyelids. "You're going to break my heart, aren't you?"

"I don't know. Let me check my to-do list. Let's see…oil change, six-month dental checkup, pick up dry cleaning…yes, there it is. Break Sarah's heart."

In spite of her efforts to prevent it, the corners of her mouth turned up. ''It may not be intentional, but you'll do it anyway. It's inevitable.'' She took a hard, shuddering breath and swiped a tear from her cheek. ''But there's something I have to say first, Father. I know it's a sin, but I can't help it. I'm a prideful woman. I will not be your regret, or a mistake you made during a moment of weakness. I won't be your midlife crisis, or—God help us both—your guilty pleasure.''

''Sarah, love, you're none of the above. What you are is my obsession.''

All the breath left her body. Outside the open door of her office, Steve and Josie went about their business as though the earth weren't buckling and trembling beneath their feet.

The phone crackled with static. ''Sarah?'' he said. ''Are you still there?''

She wet her lips, found her voice. ''Yes.''

''Just so you don't misunderstand—I'm not asking you. I'm telling you. Tonight. Nine o'clock. Be ready.''

She opened her mouth to respond, but he'd already hung up.

She left work early, stopped at the candle shop and selected three fat candles. Then she rushed home to start shoveling through the clutter. Even though he'd seen her house in its customary chaotic condition a dozen times, on this momentous occasion she wanted everything to be perfect. She washed dishes, ran the vacuum, dusted nooks and crannies she generally forgot. Tucked magazines into the magazine rack, folded newspapers and stuffed them into the trash can in the garage.

She cut a bouquet of white lilacs from the yard and placed them in the center of the dining room table, set two candles on the fireplace mantel, then spent twenty minutes choosing a diverse selection of romantic ballads and programming them into the CD player.

At seven-thirty, satisfied she'd done all she could with the house, she lit the candles, turned on the music, and went upstairs to get ready. She showered, shaved all the necessary body parts, and blow-dried her hair until it tumbled, soft and wavy, around her shoulders.

In the bedroom, she dropped her robe in front of the mirror and critically studied her thirty-three-year-old body. She was so damned ordinary, and she wondered what it would be like to be Faith Hill or Shania Twain, sleek and stunning and perfect. Leaning toward the mirror, she searched for any indication of aging—crow's feet, sagging jowls, droopy boobs—but her skin was still as smooth and supple as it had been at twenty. She couldn't find any wrinkles, and so far, nothing had started to head south. Her thighs were firm, if unremarkable, her belly flat, her waist neatly tucked. No man had ever waxed poetic over her breasts, but they were firm and high, a perfectly adequate 34C.

Oh, Lord. How was she going to survive this night without detonating like a scud missile gone awry?

She was meticulous with her makeup. He'd seen her without it, but tonight was different. Tonight was for larger-than-life romantic fantasies, and she was pulling out all the stops. While Céline Dion crooned downstairs, she applied mascara with hands that trembled so hard she had to set down the brush and force herself to take a series of slow, calming breaths. For all her worldly experience, tonight she felt like a fifteen-year-old on her first date. Except that no man, not even when she was fifteen, had ever made her tremble in anticipation.

This was it. The Big One. Everything that had come before tonight, all the frogs she'd kissed while she waited for her prince to arrive, were nothing more than rehearsal. It didn't matter that her prince was a card-carrying member of the

Catholic clergy. It didn't matter that the funeral pyre she was tossing herself onto was her own. Like a racehorse out of control, she was determined to barrel straight ahead and immolate herself in the flames. She was smart enough to recognize it, just not smart enough to figure out what she was supposed to do with the knowledge.

She managed somehow to finish with the mascara, then she painstakingly painted her lips a bloody crimson, layered them with clear lip gloss to make them shiny and wet and kissable. When she was done, she barely recognized the woman in the mirror, red lips parted in anticipation, eyes bright with a combination of excitement and terror. What she was about to do was irreversible, and terrifying on so many different levels that just thinking about it made her nauseous. Her stomach gurgled, empty and forlorn, but she didn't dare to eat for fear of upchucking and ruining everything.

She spent ten minutes deliberating her choice of undergarments. Did she dare to go without? The man hadn't seen a naked woman in eleven years, and she didn't want to be the cause of his untimely demise. On the other hand, her bureau drawers were filled with utilitarian cotton underwear, hardly sexy by any standards.

This isn't about sex, he'd said.

Right. And pigs could fly.

She decided to forgo the underwear. If she was going to play the role of vamp, she might as well take no prisoners, and if he wasn't man enough to survive it, he shouldn't have set this catastrophe into motion in the first place. *Be ready,* he'd told her. Lord only knew, she was ready, so primed she was in danger of starting without him.

She'd already picked out a dress. Her closet was crammed with lovely clothes, most of them bought with Remy's charge card. But tonight, she had no intention of wearing something paid for by another man. She'd bought the dress on sale at Filene's back in January, then she'd tucked it away in her closet and forgotten it. It was black, a soft, shimmering silk that clung to her like a second skin. She wriggled into it, reveling in the whisper of silk against her naked flesh. With nervous hands, she smoothed the fabric, adjusted the tiny spaghetti straps that held it up, tugged at the hem and trusted that her backside was adequately covered.

She stripped the bed and remade it with fresh linens. Then she turned down the sheets and spritzed perfume, subtle and floral and sweet, between crisp layers of cotton. She spritzed herself at the pulse points in her wrists and her neck, at the crease of elbow and knee, in the shadowy hollow between her breasts. Heart thudding, she crossed the room and spritzed between the sheets again, just for good measure.

Night had settled outside her window while she dressed, and somewhere nearby, a cricket had begun to broadcast his nocturnal song. She walked to the window, closed the blinds, and stepped into the black high-heel shoes she'd set out earlier. There was a box of wooden matches in the top drawer; she opened it, removed a match and struck it. With a soft hiss, it sputtered into flame, and she lit the last candle and blew out the spent match.

Surveying herself critically in the mirror, she decided there was nothing more she could do. This was as good as it got. She opened a drawer and swept her cosmetics into it. She could sort them out later. Pausing, she scanned the room to make sure the pillows were plumped, that the chair beside the window was empty, that she hadn't left any dirty undies peeking out from beneath the bed.

A flick of the lamp switch plunged her into flickering, shadowy candlelight. Through the window, she heard the purr of an automobile engine in her driveway, and her heart kicked into overdrive. With slow deliberation, she descended the stairs, afraid that if she didn't hold herself back, she'd stumble in the heels and fall ass over teakettle to the bottom. There was no room for stumbling tonight. There was no room tonight for anything but magic, the kind of magic a man and a woman could make when everything was right and the feelings were fathomless and they'd finally stopped trying to keep their hands off each other.

His footsteps crossed the porch, and he knocked on the door. Sarah stepped into the foyer, took a single, hard breath, her hand trembling on the doorknob. Then she turned the knob and swung the door open.

He waited on the other side of the screen, dark hair haloed by the porch light. His hands were tucked casually into the pockets of his jeans, the tails of his black linen jacket hitched up, crumpled between elbow and wrist. Beneath the jacket, he wore a blue dress shirt, open at the throat, just enough to reveal a glimpse of crisp dark chest hair. The effect was devastating. Her heart rate accelerated as he considered her with that enigmatic amber gaze. Gone was the humble agent of God, morphed into an exotic emissary of the Dark Side.

May the Force be with you.

She took a deep breath and said, "This is it, Father. Last chance to bail."

Those bottomless golden eyes studied her, head to toe. She waited, her chest aching with the effort to breathe. Finally, his gaze reached her face. "Five days," he said. "Five days since I last saw you, and it feels like five years."

Her heart raced as they stood there drinking each other in, electricity leaping and sparking between them, as visible as the rusted aluminum screen that separated them.

"I don't suppose I could come in?"

She returned from wherever she'd been, lost in the heady thrill of looking at him, and opened the screen door. He passed her, smelling of bay rum and altar candles. She closed the door and locked it, then switched off the outside light. They wouldn't be needing it again tonight.

Soft music swirled around them as they stood awkwardly

in the foyer, bathed in the flickering glow of candlelight, neither of them certain how to proceed.

"You look breathtaking tonight," he said.

"So do you, sugar."

As far as responses went, it was a half-witted thing to say. While his amber gaze pinned her in place, she floundered for something, anything, to say that wouldn't make her sound like the village idiot. But intelligent words weren't forthcoming, and she realized that in all her careful planning, she'd forgotten one crucial element. She'd done everything under creation to render herself irresistible, and she'd spent an inordinate amount of time dwelling on every possible permutation of the coupling that would undoubtedly take place tonight. But she'd left out a step along the way. In her customary full-speed-ahead, take-no-prisoners manner, she'd neglected to map out the route from Point A to Point B. The critical step between polite chitchat and rolling around in a sweaty tangle was a chasm she had no idea how to breach.

She seized the only lifeline she could reach. "How was the retreat?"

"Hellish." Hands still in his pockets, he paced across the foyer, then doubled back. "I walked the beach a lot. Prayed a lot. Wore circles in the carpet in my hotel room. And then I prayed some more." His shadow loomed dark on the wall behind him, exaggerated by the flickering candlelight. "I had dinner last night with an old friend. Michael Santangelo. We were in seminary together. I told him about you. About us."

"What did he say?"

He reached out, fingered a strand of her hair, its mousy brown turned a burnished gold by the magic of candlelight. "About what I expected. He took the high road of moral righteousness. He reminded me that it was Eve who was responsible for the Fall, and advised me to run as far and as fast as I could away from you. Of course, it wasn't what I wanted to hear."

Her stomach clenched. "Maybe he was right."

"He didn't understand. I'm not even sure I do." He regarded her intently, his eyes softening, warming. "God in heaven, Sarah, I don't know if you have any idea, but you look absolutely stunning tonight."

"You don't think I look trashy?" It occurred to her for the first time that in her zeal, she might have gone too far, might have stepped over some invisible boundary. The line between sex kitten and trailer park trash was sometimes blurry.

The corners of his mouth curved upward. "More like ravishing. Exquisite. Intoxicating." He reached out a single finger, skimmed her bare shoulder. Goose bumps broke out in every conceivable location, from her ears to her ankles.

Now that the moment of truth had arrived, terror took over the reins. Fighting back nausea, she said impulsively, "Dance with me."

The romantic ballad pouring from her stereo was a little outdated, and more than a little unsophisticated. But ever since she was a girl, back in Louisiana, listening with her daddy to the Grand Ole Opry on a portable kitchen radio, she'd adored Ernest Tubb's rendition of *Waltz Across Texas*.

He opened his mouth, closed it. Opened it again and said, "I don't dance."

"What are you talking about? Of course you do. Everyone dances. It's just a simple two-step. You take my right hand, I put my left hand on your shoulder, and we move around the floor in time to the music. What could be simpler?"

"Saying the Mass in Latin?"

She eyed him suspiciously. "I thought you said you wanted to be John Travolta when you were twelve years old."

"Fortunately for the future of humanity, I changed my mind. Sarah, darling, there's a reason I entered the priesthood instead of becoming the male equivalent of a Rockette. I have two left feet, and neither of them has a clue what it's doing. Trust me, it's a debacle you don't want to witness.''

''Oh, phooey.'' Having grown up in Louisiana, she'd learned to two-step almost as soon as she'd learned to walk. ''I'll lead and you follow. There's nothing to it.''

''I really think this is a mistake.'' But he let her take his hand. His palm was sweaty, and she wondered if he was nervous about the dancing, or about what would come after. ''Now,'' she said, ''you put your arm around my waist—''

He obediently followed her instructions. His warm hand brushed soft silk, sending a frisson of heat racing through her. He paused discreetly at her waist before he let the tips of his fingers trail lower, brushing against the swell of her hip with such subtlety, she couldn't be certain whether or not the move was deliberate.

His eyes gave away nothing. She rested her free hand on his shoulder and began silently counting beats in her head as she followed the steps of the dance, so familiar to her she could have performed them in her sleep. He faltered, zigged when he should have zagged, and stepped on her toe. ''Ouch,'' she said.

''I'm sorry. I tried to warn you.''

''Stop trying so hard, sugar. Close your eyes. Feel the music.''

''I can feel the music just fine. My problem is following it.''

''You just need more self-confidence. You need to—*ow!* Lord almighty, Clancy, you're supposed to be letting me lead. I'll be lucky to have any toes left.''

''Did I or did I not tell you I was hopeless?''

''You told me. I just didn't believe you.''

''Then you have no grounds for complaint.''

''Maybe we'd do better without the shoes.''

They kicked their shoes aside. Minus the heels, she instantly lost three inches of height, and they had to make adjustments. Darkly, he said, "I bet all your husbands knew how to dance."

"You make me sound like Elizabeth Taylor. I've only had three husbands, not a dozen."

"Only three. Yes. I remember."

She'd been right; it was easier without the shoes. And damned if he wasn't starting to get the hang of it. He hadn't tripped her up in at least fifteen seconds.

Softly, she said, "Sugar?"

He was busy concentrating on his feet, and it took him a moment to respond. "What?" he said distractedly, eyes still downcast, lest his feet commit some atrocity while he was looking the other way.

"You're not hopeless. And none of them counted."

He glanced up and into her eyes, lost the beat, and their feet tangled irreparably. She tripped over his ankle, and would have fallen if he hadn't caught her.

"Had enough?" he said.

"Oh, shut up. The song's over, anyway."

The CD player whirred and shifted, and the sweet, poignant strains of a classic Andy Williams tune floated free on the evening air. *The shadow of your smile when you are gone…*

Her eyes locked with his, and her pulse fluttered. "Come here," he said.

Without conscious volition, she melted into his arms, reveling in every lovely inch of him pressed against her, the full frontal contact she'd craved almost since the first moment she lay eyes on him, all those weeks ago. He snugged her tight against him, buried his face in her hair. "This kind of dancing," he murmured, "even a total incompetent like me can do."

Eyes squeezed shut, she smiled against his shoulder. Dreamily, she said, "This was Momma's favorite song. When I was a little girl, she and Daddy used to dance to it after they put us kids to bed for the night. Bobby and I used to sneak out of bed and hide behind the sofa and watch them.''

In response, he ran whisper-soft fingertips up her bare arms to the wrists that rested loosely against either side of his neck. Skimmed them back down to her shoulders, and said gruffly, ''Your skin is so soft.''

''And your hands feel so lovely against it.''

He pressed his cheek, warm and smooth and clean-shaven, against hers. His breath tickled her ear, fluttered the hair at the base of her neck. With a sigh, she inhaled his scent. In the background, Andy still crooned, the music darting little barbs of pleasure through her stomach, her pelvis, the breasts crushed so mercilessly against his chest.

''Sugar,'' she murmured, ''I think we have a problem.''

He exhaled a warm, sweet breath against her cheek. ''Why's that?''

''Because—'' she pressed her lips to his throat, drew back, studied the faint lipstick stain she'd left, pleased that she'd marked him as hers ''—I'm a very straightforward person,'' she said, her voice tremulous. ''With me, what you see is pretty much what you get. But you—'' she ran the tip of her tongue along her lower lip and raised her eyes to his ''—you have rivers running through you, dark and lovely and deep. You terrify me. I'm afraid I'll drown.''

His mouth thinned. ''I'm not all that deep. I'm really quite ordinary.''

''You're a terrible liar, Clancy Donovan. There's not a thing that's ordinary about you.'' She paused, softened. ''And I am so much in love with you I can't see straight.''

He let out a hard breath. ''This is so unfair to you. I shouldn't have put you in this position.''

''I'm here because I want to be here. There's nowhere else I want to be. Nobody else I want to be with. Only you.'' She touched her mouth to his throat again, circled his Adam's apple with the tip of her tongue. He tensed in her arms, let out a harsh, ragged breath, and then tightened his hand on the back of her neck. He lowered his head and touched his mouth to her throat, traced a moist trail from chin to shoulder. He slid aside the spaghetti strap, nipped gently at the smooth flesh beneath, and drew exquisite patterns on her flesh with his tongue.

"Sarah," he whispered.

It took her a moment to return to her body. She stroked the nape of his neck, combed fingers through his thick, dark hair. "What?"

He kissed the swell of her breast, burgeoning above the bodice of the dress. Cleared his throat. "What are you wearing under this thing?"

"There's nothing under there but me, sugar. I told you, what you see is what you get."

His eyes met hers, and heat smoldered between them like waves rising off hot asphalt. "You're a wanton woman, Ms. Connelly."

"You told me to be ready, Father Donovan."

"So I did. Are you ready, then?"

"Darlin' mine, I've been ready since I hung up the phone."

He kissed her then, a hot, wet kiss that went on and on and on. He was a world-class kisser, infinitely delectable, and she decided that if God were going to strike her dead, kissing Clancy Donovan was well worth a premature demise. He snagged his fingers in her hair, tilted her head back, and drank her in, silken tongue swirling and sliding against hers, languid, leisurely, thoroughly maddening.

They gave up all pretense of dancing. He shucked off the linen jacket, first one arm and then the other, and tossed it onto a chair. They broke apart for an instant, sucked in harsh, ragged breaths, realigned their fit and came back together with a ferocious hunger. His hands stroked her thighs, closed around them, long fingers biting into soft flesh, thumbs making teasing circles, tickling, taunting the sensitive skin just beneath the hem of her dress.

She gasped, and he swallowed the sound before it could escape. Beneath the dress, his hands edged steadily northward. Shaking like a washing machine in spin cycle, she began working frantically at the buttons of his shirt. She tugged the tails free, ran her hands up his chest, combed fingers through crisp dark hair that narrowed at his navel to point directly to paradise.

His hands reached her bare buttocks and paused. She snagged a forefinger beneath the button atop his fly, and hovered there, waiting. For an instant, time stood still as they remained in a holding pattern, blue eyes sinking into gold as shadows danced around them. Then, his eyes still trained on hers, he brought his hand around between her legs and slipped two fingers inside her.

Every muscle in her body went limp. Her eyelids fluttered closed, and she let her head fall back as she lost herself in the thrill of his touch. It might have been a long time for him, but he hadn't forgotten how to touch a woman, how to excite her, where to glide and stroke with those incredible fingers, how much pressure to use, when to back off.

The pleasure was exquisite, unbearable, yet somehow not enough. She flicked open the button to his jeans, worked the zipper down, plunged her hands inside and found him, thick and hot and as ready as she was.

She filled her hands with him, reveled in his size, his weight, the incredible heat he radiated as she stroked him. "Sarah," he rasped.

"What?"

"If you keep that up, I'll go off like a rocket."

She circled a thumb around the tip of his penis, caught a bead of moisture and teased him with it, felt him shudder in response. "I thought that was the idea."

"Not yet," he said raggedly. "Not yet."

"I'll stop as soon as you do."

"We're not going to make it to the bedroom, are we?"

"I don't know about you, sugar, but it doesn't look like it from where I'm standing."

He sucked in a hard breath. "Where?" he asked harshly.

"I don't care, baby. Just hurry."

He backed her up against the wall, lit by dancing shadows, and pressed her hard against it. Her chest rose and fell with her labored breathing as he dipped his head and took her mouth in a kiss so steamy it could have peeled the paper off the walls. She squirmed, wriggled her hips against his as his mouth roamed her face, her neck.

"Now," she demanded. "Now, please, before I die from waiting."

He tore his mouth away from her throat. "Wait. I have to—"

"No." She circled a leg around his, slid it up and down, enticing him to move closer. "Can't wait any longer."

"—condoms…"

"Don't need any. I took care of it."

"You're sure?"

"Yes!" she said in exasperation. "Oh, God, please hurry…"

He lifted her off her feet, rucked the dress up around her waist. She raised her knees and locked them around him, pulling him closer, guiding him. With a groan of surrender, he leaned forward and plunged into her.

Hot. Wet. Silk and steel. He drove deep, shoved her up against the wall so hard she knew she'd have bruises tomorrow. "Is this what you wanted?" he rasped.

"Yes. God, yes."

"More?"

"Oh, yes, sugar. I want it all."

He plunged deeper, buried himself to the hilt. Her knees

were clamped so tight around his ribs that she knew she must be hurting him, but she didn't care. He was hard between her legs and the wall was hard against her back, and he was making edgy, raw animal sounds deep in his throat. This wasn't lovemaking, this was pure jungle sex, and it felt so good, hot and sweaty and noisy. He fumbled with the strap to her dress, tried in vain to pull it down, finally gave up and yanked. Silk tore once, twice, and then he freed her breast and closed his mouth around it. She shuddered with pleasure, made a low, keening sound as his tongue tormented her swollen, aching nipple. Her last rational thought was to wonder if the music was loud enough to drown out their caterwauling, and then she forgot to wonder because his movements quickened and she heard him cry out, and the next instant her body splintered and there was nothing but him and a white-hot pleasure that threatened to swallow her alive.

They collapsed in a sweaty tangle against the wall, still connected, gasping like runners at the end of a race, too stunned to speak as aftershocks rumbled through both of them. She felt her muscles contract around him, felt his contractions inside her. His skin was sticky against hers, the smell of perspiration more aphrodisiacal than offensive.

Trying desperately to catch her breath, she said, "I do believe it was you…who said that this wasn't…about sex. Or was I thinking of…somebody else?"

His face buried in her hair, he said, "There's a distinct possibility…that I may have been…mistaken."

"That's what I thought. Time for a little…revisionist theory?"

He lifted his head, pulled a strand of her hair away from his face, reached down and attempted to pull shredded silk back up to cover her breast. "I ruined your dress."

She looked down at the dress, hanging in tatters around her. "Yes," she said. "I believe you did."

"I'm so sorry. I don't understand what happened."

"It's all right. I bought it on sale."

"Still, there's no excuse—"

"Clancy, darling…"

"—acting like some kind of animal…"

"Goddamn it, I paid fourteen dollars for it at Filene's Basement! You need to lighten up and get a sense of humor. It's a really good thing to have."

His eyes met hers, uncertain, a little embarrassed. "You're telling me there's something humorous about this situation?"

She cupped his cheek and placed a gentle kiss on his lips. "There's something humorous in just about every situation, sugar. You just have to look for it."

"I must have missed it, then. I'm sure you were impressed by my behavior. First I rip your clothes off, then I self-destruct after forty-five seconds."

She hid a smile. Toying with a strand of his hair, she said, "We were both in a big hurry this time around. It's a wonder we managed to last that long."

But he was still muttering, mumbling darkly, something about being a one-minute man. Judging by his tone, it wasn't something he wanted to be.

Heaving a mighty sigh, he said, "Sarah…love."

Her hands, stroking his face, stilled. "What?"

"I hate to have to tell you this, but I need to put you down. I can't hold you up any longer. My legs are getting shaky."

"Oh."

"Is this what it means to be middle-aged? I can't keep it up for more than sixty seconds, and to top it off, my legs aren't strong enough to lift a hundred-pound woman. What's next, diapers and a bib?"

She unlocked her legs from around his waist, disengaged, and slid down the wall to the floor. Her legs were spongy, weak and wobbly. "Speak for yourself," she said, tugging uselessly at what was left of her dress. "I'm planning on another twenty years before I hit middle age. And I weigh considerably more than a hundred pounds.''

"Where?"

She glanced up. "Where what?"

He'd pulled his boxers back up and was busy adjusting his clothing into some semblance of order. "I want you to show me all these pounds you're supposedly packing."

"I'll have you know, sugar, I weigh a hundred and twenty-eight pounds. I'm just built compactly."

"Ah. That explains it. No wonder you almost did me in. I'm surprised that with our combined weight, we didn't go right through the floor and into the cellar."

"I forgot. You do have a sense of humor. It's just slightly warped. Listen, do you think the next time around we could try for the bed?"

"So there's going to be a next time around? You're not tossing me out on my keister and singing *Hit the Road, Jack?*"

"Oh, you gorgeous, sexy, unenlightened man. We are just getting started."

She fed him ice cream in bed.

It was silly, foolish, laughably juvenile. And incredibly, undeniably sexy. He was dead certain there was no more fetching sight than that of Ms. Sarah Connelly sitting cross-legged on the mattress, bed sheets tangled around those satin thighs and candlelight drawing golden highlights from her hair. Surely nothing could be more romantic than dining à deux by the light of a single candle, sharing plump swirls of heaven on a silver spoon, punctuated by velvet sighs and sweet, vanilla-seasoned kisses.

She licked the spoon delicately and said, "I was starving. I haven't eaten a thing since lunch."

He planted a kiss on the bare knee that peeked so tanta-lizingly from beneath the sheet, and began working his way, kiss by kiss, up her silken thigh. "If you were so hungry," he said, "why didn't you eat?" He ran a fingertip along the slightly rounded contour of her belly. It was softer than he'd imagined, less firm than the rest of her sleek, toned body.

She held out a spoonful of French vanilla, and he lifted his head and took the sweet, icy confection into his mouth. "To tell you the truth," she said, "I was so nervous, I was afraid that if I ate anything, I'd throw up all over you. If nothing else, it would've been a memorable evening."

"Well," he said. "I've had some interesting experiences in my time, but I don't recall that I've ever made a woman throw up. Of course—" he studied with keen interest the row of tiny pearlescent stretch marks, barely noticeable to the eye, that crisscrossed her belly below her navel "—it's been a long time since I've been on a date. My memory could be a little shaky. But if I were to be thrown up on," he added thoughtfully, "trust me when I say that you'd be my first and only choice."

"I do believe there's a backhanded compliment in there someplace." She abandoned the spoon, stuck her forefinger into the ice cream, and pulled it out. Without waiting for an invitation, he caught her hand and drew it to his mouth, sucked in her slender finger, and swirled the sweetness away with his tongue, flicking it over the fleshy pad of her fingertip before withdrawing.

She dipped her finger back into the ice cream and said casually, "So, are you ready to talk about her yet?"

Still mulling over the paradox he'd discovered, he said, "About who?"

"Meg." She glanced up, and those blue eyes pinned him in place. "The woman whose name you have tattooed on your arm."

For an instant, he stopped breathing. Every other thought fled his mind as he waited for the old, familiar dagger of pain to slice through his heart. When it didn't, he exhaled and rolled away from her and onto his back. Staring into the shadows that danced on the ceiling, he said flatly, "Meg."

She licked the ice cream off her finger. "I asked Josie about her. She said it wasn't her place to tell me, that I needed to wait until you were ready to talk about it yourself."

"It was a long time ago."

She dug back into the ice cream. Without looking at him, she said, "So maybe it's time now for you to let it go."

He studied her open, trusting face, realized it wasn't censure he saw there, but love, mixed with something else: acceptance. However much he chose to tell or to hold back, Sarah Connelly would never pass judgment on him. Her respect for him, her admiration for him, would remain steadfast.

The knowledge was liberating. Inside him, something let go. Some stricture that had kept him tightly bound for eleven years simply opened up, with no precedent, no warning. Suddenly, it was right to talk about Meg, astonishing to discover just how much he needed to talk about her, how much he needed to share the whole bloody story with someone he trusted, someone he loved, someone who loved him unconditionally.

He reached out and took the ice cream container from her hand. Turning, he set it on the nightstand, and then he rolled onto his hip and pulled her down beside him. As she trailed caressing fingers through his hair, down the nape of his neck, he said, "You asked me once why I became a priest."

"I remember," she said. "It was the day of little Frankie's christening, when we were walking on the beach. You gave me some song and dance about how people turn to God because of unanswered questions. You danced all around the issue, but you never did give me a real answer."

A single vein blazed a blue trail beneath the soft, milky flesh of her forearm. He traced it with his lips. "I gave you half an answer," he said. "Meg was my unanswered question. Unanswered, unanswerable, and brutally painful."

They remained that way, her fingers toying with his hair, his lips a whisper away from her wrist. "Meg was beautiful," he said. "Not just on the outside, but on the inside, where it counts. She loved to laugh…" He trailed off, lost, for just a moment, in the dusty past, before he found himself again. "That's what I remember best about her, that wonderful laugh, the kind that made you want to laugh right along with her. It was intoxicating. She was intoxicating. She drew people the way nectar draws bees."

Sarah's fingers traced patterns against his scalp. "I fell in love with her when she was fourteen years old," he said. "But I was twenty, far too old for a fourteen-year-old girl. I had to wait for her to grow up. I've never been a particularly patient man, but I knew Meg would be worth the wait. So I went to UMass for a year, squeezed in courses around my work schedule. Meg knew I had my eye on her. She couldn't help but know. I tripped over my own feet and turned into a babbling idiot every time we crossed paths. While I worked and studied and suffered, Meg spent that year flirting with every fifteen-year-old boy north of Rhode Island. I think she did it just to torture me. At the end of the year, I was half crazy, she was still just a sweet teenage girl, and I was still six years older. I realized I needed to put some distance between us. What little patience I had was wearing thin, and I didn't want to ruin everything by making my move too soon. So I dropped out of school and hitchhiked around Europe for a few months. Then I went to work on a merchant ship and ended up in the Far East."

"Ah, yes. Where you learned to eat with chopsticks."

"Among other things." Some of which he would go to his grave without telling her about. "I stayed there for nearly three years. But always, in the back of my mind, I knew I was waiting for Meg."

Softly, she said, "So what happened?"

He shifted position, planted a kiss on the smooth swell of her breast. "When I came home, she was eighteen, more beautiful than ever, and I waged an all-out campaign to win her affections. It didn't take long. I suspect that all that time, she'd been waiting for me, too. Things turned serious pretty quickly. I wanted to get married right away, the summer after she graduated. I couldn't see any reason to wait; I was twenty-four years old, I'd been around the globe, seen the world. I was ready to settle down. But Meg was eighteen, and I don't think she'd ever been more than twenty miles outside of Boston. She kept putting me off. She wanted to finish college first. Four years. I couldn't imagine waiting four whole years. I pushed. She resisted. After a while, I noticed she wasn't laughing so much anymore. Then, one night in early August, she told me it wasn't going to work out between us. It was over. She was going to college in a few weeks and moving on with her life.

"I didn't take it well. I told her she was ruining her life, ruining *our* life. I told her that she'd be back, that what we had was too good to throw away. I ranted. I bellowed. I said terrible things to her." The memory, even after all these years, filled him with shame. "You have to understand, I was twenty-four years old, absolutely desperate, and stunningly, maddeningly in love."

Her fingers stilled against the nape of his neck. "What happened?"

He closed his eyes, moistened his lips. "Six days later, she was murdered."

17

It was quite possibly the first time in her life that she'd been rendered speechless. She'd expected the standard she-left-me-for-another-man-and-broke-my-heart-for-all-time tragic love story. Nothing had prepared her for the word murder. It was so cold, so hard, so final. How was she expected to respond to such a bombshell? What words could she possibly say that would convey the depth of her dismay? Or her regret at having asked about Meg in the first place? Damn it, Josie should have warned her. But of course, Josie had warned her, in a manner of speaking. She'd just chosen to ignore the warning.

"I'm so sorry," she said. The words were hopelessly inadequate, but they were the only words she could find.

"Yes. So am I. She was a lovely human being. They thought I did it."

Outrage, instantaneous and indignant, reared its furious head. "Who the hell would think such a thing of you?"

"The police. They dragged me in and raked me over the coals for hours. Followed me around for weeks. Parked outside my door. It was a sexual crime, you see. She was raped and strangled. And we'd been lovers, so I was the obvious suspect. Except that they had no evidence, because there *was* no evidence. As if I could have put my hands around that beautiful, vulnerable neck, and—" he stopped, rolled away from her, sat up on the edge of the bed and ran his fingers through his hair "—it was the darkest moment of my life."

Sarah took a breath, tried to smother the pain that was a bright flame in her chest, and followed him. She folded her arms around him from behind and pressed herself up against his back. Held tight until she felt him relax against her. Then, she said softly, brokenly, "So you turned to God."

"I turned to the bottle. I got stinking drunk, and I stayed that way for three months. The tattoo made its appearance while I was endeavoring to bring home the gold in the drunkard's Olympics. I don't even remember getting it. I woke up one morning after a particularly nasty night before, and there it was, in living color. My permanent memorial to a dead lover. I was lucky, you know. In spite of my determined efforts to commit slow suicide, God was at work in my life. It was Father O'Rourke, the old tyrant, who saved me. He sobered me up, wiped the snot from my nose, and told me what a disappointment I was to God. If it wasn't for him, I'd probably be dead now."

In the flickering shadows, she held him close to her breast, her breathing synchronized with his, her hands curled into tight fists against his bare chest. "I think a good part of what drove me," he said, catching her hand and bringing it to his mouth, "was guilt, and the need for atonement. If I could devote the rest of my life to God, I could somehow make up for my own sin, my own part in what happened to Meg." He unfurled her fingers and kissed her knuckles, one by one.

"But it wasn't your fault."

"Somehow, I felt as though it was, and somehow, I needed to make it up to her. And to God. So I entered the priesthood."

"Do you regret it?"

He turned, drew her into his arms. "Becoming a priest? No. The frustrations are legion, but overall, the experience has been phenomenally rewarding. To be able to touch so many people's lives in such a significant, positive way." He drew her head down to his shoulder, cradled it there, rested

his chin against her cheek. "I wonder sometimes, if Meg and
I had married, where I'd be now. I've been a part of the
Church for so long now, I can't imagine what else I might
have done. In spite of its shortcomings—" he pulled a blanket over them, wrapped it around her "—the Catholic Church
has been good to me. And most of the time, I like what I do.
I don't always agree with the Church, but I'm good at being
a priest. But going home at the end of the day to a single
bed in an empty room, night after night…it gets lonely."

"I know."

"Until you came along, I hadn't realized how lonely I was.
I knew something was wrong, I just couldn't put my finger
on it. I'm sworn to a life of servitude; I'm not used to thinking about my own needs." He tilted her face up to his,
touched his mouth to hers in a gentle kiss. She cupped his
cheek, ran a fingertip up to his eyebrow, traced the line of
hair at his temple. "Your hands," he murmured, "they feel
so good. On my face…in my hair. That's what I've missed
the most, you know. More than the exquisite pleasure of being inside a woman. More even than that violent rush of
rapture at the end. Simple human touch."

"That's so sad."

"It's just the way of the Church. Touching isn't forbidden,
of course. But we're encouraged to live apart from the world.
That's the facet of priestly celibacy most people don't understand. It's not just about sex. It's about setting ourselves
apart from the rest of the world, living for the spirit instead
of the flesh. Touching is worldly and carnal. We're supposed
to be above that."

"I don't know, sugar. It sounds to me like a damn lonely
place to be."

"I'm not even sure it's right, or proper, despite what we
were taught in seminary. It's said that infants can die without
loving human touch. Failure to thrive. That's how I feel. All
these years, I've been failing to thrive."

"Not anymore," she said. "Not if I have anything to say about it."

"Sweet Sarah." His eyes gazed deep into hers. "You have more heart than any other woman I've ever met."

She turned her face into his palm, kissed it, felt him shudder in response. "God, Clancy," she said. "What are we going to do?"

"I don't know about tomorrow, or the next day. But for tonight, at least, we can love each other."

When she awakened, the other half of the bed was empty. She glanced at the clock on the dresser. Its glowing red digits read 1:53. It was the middle of the night. Had he left without saying goodbye?

With dread forming a hard lump in her stomach, she rolled out of bed and pulled on a robe. Belting it around her, she walked to the window and drew back the curtain. She hadn't realized she'd been holding her breath until the sight of the blue Saturn still sitting in her driveway sent it rushing from her chest. Her stomach unclenched, eased. He hadn't run away. So where was he?

She moved easily through the darkened house. The fourth stair from the top squeaked as she descended, a familiar and comforting sound. The living room was empty, bathed in night air, a good twenty degrees cooler than it was upstairs. Until she'd moved here, she'd always thought New England summers were cool and dry. But the first summer heat wave, which had arrived in early May, had quickly disabused her of that notion. In a two-story house, especially one that lacked adequate insulation, heat was bound to rise and, on these hot nights, the upstairs of her house bore a striking resemblance to the sticky, steamy atmosphere of the shack where she'd grown up in Bayou Rouillard.

The kitchen door was thrown open to the night air. A breeze played cool fingers through her hair as she stood at the screen door and listened to the chirping of crickets and the rusty creak of the backyard glider. In the moonlight, his features were indistinguishable; she saw only dark hair and the pale glimmer of his face in the darkness.

She opened the screen door and stepped outside. The grass was cool and damp and prickly against her bare feet as she crossed the yard to where he sat. "Here you are," she said, sitting beside him on the glider. "I wondered where you'd disappeared to."

"I suffer from chronic insomnia. I spend a lot of time sitting in the dark, thinking."

"You can call it thinking if you want, sugar. I prefer to call it brooding. And brooding is bad for your health. It'll give you ulcers. A heart condition. Maybe even impotence."

His smile was wry. "Now there's a terrifying thought." He raised his arm, looped it around her shoulders. "I'm afraid there's no help for me. I'm Irish. We've elevated brooding to an art form."

She drew her legs up around her and settled against him. "So what are you brooding about?"

"Oh, the usual. Sin. Redemption. Divine grace, or the lack thereof."

"Of course. All the usual stuff people think about at two in the morning."

"I'm supposed to provide spiritual guidance to my flock. I'm supposed to be a role model. Lead them away from sin and toward a state of grace. But I can't even keep my own house in order."

She was silent for a moment before she said, "Are you having regrets?"

"There's a part of me that wishes I were."

In the darkness, she took his hand. His skin was cool and smooth. They laced fingers. "I'm sorry," she said.

"Don't be. It would break my heart." He sighed and rubbed her knuckles with his thumb. "I broke a vow," he said. "The Church would say that what I've done is a sin. Most people would agree. But if it's a sin—" he paused, turned to examine her face in the moonlight "—then why does it feel so right?"

"It does, doesn't it? We're an ideal match. A three-time loser and a Catholic priest." She raised her face to the vast, starry sky. "Momma's undoubtedly rolling in her grave right now, knowing that her Jezebel of a daughter seduced a holy man and toppled him from his pedestal."

"I'm not a holy man, I'm just a man. I don't belong on any pedestal. And you didn't seduce me. I seduced you."

"Actually, it wasn't so much seduction as it was marching orders."

"I wasn't about to take the chance you'd turn me down."

They were both silent for a time before she said softly, "What'll they do to you if they find out? Could you be defrocked?"

"For having sex with a woman? It's highly unlikely, considering the number of priests who haven't been defrocked for having sex with little boys. When you put it into perspective, what you and I are doing is pretty tame. The Catholic Church has a long and glorious history of selective blindness when it comes to things they don't want to see. If they got really ticked off, I suppose they could transfer me to a parish in Oshkosh. More likely, as long as I'm not making a total ass of myself in public, they'd probably turn a blind eye to the whole affair."

"Is that what this is? An affair?"

"Sarah, darling, I meant it in the broader sense." He ran a thumb lazily up and down her bare arm. In the distance, an eighteen-wheeler whined as it shifted gears out on Route 1A. The night breeze, ripe with the scent of lilac, caressed her cheek. "I need to ask you a question," he said.

She lay her head against his shoulder. "What's that, sugar?"

"Why didn't you tell me the truth?"

She sucked in a sharp breath. Her heart began to do an odd little dance inside her chest. Carefully, she said, "What truth would that be?"

"The truth about Kit. Why didn't you tell me you're her mother?"

Needles of grief and loss darted in and out of her heart like flames, licking and destroying. She pulled away from him slowly, bent forward, and cradled her head in her hands. Not bothering to disguise the tremor in her voice, she said wearily, "How long have you known?"

"I guess I'm a little slow. I just figured it out tonight."

She told herself it wasn't hurt she heard in his voice. Rubbing at her temples, at the headache that had suddenly sprung up there, she said, "You're far too perceptive, Father Donovan."

"It wasn't all that difficult to figure out. You've been so determined to find her. A lot of women would have given up by now. And there was the marriage thing."

Still not looking at him, she said, "What marriage thing?"

"It didn't make sense to me that you would have left Remy because he didn't get along with your niece." He toyed with a strand of her hair, lifted it and let it fall. "She looks just like you, Sarah. Tonight, I saw the final piece, and it all fell into place. When a woman's given birth, it's hard for her body to hide the evidence from a lover."

"I suppose so," she said, "if he's an attentive lover."

"The truth was there all the time, sitting in front of me, like a giant jigsaw puzzle. I just had to put the scattered pieces together before I could see the whole picture." He caught one of her hands in his. She pressed her free hand over her eyes, still unable to look at him as he threaded fingers with her and pressed his palm, warm and comforting, against hers. "It must have been agonizing," he said, "having to hold in your true feelings all these years. Trying to achieve that delicate balance between showing enough interest in her life and showing too much. Watching her grow, experiencing her achievements and failures as a spectator, when all you wanted was to be her mother.''

Tears, harsh and unexpected, welled up in her eyes. "I'm sorry," she said. "I'm sorry I lied to you. But Kit doesn't know the truth. After Ellie died, we all felt it would be best to let sleeping dogs lie. She's Bobby and Ellie's daughter. Period. In the eyes of the law, I'm nothing more than her aunt.''

"You could have told me. You could have trusted me.''

"In the beginning," she said softly, "you were a stranger. There was no reason to tell you.''

"And later? After we became a little more than strangers?''

"Later," she said, "I was afraid to tell you. Afraid you'd think less of me.''

"For being her mother instead of her aunt?''

"You're a man of God. Morally upright. To put it delicately, I have a checkered past. I didn't want to lose your respect.''

"Damn it, Sarah. Look at me.''

Like a naughty child, she turned to face her accuser. "If you don't trust me," he said, "this isn't going to work.''

A single tear broke free and ran down her cheek. "Tell me, Father, just how is it supposed to work? You're married to the Catholic Church. No matter what happens between us, there'll be no happy ending for you and me.''

He released her hand, ran both of his hands through his rumpled hair. "This is some mess we've created, isn't it?''

"The ultimate love triangle. You, me, and God. Tell me, Clancy, how the hell am I supposed to compete with God?''

"I don't know," he said wearily. "I wish I did.''

They decided that if there would ever come a time when they both needed alcoholic fortification, this was it, so they opened his forty-dollar bottle of wine. Sarah lit a single candle on the mantel and they settled in the living room to face each other across a room filled with flickering shadows.

"I was a rotten kid." She slowly twirled the stem of her wineglass between slender fingers. "A real hell-raiser. I drank beer, smoked dope, spread my legs for just about any young buck who'd smile real pretty at me and take me to McDonald's for a chocolate shake."

She took a delicate sip of wine and swallowed it. Crossed her legs and stared into the glass. "When I was sixteen," she said, "I met Sonny Evans. He worked at his daddy's garage, a couple of towns over. He was five years older than me, a real wild boy. Momma hated him on sight because he wore a leather jacket, he always had grease under his fingernails, and he had a reputation as a hard drinker. She kept telling me he'd never amount to a piss in a windstorm. She couldn't understand that all the things she hated about him were what made him so irresistible to me."

She leaned back against the couch. "The more she hated him, the more I believed I was in *Love*, with a capital L. It just about drove her crazy. Of course, underneath it all, that was probably my primary motivation. At that age, you live to torment your parents. One fine day, after a particularly nasty battle, I packed all my stuff and moved in with Sonny. It was a stupid thing to do, but like I said, I was sixteen. At sixteen, you have all the answers. You're just not smart enough yet to realize they're all the wrong ones." She stared into her glass, lifted it and took a long, slow swallow.

Quietly, he said, "What did your mother do?"

"She stopped speaking to me. As far as she was concerned, I'd made my own bed, and now I could lie in it."

"Tough love."

"And then some. At first, I didn't mind. I was all grown up and living my own life, and having one hell of a fine time of it. One party right after another. For a few months, I really thought I was hot shit.'' She smiled ruefully. ''But after a while, the glitter started to rub off. I got tired of the partying, and Sonny got tired of my nagging. I was cramping his style by daring to suggest that he might occasionally spend an evening home with me, instead of out drinking and chasing skirts with his friends.

''Then I found out I was pregnant. I was young enough, and gullible enough, to believe he'd be happy about the baby. I thought it would save our rapidly deteriorating relationship.'' She took another sip of wine.

Softly, he said, ''What happened when you told him?''

She looked at him over the rim of her wineglass. ''He called me a few choice names and said the baby probably wasn't even his. Considering how much time I'd been spending at home while he was out sowing his wild oats, I could easily have been…shall we say…entertaining other gentlemen…in his absence. After all, according to him, I was a legend around Bayou Rouillard. There wasn't a guy in the parish who hadn't nailed me at some point in time.''

He winced, felt the pain she tried to disguise behind an offhand manner. ''Cruel words,'' he said.

''I warned you it wasn't a pretty story. He tossed me out on my rear. I was devastated. I really thought I was in love with the guy. I was so young.'' She shook her head, sighed. ''So there I was—no man, no roof over my head, no job, no marketable skills. I didn't even have a high school diploma. All I had was this little baby growing inside of me. I did the only thing I could do. I tucked my tail between my legs and ran home to Momma.''

He let out a hard breath. ''And she took you in?''

''What's that old saying, about home being the place where, when you have to go there, they have to take you in? I'll give her credit. She never once said, 'I told you so.' But she was mortified. We might have been dirt-poor, but we

weren't dirt. Momma went to church faithfully, every Sunday
of her life. She'd always been able to hold her head up in
public, and she wasn't about to give that up. So she took
care of everything for me. She sent me here, to stay with
Aunt Helen, until the baby was born. I was so young and
scared and confused, so grateful she hadn't turned her back
on me, that I let her run the show. I shut my mouth and did
whatever she told me, even when she told me that Bobby
and Ellie wanted to adopt the baby. They'd been trying for
a couple of years, but Ellie couldn't conceive. Something
about a tipped uterus. My brother was so much in love with
his wife, he would've roped the moon for her if she'd asked.
And she wanted a baby so bad she could taste it. So I gave
her mine.

"It was the hardest thing I've ever had to do," she said.
"Because, you see, I fell madly in love with that little girl
the instant I laid eyes on her. I hadn't understood about
mother love. I think it's something you have to experience
to really understand. But I did what Momma said was best
for everyone concerned. My life was a big zero. I had nothing
to offer Kit. Bobby and Ellie could give her a home, with
two parents I knew would dote on her. Sure, Bobby had a
little growing up to do. But his heart was in the right place,
and I knew Ellie would be a good enough mother to more
than make up for any of my brother's inadequacies. You
should have seen her face the first time they put that baby in
her arms. Like she'd just seen God. And I figured that at
least I'd still get to be a part of Kit's life. I could still see
her regularly, play the part of the doting aunt. I was seventeen. What did I know?" A single tear trickled down her
cheek. "I thought that would be enough."

He got up from the chair and crossed the room to where
she sat on the couch. Kneeling in front of her, he took her
wineglass and set it on the floor, then clasped both her hands

in his. "It must have taken tremendous courage," he told her, "to do what you did."

"I didn't have a choice, don't you see?" She swiped a strand of hair back from her face. "Courage had nothing to do with it! I did what I had to do, what was best for Kit. I handed over my daughter to my brother and his wife, pretending my heart wasn't all bloody and battered."

He eased closer, between her parted knees, and drew her trembling body into his arms, trying to absorb her pain, to carry some of the load for her. "I'm so sorry," he said.

She pressed her damp cheek against his shoulder. "Every day of my life," she said, "for the last sixteen years, I've regretted what I did. Two years ago, when Bobby finally brought her to me, I thought it was the second chance I'd been praying for. I was finally going to get to know my daughter. To influence her life. To be her mother. But the joke was on me, because she's just like me. Headstrong, careless, and determined to make all the same mistakes I made, plus a few of her own that I was too naive to think up at her age. And I can't even tell her I'm her mother. That's the cross I have to bear for my sins. She's built this whole fantasy around Ellie. I don't have the right to tear that down."

"You don't think she has a right to know the truth? To understand the sacrifice you made for her because you loved her enough to give her up?"

Softly, against his neck, she said. "I don't know. I truly don't know."

"I think you're underestimating her."

She toyed with a button on his shirt. "What if I tell her the truth and she ends up hating me? What if she thinks I gave her up because I didn't want her? We've lied to her for her entire life. How the hell do I tell her that her father is really her uncle, and her real father was a coked-up grease monkey who refused to even acknowledge that she was his?"

He stroked her hair with gentle fingers, more determined

than ever to bring her daughter back to her in one piece. "You'll find the words," he said. "When the time comes, you'll find the right words."

"What if she ends up hating us all?"

"It's a chance you'll have to take." He brushed a strand of damp hair away from her cheek and redeposited it behind her ear. "You can't change the past," he said. "You can only move ahead. We've all done things we're not proud of." He thought of his own past, and firmed his resolve. "What counts isn't where we're coming from, but where we're headed."

"I feel like I'm headed nowhere. I'm just spinning my wheels. All these weeks, and we're no closer to finding her than we ever were."

He kissed her cheek. "It'll happen," he said. "I suspect we're closer than we think. All we need is the right puzzle piece, and it'll all fall into place. That one single piece of information that will lead us to her. I think it will come when we least expect it. But I promise you one thing: it *will* come."

His cell phone rang just as the birds outside the bedroom window were starting to greet the day. He groaned, tugged uselessly at the sheets caught in a hopeless tangle around his lanky legs, and thrust an arm into the early morning shadows to snag the phone. With a soft, incoherent murmur, Sarah pressed closer and wrapped a slender leg around his thigh. He returned to her silken warmth and clumsily pressed the button to silence the ringing phone.

She pressed her face against his back. He slipped his free arm through hers and cleared his throat. "Hello?"

"Father Donovan?"

Still half-asleep, he fumbled for the correct answer to the question. "Yes."

"It's Terry."

In his incoherent and disoriented state, it took him a moment to process the name. "Terry?" he said.

"Terry Jackson. You gave me your card and that flyer a couple months ago in Kenmore Square."

Ah, yes. Terry. Short black skirt, no coat, needle tracks running up the inside of her arm. Still fumbling, he said, "Terry, it's—" he squinted to read the bedside clock "—four-thirty in the morning."

"I would've called sooner, but I just remembered where I saw her face before."

He rubbed his forehead with his free hand and murmured, "Whose face?"

"Kit. The missing girl. The one on the flyer you gave me."

Full consciousness slammed into him. He smoothly disentangled himself from Sarah's limbs, twined with exquisite abandon around his, and sat up in bed. "You've seen Kit?" he said.

"Yeah," Terry said. "But like I said, it took me a while to figure out she was the same girl."

Beside him, Sarah raised herself on one elbow. Their gazes locked. "Where?" he said. "Where did you see her?"

"At a porno shoot about ten days ago, in one of them sleazy no-tell motels out on Route 1 in Peabody. This guy Rio, he got himself a little business shooting home movies for slicked-up rich dudes looking for a little outside action, if you get my drift. Sometimes, he gives me a call when he's looking for something special. I'm a specialist—" she drew out the word, gave it a few extra syllables "—in pain management."

"Pain management," he said blankly.

"Yeah, you know, S&M? He got this regular client who likes to be tied up and abused. He really gets off on it."

"What does this have to do with Kit?"

"She was there."

"You're sure it was her?"

"It was her, all right. Rio's always got some new cookie on his arm. I usually don't pay no attention. I don't even know why I'm telling you this now. We both know that I ain't no good Samaritan, and I'll be damned if I can figure out why I should care. But that dude is bad news, and it gets old, watching him take advantage of young girls too stupid to figure out what he's up to. And Kit, she was a real babe in the woods. She didn't even figure out we were shooting a porn movie until she got a look at Mistress Terry all done up in her dominatrix attire." Terry let out a short, harsh bark of laughter. "Once upon a time, I was probably as innocent as she is. When I was about eight. A girl like that, Rio'll chew her up and spit her out. And his girlfriends have this habit of disappearing permanently once he's done with 'em."

"How do I get in touch with Rio?"

"Don't nobody get in touch with Rio. He gets in touch with you."

"Somebody must have access to him. Who else was there?"

"Just Nate and me, and—"

"Nate. Who's Nate?"

"The techie. He sets up the camera and the lights and stuff. He's been at every shoot I ever did with Rio."

"I don't suppose Nate happens to have a last name?"

"I imagine he does, but I ain't privy to that particular piece of information. Anyway, like I was saying, it was just Nate and me, and the client."

"The client," he said. "You don't happen to know his name?"

Terry went abruptly mute.

He waited out the silence. "Look," she said, "if Rio ever catches me blabbing the name of one of his high-profile clients, he be wiping my face all over the bricks in City Hall Plaza."

"So you do know his name?"

"I might," she said cagily. "What's it worth to you?"

"A young girl's life, Terry. You don't want Kit to disappear permanently, like all those other girls."

At the other end of the line, there was silence. "You know," she said finally, "I ain't nothing but a cheap junkie whore. But you did me a favor once. You took me in off the streets and told me I was worth something. I owe you for that. But this is it, Father. No more favors. We're even. The slate's wiped clean. Understand?"

"I understand."

"Just remember I wasn't the one that told you this. That high-profile client? His name's Tommy. At least that's what I call him. But you'd know him better as Tom Adams. Senator Tom Adams."

18

The Adams for U.S. Senate campaign headquarters was tucked away in a narrow storefront on a West End side street, in the shadow of the State House perched high atop Beacon Hill. The early afternoon sun reflected off gleaming windows plastered with campaign posters bearing slogans like *Adams for Senate in 2004* and *Tom Adams—Standing Tall for Massachusetts.* Inside, fresh-faced, eager young campaign workers stuffed envelopes and typed letters and telephoned voters to enthusiastically urge them to cast their gubernatorial ballots for State Senator Thomas Adams, the Great White Hope of the people of Massachusetts.

Clancy lingered on the sidewalk outside the door. He and Tom Adams had sat on countless committees together, had stood side by side at a downtown soup kitchen, spooning food onto paper plates for the homeless. Together, they'd argued with the Licensing Board—and won the battle—when a local businessman had applied for a permit to open a new strip club in the heart of Chinatown. He'd been to Tom's house, had dined with Tom's pretty freckle-faced wife, Bess, and their two giggling daughters. The two of them had played racquetball together on occasion, had met for lunch a few times at Durgin-Park. They'd been friends, and there was nothing of the Tom Adams he knew, the clean-living, hard-working, caring family man, in the Tom Adams Terry had described, a man caught up in sin and darkness and degradation.

Sarah touched his arm, bringing him out of his reverie. "You okay?" she said.

He turned to look at her, wondered if the vulnerability in his eyes matched what he saw in hers. She knew as well as he did that this could be the link that would bring them to Kit. Or it could turn out to be simply another dead end. He took her hand and squeezed it. "I'm fine," he said. "You?"

"Are you kidding, sugar? I'm a tough old broad. I can handle anything."

He drank in her sweet face, memorized each line. "Tough, maybe," he said. "Old, never. And I imagine you can handle just about anything. All right, then, let's do it."

A half-dozen smiling young faces looked up when they came in. He chose the nearest one, a twentyish girl with a buzz cut, a variety of earrings, and a Harvard sweatshirt. "Is Tom in?" he said.

"Back office," she said, "straight ahead."

He followed her directions to the open door at the back of the room. Tom sat at a polished walnut desk, one hand rubbing the nape of his neck, the phone balanced between his ear and his shoulder. His white dress shirt was wrinkled, open at the collar, his tie loosened. When he saw them, a broad smile crossed his handsome face, and he waved them inside. "I have to go, Jerry," he said into the phone. "I have visitors. I'll touch base with you later."

He hung up the phone and stood. "Clancy," he said heartily, reaching over the desk to shake hands. "Don't tell me you're here to volunteer. We could use a couple more warm bodies to stuff envelopes. Or maybe you'd like to make a campaign contribution."

Clancy briefly clasped the senator's hand and managed a weak smile. "Tom," he said, "this is Sarah Connelly. Sarah, Tom Adams. We need to speak with you."

While the two shook hands, Clancy glanced through the door into the room beyond, then closed it behind him.

Tom raised an eyebrow. "Why the closed door?"

"I suspect you might not want this broadcast to the entire world."

Tom's smile lost a little wattage, but held steady. "Grab a chair," he said. "Sit down. What can I do for you?"

Silently, Clancy and Sarah settled into metal folding chairs. On one corner of Tom's desk was a framed photo of Bess and the girls. Sweet, wholesome, smiling. The perfect family.

"There's no way I can soft-pedal this," he said, "so I'm just going to jump right in. According to my sources, you've recently developed an interest in filmmaking."

Tom clasped his hands on the desktop and furrowed his brow. "Filmmaking?" he said. "I don't know what you're talking about."

"I'm talking about the little home movie you made a couple of weeks ago in Room 17 at the Starlite Motel in Peabody. I'm talking about a man named Rio with a camera, and a woman named Terry with a riding crop. Is any of this starting to sound familiar?"

Tom's face paled, but his smile remained in place. "You're kidding, right? This is some kind of joke."

"I understand there were two other people in the room that night. A sound and lighting technician named Nate, and a blond, blue-eyed sixteen-year-old girl named Kit. The same girl I've been looking for since March. The same girl we talked about just a few weeks ago. The one you promised to help me find."

Tom's complexion had turned to a sickly gray pallor, and he'd begun to sweat. "You have to understand—"

"I expected better of you, Tom. I thought you were an honorable man. But now I realize that the man I thought I knew doesn't exist. He's nothing more than a media creation designed to further your political aspirations."

Fiercely, Tom said, "You have no right to judge me."

"No," he said. "Only God has that right. But I do have a right to certain expectations, among them, honesty."

"I've never been dishonest with you."

"You've been dishonest with everyone. You've been dishonest with me, with your family, with all the people who are so eager to send you to Washington. How will you answer to them, Tom? What'll you do if the police arrest Terry for prostitution and your name shows up in the *Globe* as one of her regular johns? What do you think that would do to Bess and the girls? Have you even thought about them at all?"

Tom's face went slack as his tough, shiny facade began to crack, one smooth brick at a time. "Jesus," he said, and buried his face in his trembling hands. "Christ Jesus."

It wasn't easy, watching a man he'd trusted, a man he'd admired, a man he'd considered a friend, crumbling like week-old bread. But he sat in silence and waited for Tom to pull himself together.

It took a while. Eventually, Tom got up and walked to the window. He stood looking out, his dress shirt ringed with sweat, his shoulders quivering. Bleakly, he said, "All my life, I've done the right thing. Went to the right schools, earned the right degree, dated the right girls. Got the right job. Married the right woman." He shoved his hands into his pockets and absently jingled a fistful of change. "Bess is pregnant again, you know. Number three."

He turned away from the window, a rivulet of sweat trickling from his forehead. "I love my wife and my girls," he said hoarsely. "More than anything. If they find this out, it'll kill them. If the rest of the world finds out, my career will be down the toilet. It's such a small thing, really. Once in a while, I just need something a little…more. Something I'd never ask Bess to give me. I—" He paused, looked at them both beseechingly. "Is that really so awful?"

Quietly, Clancy said, "You're playing with fire, Tom. Did you really think you wouldn't get burned?"

Tom had aged ten years in the past five minutes. He looked old. Defeated. "She was with Rio," he said wearily. "I hardly looked at her. We never even exchanged words. I didn't realize she was the same girl. If I had—" He closed his eyes, shoved his fingers through carefully arranged hair. "I'd never touch a girl that young," he said. "You know that. She's not much older than my own girls. I'd kill anybody who touched one of them."

Clancy leaned forward in his chair. "Then you should be able to understand our determination to get her away from Rio. This man is trouble, Tom. Poison to a young girl like Kit."

A new thought appeared to occur to Tom. "Good God," he said. "You mean to tell me it was *Rio* who beat you up?"

"Not in person. But his message came through loud and clear."

"That son of a—" Tom paused, shook his head. Although his color had begun to return, his cockiness was gone. Clancy suspected it might be some time before it reappeared. If it ever did. "What is it you want?" Tom said. "What can I do to help?"

"You can get in touch with Rio," Clancy told him. "And set me up for one of his video extravaganzas. With Kit."

The seconds ticked away while the two men locked gazes. Neither spoke, neither gave an inch until, without a word, Tom reached out and picked up the telephone.

Clancy paced the tiny office, hands in his pockets, and listened as Tom wove an elaborate tale about an out-of-town friend who liked his girls young and blond, and who'd pay whatever it cost to get a couple of hours in front of the camera with the hot young blonde who'd been with Rio the other night. He was so convincing, so sincere, that Clancy nearly believed the story himself. But then, he'd never had reason to doubt Tom's veracity until now. While he paced, Tom and Rio settled on a price, a time, a location. Tonight, 9:30, the Starlite Motel. Three thousand dollars cash. The price of a young girl's innocence.

Now there was nothing left to do but wait.

They were both subdued when he dropped Sarah off at Bookmark an hour later. In the privacy of his car, she took his hand in hers, rubbed a soft fingertip over the fleshy base of his thumb, and threaded their fingers together. "I'm sorry," she said. "I know he was your friend."

He turned their clasped hands upside down and examined their entwined fingers. Brought her hand to his lips and kissed it.

"Don't," she said. "Somebody will see."

"To hell with them. To hell with all of them." There in the parking lot of the Northgate Mall, in broad daylight and in full view of the world, he kissed her with desperate intensity. He buried his face in her hair and drew a hard, shuddering breath. Backed away and tucked her hair behind her ear. "Go," he said. "I'll see you tonight."

His stomach churned all the way back to Saint Bart's. Melissa took one look at his face and sighed. "I knew it was too good to last," she said.

He didn't bother to answer. Inside his study, he locked the door behind him and reached into the candy jar on his desk for a hit of cinnamon and sugar. He plopped heavily onto his chair, picked up a paper clip from the container on his desk, and began twisting and bending it with ferocious intent.

He destroyed paper clip after paper clip as he played and replayed the last twenty-four hours of his life, like a videotape in his head. Play, rewind, fast-forward. Play, rewind, fast-forward. No matter how often he replayed the tape, the pictures always came out the same. Sarah, lush and earthy and sweetly, agonizingly tender. The scent of her perfume played in his head like the wispy strains of a half-remembered melody. Velvet skin, velvet sighs, velvet kisses. He'd thought he remembered what it was like, this damning combination of tenderness and lust that brought a man and a woman together in a fiery conflagration, but his memories were dusty, insubstantial. They bore no resemblance to the exquisite reality of loving Sarah. What he'd felt for Meg had been nothing compared to this. He'd been a boy then, hot-tempered and hot-blooded, determined to win the prize no matter what the cost. Now he was a man, with a man's appetites and a man's capacity to love. And last night he'd tasted heaven, even though he knew that grasping it was an impossibility.

He pulled a sheet of paper from the desk drawer, crumpled it into a ball, and let it fly. It reached the far wall of his study before it crashed and burned. After years of exposure to the streets and the people who populated them, he'd thought himself beyond idealism, immune to the disappointment one human could cause another. But apparently that idealist still dwelt somewhere inside him. And he was heartsick about this mess with Tom.

They weren't really so far apart, Tom and he. Not when you looked past the outer trappings and dug down to the heart of the matter. Tom had made a vow to Bess, a vow he'd broken by participating in adulterous sex. Clancy had made a similar vow to God, and he, too, had broken his vow. Did it make him a better person than Tom because he'd broken that vow with a woman he loved instead of a prostitute? A vow was a vow, and come Judgment Day, he didn't expect he'd be getting any brownie points just because he happened to be in love with the woman in question. God wasn't the IRS, with exceptions and sub-paragraphs and exemptions from responsibility for those who needed them the least. His laws were clear, straightforward, unbendable.

Elbows propped on the desktop, Clancy raked his hands

through his hair. He'd come to Sarah's bed with a clear head and a clean conscience, and though all the demons of hell might torment him for eternity, he would carry no regrets away from it. For one night, he'd been reminded of what it meant to be fully alive, and he would carry the bittersweet memory with him for the rest of his days. But the ending to their story was already written, cemented by fate and his station in life. Michael had been right. No matter what a man chose to do, no matter whether he chose good or evil or something that lived in the shadowy area between the two, there were consequences to face. There always had been, and always would be, a piper to pay. How he chose to make that payment—and to whom—determined whether or not a man was capable of meeting his own eyes in the mirror each morning for the rest of his days.

He couldn't have it both ways. He couldn't continue to live with one foot in the Church and the other in the secular world. It was tearing him apart, and merely prolonging the inevitable. He and Sarah couldn't be together. Not the way he wanted to be, not if he wanted to remain a priest. It was time to make a choice.

He picked up the telephone and called Bishop Halloran.

She was sitting on the couch, watching *Wheel of Fortune*, with Pixel's soft muzzle cradled in her lap, when Rio came in whistling. Kit eyed him suspiciously. Ever since the night Gonzales had come to the house, the night Rio'd dragged her out to that awful motel, the two of them had existed in a state of armed truce. She'd treated him with the same distant courtesy she would have shown a stranger. Although he'd wheedled and cajoled and tried just about everything he could think of to win back her favor, she hadn't budged an inch. She'd been a fool to trust him in the first place, a fool to fall for his boyish smile and his winsome ways. Now she was a prisoner who wouldn't even be granted parole.

But she hadn't given up hope. Her brief, furtive phone call to Aunt Sarah had renewed her faith. Sarah had broken down and cried at the sound of her voice. That, more than anything, had told Kit that her aunt would continue ceaselessly to pursue Rio's trail. Sooner or later, this nightmare would come to an end. Sarah would find her. And if she didn't, as long as Kit stayed quiet, as long as she didn't rock the boat, as long as she remained vigilant, sooner or later the opportunity for escape would present itself. Sooner or later he'd make a mistake, turn his back on her, leave her unattended. And then she would run, as far and as fast as her legs would carry her. Back to the ugly blue house in Revere—which didn't seem quite so ugly anymore—and back to Aunt Sarah, who'd treated her with more kindness and warmth than anybody else ever had.

Rio crossed the room in front of her and picked up the remote, silencing the television with the click of a button. "Great news," he said. "Remember the client from the shoot we did a couple weeks ago?"

Would she ever forget the distinguished-looking gentleman who'd paid an exorbitant fee to be abused by Terry? Not likely. "Why?" she said.

Rio picked up a plum from the bowl on the coffee table, polished it on his shirt, and bit into it. Juice squirted in every direction. He wiped his chin carelessly with his sleeve. "Apparently, he was quite taken by you."

Her heart began to beat a little faster as she pondered the implications of his words. "I didn't think he even noticed I was there."

"He noticed, all right. He mentioned you to a friend who's in town on business. The guy scheduled a session with you for tonight."

She shoved Pixel's head aside and leaned forward. Pix woke abruptly and looked around, puzzled at having been cast aside so thoughtlessly. "With me?" she said, horrified.

Rio turned his back on her, headed to the kitchen and opened the refrigerator. Kit got up off the couch and dogged his footsteps. He took out a quart of milk, poured himself a glass, and drank it. Refilling the glass with the last of the milk, he said, "You don't have to worry. He's a lawyer. Loaded with money, class all the way. Tom wouldn't have recommended him if he was a pig."

He kneed the refrigerator door shut and tossed the empty milk carton into the trash. Leaning against the counter, he said, "Now, why are you looking at me like that? You wanted to be in show business. Here's your chance."

"I'm not taking off my clothes in front of your camera, and I'm not having sex with some strange man."

He squared his jaw. "Seems to me, kitten, as though you don't have much of a choice. In case you've forgotten, I'm the one who calls the shots around here."

"You're crazy. Absolutely bugfuck."

"Not much you can do about that, is there?"

She shot him a dagger-sharp look. "It won't be that bad," he said. "You won't have to do the stuff Terry does. This guy's a marshmallow. Straight sex. Nothing kinky. I'd never let him near you if I thought he wanted to hurt you. One hour, Kit, and we've made our three grand. I'll split it with you, 60-40. How does that sound?"

Pix padded into the kitchen and stood forlornly watching them. "I don't want your filthy money," Kit said.

Color crept up his cheeks. "But you've sure enjoyed the benefits that come with it, haven't you, Princess? The digital cable, the stereo, the hot tub. The filet mignon." He glanced at Pix. "Even the freaking dog I bought with the fruits of my labor. I don't see you squawking about that stuff."

"I didn't know! And it's not exactly *your* labor we're talking about. You're nothing more than a rich pimp!"

Anger flushed his cheeks even redder. "And you're a really stupid teenage girl," he said. "Here's the bottom line, tootsie. You'll do as I say, like it or not. Let me tell you a little story. Your aunt has this friend. He's been snooping around, nosing in my business, making a real nuisance of himself. A couple of weeks ago, Luis and Tico paid him a visit. They taught him a lesson he won't soon forget."

"And your point is?"

"My point, sweet thing, is that if you don't cooperate, your aunt is next on their list."

Sarah had just climbed out of the shower when she heard someone banging at her door. Wrapping a towel around her head, she slipped into her terry-cloth robe and hurried to answer it.

Clancy stood on her front porch, hands in the pockets of his jeans. "You're early, sugar," she said, toweling her tangled curls. "I didn't expect you for another couple of hours."

Those amber eyes studied her somberly before he said, "We need to talk."

She froze, the towel still in her hands. Her stomach went into free fall, plummeting like a roller coaster on a hot July noon. She wasn't going to like this. Somehow, she knew she wouldn't like it. "Come in," she said. "We can talk in the kitchen."

Droplets of water ran down the back of her neck. She slung the towel around her shoulders to catch the runoff and leaned against the sink for support. Hands braced against the edge of the countertop, she said, "This sounds serious."

He stood in the doorway, halfway between kitchen and living room, as though he couldn't make up his mind which way to go. "A few days ago," he said, "Bishop Halloran called me into his office and offered me a transfer to a parish in Detroit." He paused, while her heart fluttered madly in her chest. "This afternoon, I called him and accepted it."

Everything went still inside her. He continued talking, but his words didn't really register. *Inner city...needy parish...*

gang activity...retirement...prostate cancer...desperately need the hand of God in their lives...

"Would you please say something?" he said desperately. "I feel as though I'm standing here babbling to myself."

She was holding on to the edge of the kitchen counter so hard she would probably leave her fingerprints embedded in the Formica. She wet her lips and whispered, "When?"

"A few days. A week at the most. They want me there by the fifteenth."

Let me check my to-do list...yes, there is it. Break Sarah's heart. Twenty-four hours ago she'd been giddy as a teenage girl, practically dancing on air. Now, with a single sentence, he'd crushed her hopes and left her battered and bleeding. What was it that old song said? *What a difference a day makes.* Whoever wrote that knew exactly what he was talking about.

She struggled for oxygen, fought against the burning pain in her chest. "Tell me, Father. Is there a sign tattooed on my forehead that says Loser?"

"Sarah, darling. Don't be angry. Please."

"Angry? I'm not angry. Hurt, maybe. Stunned, for sure. I imagine the word devastated would even be appropriate." She turned away from him, took a plastic tumbler from the cupboard, and turned on the cold water tap full blast to fill it up. "Why would I be angry? I'm a modern woman." She drank the cold water in a series of fast, angry swallows, then slammed the plastic tumbler into the sink and turned on him. "I understand, sugar. I understand that last night was nothing more than a roll in the hay."

She registered his wounded expression, took a moment's satisfaction in knowing she'd hurt him. "You know better than that," he said quietly. "If all I'd wanted was a roll in the hay, do you really think I would have waited eleven years? Last night was incredible, the most amazing night of my life."

"Yet you're still leaving. Maybe you could explain that to me, because I just don't seem to be smart enough to get it."

"It has nothing to do with my feelings for you." He crossed the kitchen, looked out the back door. Walked back across the room to where he'd started. "And it has everything to do with them."

"Make up your mind, Father," she said tartly. "You can't have it both ways."

"That's just it." He stopped pacing to look at her. "After we talked to Tom this afternoon, I looked in the mirror, and I didn't much like what I saw."

"Are you implying that you're like him? Because if you are, that's bullshit! You aren't anything like him. If you were, I wouldn't—" She stopped abruptly, fearful that if she didn't rein in her fury, she'd turn the full extent of it on him. It wouldn't be a pretty picture.

"But how long would it take before I turned into him? God, Sarah." He heaved a sigh and ran his hands through his hair. "If I didn't care so much for you, it wouldn't matter. But we both know that if I stay in Boston, we'll end up sneaking around to be together. It'll turn something beautiful into something tawdry, and that would kill me. I'm not the kind of man who can live with something like that. And you deserve better."

"Stop trying to save me from myself, Clancy. That's the same thing Remy did, and it got real old, real fast. I'm a big girl, I don't need saving. Matter of fact, I'm big enough to read the writing on the wall. I asked you how I was supposed to compete with God. Now I have my answer. God one, Sarah zero. The math is pretty simple."

"It's not that simple!" Emotion turned his golden eyes to molten lava. "It's not a matter of choosing one over the other. I am what I am, Sarah. I don't know how to be anything else. I made a commitment a long time ago. If I cave the instant temptation comes along, what kind of priest does that make me? What kind of man?''

''The kind that runs away when he doesn't know what to do?''

He stood before her, chest heaving. ''That's not a very complimentary description,'' he said, ''but it's probably accurate. The way I feel about you…it terrifies me.'' He took a step toward her. ''I want to be with you so much it hurts. But I'm not ready to give up the priesthood, and the two are mutually exclusive.'' He moved closer, enveloping her in his body heat. ''The problem isn't between you and me,'' he said softly, fingering a strand of her wet hair. ''It's between me and the Catholic Church.''

She'd given up on men before, more times than she cared to remember. Usually not because it was what she wanted, but because it was the right thing to do. Breakups always hurt, some more than others. It had nearly killed her when she'd left Jackson. And the split with Remy had torn a hole in her heart. But this—this was a hundred times worse than both of them put together. ''You want to know what the hardest part is?'' she said brokenly. ''I know you're running for your life. I want to hate you, but I can't, because there's a part of me that understands where you're coming from.''

He closed the gap between them and buried his face in her sodden hair. ''I'm so sorry,'' he said.

''That makes two of us, sugar.'' She wound her arms around him, rested her head on his shoulder, and absorbed his warmth, his scent, the feel of his hard body against hers. ''Make love to me,'' she whispered.

Hand in hand, they climbed the stairs to her bedroom. The bed was still unmade, still smelling of perfume, and of last night's lovemaking. In the fading light of early evening, they undressed and crawled beneath the tangled bedcovers.

Last night had been about passion, about a frenzied mating of bodies too long denied. Tonight was a mating of souls.

They moved together with exquisite harmony, hands exploring, mapping, imprinting. His breath was hot and sweet
against her face, his words of love swallowed by her greedy
mouth. Torture, slow and sweet, made even more poignant
by the inevitability of parting that hung over them like a
double-edged sword.

With a fingertip, she traced the heart tattoo that bore another woman's name, insanely jealous because she wanted to
be the one he carried with him forever instead of some long-
dead eighteen-year-old girl. Then he rolled over, taking her
with him, and she forgot jealousy as he rocked her hard and
fast and blistering hot until she reached flashpoint and exploded in a conflagration that burned hotter than the fires of
Hell.

Lord have mercy.

As dusk turned to darkness outside the window, they lay
together, warmth to warmth, in the sticky aftermath of love.
His heart beat strong and steady beneath her cheek, and those
lovely fingers of his stroked her with exquisite tenderness.
For as long as it lasted, she pretended this moment would
never end.

But, as all good things do, eventually it had to end.
"Sarah?" he whispered. "It's time."

She peeled her sticky flesh away from his and turned to
look at the bedside clock. In just over an hour, he would
come face to face with Rio. He would either rescue Kit, or
die trying.

It was a terrifying proposition.

She leaned to kiss him. "I'll shower first," she said, and
left him alone in her bed.

19

They sat in a rented car, parked in the shadows outside the Starlite Motel, watching traffic pass by on Route 1. On the radio, Steven Tyler sang softly. *Hey, j-j-jaded.* The night was dark, ripe with the sounds and scents of early summer. The dashboard clock read 9:13. Her palms were damp, her stomach queasy. This would be their only chance. If they blew it, she might never see Kit again.

From somewhere, Clancy produced a .38 revolver. He checked the chamber for bullets, then closed it. "Do you know how to use one of these things?" he said.

"Are you kidding, sugar? I grew up in Louisiana. I learned to shoot before I learned to read. But where'd you get it?"

"Better if you don't ask." He handed it to her. "If anybody comes after you..."

She was sending him into danger to bring back her daughter. She hadn't wanted to face that truth. But the weight of the gun in her hand negated her denial. "What about you?" she said. "Don't you need it?"

"I'm going in unarmed. All Rio knows about me is what Tom told him. He can't afford to be too trusting. Where's the money?"

"Right here." She opened her purse, took out a manila envelope stuffed with cash and handed it to him.

He tucked it into the pocket of his suit coat. "The money will buy my way in," he said. "I can't guarantee you'll get it back."

"I don't care about the money. All I care about is getting Kit back."

He touched her cheek with his hand, and she turned her lips to his palm and kissed it. Beyond his shoulder, she watched a red BMW slow and turn into the motel parking lot.

"It's showtime," she whispered tersely. "He just drove in."

Rio parked the car, turned off the engine and the lights, opened the driver's door and got out. He walked around to the passenger side, and Sarah held her breath as he opened the door and her daughter stepped out of the car. Kit took a long, sweeping glance around the parking lot. She was too far away for Sarah to read the expression on her face, but her body language spoke volumes. She clearly didn't want to be here. "Oh, God," Sarah said.

"Is that her?"

"It's her. My baby."

Rio took Kit by the elbow and steered her in the direction of the motel room door, swung open the door and shoved her through it.

"That son of a bitch," Sarah said, reaching instinctively for the door handle of the rented Alero.

Before she could open it, Clancy's fingers clamped tight around her wrist. "Wait," he said.

"I've waited almost three months! Isn't that long enough?"

"We don't know what might happen," he said in a maddeningly reasonable tone. "This whole thing could blow up in our faces. I'm trying to prevent that from happening. Let's do this the way we planned. Are you with me?"

Every atom in her body screaming resistance, she said bitterly, "Do I have a choice?"

Clancy released her wrist. "Keep watch," he said, unclipping his cell phone and handing it to her. "If anything goes wrong, you're to call the cops and then get the hell out of here. Do you understand?''

''And leave the two of you alone in there with him?''

''Sarah.'' He caught her chin in his hand and forced her eyes to meet his. ''If there's any trouble, I don't want you in the middle of it. Do you understand?''

''Yes! Damn you.'' She reached up to pull away his hand, but at the last minute, wrapped hers around it instead. ''Be careful,'' she whispered.

He kissed her, hard. ''Time to rock and roll,'' he said, and climbed out of the car.

She watched him cross the parking lot, watched him knock on the door of the motel room. The door opened a crack, and he exchanged a few words with Rio. Light spilled out onto cracked asphalt as Rio slowly, cautiously scanned the deserted parking lot. Satisfied, he opened the door wider. Clancy stepped inside, and it closed behind him.

And the wait began.

It looked just like every other cheesy motel room he'd ever seen. A double bed, stripped because they'd used the bedding to cover the window. A mattress stained with God only knew what. Above the bed, a nondescript landscape painting, a trio of three-masted schooners with billowing sails.

''Mr. Bryant?'' Rio said. ''I'm going to have to check you for weapons. Can't be too careful.''

''Of course. I understand.''

He stood stiffly while Rio patted him down. ''You seem nervous,'' Rio said.

''Damn right, I'm nervous. If my wife finds out about this, I'm dead meat.''

Rio chuckled. ''Not much chance of that,'' he said. ''With you being here, and her being…where was that again?''

''Phoenix.''

Rio's cool blue eyes studied him with open speculation. "I don't hear a Southwestern accent."

"Always this suspicious, are you, Mr.—ah—I never did get your name."

Rio didn't take the bait. "You don't need to know my name. And I'm being cautious for a reason. If I make a mistake, I'm out of business."

Clancy nodded agreement. "Fair enough. I'm originally from the Boston area. Somerville. It's my wife who's from the Southwest. Her parents are in their seventies. We settled in Phoenix to be near them." He gave Rio his most engaging, comrades-in-arms smile. "And to get away from the cold winters."

"Those New England winters can be a bitch," Rio agreed. "You have the money?"

"Of course." Clancy fished the manila envelope from his pocket, handed it to Rio, and watched him count it.

"Excellent. So you're a friend of the senator's."

"That's right. We were in college together. Harvard Law."

"And you're in town for...?"

"Business." Again, he turned on that conspiratorial smile. "And a little fun while I'm at it. So where's the girl?" He glanced around the room, took careful note of the stripped bed, the lights, the camera, the notable absence of Nate, the techie Terry had told him about.

"In the bathroom. She's a little bashful. Inexperienced. She might need to be coaxed a little. Tommy said you were looking for something extra-special, and that's just what Kit is. Young and innocent. Just like you ordered."

"She's clean, I trust?"

"Don't insult me, Mr. Bryant. I run a quality operation. And I already told you she's inexperienced. As a matter of fact—" Rio's grin was cool and self-satisfied "—you'll be her first."

"I'd like to talk to her."

Rio's smile vanished. He studied Clancy cagily. "Talk to her," he said.

"If I'm going to be, ah—intimate—with the girl, I'd like to talk to her first. Get to know each other a little before the clothes come off and the camera starts rolling. After all…this is my first time, too. She's not the only one who's nervous."

Rio clearly wasn't comfortable with the idea. In his world, it apparently wasn't a common expectation, that two people might exchange a few words before they exchanged body fluids. He moved to the bathroom door and rapped twice. "Kit? The client wants to talk to you. Open the door and come out."

Clancy cleared his throat. "I, um—I'd prefer to speak to her in private. I hope that's not a problem. This is all so new to me, I don't know what the boundaries are. I don't want to step on anybody's toes. But Tom told me that for my three thousand dollars, you'd give me whatever I wanted. It's a lot of money. I want to make sure it's well spent."

"Trust me, it's well spent. Kit's special. She'll blow your freaking mind."

"I'm in Boston five or six times a year. If I decide she's worth my while, I'll come back the next time I'm in town."

Clearly torn between greed and whatever ethical code he adhered to, Rio debated his options while a trickle of sweat rolled down Clancy's spine. He was walking a fine line here, and if he took a single misstep, the game would be over. On the other hand, although Rio didn't trust him, the pimp was enough of an entrepreneur to realize that if he insulted a customer, there would be no repeat business. And Clancy suspected that repeat customers were the lifeblood of this particular enterprise.

Rio reached a decision. He turned away from Clancy and said to the closed bathroom door, "Kit? I'm sending him in so the two of you can play *let's get acquainted.*"

Relief flooded him, and Clancy tried not to let it show. Rio opened the door and motioned him inside. "Two minutes," he said. "Then we either get this shoot underway or we call it off. Either way, I keep the three grand."

The bathroom was tiny, and carried a faint scent of urine that a heavy dose of disinfectant hadn't quite been able to mask. Somebody had opened the window a crack, most likely to air the place out. Kit sat cross-legged on the commode, looking like something out of a Britney Spears video: red and black plaid pleated skirt, knee-length socks, and a mid-riff-baring white blouse. Defiance and fear oozed from her every pore, so palpable he could smell it in the air as she stared at him with enormous blue eyes, Little Red Riding Hood, waiting for him to swallow her alive.

"Hi," he said in a brisk voice he hoped would convey earnestness, tempered by nerves, through the door to Rio. "It's Kit, right? I'm Ed Bryant. I thought we could talk before we get started. Break the ice a little."

Those blue eyes accused him as he held a finger to his lips in a *shh* gesture. He walked to the window, tested the strength of the rusted screen, and ran his fingers along the wooden frame, mentally measuring the opening. It was a narrow window, about ten inches high and maybe fifteen inches wide. He might get Kit through it, but there was no way his shoulders would ever fit through that small an opening. Even if he could somehow squeeze her through, it would be a long shot. There was no way of telling what lay beyond, how far a drop it was to the ground, or what she'd find when she got there.

So the window was out. On to Plan B. He knelt on the floor in front of her. "I am *so* happy to see you," he whispered. "My name is Clancy, and I've been looking for you since March. I'm a friend of your Aunt Sarah's. She's waiting outside, in the car."

She studied him mutely, trying to decide whether or not

to trust him. "Kit?" he whispered. "Do you understand what I'm telling you?" He took her hand in his, tried to rub some warmth into her cold, clammy fingers. "I'm here to take you home."

For the first time, he saw something resembling hope in her eyes. Guarded hope, but hope nevertheless. "You're that priest," she whispered. "The one Gonzales beat up."

"That's right. And I'm going to get us out of here. But I'll need your cooperation. Are you with me?"

She hesitated, and he offered up a silent prayer: *God, please don't let me fail in this endeavor. Please give me strength and wisdom. And if You're willing, a strong dose of luck.*

Her fingers closed around his. "Yes," she said. "I'm with you."

"Good girl," he said. "I hear you want to be an actress."

Outside the door, Rio knocked. "Your two minutes are up, Mr. Bryant. Time to come out."

"Yes," she whispered. "Why?"

"You're going to get a chance to audition for the Academy Award."

He'd been in there for hours. She didn't care if the dashboard clock said it had only been eight minutes. In the tortured world she now inhabited, those eight minutes had taken hours to pass. Sarah lowered the window to allow the night air inside. She was sweating heavily, her heart galloping like a racehorse at Suffolk Downs.

On Route 1, traffic whizzed by at a pace far beyond the posted speed limit. She drew in a deep breath of air tainted by exhaust fumes. What could be going on in there? The two people she loved most in the world were inside that motel room, while she'd been relegated to the exalted position of sentry. The indignity didn't sit well with her. Nor did the frustration of not knowing. She should be in there with him.

Kit was *her* daughter, not his. But this was a one-man mission, and unfortunately, she didn't have the proper equipment for the job. Like it or not, her only option was to trust him. And maybe pray a little. She'd never been a particularly religious person, but if there ever was a time to take up religion, it was now.

What in hell was taking him so long?

An eighteen-wheeler passed by, grinding gears as it slowed for its exit. Behind it, a low-slung black Camaro blinked and turned into the motel parking lot. The car passed her and shot into an empty slot beside Rio's BMW. Sarah sat a little straighter, her stomach jumping all over the place as two men got out of the car and closed the doors. For an instant, the glow from one of the overhead lights illuminated the gold chains the driver wore looped around his neck. Then Luis Gonzales pocketed his car keys, and both men walked directly to the door Clancy had disappeared through about a year ago.

"Sweet Jesus," she whispered.

Clancy unlocked the bathroom door and swung it open. Rio waited impatiently on the other side. "Move it," he said. "I'm renting this place by the hour."

Like the sixteen-year-old that she was, Kit plopped onto the bare mattress. Clancy stood awkwardly beside the bed, hands in his pockets, rocking on the balls of his feet as though he wasn't quite sure what his next move should be. It was pretty close to the truth.

Adjusting the angle of the camera, Rio said, "Any time you two kids are ready."

Kit sat up straighter and crossed her arms. "I'm not doing this," she said.

Rio froze, then straightened to his full height and studied her with cool deliberation. "What did you say?"

Squaring her shoulders, she said, "I…am…not…doing…

this." She swallowed hard, and tears welled in those blue eyes, making them look twice their size. Bursting into tears, she wailed, "And you can't make me!" She buried her face in her hands and began sobbing uncontrollably.

"Oh, for Christ's sake," Rio said. "What's this all about?"

"Yes," Clancy said, "just what is this all about? You told me she needed coaxing. You didn't tell me she wouldn't go through with it."

Rio raked a hand through his hair. "Give me a minute!" he snapped. Turning back to Kit, he said firmly, "We talked about this already. We came to an agreement."

She glared at him through red-rimmed, watery eyes. "I changed my mind."

"Did you forget the little talk we had about consequences?"

Kit clenched her fists in the folds of her skirt. "You threatened me," she said. "You threatened my aunt. What did you expect?"

"This isn't the time to air our dirty linens, babe. We'll discuss them later, *when we're alone*. Right now, we have a movie to make. Mr. Bryant has paid good money for you, and—"

"Leave me out of it," Clancy said. "I've never forced a girl yet, and I'm not about to start now. If the lady's not interested, neither am I. I'd like my money back."

Rio let out a bark of incredulous laughter. "Are you nuts? That money's already changed hands. You're up the creek, Bryant."

"Not the way I see it. You promised me something, and you failed to deliver. In my book, that's a clear breach of contract. The money's mine, and I'm not leaving until I get it."

"Good luck finding a judge who'll back you up. In case you hadn't noticed, what we're doing here is illegal."

Kit sobbed dramatically, ended on a hiccup. "He black-mailed me, Mr. Bryant! He said if I didn't go through with this, he'd kill my aunt! You have to help me."

She might have been making up the script as she went along, but Clancy suspected the details came direct from real life. "What kind of operation are you running here?" he said to Rio. "Tom told me I could trust you. Now I find out you're using threats to coerce your girls into performing?"

"She's lying," Rio said. He was starting to sweat, starting to lose his cool. "I swear on my mother's grave that I never threatened anybody. And I've never coerced any of my girls. If you're willing to wait a few minutes, I can have somebody else here. Somebody who'll be happy to fulfill our, ah—contractual agreement."

Clancy feigned deliberation. "Why should I trust you after this fiasco?"

"Because Tom gave me a glowing recommendation, and he's a regular client. Because nothing like this has ever happened to me before. Because I admit to poor judgment." Rio's smile was ingenuous, ingratiating. "I should have known Kit wasn't ready for—"

A knock on the door interrupted his words. All three of them froze. Then three heads turned in the direction of the door. This wasn't in the script, Clancy thought. He and Kit exchanged brief, panicked glances as Rio walked to the door and glanced through the peephole. While inside Clancy's stomach, butterflies danced the tango, Rio turned the dead bolt and undid the chain.

And opened the door.

The emergency operator had been a nincompoop, and Sarah could only pray that she'd gotten the message right. Especially the part about calling Vince Paoletti. But she didn't have time to stew over it. Or to wait for the cavalry to arrive. She was on her own. Hopefully she'd learned a thing or two from those *Charlie's Angels* reruns she'd overdosed on as a kid.

The .38 heavy in her hand, she stuck to the shadows at the edge of the parking lot. She circled a huge green Dumpster and began wading through waist-high weeds. It had been a hot day, and the pungent stench of old garbage turned her stomach. Somebody must have mistaken the area behind the motel for the city dump. Moonlight glittered off shards of broken glass. A bag of garbage, overflow from the Dumpster, had been ripped open and scattered by members of the local wildlife population.

The land dropped away sharply just a few feet from the building, and to keep from tumbling ass over teakettle into the gully, she was forced to cling to the slender saplings that grew tight against the cement walls. She tucked the .38 into her waistband so she wouldn't drop it and accidentally shoot herself. Her foot tangled in a coil of wire that tore a deep slash in her ankle, bringing hot tears to her eyes. She blinked them away, shook off the wire, and kept moving. Counting windows as she went, she stumbled and nearly fell over an old television that somebody had discarded.

A bramble caught at her sleeve, and she yanked it free, barely aware of its prickles against the soft flesh of her forearm. She reached the backside of the fourth unit from the end, and looked helplessly at the bathroom window that was a good two feet above her head. "Shit," she muttered. "Now what?"

Sweat trickled through the valley between her breasts. Somewhere out there in the weeds, a cricket chirped merrily. Glancing around, she spied the black hulk of the television, barely visible in the darkness.

It took some slick maneuvering to wrestle it into place without shooting herself or dropping it down the embankment, but she finally succeeded. She jostled it up against the wall, wiped the sweat from her brow, and climbed atop her wobbly makeshift stepladder.

The window was cranked open a couple of inches. Sarah grabbed the wooden frame in both hands, wiggled it, then pushed it upward as hard as she could. It refused to budge. She tried again. Again, the crank held firm. Holding in the cuss word that formed on the tip of her tongue, she gave up on the window and applied herself to the rusted screen.

If only she'd thought to bring the nail file she carried in her purse, this would have been a breeze. Instead, she had to use a sharp stick to poke a hole in the screen. The rusted mesh gave, and she dropped the stick and widened the tear so she could get her hand through it. Feeling around inside, she located the window crank.

It seemed to take forever to crank the window open, but in reality it couldn't have been more than twenty seconds. When it was fully opened, she tore the rest of the screen from the window frame and tossed it on the ground.

Now came the hard part.

She should never have quit aerobics class. Panting like a sheepdog on a hot July day, she hoisted herself, inch by painful inch, up the cement wall. She wished, not for the first time, that she were a size three. A big-boned size ten, she wasn't even sure she'd make it through the window. But she didn't have a choice. Her daughter, and the man she loved, were both depending on her. She couldn't allow herself to fail.

Her belly scraped on the jagged pieces of screen she'd left behind as she squeezed through the tiny opening. She heard fabric tearing, but didn't stop to check. She was halfway through the window when she realized she should have gone feet first. But it was too late to turn back now. She'd just have to dangle upside down like a slumbering bat and try not to break her neck. The window crank drilled into her hip as she squeezed her rump through the opening. Still upside down, she pulled in first one leg and then the other. With a thud they probably heard in Portsmouth, she dropped clumsily to the floor.

Heart hammering, she froze, afraid to breathe. If they'd heard the noise…if they got suspicious…but after a moment, when nobody came to check, she took a deep breath and tiptoed carefully to the door. One hand on the doorknob, the other on the .38, she pressed her ear against the door and opened it a crack so she could hear what was happening on the other side.

Clancy's stomach turned inside-out at sight of the two men who walked into the motel room. One was tall, scrawny, stupid-looking. The other swaggered into the room, a half-dozen gold chains around his neck and shiny black boots with pointed toes on his feet. Luis Gonzales gave Clancy a hard little smile and said to Rio, "Your instincts were right, *amigo*. It's him."

"Goddamn it! I knew it smelled like a setup! Tom Adams is a dead man." Rio's face went a sickly gray as his gaze darted frantically from one piece of expensive electronic equipment to the next. "Shit," he said. "He probably has the cops on the way. We have to get this stuff out of here." He knelt beside the bed and began disconnecting his camera from its tripod. "Tico!" he barked. "Help me pack up this equipment!"

Santana blinked twice, then started unplugging lights and coiling the cords. Gonzales reached beneath his leather vest and smoothly pulled out a Beretta semiautomatic. Pointing it directly at Clancy's heart, he said, "So, padre, we meet again. It's a shame you ignored my last warning. It truly pains me to have to kill a man of God. I'll be in confession for a year."

Clancy stared down the barrel of the loaded gun, surprised

to realize that should he die here, on this balmy summer evening in this miserable excuse for a motel room, he would meet his maker without fear or regret. He would be a little miffed at having been cut down in his prime, while his work here wasn't yet done. There were so many things left to do. So many people he wasn't ready to leave behind. But he didn't fear death. He knew with absolute certainty where he was headed, knew with equal certainty that when he got there, he wouldn't run into either Rio or Gonzales. That was enough for him.

But he didn't intend to take Kit along for the ride.

He met her eyes across the room. Pressed up tight against the headboard, she looked terrified at the sight of Gonzales pointing that gun at him. "Let the girl go," he said. "I don't care what happens to me, but let her go. She's only sixteen years old." He thought of Meg, who would remain eighteen forever, and strengthened his resolve. "She's done nothing wrong. Let her go home where she belongs. My sins are my own. She doesn't deserve to pay for them."

"Shut up," Rio said, zipping his precious video camera into its vinyl carrying case. "Stay out of it. Kit's my property, and I'll do with her whatever I choose."

There was a faint thump from the vicinity of the bathroom. Heedless of the sound, Rio and Santana continued packing lights and stands and electrical cords. Had they not heard it? Or had they all, Gonzales included, attributed the thud to the commotion from the hasty packing? He glanced at Kit. She stared back through unblinking blue eyes. She was either paralyzed with terror, or the gutsiest kid he'd ever met. Maybe a little of both. "Give it up, Rio," he said. "Or Roger, or whatever your name is. Let us go. Too many people know the truth, including a BPD detective named Paoletti. If anything happens to me, who do you think they're going to come to first?"

"I told you to shut up!" Rio was sweating, his underarms

damp, his face dripping. "Get him out of here, Luis. Take him someplace and get rid of him. This time, make sure you do it right. I don't want any evidence left behind." He snatched up his tripod, his camera. "Tico, get the rest of this equipment into the Camaro. You know what to do with it." Shouldering the camera bag, he turned to Kit. "You, come with me. We're getting out of here." When she didn't move, he barked, "Now!"

"No," she said. "I'm not going with you."

"Move it! I don't have time to argue!"

She folded her arms and held her ground. "I told you, I'm not going."

"There you go," Clancy said with a cheerfulness he was far from feeling. "Dissension within the ranks. Whether you kill me or not, Rio, your little empire is about to come tumbling down on your head."

The look Rio gave him would have vaporized a lesser man. The pimp darted a glance toward the door. In a tone just short of pleading, he said to Kit, "I thought we had something really good going here. Don't do this to me."

With a poise that was amazing under the circumstances, Kit said, "I'd rather die than spend another minute with you."

Rio's face hardened. "Fine!" he said. "Take her along for the ride, Luis. It's a damn shame, you know, kitten. You had potential. We could have gone places together."

"I told you, *amigo*. Sooner or later, they all become liabilities." Gonzales waved the gun in the direction of the parking lot. "Move! Both of you!"

The bathroom door opened silently, and Sarah stood in the doorway, Clancy's .38 trained directly on Gonzales. Her hair was a tangle of twigs and leaves, and her shirt hung in tatters. A clump of burdock clung to her sleeve, and a drop of blood trickled down her forearm. Clancy had never seen a more beautiful sight. "If I were you, sugar," she said in a decep-

tively soft voice, ''I'd drop the gun. If I pull the trigger on
the one I'm holding right now, the only thing you'll be good
for is guarding the sultan's harem.''

Gonzales froze. Santana paused to gape at her, a heavy
box clutched to his chest. ''Aunt Sarah!'' Kit said.

''Come here, baby. Go in the bathroom and shut the door,
and don't come out until I tell you it's safe.''

''But—''

''Go on,'' Clancy said gently. ''It'll be all right.''

The girl hesitated for an instant, then scrambled to obey.
Rio came out of his stupor and began edging toward the door.
''Move another inch,'' Sarah said sweetly, ''and I'll blow
you away. I've waited months for the privilege.''

Rio froze. ''Luis,'' she said, ''be a good boy now and drop
the gun. I'd really hate to have to shoot you. I detest
messes.''

Scowling, Gonzales bent and placed his gun carefully on
the floor. ''Wise choice,'' she said. ''Now kick it across the
room.''

He shoved the gun with his foot. It skittered across the
floor. Clancy bent and picked it up, unloaded the ammuni-
tion, and tucked it into his belt. In the distance, he heard the
wail of a siren. ''Santana's carrying, too,'' he said.

''Then perhaps you'd best disarm him, sugar. Tico, just
keep on holding that box. If you drop it, I'll have to shoot
you.'' She smiled wickedly. ''Just because I can.''

His gaze darting wildly around the room, Santana swallowed, his Adam's apple bobbing up and down. He raised
the box slightly so Clancy could remove the gun at his hip.
Pocketing it, Clancy said, ''I don't think I've ever been quite
this happy to see anybody.''

Across the room, Sarah held his .38 steady, without so
much as a tremor. ''The feeling's mutual, sugar. By the way,
you got a permit for this thing?''

Outside, tires squealed and the siren he'd been hearing squawked to a stop. "Yes," he said. "Why?"

"I just thought it might be a good idea for it to be in your hands when Paoletti gets here."

20

20

His bags were packed, the detritus of thirty-five years of living packaged tidily in four cardboard boxes that barely weighted down the trunk of his Saturn. He didn't have much to show for those thirty-five years. Just his clothes, his stereo, a few books and personal items. He'd never been one to accumulate material possessions. After a while, things came to own you, instead of the other way around. Having few belongings made it simpler to move on.

On Sunday, he'd conducted his final Mass at Saint Bart's. In the intervening days, he'd tied up all his loose ends, said his farewells. He'd resigned from a multitude of committees, had found somebody to take over his coaching duties, had made sure parish affairs were in order for a smooth transition to his wet-behind-the-ears successor. He'd given Fred and Barney to Melissa. The goldfish would never have survived the seven-hundred-mile trip, and she'd been ridiculously pleased by the gesture. Afterward, he'd patted her hand and kept her supplied with tissues until her tears dried up.

Yesterday afternoon, he'd driven Jamal over to Huntington Avenue where, amid the whine of electric saws and the incessant hammering of nails, he'd introduced the kid to Ruth. It was a marriage made in heaven. She needed warm bodies to help with her new project, and Jamal needed something to keep him off the streets. Spending his days with Ruth and his nights with Fiona, Jamal would be too busy to stray from the straight and narrow. And if he did, there'd be two un-happy women to contend with instead of one.

His last night in Boston, Clancy had eaten dinner with the Raffertys. There'd been laughter and tears, tender reminis-cences and good-natured ribbing. When he'd gone to the kitchen to pour himself a cup of after-dinner coffee, Fiona had cornered him. "Are you sure you're doing the right thing?" she said.

He stirred sugar into his coffee, lifted the cup and took a sip. "No," he said.

"Then why are you doing it?"

"Because I have to. Because if I don't, I'll never know. I have a great deal of thinking to do, and I have to do it away from Boston. Away from Sarah. It's the only way I can main-tain any kind of objectivity."

"Have you told her that?"

"What am I supposed to say to her? Please wait for me, just in case Detroit doesn't work out?" He dropped his spoon into the sink. "That's a little too much like stacking the deck. I have to proceed under the assumption I've made the right decision. Asking her to wait would be grossly unfair to her. She needs to move on with her life. And so do I."

Now, on this bright, sunny May morning, he had just one more stop to make. He pulled into the Northgate Mall and parked the car. As he approached Bookmark, he could see Sarah and Josie inside. He tried the door and found it locked, checked his watch and realized the store wouldn't open for another forty-five minutes. He rapped on the glass with his car key, and Sarah looked up and saw him.

For what seemed an eternity, they stared at each other through the window. Then she came to the door and opened it. "Hi," he said softly.

"Hi."

He had no idea what was going on behind those blue eyes, couldn't tell whether she wanted to kiss him or kick him.

"May I come in?" he said. "I couldn't leave without saying—" He stopped, unable to make his lips form the word *goodbye*.

She stepped aside so he could enter, then led him wordlessly to her office at the back of the store. "How's Kit?" he asked.

Sarah sat on the edge of her cluttered desk. "Quiet," she said. "Polite. She spends a lot of time alone in her room." She folded her arms across her chest, absently rubbed her elbow, and sighed. "I don't seem to be getting through to her."

"Give it time. She's been through something immensely traumatic. She needs time to process it. Time to heal. I brought you something." He fumbled in the pocket of his suit coat, pulled out the paper he'd had Melissa type up for him. "It's a list of family therapists," he said, handing it to her. "I know each of them personally, and they're all good at what they do."

"Thank you." Sarah unfolded the list, quickly skimmed the names, then dropped it on the desk and raised her eyes to his. "How's Tom?"

"The esteemed Senator Adams has suddenly and inexplicably dropped out of the congressional race." He drank her in greedily, memorizing her eyes, blue as a summer sky, her smooth, milky complexion, all that wavy brown hair that fell wild and loose around her face. This was the picture he would carry with him, the mental snapshot of Sarah that he would pull out to comfort himself with when he missed her so much he ached with it. The heartache was inevitable. He hadn't even left yet, and already he missed her.

A tear slipped from the corner of her eye and began a slow slide down her cheek. "Damn it all," she said, "I swore on Momma's grave that I wouldn't cry."

He took a step forward, lay a hand on her damp cheek. She leaned into his caress, pressed her cheek against his palm. "Thank you," she said. "Thank you for giving me back my daughter."

"No," he said. "I should thank you for giving me back my life."

"No regrets?"

"Not a one."

"Me neither." She straightened, took his face between her palms, and kissed him tenderly. "Get on out of here," she whispered, "before I make a damn fool of myself and beg you not to go."

"I love you," he said. "It was never a matter of not loving you."

"I know that, sugar."

"You're a strong woman. You have Kit to worry about now. You'll get past this."

"I know that, too. Go. You have a long drive ahead of you."

He backstepped, away from her. "See you around," he said.

"Sure thing," she said. "Next time you're in town, give me a call. We'll have dinner or something."

"Or something," he echoed.

He walked away without looking back, afraid that if he did, he would change his mind. Sarah Connelly was tough and strong and resourceful. A survivor. Smart enough to realize that what they'd shared couldn't possibly last. She would put this behind her and move on with her life. And when she thought of him—if she ever thought of him—it would be with affection instead of bitterness.

The door swung closed behind him and the lock snicked into place. On the sidewalk outside the bookstore, he took a long, deep breath to steady himself. He hadn't expected it to be this difficult. Hadn't expected that as he walked away from her, every atom in his body would scream at him to stay.

It was a beautiful, sunny day, a perfect day for a new start. He'd made a promise to God and the Church. He had responsibilities, commitments. A parish in Detroit that waited for him. He couldn't screw it up now. It didn't matter that his gut was twisted and his hands were shaking. It didn't matter that with each step he took closer to his car, drawing breath became increasingly difficult. No matter how much he wanted her, no matter how difficult it was to leave her behind, he had to face the truth like a man: *It's not going to happen.*

He unlocked the Saturn, sat in the driver's seat, and closed the door. Fastened his seat belt and slid the key into the ignition. His fingers hesitated as he struggled with the panic that lay low in his belly. "You can do this," he said aloud, and turned the key. The engine roared to life, and he put his hand on the gearshift and prayed to God for the strength to walk away from her.

With renewed determination, he shifted the car into Drive. And drove away.

21

When the plane touched down at New Orleans International, she breathed a sigh of relief. It had been a long flight. Kit hadn't uttered more than three words since they'd left Boston. These days, that was standard behavior. The sullen, antagonistic Kit who'd run away from home had disappeared, replaced by one who was polite, distant, and for the most part silent. Sarah wasn't sure which was worse. After seven months of family counseling, she still hadn't been able to breach that wall of silence, and she'd begun to despair of ever getting through to the girl.

Three weeks ago, she'd talked it over with their counselor, Dr. Ferguson. He had agreed that she couldn't begin to move forward with her life until she unburdened herself. He'd also agreed that Kit was strong enough at this point to hear the truth. Sarah knew the risks, knew there was a chance it might drive a permanent wedge between them. But she couldn't live a lie any longer. Seventeen years was long enough. It was time to tell Kit the truth.

But she couldn't do it in Boston. Their story had begun in Bayou Rouillard, and that was where it should end. Full circle. Back to the beginning. So she'd called Remy, asked if he'd be willing to put them up for a few days. "Of course I will,'' he'd said. "It's high time you told her the truth. It's been eating at you for years. Come for Christmas, sugar. Stay a few days. It'll be like old times.''

He was wrong about that. It couldn't ever again be like old times. She and Remy would never again share a bed. That aspect of their relationship was history. But she still loved him dearly, still considered him her oldest and dearest friend. So she'd packed up Kit and a suitcase full of Christmas gifts, and here they were.

She rented a car, and they silently loaded their luggage into the trunk. She left the airport and got on the highway heading west, away from the city. Kit glanced at a passing road sign and said, "I thought we were going to Remy's.''

"We are, sugar. But there's somewhere else we need to go first.''

Kit didn't question her further, just hunkered down in the passenger seat and stared out the window. They drove for an hour in a weighty silence. Sarah's stomach grew increasingly queasy as she drew nearer to her destination. Homecomings were often difficult. But the homecoming of this prodigal daughter was more poignant than most, for nobody was left to greet her except the ghost of a frightened seventeen-year-old girl who had grasped desperately at the only route she was offered out of a hopeless situation.

She glanced over at Kit, who stared wordlessly at the passing scenery. Would her daughter understand what she'd done, and why? Or would her confession simply drive Kit farther away from her?

Her knuckles bone-white on the steering wheel, she took the familiar exit off the highway and began the trek down a two-lane blacktop road leading deep into the heart of bayou country. She passed a cluster of rusted trailers, a ramshackle store with long-defunct gas pumps. Near the little wooden Baptist Church perched at the crossroads that passed for the center of town, she turned left, onto a dirt road that plunged her into a forest so dense that little light managed to penetrate the overhead canopy. What light did come through was a murky, grayish-green.

She almost missed the driveway, it was so overgrown with vegetation. She clicked on her blinker and eased the rental car over a series of grassy ruts, then came to a stop in a small clearing.

The little house still stood at the edge of the bayou. Weathered by time and the elements, it tilted precariously on posts driven into the boggy ground decades earlier. The roof shingles were nearly gone, and the window glass had all been shattered, most likely by kids with nothing better to do. "What's this place?" Kit said.

She gripped the steering wheel tightly and threw back her shoulders. "This is where I grew up, sugar."

Kit took a second look at the decaying shack and said, "Doesn't look like much."

"Mmm. Didn't look like much when I was growing up here, either. You lived here for the first four years of your life."

"I did?"

"You don't remember?"

Kit shook her head. "Is this where I lived with Momma?"

Pain was a bright, hard thing fluttering in her chest. Or maybe that was her heart. Either way, it hurt like hell. "Yes," she said. "And that's why we're here. I have a story to tell you. But first, I wanted you to see this place. I wanted to see it again myself. I wanted to remind us both just how far we've come. And exactly where it is we're coming from."

"Okay," Kit said, in that tone teenagers reserve for particularly moronic adults.

"Bear with me, sugar. It'll all make sense to you in good time." She clicked her fingernails against the steering wheel and took a deep, cleansing breath. "Once upon a time," she began, "there was this young girl. She came from nothing, just a little tar-paper shack at the edge of the bayou. She was a bit of a wild child. Headstrong and willful, and absolutely sure she had all the answers. If her Momma said green, she'd say red, just because she could. One day, when she was sixteen, she met a boy and fell in love with him. He was tall and good-looking and everything her Momma found vile and detestable. So of course, she ran away from home to be with him. Everything was peachy keen until she got pregnant and her Prince Charming turned out to be a frog. He told her she couldn't prove the baby was his. Why, she could have been fooling around with all kinds of other boys behind his back. So he threw her out on the street."

She hazarded a glance at Kit. The girl was listening intently, but her face gave away nothing. "So there she was, penniless, pregnant, and terrified. She was just seventeen years old, Kit. The same age you are now. She didn't know what to do, so she went home to her Momma. Momma said she'd fix it all up so nobody'd ever have to know about her shame and her disgrace. Momma said, 'Your brother and his wife want a baby and they can't have one. So we'll fix it so you can give them yours, and it'll work out to everyone's benefit, and life can go back to the way it was before.'"

Sarah wet her lips with her tongue. "The girl was so scared. She didn't have anything to give that little baby. She hadn't even finished high school. She was too young and too weak to fight her family, so she listened to her Momma. And when her own sweet little girl was born, even though she loved that precious baby more than life itself, even though it tore a big old hole in her young girl's heart, she turned the baby over to her brother and his wife to raise." She glanced over at Kit, who was looking at her now with fear and confusion and astonishment on her face. It killed her to think she was responsible for that look, but there was no turning back now. She'd already passed the point of no return. Kit was young and resilient. She would bounce back from this. She had to. Anything else was unthinkable.

"When Ellie died," she said softly, "I begged your father—my brother—to leave you with me. But he wouldn't hear of it. You were his little girl, and that was that. It didn't matter that he wasn't your biological father. He loved you. And I had no rights. I might have been under pressure from the family when I signed my name on that dotted line four years earlier, but I'd still signed it. Nobody'd had to break my arm to make me do it. So he took you away, and I didn't see you again for ten years. Ten years, Kit. Do you know how long that is to live without something you need as much as you need air and water and sunshine?

"Then, after ten years, one day a miracle happened. He brought you to me, and I got down on my knees and thanked God for giving me a second chance with you. I thought everything would be perfect this time around. But you and I, we're too much alike. I fought with you worse than I ever fought with Momma. And I got my payback for all the rotten things I did to her. History repeated itself. You ran away from me, just like I ran away from her when I was your age." She took a deep breath. "Only I did something Momma didn't do. I went after you. I never gave up on you, Kit. No matter how hard it got, I never gave up on getting you back."

She was crying now, fat tears that rolled down her cheeks and dampened the collar of her shirt. "We've both done some really stupid things," she said, "but none of that matters as long as we love each other. A very wise and wonderful man once told me it's not where you're coming from that matters, it's where you're going. We can't change the past, Kit, we can only learn from it and try to do things a different way in the future. I'm hoping you can find it in your heart to forgive me for everything I've done wrong. I wouldn't blame you if you hated me, but I just want you to understand one thing. You were never my disgrace or my shame. Right from the instant I knew I was pregnant, you were never anything less to me than a miracle. There wasn't a minute of that entire nine months that I didn't want you. I did what I did because I loved you so much and I wanted you to have things I couldn't possibly give you at seventeen. And there hasn't been a day since that I haven't regretted giving you up."

Kit was staring out the window now, away from her. Sarah studied the back of her daughter's head, the slender neck, the vulnerable shoulders, too young to carry such a heavy burden. "I know this has been a shock to you," she said, "and I imagine you'll need a little time to think it over. So I'm going to leave you alone for a bit. I'll be wandering around the grounds outside. If there's anything you want to know, anything at all, you come find me and ask. No matter how much it might hurt me, I'll tell you the truth. The years of lying are over."

She got out of the car, closed the door quietly behind her, and walked around the house, where the grass grew tall and the ground was spongy. Above her head, birds flitted from tree to tree. A shaft of sunlight filtered through the trees and reflected off the glossy wet head of an otter who swam in the murky water of the bayou. The sights, the sounds, the scents of the bayou shot a surprising stab of nostalgia through her.

She stood for a time, watching the otter swimming in the black water. He reached a cypress knee that poked skyward, dove, and disappeared into the murky depths. Behind her, on the other side of the house, a car door opened and closed. Sarah crossed her arms and raised her face to the sky, studying the sway of the Spanish moss draped from a live oak at the water's edge.

Kit came and stood next to her. Side by side, they gazed into the bayou. "At night," Sarah said softly, "it comes alive. I used to fall asleep every night listening to that sweet chorus of sound. It took me a long while to adjust to city living, to the sound of trucks and sirens instead of the birds and the frogs and the other wild creatures.''

Silently, Kit slid an arm through hers. "I don't know what to call you," she said.

"Call me Sarah. It's my name."

"My mother—I mean, my adoptive mother—"

"Ellie."

"I don't remember much about her, except the singing."

"Ellie was the sweetest, kindest person who ever walked this earth. If she hadn't been, I would never have handed my baby girl over to her, no matter how hard Momma pushed. She loved you more than life itself."

"I always used to wonder…when I looked at pictures of her. I used to wonder why I didn't look like her at all. Now I know why. It's because I look just like you."

She took a deep breath. "That's what people keep telling me."

"I'll have questions," Kit said. "I know I will. But I need more time. Is that okay?"

Her heart contracted. "Of course it is, sugar. You take all the time you need to process this. I'm here for you whenever you need me. Any time, day or night." She gazed at the muddy water of Bayou Rouillard and took a deep breath. "You and me," she said, aiming for a casual tone, "are we going to be okay with this?"

She waited breathlessly for her daughter's answer. Kit considered the question at length. Then she lay her cheek against Sarah's shoulder. "Yes," she said. "Yes, I think we are."

Buying the Celica was the most impulsive thing he'd ever done.

The car was bright red, a Boston driver's dream, with a 1.8-liter DOHC 16-valve engine and a 6-speed manual transmission that would take him wherever he wanted to go in as little time as possible. It had all the bells and whistles, including a JBL premium stereo system that at full volume would probably blow out the windows. The car was too flashy, too fast, loaded with too many expensive and unnecessary toys. It was an outrageously inappropriate vehicle for a Catholic priest to drive, loud and aggressive and blatantly, inexcusably sexy.

It had cost him the moon, but then he'd been frugal with his money all these years. He'd tucked a portion of it away in savings, had shrewdly invested another portion. His frugality had paid off. He'd been able to pay cash for the car and still have a substantial sum left in his bank account. That was a good thing, since he was now officially unemployed, and might have to live off his savings until he found work.

No regrets. That was what he'd promised Sarah seven months ago, and what he'd promised God two weeks ago when he walked into Bishop Livingston's office and tendered his resignation. He'd expected to meet with resistance, but the bishop had been surprisingly supportive of his decision.

"When you came here seven months ago," Livingston said, "it was made clear to me by Bishop Halloran that you were undergoing some kind of personal crisis and needed the time and space to mull it over. Of course, I'd hoped you'd choose to stay, but I took you on fully understanding that your choice might be to leave the priesthood."

"Then you won't try to talk me into staying, Your Excellency?"

"It's a decision only you can make, Father, and it appears as though you've already made it. You've been an asset to the priesthood, and I'm sure you'll be successful at whatever you attempt in the secular world. If there's anything I can do to help ease your transition, please let me know. Go with a clear conscience, and may God go with you."

He'd stayed through Christmas. Somehow, it had seemed

fitting that he should remain long enough to celebrate the Lord's birthday with his parish. He'd made a few friends during his seven months in Detroit, people whose faces and kindnesses he would remember fondly, and he made sure to give each of them a personal farewell. Some of his parishioners urged him to stay. But the ailing parish needed someone he could never be: a priest who could dedicate himself, heart and soul, to rebuilding and restoring a needy inner-city parish. His soul might have belonged to God, but his heart belonged to the woman he'd run away from. He'd put seven hundred miles between them, thinking it might make a difference, but he'd found he couldn't outrun her reach. She'd simply followed him, haunting his sleep and distracting him from his daily routines and responsibilities.

It had taken a great deal of soul-searching, a great deal of prayer, before he was able to admit it was time to move on. He was no longer effective in the role he'd chosen to play. Whatever God's future plans for him might be, they didn't include the priesthood.

It still hadn't hit him. Not really. He'd packed his vestments and taken off his collar, but he couldn't shake off the mantle of priesthood quite as easily as he could remove the outer trappings. There were ingrained patterns of thought and behavior that had taken years to form, and that would take as many years to erase. It was both liberating and terrifying to realize that for the first time in twelve years, he had no expectations placed on him, no schedule or rigid rules to follow. There was no place he had to be, nothing he had to do. He no longer held in his hand the weighty responsibility of the souls of two hundred people. His relationship with God had moved from the professional arena to the personal, and it would take him some time to fully grasp that transformation. He suspected it would take even longer to adjust to being called Mister instead of Father.

He left Detroit the day after Christmas. Traffic was light,

as most travelers hadn't yet begun the post-holiday trek home, so he opened up the Celica and let her run those seven hundred miles of highway between Detroit and Boston. Ten hours later, with the sun hanging low over the western sky, he arrived in Boston. He drove straight through the city without stopping. There were places he wanted to go, people he wanted to see. But first, there was a woman in Revere who held his future in the palm of her hand.

He had to find out if she still wanted him.

The mall was dressed up in Christmas attire, and when he stepped through the door of the bookstore, sleigh bells tinkled overhead. Josie was working the counter. A pair of earrings shaped like Christmas tree bulbs dangled from her earlobes, and on her head she wore a ridiculous pair of red and green reindeer antlers. She glanced up and saw him, and her face lit up like a Las Vegas summer night. "All the bookstores in all the malls in all the world," she said, "and he has to come walking into mine."

He returned her grin. "Hello, Jose. Is Sarah around?"

Josie's smiled disappeared. "You missed her, hon. She left two days ago for New Orleans."

Bitter disappointment flooded his body. "New Orleans?" he said. "What's she doing in New Orleans?"

"She and Kit flew down to spend Christmas with her ex-husband. They won't be back until January."

A hard knot settled in the pit of his stomach as he pondered the significance of this development. Could she be planning to reconcile with Duval? Was he too late? Had he completely blown any chance he might have of getting her back?

His face must have read like an open book. "Look," Josie said, leaning on both elbows over the counter. "That lady has one tough hide. But it's not bulletproof. I've seen the scars. After you left…" She paused, shook her head. "Let me just say one thing. If you let her get away, you're a damn fool."

He released a pent-up breath. "Then I'm not too late? She hasn't gone down there to—" He paused, unable to continue.

"You mean Remy? I imagine he'd take her back in a heartbeat, but I honestly don't see it. Since the day you left, she's never so much as looked at another man. She's a one-man woman. Unfortunately, that one man happens to be a good-looking, hardheaded priest who's too blind to see past the nose on his face and realize what he walked away from."

"I've taken off the blinders, Jose. And I'm not a priest anymore."

"Then go after her. Make the gesture. She's a woman, Clancy. We appreciate romantic gestures. If any man ever chased me all the way to New Orleans…well, let's just say I'd find him pretty hard to resist."

The sun was going down as he drove back to Southie. M Street wore the rosy glow of an early winter dusk. As he approached the Rafferty house, he saw Jamal standing in the street, talking to another kid, both of them leaning against Caro's Mitsubishi. Clancy winced and shot a quick glance at the second-story window. If Carolyn saw the kids anywhere near her car, she'd probably skin them both alive. For the first time ever, he understood.

He pulled up to the two boys. With the flick of a button, he smoothly lowered his window. "Good afternoon, boys," he said.

Jamal's mouth fell open. "Holy shit," he said. "I thought you in Detroit."

"I was," he said. "Now I'm here."

Jamal eyed the Celica with open appreciation. "This your car, dude? You finally get rid of your old lady car?"

"I did. What do you think?"

"I think we overdue for a ride. Way, *way* overdue."

"Funny you should mention that, because I was thinking you might be interested in a little road trip. If we can get Fiona's permission, of course."

Still gaping at the car, Jamal was slow to process his words. "Road trip?" he said, and glanced up with keen interest. "You and me? In this car? Where we going, dude?"

He leaned back in the driver's seat and stretched out his legs. "Well," he said, "if Fiona doesn't object too loudly, I thought you might like to come to New Orleans with me."

Somewhere on the outskirts of the city, he pulled into the parking lot of a ramshackle diner with a peeling hand-painted sign advertising crawfish caught fresh daily. He and Jamal walked past a line of dusty pickup trucks to the entrance. Inside, on the jukebox, Alicia Keys wailed soulfully about falling in and out of love as they slid into a red leather booth and picked up sticky menus.

The place wasn't fancy, but the food was good, the servings massive, and the waitress friendly. "You boys from up north?" she said when she heard their Yankee accents.

"We're from Boston."

She flashed him a killer grin. "Well, then, sugar, welcome to New Orleans."

They inhaled their food, just two growing boys on a road trip, and he topped off his meal with a cup of coffee while Jamal slurped the biggest root beer float he'd ever seen. Watching a dented vintage GMC pull into the parking lot, he told the kid, "We probably should check into a motel."

Jamal eyed him over the root beer float. "Don't know 'bout you, but if I was the one come all this distance to see my woman, I be headed straight to her house."

"We have to find her first. I don't even know where the man lives."

"That's why God made phone books, dude."

The waitress pointed him in the right direction, and he sat on a high stool beneath the pay phone and paged through the telephone directory. There were five Remy Duvals. He folded back the pages of the directory and took it to the waitress.

"I'm looking for a Remy Duval who lives in the French Quarter. Can you tell me which address might be the right one?"

She squinted, then pointed. "This one for sure, *cher*."

He went back to the pay phone, pumped in a couple of coins, and waited, his heart thudding double-time. When a man answered, he said, "I'm looking for Sarah Connelly."

"She's not here." There was a measured pause. Then, "Who's calling?"

"My name's Clancy Donovan. I'm a friend of hers, and—"

"I know who you are."

It was his turn to pause. He hadn't expected the ex-husband to recognize his name. Nor had he expected to be received with open hostility. "Look," he said, "I just drove all the way from Detroit, by way of Boston. I have to see her. Can you tell me—"

"She went out shopping a couple hours ago. I imagine she'll be coming round pretty soon. You say you're here in New Orleans?"

"Yes. I'd like to come over."

"I can think of a thousand reasons to say no, but if Sarah found out, she'd fillet me and make gumbo out of my hide. She prob'ly wouldn't kill me first, either. You got a pen?"

"I don't need one."

Remy Duval gave him crisp, concise directions. "You got that?" he said when he was done.

"I've got it."

"Good for you." And the man slammed down the phone without saying goodbye.

"Holy shit," Jamal breathed as they pulled up in front of what could only be termed a mansion. "You think she gonna give up something like this for the likes of you, dude, one of you got some serious brain damage."

Laurie Breton

Built of burnished red brick with an elegant white portico fronting on a semicircular drive, the house possessed a warmth and charm that spoke of good breeding and old money. Evergreen garlands decorated with tiny red bows wound around massive white porch columns in honor of the season. Clancy turned off the ignition, removed his keys. "It's not hers," he said. "It belongs to her ex-husband. And I appreciate the support."

"Any time." Eyeing the eighty-thousand-dollar Mercedes S500 sedan parked in front of them, Jamal said, "Cheer up. You may be out of work and not much to look at, but your ride is way cooler than his."

"Ah, youth. Keep your mouth shut and try not to embarrass me. Got that?"

The kid rolled his eyes. "Yes, Massuh."

To his surprise, Remy Duval opened the door himself. In a house this size, he'd have expected servants. Duval was in his mid-forties, with wavy blond hair going prematurely gray, and cool green eyes that bored into him as though he were day-old garbage. There was a softness to the man, a boyish pudginess to his face that probably came from forty years of easy living.

"Do you suppose there's some unwritten rule of etiquette," Duval drawled, "that says I have to let you in, Boston?"

"Absolutely not. We can wait in the car if that's what you'd prefer."

Duval looked past him, sniffed an opinion of the Celica that had nearly bankrupted him, and stepped aside. "Might as well come inside instead of letting the heat out." He eyed Jamal as though he were some exotic zoo animal. "Who's this?"

"My faithful manservant. Jamal, say hello to the nice man."

"Yo, dude. This some crib you got here." The boy's eyes

were the size of dinner plates as they took in the massive foyer, complete with marble-tiled floor, crystal chandelier, and a massive winding staircase with gold-painted wrought-iron railing. The Renoir on the opposite wall, a delicate still life, appeared to be real.

Duval shut the door behind them just as the roar of some god-awful music floated down the staircase. All three of them raised their heads at the intrusion, but it was Jamal who spoke.

"Nine Inch Nails," he said in outrage. "Who listening to that crap, man?"

"Kit?" Clancy guessed.

"Kit," Duval confirmed.

Jamal shook his head in exasperation. "That girl got no taste at all. She as honky as you, dude. She be needing a serious music education."

For once, they agreed on something. "You want to go up and see her?" He glanced at Duval for permission.

Duval shrugged. "Go," he said. "Second door on the left."

Jamal strolled across the foyer, the ultimate in hip, the epitome of bad. "Shoes," Clancy ordered, totally demolishing his coolness. With an exaggerated roll of his eyes, the boy came back and kicked off his size thirteens while Remy Duval looked on with mild horror. "And don't be getting any ideas about stealing the silver while you're here," Clancy added. "You get in any trouble, I'll feed you to the gators."

"You sure know how to ruin a brother's day," Jamal grumbled cheerfully, and sprinted up the staircase.

Duval looked after him, his face a shade or two paler than it had been when they arrived. "Should I be worried?"

"He's nowhere near as bad as he'd like you to think. The kid has a heart the size of Texas." *And a pocketful of hip-*

hop CDs, he thought, but didn't say it out loud. Duval would find out in due time.

"So, you're a priest."

"Yes. I mean no. Well, sort of. It's complicated."

Duval's green eyes narrowed. "Well, which is it, Boston, yes or no? Seems like a pretty simple question."

"I've resigned from the active priesthood. But I'm still a priest. It doesn't go away."

"I suppose you realize you broke her heart."

"That was never my intention."

"What is it they say about the road to hell? I suppose you also know that in spite of six years of marriage, I was never able to do what you did in just a couple of months. It sticks in a man's craw, that kind of thing. She never loved me, you know. That's the difference. She loves you."

Duval paused, studied him keenly. "Since her Daddy's no longer among the living and her brother's taking up breathing space that should have been allocated to somebody who's evolved beyond Neanderthal status, I suppose that means it's my responsibility to be asking you what your intentions are."

"I could ask you the same question, Duval."

"Doesn't really matter, does it? You're the one she's in love with. How's this? Hurt her again, Boston, and I'll have you killed. I have friends in high places."

He bit back a smile. "I suspect my friends in high places beat yours any day."

Duval uttered a long-suffering sigh. "I imagine you're right."

Upstairs, the music abruptly stopped. They both glanced heavenward. "Praise be to God," Duval said.

"Don't start praising too soon. It's about to get worse."

"There's worse?"

As if in answer to his question, the deceptively innocuous opening bars of *The Real Slim Shady* filled the air. "What the hell is that?'' Duval said, and then Marshall Mathers opened his mouth and removed all doubt.

"He calls himself Eminem. I prefer to think of him as an equal-opportunity offender. It's been an interesting trip.''

"Oh, shit.'' Duval rubbed his head. "I think I need a drink.''

The after-Christmas sales had yielded some wonderful bargains. She'd picked up a couple pairs of jeans for herself, a gorgeous blue turtleneck sweater for Kit, some kind of stylish hair clasp to bring home to Josie. Now she was all shopped out, ready to kick off her high heel boots and relax with a cold one.

She pulled into the half-moon drive and parked her rented Oldsmobile directly behind a fire-engine-red Toyota Celica with Michigan plates. Remy had people over to the house all the time. He was a regular social butterfly, and she wondered who he could possibly know from the frigid Midwest. If she was really lucky, she'd be able to sneak upstairs before he noticed she was back. Otherwise, he'd corral her and try to drag her into their little social exchange. These days, socializing with strangers wasn't high on her list of favored activities.

The jagged, syncopated rhythm of hip-hop hit her as she walked through the door. Lord love a duck. She knew kids bounced all over the place with their musical tastes, but she'd only been gone for three hours. It hardly seemed possible that Kit's CD collection could have undergone such a drastic transformation in the space of one short afternoon. Remy must be having a cow.

She set her bags on the bench in the foyer, bent and slipped off her boots. They were ankle high, black suede, with zippered sides and little stiletto heels, killer boots that had cost her a fortune at Macy's Downtown Crossing store. The problem was, they were killer boots in more than one way. She should have known better than to wear them shopping. Three hours of standing on the damn things had probably crippled her feet permanently.

She felt his presence before she saw him, a faint prickling at the back of her neck that had her raising her head and straightening, still holding a single boot in her hand. The man who stood in the parlor doorway, dressed in a simple black shirt and jeans, was both intimately familiar and a total stranger. Hands thrust into his pockets, he studied her with bone-melting intensity while she tried to take in enough oxygen to keep her upright.

Michigan plates. She should have figured it out right away. She'd studied geography in fifth grade. Unless they'd moved Detroit since then, it was still in Michigan. But the truth hadn't even occurred to her. He was, after all, driving a strange car. And never, not in a million years, would she have expected him to follow her all the way to New Orleans.

Bittersweet joy ricocheted through her as she realized there could be only one reason why he'd come.

He'd cut his hair, all that beautiful dark hair she so loved to run her fingers through. A part of her mourned its loss even as another part of her admired how attractively the crisp new cut followed the contours of his head. Two hundred and twenty-seven days. It had been two hundred and twenty-seven days since she'd touched him, and she'd counted every one of them. At times, she'd wondered if she would spend the rest of her life counting. Seven and a half months should have been time enough to dull the knife blade a little, to take away some of the sting. But it still cut with breath-stealing precision.

No way was she going to make this easy on him. Not after all those months of crying herself to sleep every night. Her fingers twisted on the soft leather of the boot she held in her hand, and she straightened her spine.

"Nice car," she said. "Midlife crisis?"

"No. I suspect it's more a case of the real me finally being allowed to run free."

Her hands trembled, those damn treacherous hands, bent on betrayal. She turned, set down the boot, lined it up with military precision beside its mate on the floor beneath the bench.

"What are you doing here, sugar?" she said. "I thought you were in Detroit, battling Satan or some such thing."

"I was. It didn't work."

She glanced up and fell into those golden eyes of his. Trapped in their relentless whirlpool, she trod water, struggled to stay afloat. "Battling Satan?" she said.

"Detroit. I thought if I put enough miles between us, you'd stop waking me up at night. I was wrong."

The tightness in her began to uncoil, one slender strand at a time. "So," she said. "Here you are."

"Here I am. Sarah, I've left the priesthood."

Inside her, jubilation warred with blame, elation with guilt. "Because of me," she said.

"I don't want you to feel responsible. You were only part of it. A big part, but I was dissatisfied long before you entered the picture. You were simply the catalyst. You gave me the courage to act, the courage to admit I was in the wrong place."

"So you just walked away? Just like that?"

A faint smile touched his lips, softened his eyes. "It's not quite that simple," he said. "The priesthood is a bit like the military. You don't just walk away. You can take off the uniform and go AWOL, but that won't alter your status as a soldier. I've applied to Rome for laicization."

"Laicization," she repeated, unfamiliar with the word.

"You'd be more likely to think of it as a dispensation. It'll officially relieve me of my clerical duties and my promise of celibacy, and allow me to go back to living as a layman."

She wondered if he could hear her heart thudding, all the way across the room. "So you won't be a priest anymore."

"I'll still be a priest. Holy Orders is irreversible. But I won't be allowed to perform the sacraments any longer. Of course, as a failed priest, I'll be pretty much *persona non grata* in the eyes of the Church. A black mark on her record, at a time when she can't afford many more black marks."

She took a deep breath, filled her lungs with blessed oxygen. "And you're all right with this? You're sure you've done the right thing?"

"Absolutely certain. In spite of my status as a boil on the arse of the Church, God and I have come to an understanding. I hadn't realized how constricted my life had become until I took off the collar and walked out the door a free man. Free to be who I really am, free to live up to my potential." He paused. "Free to marry you, if you'll have me."

She fought back tears. "You know what a lousy risk I am, sugar. I've been divorced three times. I'm not sure I have what it takes to get it right."

"I don't give a damn how many husbands you've had before me, because I'll be your last. That's all that matters."

With unerring precision, his words arrowed swiftly and directly into their intended target. Releasing a pent-up breath, she gave in to the truth her heart already knew. He'd been hers from the first moment they set eyes on each other. It had just taken him some time to work it out in his own mind, some time to get to the place where he could accept the curveball destiny had thrown him.

With slow deliberation, she crossed the room and wrapped her arms around him, pressed her cheek against his and breathed in his essence: warmth and solidity, strength and honor. Bay rum and altar candles. It was an impossibility, but the scent clung to him, emanated from his pores. Or maybe it was just inside her head, a scent she would associate with him for the rest of her life.

He embraced her, closing the circle, and drew her close. "Don't cry," he said into her hair. "Sarah, darling, please don't cry."

"I've shed enough unhappy tears over you to fill Lake Ponchartrain." Her voice sounded unfamiliar, like coarse-grade sandpaper. "These are happy tears. Let me have my little luxury."

His fingers tangled in her hair. "The adjustment won't be easy," he said. "There'll be talk. A priest leaving the Church to get married. A lot of people won't understand."

"I understand. You understand." She raised her face, met his eyes, forgot to breathe as his breath gusted warm and sweet against her face. "To hell with everybody else."

With his thumb, he wiped a tear from her cheek. "I also happen to be unemployed. I may have to go back to school for a while. I suspect my Master of Divinity degree won't be terribly useful in the job market."

"You'll find something. There's nothing you can't do. And I'll support you until you're on your feet."

"It's a lovely offer, but I'm not sure how I feel about being a kept man."

"Don't worry. If I think you're getting too used to it, I'll just put a For Sale sign on that gas-guzzler sitting out in the driveway. That should motivate you to find gainful employment."

He took her face between his hands and stepped closer. "You really know how to hurt a man," he said, and crushed his mouth to hers.

It wasn't possible that she'd forgotten how it felt to kiss him, forgotten how his mouth left her breathless and aching and raw. It wasn't possible that she'd forgotten this terrifying, intoxicating tangle of tenderness and bone-deep sexual longing that reached inside her and wrapped clutching fingers around her heart. Like the scent of altar candles that clung to him despite every shred of common sense in her telling her it couldn't, forgetting these things was an impossibility.

His mouth reminded her. She combed fingers through what was left of his hair and lost herself in him. His body pressed hard against hers with aching familiarity, evoking poignant memories of humid summer nights spent tangled in the sheets with a man she wasn't allowed to love. She'd loved him anyway, and for that sin, she'd paid with seven long, torturous months of solitude. Momma used to say that anything worth having was worth suffering over. Maybe loving him wasn't supposed to be easy. Maybe it was the pain of getting to the goal that made the prize all the sweeter.

A fresh assault of urban hip-hop tumbled them both back to hard reality. With a sigh, he broke the kiss. She pressed her face against his throat and murmured, "What on God's green earth is that caterwauling?"

"It's my fault. I brought Jamal with me."

She opened her eyes, drew back, and looked at him in astonishment. "You brought Jamal to New Orleans?"

He tugged her back against him. "I did. And if I can work it out somehow, I'm going to bring him to live with us. That is, unless you have some objection. He's a great kid, he just needs a break. I'd like to give it to him."

She studied him keenly. "Gotten attached to the boy, have you, Father?"

"I—" he paused, looked embarrassed "—I suppose I have."

"Don't worry, sugar. I won't reveal your secret."

"I think the attachment's mutual. On the other hand, it could just be my car."

"It's your charm. Nobody can resist it. That, and your slightly twisted sense of humor." She paused, sobered. "It's a big responsibility, and I have Kit to think about. I'll have to give it some thought before I can say for sure."

"Fair enough. But there's one thing I won't back down

on. We have to get married as soon as it's allowed. There's no way I'm going to be able to stay away from you, and there is the little matter of that agreement I made with God. I'm not crazy enough to push it. I've been given a second chance. This time, I intend to do it right.''

She lay her palm against his face, that beautiful face she would wake up to every morning for the rest of her life. Against her chest, his heart beat strong and steady. She'd thought she knew about love, but what she knew was nothing until Clancy Donovan walked into her life and made her love him in spite of all the reasons she mustn't. Call it destiny, call it fate, call it the hand of God. She didn't know which, and she didn't really care. All she knew was that she'd been given another chance. And this time, she intended to do it right.

She cupped his face, drew his mouth down to hers and kissed him with exquisite tenderness. "Today, tomorrow, yesterday," she said. "New Orleans or Boston or the moon. I don't care which, sugar, as long as you show up. You pick the time and the place, and I'll be there."

New York Times bestselling
author Maggie Shayne returns
us to the dark, erotic world of
Wings in the Night

MAGGIE SHAYNE

His name is Edge and vengeance is his
obsession. He is the last of a band of
Immortals hunted down and murdered
by Frank Stiles—an enemy determined
to unlock their deepest secrets. To
claim his revenge, Edge must find
Amber Lily—the only half human,
half vampire ever born.

Amber shares Edge's need to get to
Stiles, and is drawn into his hunt. By
joining him, she will cast her fate to
the wings of the night, to a passion that
may be her destiny, to an evil she may
not be able to defeat—to the edge of
twilight where only Immortals belong.

EDGE OF TWILIGHT

"Maggie Shayne demonstrates an
absolutely superb touch, blending
fantasy and romance into an
outstanding reading experience."
—*Romantic Times* on
Embrace the Twilight

*Available the first week of March 2004
wherever paperbacks are sold.*

MIRA®

Visit us at www.mirabooks.com   MMS2022

With a wise, insightful voice,
USA TODAY bestselling author

SUSAN WIGGS

creates a moving novel about family, second
chances and the healing power of love.

HOME BEFORE DARK

"Wiggs' strongest and most vivid writing, a novel that bites into
such loaded issues as adoption, estranged sisters, difficult
teens…family secrets…." —*Seattle Times*

*Available the first week of March 2004
wherever paperbacks are sold.*

MIRA®

Visit us at www.mirabooks.com   MSW2019

New York Times **bestselling author**

CHARLOTTE VALE ALLEN

For twenty-seven years Lucinda Hunter has been a virtual recluse.
It sometimes takes her days to summon the courage to venture
past her front door. Then, one July morning, a motion in the
garden catches her eye. Looking out, she sees a little girl admiring
the overgrown flower beds. Lucinda goes outdoors to make the
acquaintance of nine-year-old Katanya Taylor who, courtesy of
the Fresh Air Fund, has come to spend two weeks in Connecticut.
Taken with the girl's sweet nature, intelligence and generosity,
Lucinda finds herself gradually, painfully drawn back into the world.

fresh
air

"The fluidity of [Allen's] prose and her easy narrative
skills are persuasive, and there's no doubt that readers
will find her characters immensely appealing."
—*Publishers Weekly*

*Available the first
week of March 2004
wherever paperbacks
are sold.*

MIRA®

Visit us at www.mirabooks.com

MCVA2023

MIRABooks.com

We've got the lowdown on your favorite author!

☆ Read an excerpt of your favorite author's newest book

☆ Check out her bio

☆ Talk to her in our Discussion Forums

☆ Read interviews, diaries, and more

☆ Find her current bestseller, and even her backlist titles

All this and more available at

www.MiraBooks.com

MEAUT1R3

New York Times
bestselling author

SUZANNE BROCKMANN

All her life, foreign aide
Melody Evans wanted to
marry a plain, average man
who didn't take risks. But
when the foreign embassy is
taken over by terrorists and
she's rescued by a daring
navy SEAL, Melody blames
the extreme circumstances
for their ensuing passion.
When it comes to ordinary,
Harlan "Cowboy" Jones is
anything but, and their
encounter leaves Melody with a
little more than just memories....

Seven months later, Cowboy
pays Melody a visit and is
surprised to find her pregnant—
with his child. Now all he has
to do is convince her that they
are meant to be together and
he can be as ordinary as the
next guy. The only problem is,
once a hero, always a hero....

EVERYDAY, AVERAGE JONES

"Everyday, Average Jones is
the kind of book you would
get if you mixed Tom Clancy...
with a romance novel."
—*All About Romance*

*Available the first week
of March 2004 wherever
paperbacks are sold.*

MIRA®

Visit us at www.mirabooks.com

MSB2014

New York Times bestselling author Heather Graham choreographs a sexy thriller of passion and murder....

HEATHER GRAHAM

Accomplished dancer Lara Trudeau drops dead of a heart attack brought on by a lethal combination of booze and pills. To former private investigator Quinn O'Casey, it's a simple case of death by misadventure, but experience has taught him not to count on the obvious when it comes to murder. Going undercover as a dance student, Quinn discovers that everyone at Lara's studio had a reason to hate her—a woman as ruthless as she was talented. As a drama of broken hearts, shattered dreams and tangled motives unfolds, Quinn begins looking for a killer....

DEAD ON THE DANCE FLOOR

"Graham's tight plotting, her keen sense of when to reveal and when to tease...will keep fans turning the pages."
—*Publishers Weekly*
on *Picture Me Dead*

Available the first week of March 2004 wherever books are sold.

Visit us at www.mirabooks.com

MHG2027

LAURIE BRETON

66660   FINAL EXIT   ___ $6.50 U.S. ___ $7.99 CAN.

(limited quantities available)

TOTAL AMOUNT	$_____
POSTAGE & HANDLING	$_____
($1.00 for one book; 50¢ for each additional)	
APPLICABLE TAXES*	$_____
<u>TOTAL PAYABLE</u>	$_____

(check or money order—please do not send cash)

To order, complete this form and send it, along with a check or money order for the total above, payable to MIRA Books, to: **In the U.S.:** 3010 Walden Avenue, P.O. Box 9077, Buffalo, NY 14269-9077; **In Canada:** P.O. Box 636, Fort Erie, Ontario L2A 5X3.

Name:_____

Address:_____ City:_____

State/Prov.:_____ Zip/Postal Code:_____

Account Number (if applicable):_____

075 CSAS

*New York residents remit applicable sales taxes.
 Canadian residents remit applicable GST and provincial taxes.

MIRA®

Visit us at www.mirabooks.com   MLB0304BL